COURTING TROUBLE

www.transworldbooks.co.uk

Courting Trouble

Kathy Lette

BANTAM PRESS

LONDON • TORONTO • SYDNEY • AUCKLAND • JOHANNESBURG

TRANSWORLD PUBLISHERS
61–63 Uxbridge Road, London W5 5SA
A Random House Group Company
www.transworldbooks.co.uk

First published in Great Britain
in 2014 by Bantam Press
an imprint of Transworld Publishers

A CIP catalogue record for this book
is available from the British Library.

ISBNs 9780593071335 (hb)
9780593071342 (tpb)

Addresses for Random House Group Ltd companies outside the UK
can be found at: www.randomhouse.co.uk
The Random House Group Ltd Reg. No. 954009

The Random House Group Limited supports the Forest Stewardship Council®
(FSC®), the leading international forest-certification organisation. Our books
carrying the FSC label are printed on FSC®-certified paper. FSC is the only
forest-certification scheme supported by the leading environmental
organisations, including Greenpeace. Our paper procurement policy
can be found at www.randomhouse.co.uk/environment

Typeset in 11.25/15pt Palatino by Falcon Oast Graphic Art Ltd.
Printed and bound in Great Britain by
Clays Ltd, Bungay, Suffolk

2 4 6 8 10 9 7 5 3 1

Dedicated to my inspirational friend
Helena Kennedy, QC, who
has promised to defend me
when I kill my first book critic.

Contents

Preface

Rap Sheets

Ladies and gentlemen of the jury, I left school with the intention of being either a lawyer or a mistress of espionage. As I hate pain and can't keep a secret, I achieved only one of these ambitions. (Well, that's what I have to tell you . . . unless you use my code name, of course.)

Today, I am prosecuting myself. The case you must judge involves a moral dilemma. My role is to lay the evidence before you. What you must decide is simple – is it ever right to take the law into your own hands? Especially if you're a lawyer.

This is a tale of emotional breaking and entering and acute lust in the third degree. As well as these crimes of the heart, this is also a story of violence, vengeance and betrayal. But it's up to you to decide where to lay the blame and whether to find me guilty.

So firstly, let me introduce you to the witnesses and defendants in this immorality tale.

If I were to show you my own charge sheet it would read:

Matilda Devine

35, accident-prone mother of one and barrister-at-law, 5'7",
red hair, green eyes, size ten – well, eleven after a chocolate
binge.

Convictions: that my arch-rival and frequent opponent in
court, Jack Cassidy, is an A-grade ratbag.

Previous convictions: that Jack Cassidy was an A-grade
ratbag way back when I first met him at law school and he
always will be.

If I were writing a rap sheet for Jack Cassidy it would read:

Jack Cassidy

38, barrister-at-law, tall, dark embodiment of handsomeness,
fluent in three languages – English, Sarcasm and Flirtation.

Convictions: tried and found guilty of relationship hit-and-
run.

Jack was a couple of years ahead of me when we were
studying law at Oxford. I had the misfortune of briefly falling
in love with him before realizing that his specialist area was
lying and heartbreak.

Like some corseted, cosseted heroine from a Victorian
melodrama, I was late to lose my virginity. It didn't happen
till university. Which is a surprise, I know. I mean, what
typical, tattooed, rock-and-roll-lovin', inner-city-London
state-school boy wouldn't want a nerdy, flat-shoed female
wimp who was always in the library studying Latin and
jurisprudence? It defies logic, clearly.

It wasn't long before Jack carved another notch on his
bedhead – a notch with my name on it. If only I'd discovered
the cad was sleeping with three other women before I fondled
his metaphorical gavel.

After Jack's carnal double-cross, I'd planned to devour a whole smorgasbord of blokes, but immediately drifted into a relationship with Steve. I was like a holiday-maker who arrives full of intentions to set out on scintillating sightseeing trips, then finds herself simply sinking into the empty sunlounger by the pool and ordering a pina colada. If I were writing a charge sheet for Steve it would read:

Stephen Myer
40, psychiatrist.
Looks: a charmer of the old-school variety, with a leather-elbow-patched poetic streak. Natural habitat – his study, sipping Burgundy and listening to a Bartók quartet.
Traits: on our first date he told me that he found long-term relationships to be as annoying and repetitive as bad wallpaper . . . Needless to say, we married shortly afterwards.

Well, accidentally falling pregnant sealed that deal. I did not want Portia (now thirteen) raised in a single-parent family, like me. Portia (named after Shakespeare's legal heroine rather than de Rossi) obviously can't have a rap sheet as she is completely innocent, beautiful and the light of my life. No, rap sheets are reserved for people like Petronella. If I were writing a rap sheet for Petronella it would read:

Petronella Willets
35, barrister-at-law, piranha in Prada.
Looks: blonde; Viking goddess. More groomed than a pedigree poodle at Crufts . . . Only much more bitchy.

When not in court, I tend to dress as though I've been hired to de-algae your aquarium. But Petronella Willets always looks sleekly elegant in black, pinstriped pencil skirts and immaculate white shirts. While I tend to gobble down chocolate at any opportunity, health-nut Petronella has her own nutritionist and acupuncturist – hell, she probably has a faecalist who feng shuis her faeces. I refuse to spend a fortune on face creams, believing that the secret of great skin is to be, well, Mediterranean. But Petronella tends to have every tanned pore individually pampered.

The piranha's true antithesis is my mother. It feels strange to write a rap sheet for Roxy, as she's guilty of only one thing – an over-protective, lioness-type love for her family. But if I *were* to write her a charge sheet, it would read:

Roxanne Devine

55, but depends who's asking. If it's a toy boy, then she's approaching 40, only she doesn't say from which direction. My mother's appetite for men borders on the carnivorous. Her motto is 'Have Your Beefcake and Eat It, Too'. Her latest beau, a 30-year-old DJ, is so good in the sack that he regularly launches her into the stratosphere. She calls him Cape Canaveral. 'Let's do launch,' she texts him on a nightly basis . . . Which is way too much information for any daughter to cope with.

Looks: at five foot one and ten stone, she's a butterball, with skinny, miniskirt-clad legs tapering off into leopardskin wedges. Her wild, dyed-blonde hair is piled high on her head in a skew-whiff beehive. My mother has the kind of walk that should always be accompanied by a brassy saxophone solo. She dances everywhere, with everyone – on tables, in aisles. And often in an alarming amount of gold lamé. Resilient, strong, indomitable – in other words, Australian.

History: if what doesn't kill you makes you stronger, then my mother is made of titanium. Roxy ran away from her conservative Irish Catholic family in Sydney to Britain aged

18, to take part in the anti-nuclear demonstrations. Here, she fell in love with an environmental activist called Danny. After a passionate three-year relationship, he told her he had to disappear for a while as the police were after him, but promised to send for her soon, as he loved her so deeply. It was after he'd gone to ground that Roxy discovered she was pregnant with me. Her strict, religious parents disowned her. She waited and waited, but Danny-boy never returned.

My sassy and sexy mother now maintains that men have only two emotions: hungry or horny. 'If you see him without an erection, make him a sandwich' was her only dating advice. **Career:** heartbroken by my father's abandonment and determined that nobody would ever take advantage of her again, Roxy put herself through law school to become a solicitor. 'Making me self-tort', is her Twitter-profile legalistic quip on the subject.

My mother has 'Do Not Resuscitate' tattooed across her chest and, in case medics don't see the message, 'PTO' on her back. She's stipulated in her will that she'd like her ashes to be fired into the sky from a cannon. 'When I die, I want to be covered in scars, glory, scandal, totally zonked, declaring loudly, "What a bloody great ride!!"'

When my husband, Stephen, a very smug non-smoker, nagged my mother to give up cigarettes, her response was to challenge him to a race up Parliament Hill. When he declined with the comment, 'That's so silly, Roxanne, at your age!' Roxy upped the ante and offered to smoke during the race. When Stephen arrived at the top five minutes after she did, my mother just couldn't resist lighting another fag from the one she'd sucked to the filter, and cackling, 'What kept you, possum?'

But I admit, my mother can be borderline too much of a

good thing. The woman takes no prisoners – unless she's performing a citizen's arrest on a drug dealer or has tied a toy boy to her bed with silk stockings.

Her heart is pure gold. An old hippy, she grows her own vegetables, dispensing herbal cures to local crackheads and, as well as saving the orang-utan, lion and humble bumblebee, is a foster-parent for traumatized dogs. 'Nobody wanted him. He'd been in the pound for ten years and yet he's so adorable!' Needless to say, what she sees as a harmless unloved pup, I see more as the Hound of the Baskervilles. And yet, although my mother and I are opposite in every way, we love Portia with equal passion.

As well as the main defendants in this case, there's also a granny with a grudge, a few crims with testicular trauma and an entire den of thieves – and that's just in my law firm. But one thing's for sure. There'll be a waterproof-mascara shortage after I've presented all the facts in this curious tale.

It all began two years ago, on the worst day of my life. When everything that *could* go wrong *went* wrong . . . and my world changed for ever.

1

Courting Disaster

The question on most women's minds is – why doesn't chocolate go straight to your boobs? It may not be particularly Einsteinesque or existential, but it was definitely the question consuming me as I consumed my second block of Green and Black's hazelnut milk to alleviate the pain of losing my court case to my arch-enemy; my barrister's job at Diplock Chambers; my domestic stability; and quite possibly my sanity. And all on the same dismal day.

As I cracked open the silver foil on block number three, I tried to ward off despondency, depression and feelings of worthlessness by reminding myself that I was once the fastest, most victorious little sperm out of millions . . . But I was beginning to think of that as my one moment of glory. How had it come to this? That I, Matilda Devine, law graduate, feminist, voted Best Legs in law school (I feigned disdain while secretly thrilled), cryptic crossword queen and 33-year-old mother of an eleven-year-old darling daughter – would be curled up in the foetal position in my pyjamas, crunching my way through an entire cocoa plantation while sobbing hysterically to Puccini's *Madame Butterfly* death aria.

The dreadful day began when I asked my husband, over tasteless organic cereal (*his* choice; Stephen says it's important to massage your bowels daily with bran flakes), what time he'd be joining me to watch our daughter, a tap-dancing cupcake, performing in the school musical. I was so excited about Portia's stage debut that only a Red Arrow fly-past would suffice by way of celebration.

Steve had grunted between spoonfuls that he couldn't make it, as he had to give a presentation at the Anna Freud Centre that evening.

My muesli-laden spoon stopped mid-air. 'At our wedding, the celebrant should have said, "I now pronounce you man and briefcase." You are married to your work of late, Steve.'

I waited for a response. I'd recently mentioned wanting another child, and all I'd seen of my husband since were his dark eyes glaring at me over the top of his *Psychology Today* magazine.

'You know how you're a shrink, Steve? Well, I think it might be time to book an appointment with yourself.'

Cue more glaring.

'A parent must always attend their child's school concert . . . whether you need the sleep or not,' I joked.

Still nothing.

Working from home seemed to assure Steve diplomatic immunity from all domestic chores, and so, as usual, I made Portia's breakfast, which she gigglingly referred to as her 'Freud eggs', found her sports kit, checked her homework, unpacked the dishwasher, folded the laundry, sorted the recycling and took out the rubbish, then did the school run before parking the car near Angel station and storming off to court, getting more and more steamed up on the Tube on the way ... Which is possibly why I lost my temper with the large, grey edifice that is Judge Jaggers.

On this day, County Court 6 was the scene of a property dispute between two ex-spouses. I was representing a 26-year-old minor starlet from a reality-TV show who was being sued by her ex-boyfriend for the money he'd spent on her breast enlargements. He claimed that her new boyfriend was getting all the benefit.

Judge Jaggers, who'd obviously graduated from Cambridge in Advanced Pomposity, was so blatantly dismissive of me all morning, rejecting my points of law and granting every challenge made by the claimant's barrister, that my blood pressure was soon reaching nuclear meltdown. Just before we broke for lunch, the judge interrupted my best point about possession being nine-tenths of the law to peer down his florid nose at me and boom in a voice dripping with condescension, 'Perhaps undertaking a refresher course at law school for a week might prove useful.'

'This judge is about as *useful* as a solar-powered vibrator on a rainy day,' I whispered to my acned solicitor seated behind me. 'If Judge Jaggers were any more moronic we'd have to water him once a week.'

Impetuosity. It's a trait I inherited from my Australian mother – the art of saying what you're thinking *without* thinking. I presumed I'd muttered my retort to the judge's outrageous comment in a discreet Rumpolesque aside. But judging by the machinegun-fire of laughter which erupted from the starlet, it was obviously a whisper that could be heard in the Outer Hebrides. When I'd first met my client, I'd reasoned that her survival in the reality-TV jungle (she'd beaten a fire-eating transsexual and a yodelling dwarf to win the competition) was because she could so easily escape by taking an inflatable-raft trip down the rapids on her own lips.

As she laughed, the disputed property – two round, creamy breasts nestled in low-cut, pale-pink silk ruffles – began to wobble so violently I was worried they might puncture, causing her to zoom around the court like a deflating party balloon.

But my client wasn't to laugh for long. Her merriment was quite abruptly curtailed when I lost the case and she was ordered to pay her ex £8,000 and his court costs. Even worse, the judge said he could charge me with contempt of court for calling him a moron. Even more upsetting, though, was the fact that I had lost the case to my arch-rival, Jack Cassidy.

It was the first time I'd encountered Jack since I'd graduated and been called to the Bar eight years earlier. Seeing him again, under these humiliating circumstances, I felt a strong call to another kind of bar – the one with swizzle sticks and swivel stools. (Try saying *that* when you're pissed.)

As Court 6 drained of people and the judge harrumphed off to call my Head of Chambers to complain, Jack winked at me. 'Well, I think Clarence Darrow can sleep soundly at night The reason there's a penalty for laughing in court is because, otherwise, the jury would never be able to hear the evidence . . . Still, no one can ever accuse you of being dull, Matilda. You obviously haven't changed a bit.'

Chuckling lightly, Jack removed his springy lawyer's wig. I looked for any change in him. His thick mop of dark wavy hair now had a tinge of silver shimmering on his temples but other than that he looked just the same. As he shrugged off his long black gown, I gave my ex a good ocular going-over. Despite the fact that he held pride of place on my top-ten list of Least Likable Men on the Planet, after Mugabe, Putin and Rush Limbaugh, my insubordinate heart skipped a beat. The man must have been taking handsome lessons: he was looking lip-moisteningly better than ever.

Since moving back to London and joining Diplock Chambers, I'd heard that women stalked Jack Cassidy with everything except a net and a tranquillizer dart. I'd also heard that he'd sold out. Once, he'd been a radical student, but he had lost his socialism along with his distinctive Yorkshire burr. I had loved his accent. It sounded like syrup on sandpaper. But the man now had pinstriped principles to match his new velvet vowels. He used to be so idealistic that everyone had presumed he'd become a human rights lawyer or go to New York to run the UN. Instead, the man had developed a talent for rushing to the defence of the winning side. He was charming, debonair, lazy; his colleagues referred to him as 'Sir Lunchalot'.

'Why don't I take you out to lunch and give you some tips on how to manage your anger,' Jack suggested, loosening a few buttons at the top of his shirt.

'I wouldn't need to manage my anger, Mr Cassidy, if people would learn to manage their idiocy. That judge is a misogynistic cretin. He rejected every reasonable point I made while favouring every inane argument you dredged up.'

As I shed my robes, I felt his gaze running up my legs and body. I turned to meet his eyes just as they locked on to mine.

'Do you know the difference between a good lawyer and a great lawyer?' Jack said to me, smiling wryly. 'A good lawyer knows the law. A great lawyer knows the judge. Judge Jaggers is so far back in the closet, you can see Narnia, a white witch and snow. I just batted my lashes at him – in a manly way – and he was mine.'

This kind of cynicism sums up everything I loathe about Jack Cassidy . . . That and the fact that he's seen me naked.

'What happened to you, Jack? I . . . well, *we* all thought you were going to stride the globe, righting wrongs, liberating underdogs from their kennels . . . But you haven't exactly taken the world by storm. I think your "storm" got downgraded to "light drizzle".' I picked up my stack of files. *'You're* the one who should be accused of contempt of court, for the contempt with which you view your profession and your talent.'

I executed a pretty formidable flounce from the room, considering I was wearing high heels. Despite the fact that high heels make me walk like a dressage horse, I wear them in court to enable eyeball-to-eyeball contact with opposing, condescending male barristers.

'I like your shoes, Matilda . . . Of course, the reason men created stilettos is so that women feel good lying on their backs no matter what,' my narcissistic nemesis called after me.

Laugh, and the world laughs with you. Fall flat on your face, and the whole world laughs – whether you've grazed your knees and snapped one heel or not. If ever I'm a contestant on *Mastermind*, 'Humiliating Moments Witnessed by Jack Cassidy' will be my specialist subject. As I swivelled to zing back a stinging retort in his direction, I'd lost my balance in my stupid shoes and was now spreadeagled on the landing, halfway down the stairs.

The law of probability states that the likelihood of being watched is directly proportional to the embarrassingness of your action. Jack skipped lightly down the stairs to pick me up off the floor.

'You would be watching, wouldn't you?' I grumbled.

'Do you know what's behind every great woman? A man checking out her peachy posterior.' Jack winked.

I was very restrained. After all, I didn't stuff my broken stiletto up his nose. But, gathering my scattered papers, I was beginning to feel that the whole world was against me – which was totally irrational and paranoid. I mean, Sweden is neutral, right?

'Have a good day,' the security guard commented as I limped by. To say I was *not* having a good day was like saying that the members of the National Rifle Association are sane, rational, peace-loving liberals. But I should have stopped then and there to strap on a bulletproof bra, because, on this particular day, fate was clearly using me for target practice. It was only October, but London was already in the grip of a deep, early winter, with the sun hanging low among the bones of the trees.

Too dejected to take the Tube, I splurged out on a taxi. Alighting near Chancery Lane, I changed back into flat shoes before trudging through the rain to my Chambers. Lincoln's Inn was built in 1422 by churchmen, who were the lawyers of their day. This explains why the picturesque squares and cobbled courtyards resemble medieval cloisters. But the vine-entwined arbours, fragrant rose gardens and graceful, four-square sandstone buildings with their arched windows and Juliet balconies belie the cut-throat struggles that go on within these ancient walls.

Word of my morning's performance had spread like – well, like the genital lice which no doubt plagued the pious churchmen who once practised here. My Head of Chambers asked to see me the moment I had shed my coat, gloves and hat. I'd been on probation for a while now. Because I am nothing if not an amazing businesswoman, I'd actually made a loss in the last quarter. This was mainly due to the fact that I'd taken on too much work for free. As far as my Chambers is concerned, the terms 'pro' and 'bono' should be used only when referring to a penchant for the lead singer of an Irish rock band and not when working for free on Death Row cases in the Caribbean. My breast-implant-ownership case was supposed to have been a step towards landing more lucrative cases. But Judge Jaggers' call, threatening to report me to the

Bar for unprofessional behaviour, proved the final nail in my commercial coffin.

Of course, my Head of Chambers, who has the sort of face you wouldn't wish on a bull terrier, didn't call it 'getting the sack'. Mr Phibbs, which was a perfect name for a lawyer so adept at bending the truth, referred to his request that I vacate Chambers as a 'career-alternative-slash-enhancement opportunity' and a chance to 'vocationally relocate'. Whatever way you looked at it, with my legal practice kaput, to continue with his euphemisms, I was now 'economically marginalized' and, with mortgage payments to be met, soon to be 'under-housed'. Unless my husband started to pull his financial weight, that is. Not only was Steve into his second year of researching some academic tome which would never sell, but he'd inherited his father's old Porsche and was spending a fortune fixing it up. He was committed to that car, in sickness and in health. I would go straight home and insist that he put his opus on hold and take on more clients. 'You have responsibilities now,' I would say. 'You have an unemployed wife and a car to support!'

I was halfway out of Phibbs's room when I turned back to throw myself on his mercy. I approached the large mahogany desk and the cold stare of its occupant in the hope of winning a stay of execution. But, if I really *had been* a spy, my code name would be 'Bloody Idiot', because my Head of Chambers interrupted my plea bargaining to remind me brusquely of the calibre of former members of the Inn, from Sir Thomas More and John Donne, to Prime Ministers Pitt the Younger, Disraeli, Gladstone and Thatcher ... Was it any wonder that my boxes had to be packed? I was two months behind in Chambers rent and had until the next day to move out. A high-earning barrister who had applied from another Chambers was moving into my room forthwith.

Numb with disbelief, I descended into the fuggy air of the Tube. No more taxis for me. On Holborn platform, I just stood staring into the black tunnel waiting for the myopic eye of the train. A mouse twitched along the track. I momentarily envied his busy, purposeful little life down there in the semi-dark.

As the Tube hurtled me home to Islington, I steeled myself not to sob until I was wrapped up in the warm, protective arms of my husband. After all, the man was a professional. He knew how to cope with a person in psychological crisis. Despite everything, we had always taken comfort in each other's arms. I'd come home hurt from the small humiliations I'd endured in court to find Stephen burdened down by patients' complaints, and we'd somehow turn all that emotion into desire. Stephen's office is in the front room of our tall terraced house in Cranbrook Crescent. I knew from the communal calendar we keep in the kitchen that preparation for the Anna Freud event had required him to cancel that day's sessions – which is why I opened his closed door without knocking.

I'd always joked that psychiatry really is a terrible waste of couches. Well, my hubby obviously thought so, too, as he was putting his own couch to much more imaginative use. It was more bonkette than banquette, judging by the vigorous up-and-down motion of his pale buttocks. Stephen always said he'd married me because he admired my morals and integrity, and yet here he was, pumping away at a woman whose moral integrity couldn't be located by the Hubble telescope. Petronella Willets had been my room-mate at college. We'd been fierce rivals at law school, vying for the highest marks, and had kept in competitive touch ever since.

When my eyeballs stopped sending SOS signals to my cerebral cortex, I relocated the power of speech. I wanted to say, 'That's all for today. Your allocated time is up,' or some other aloof spoof of shrink jargon, but instead heard myself shriek, 'What the hell, Stephen? What the fucking hell?'

I now watched in stunned disbelief as Petronella propped herself up on her elbows, her highlighted blonde hair streaming back from her face like the goddess at the prow of an invading Viking ship.

'I'm sorry you had to find out like this, Matilda,' she replied, with her carefully cultivated air of languor. 'But it's clear that you just can't give Stephen what I can—'

'What? An incurable genital disease?' Not my best line, but I hadn't had any chocolate at this stage.

'Why are you home so early?' Stephen said, as though it was me who was at fault.

'Why are *you* so lazy?' I retorted. 'I mean, if you wanted to have an affair, couldn't you have at least got dressed and strolled to the end of the street – instead of using any old thing that was *lying around the house*?' I said pointedly, glaring at Petronella. 'Get out!' I yelled at her. 'Get out of my home! And never come near us again.'

Neither of them moved. My college room-mate was still pinned beneath my husband like an exotic butterfly on an entomologist's board.

So much for selling Steve's vintage car to help with the mortgage. It was clear that Petronella was the type of woman who would lick his Porsche all over as part of their foreplay. And foreplay, after all, was her forte. I'd topped the year in the written Bar finals, but Petronella had pipped me at the performance post in the Advocacy exams simply by pouting provocatively at the aged male assessors who obviously required urgent counselling for lipgloss addiction. What I learnt back then is that when Petronella smiles at you for no reason, there's a reason.

'You have to choose right now, Stephen. Is it her or me?'

She smiled up at my husband, then they both went into Trappist-monk mode. I turned on my heel, scrambled into my car and drove straight to my mother's modest little solicitor's practice above a butcher's shop on Camden High Street, sandwiched between a hairdressing salon and Oxfam. Roxy (she prefers to be called by her Christian name) mainly spends her time chasing fathers who haven't paid their child maintenance, taking on local councils to help secure disability benefits or sorting out non-molestation and restraining orders for victims of domestic violence. Today, she might be advising me on how to claim that it was PMS that made me kill my husband and cut him up into teeny-weeny pieces.

2

Till Homicide Do Us Part

'Promise me you won't say "I told you so,"' I announced, kicking her office door shut and flumping down on her sofa in a fugue of shock.

Roxy looked up from her case files. 'Of course not, possum. Now tell me everything . . .' I regaled her with my morning's woes. 'I told you so!' she erupted Vesuvially. 'That needle-dicked numbskull was never good enough for you, Tilly.' She was up and out of her chair with the speed of a ninja to wrap her strong, firm arms around me.

'Why has Steve done this to me, Mum?' I bawled, only it came out as 'Ughgg assteeeve darn tumey mmeerm', as my face was firmly buried in her ample cleavage.

'Where is the snotty, swotty, piss-weak wanker?' Roxy finally broke the seal that suctioned me to her and started fossicking around in her voluminous handbag. 'I know I have a Taser gun in here somewhere.' Frustrated, she upended the bag on to her desk. A colourful detritus cascaded forth. Crossword puzzles, rape whistle, screwdriver, nail varnish, hair straighteners, handcuffs for work or pleasure, HRT

26

patches, a diamanté tiara ('Nobody can be mean to you when you're wearing a tiara, darls'), a hardback biography of Emmeline Pankhurst ('My secret weapon, possum. When it's Handbags at Dawn, I can bring a man down with a quick thwack to the side of the head'), organic dog biscuits, a silver vibrator, a capsicum spray, a Taser gun and flat shoes, for running between high-heeled appointments. 'How come they can put men on the moon but not invent a heel which goes up and down? I've already thought of a name for it – "The Social Climber",' she told anyone who cared to listen.

'A vibrator, Mother? Really?'

'Well, you never know when you'll be at a loose end and in need of a little relaxation.'

I slumped my head into my hands. 'Do you think Steve is really going to leave me?'

'A beautiful, clever girl like you, Matilda? Never.'

My voice dropped to a despondent whisper. 'It takes two to make a single mother . . . Obviously, I wasn't enough for him.' A sob was lurking just behind my tonsils.

'That's ridiculous. You've busted a gut for that bloody man . . . Even though, to be honest, I've often thought you should be committed for ever loving a bastardly boof-head like him. The question is do *you* still want *him*?' she asked tenderly.

'I love him. He's the father of my child. And I love my family.'

'Men are so stupid. We really should take the "men" out of "Mensa".'

'The worst thing is . . .' I was really weeping now '. . . Steve's a shrink. He knows what my greatest fear is.'

'Wearing a thong two sizes too small on a first date and cutting off all circulation to your whatnots?' my mother hazarded, in an attempt to raise my spirits.

'Turning into my mother.'

The wind went momentarily out of Roxy's monumental sails. 'Oh.'

'. . . When I was in the antenatal group, the health visitor asked me what was my biggest fear? And I said, "To turn out like my mother."' I blurted this out between huge, gulping howls. 'I'm sorry, Mum, but I don't want to bring up Portia the way you brought me up. I want a stable, normal home for my daughter, with bedtime rituals and Sunday roasts and a mother and a father. I'm a 33-year-old woman who's never met her dad. I have no idea what happened to him. I don't want Portia always to be looking for her father's hand to hold walking home from school or in the scary dark.'

I hadn't meant to cut my mother to the quick. It had all just tumbled out the wrong way. My mother retreated from me faster than if she'd caught her bra strap in a train door. She sat back down at her desk, deflated. She braved a smile, but it clung to her lips like biscuit crumbs. 'Baby kangaroos live in single-parent homes and they're pretty okay,' she said briskly. 'So, what are you planning on doing?'

'Nothing much. I just thought I might cry hysterically into my pillow and pray for the sweet release of death.'

My mother doesn't believe in feeling depressed. She will admit to the occasional bout of ennui, which is really just depression in a pair of satin mules and silk scanties. But she could knock ennui on the head after just one iddy-biddy night out with the girls, croaking karaoke, which is why she now said, 'Well, aren't you the most adorable black hole of need! Yes, Stephen's behaving like a selfish prick, but you are of pioneer stock.'

'But if Steve leaves, how do I pay our mortgage? And Portia's school fees? My Head of Chambers has asked me to vacate the premises. And I can't afford the fees to set up in any other Chambers. I can't even think of any set of

Chambers that would offer me a seat right now. Not with my reputation of late and my low earnings.'

'Oh, possum, I wish I could offer a more effective remedy than a hug, a barbecue and a bedroom. But these, at least, are yours,' Roxy said. Although my mother lives in a modest Georgian cottage in a Camden backstreet, her heart, meals and generosity are enormous. 'We'll go and see Portia being a tap-dancing cupcake, then you'll both stay the night. We'll watch silly movies, eat ice cream, drink plantations of my home-grown camomile tea and reassess in the morning. Okay, darl?'

I passed the night in a fog. I woke from a fitful sleep with a hangover – only I hadn't drunk anything the night before. It was as though my heart had indigestion. I booted up my laptop and checked my inbox, hoping for hand-wringing apologies from both Steve and Petronella. But the only email I'd received was one of those 'Ten Reasons Not to be Depressed' lists encouraging me to send it on to ten of my closest friends and colleagues. Sadly, I could think only of my psychiatric doctor husband . . . and the woman whose temperature he'd been taking with his fleshy thermometer.

When I sloped into the kitchen on the hunt for coffee, my mother clapped her hands in joy.

'I've had a brainwave!' She poured out espresso and dished up Danishes. 'If Diplock Chambers really have been stupid enough to throw you out, why don't you join my law practice? The fees are modest. And legal aid is a pittance. But there's enormous satisfaction to be had from helping the locals. Leaving that stuffy, uppity Chambers of yours could be a blessing in disguise. It's not as though you were happy there.'

I looked at my mother. Was early senility setting in? 'Mum, it may have escaped your notice, but you're a solicitor and

I'm a barrister. Your job is to liaise with the client. Mine is to represent them in court.'

'Exactly. So why not offer both legal services under the one roof?'

I took a scalding sip of my espresso. 'That's ridiculous. It would be like a specialist surgeon setting up shop with a GP.'

'Yes. And imagine how time-saving that would be.'

'But Mum, it's not the done thing.'

My mother rolled her iridescent, green-lidded, thickly mascaraed eyes. 'Oh, how I hate that British expression. Once we do it, it's done, so then it is "the done thing".'

'Mum, huge solicitors' firms can hire a barrister inhouse, but a two-person joint practice doesn't make sense as a business model,' I said, practically. 'Plus it would create so many ethical problems. I mean, think of the dilemmas. Solicitors get too close to their clients. Especially you, Roxy.'

'And you barristers don't get close enough. Especially you, Matilda,' she retaliated. 'Your trouble is, you keep trying to fit in, when you were born to stand out. Ours could be a law practice where we champion only women's causes.'

'Mum, I love you, but we could never work together. Apart from yesterday's backchat to the judge, when my inner monologue somehow bypassed my firewall of British courtesy, I'm a stickler for the law, while you break all the rules.'

'Which means we would complement each other perfectly. I want to be the patron saint of fallen women.'

'Did they fall? Or were they pushed?' I commented bitterly.

'You see? Even though our approach to the law is very different, darl, we do both agree that it's a man's world and that the bastards get away with it far too often. I mean, women still don't have equal pay. Plus, we're getting concussion from hitting our heads on the glass ceiling.'

'I know – and we're s'posed to clean it while we're up there.' Despite the fact that my mother sounded like a bumper sticker, I couldn't help but join in.

'Exactly. Which is pure bloody heaven compared to what happens in the developing world, where women are fed last and fed least.'

'Apparently, a billion women will be beaten up or killed by men during their lifetime. That's one in three.' I shuddered, clearly going for first place in the Long-distance Cross-bearing competition.

Roxy beamed. 'You see? Yes, we're opposites, but we're united in our desire to help women who've been cheated, abused, abandoned, bushwhacked or just plain buggered up by blokes . . . We could call it the "All Men are Bastards Bureau . . . Except George Clooney Who Is Crumpet" . . . Or what about the "Charlie's Fallen Angels Agency".'

'Or the "Wash that Man Right out of Your Hair Organization",' I riffed. '"The hair you will never again have to wax".'

'"Goddesses R Us",' Roxy enthused, pouring more coffee into my cup.

'"Pest Control for Love Rats" . . . Or, better still, "Love-rat Fumigation Services".'

'"Lady Godiva's Chambers . . . Only We ain't No Ladies".'

I laughed for the first time in twenty-four hours – although, admittedly, it was the sort of laugh that goes with a strait-jacket and incessant hair-braiding.

'So what do you say?' my mother prompted. 'Take a risk for once. You always take the safe option. That's why you married Stephen. And look how well *that* worked out.'

Talk of Steve brought me back to earth with a thud. I checked the clock. It was time to get Portia up for school and then win back my errant husband, if only for the sake of our darling daughter. I adore my mother, but she's not a good influence. Roxy is a let-them-eat-cake-in-the-bath-type granny, meaning that I have to be the uptight one who is always banging on about broccoli. Roxy always babysat if I had a case on and Steve was away at a conference. Portia, at only eleven, already seemed to be taking after her maverick and mischievous gran. I love my mother, don't get me wrong, but sometimes, distant relatives are the best . . . and the more distance between you the better.

'Oooops. Look at the time. It's school o'clock. Thanks for the offer, Mum, but no thanks.' After breakfast, I buckled my daughter into my sensible car, an A-class BMW which, I admit, does look a lot like an orthopaedic shoe, but at least it won't crumple like a cigarette packet upon impact. I glanced back at my mother's house. It was the last in a row of crooked little cottages leaning secretively in together around a communal garden. Each door is painted a different colour – mauve, pink, green, pistachio, peach – like a row of doll's houses in a toyshop. It was time to go back to the real world. Of late, life had been giving me a ride as though it were a bucking bronco. I left, determined to rein things in.

The most dangerous thing about being thrown from a horse is to avoid a kick in the head from a flying hoof. In my case, I most definitely did not see it coming. It wasn't until I'd dropped Portia at school and paused at a supermarket cash machine that I discovered our joint account had been cleaned out. And that wasn't all. When I walked into our three-storey red-brick Victorian house, I found that all Stephen's possessions were missing. And many of our shared things, too. Apparently we didn't even have joint custody of the coffee-maker.

You must be asking yourself how I could not have noticed

that my husband had fallen in love with someone else. But he hadn't taken up any strange new hobbies that kept him out at night or at weekends. Nor had he started taking his phone into the shower. Or using two phones ... Although, now I thought about it, he had started a new grooming regime and his sexual repertoire had suddenly extended. Plus, there had been an upgrade in the underpants department. And so many 'conferences' requiring overnight stays ...

How long had it been going on? The note he'd left said '*I'm clearly having some kind of mid-life crisis. I know it's clichéd. Especially given my profession.* [You're right there, mate. Who did you train under? Dr Seuss?] *I just need some space.* [The space between Petronella's thighs, obviously.] *Tell Portia I'm sorry. It's not her fault. I'll be in touch soon. Will pay you back when I can.*'

Sifting through a flutter-click snapshot of our marriage – my accidental pregnancy, his grudging agreement to become a father, his slow drift away from us, I was well on the way to demolishing a fourth block of Lindt chocolate when Roxy arrived. I heard her before I saw her. My mother drives an MG Midget, which she bought at a bargain price because it doesn't go in reverse and sometimes the soft top gets jammed halfway up or down. At five foot one, my mum is so short, oncoming drivers can't see anything but her hands gripping the wheel. She careers around London's streets like the headless horsewoman. I've tried to convince her to drive a sensible car. But nobody tells my mother what to do.

'Did that mongrel really take all your money?' she said, bursting through my door like a gun-slinger in a Wild West saloon, only vertically challenged and in lime-green leopardskin.

'I inserted my card into the cash machine and it just laughed and spat it out.'

'That mingy, stingy, two-faced dog turd. How can he have a mid-life crisis when he's clearly never left puberty?' Although she wasn't really all that surprised. Roxy was burnt so badly by my father's disappearance that her philosophy has always been: If everything's going well, you have obviously overlooked something. Her immediate solution was to refloat our joint legal venture. 'Your life's going down the gurgler, love. How else are you going to pay your bills, Matilda?'

'Something will turn up.' I'll say it again. I love my mother. But the chances of me setting up in practice with her were as likely as King Herod being asked to babysit.

Diplock Chambers at Garden Court was expecting me to collect my belongings. The humiliation was so overwhelming I was tempted to call the clerks to explain that I wouldn't be able to make it in today, due to the fact that I was deceased. But I fortified myself by eating my own body weight in brownies, then plodded out to my car. A chill wind burrowed into my skin like a worm. Teeth chattering, I drove on automatic pilot, down through Clerkenwell to Lincoln's Inn Fields.

It was here, in 1586, that Babington, the man who tried to assassinate Elizabeth I, was hanged. (In those days, justice came with strings attached.) Babington's body was then drawn and quartered, which involved extracting his entrails and burning them before his goggling eyes. The punishment proved so gruesome, the stench of burning bowels so overwhelming, that Elizabeth mercifully allowed Babington's thirteen accomplices merely to be hanged. Well, today I knew just how old Babington must have felt.

I slunk into Chambers unnoticed. I was knee deep in half-full cardboard boxes when I heard a knuckle rap on wood as the door snapped open.

'Why do you bother knocking when you just barge right in anyway?'

'I was hoping to catch you unawares, preferably changing into a bikini,' said Jack Cassidy.

'In the middle of an arctic London winter . . . Right.'

'A boy can dream. There are many people I would pay money not to see naked. You are definitely not one of them. From what I remember from our student days, that is . . .'

I felt a hot colour rising on my neck. Even though my mother walks around naked all the time – scaring neighbours, Jehovah's Witnesses and pollsters – I am more the Loch Ness Monster of nudity, but there are *no* sightings. I haven't even seen *myself* naked. Which made the memory of my first encounter with Jack Cassidy on the streets of Oxford even more nail-gnawingly humiliating.

'I believe the police report stated that a pretty eighteen-year-old woman, stark naked with a traffic cone on her head, had been arrested,' Jack reminded me. 'Her defence was that she was fresh out of the shower and had darted on to the secluded private balcony of her ground-floor student room to retrieve a drying towel . . . Only the towel had blown away. Then the balcony door slammed and locked behind her. When banging and yelling didn't rouse her fellow students, she feared hypothermia and so scaled the small brick wall and grabbed the nearest cover, which just happened to be a rubber, cone-shaped roadside bollard, which she put on her head to hide her identity before darting down the lane and around to the front of the building to frantically ring the bell . . . It was then that the traffic cone slipped down and she found herself wedged in the "Keep Left" sign and then got lost.'

I busied myself packing up another box of my possessions so that he couldn't see my discomfort. Of all the people to bump into naked with a traffic cone on your head, the fickle Fate Fairy would make sure it was Jack Cassidy, wouldn't she? Although Jack did manage to convince a suspicious policeman that he should not arrest me for indecency . . . but simply hold my coned head while Jack wrapped me in his jacket, before tugging at my bare legs to set me free. I was so discombobulated with gratitude that I accepted his invitation to dinner – an experience which proved so deliciously, decadently, erotically pleasant that, three weeks and ten dates later, I gave him my briefs – the lacy, not the legal, kind. Over the next month we basically became human origami – well, orgasmic origami, really.

I was well and truly in love by the time I found out that he'd had three wives already. None of them his own. Turns out Jack Cassidy had bedded one female professor on campus and the wives of two others.

'In retrospect, knowing the exact location of all officers of the law within the immediate vicinity is obviously the minimum precaution one should take before exposing one's genitalia to the elements,' I said to him now, in my crispest tones. 'And I thank you for assisting me. But there's been a lot of sewage under the bridge since then. So, did you come here for any purpose other than to gloat?'

'Well, from what I hear on the grapevine . . . the sour-grape vine . . . your husband has absconded with all your money and your college rival, Petronella Willets, who, unlike you, is in great demand at the Bar. Not only has she not been sacked from her Chambers but it's rumoured she's about to get Silk.'

'Being an unmitigated failure is not as easy as it looks, you know.'

'Is it true? About your husband?'

I felt a sharp pang of embarrassment that word of my marital humiliation had travelled so fast. 'Let's just say Stephen flunked the practical exam for his marriage licence,' I replied glibly.

'What a bloody idiot . . . Anyway, I just thought you could do with some help.'

'I'm fine.'

'Fine? Really? Remember, you don't have a traffic cone on your head right now, Matilda. I can see your face, you know.'

My cheeks were now blazing red, two expressionist splotches of colour. 'Okay, I admit it. Things are a little fraught . . .'

'In the circumstances, "fraught" reminds me of that British chap who was asked what the Second World War was like and said: "My dear, the *noise*. And the *people*."'

'All right already. "Fraught" may be an understatement. Sadly, no one at present seems to find offering me a full-time job absolutely necessary. But something will turn up.'

'Yes. Me. That's what I came here to tell you. I could smooth the way for you to join my Chambers.'

'Regal Helm Chambers? Don't be ridiculous. I could never afford the rent.'

'I could pay your rent until you established yourself. For the amusement value alone it would be so worth it.' He grinned.

I stopped packing and turned to appraise the man who had tricked me out of my virginity. Maybe he had changed? Perhaps I was looking at a Born-again Human Being. I knew for sure there was a kind side to the man. When we were dating he never passed a woman with a pushchair without helping her up or down the stairs. He'd emptied his wallet for beggars on numerous occasions. And I felt sure there'd been a sponsored goat in a village in Africa somewhere. 'Really? You'd do that? Pay my Chambers rent until I get on my feet again?'

'Yes . . . If you'll agree to go out with me.'

I placed my hands over my ears. 'Hear no evil, see no evil, date no evil.'

'Contrary to popular feminist belief, not all men are hideous bastards, Matilda.'

'Yes, you're right. Some of them are dead.'

'Seeing you again yesterday morning – well, it really stirred me. You broke up with me at Oxford before we even got started.'

'Well, that's because you'd obviously *started* with so many others. I gave you my heart, not to mention other parts of my anatomy, only to discover that you were also sleeping with a professor and two professors' wives, while also shacked up with a gym-junkie aerobics instructress. Which reminds me, have you ever noticed that I'm not your type? I didn't make it to the gym today. That makes it, oh, ten years in a row.'

Jack gave the kind of cavalier, lusty laugh last heard in a swash-buckling Errol Flynn movie. 'You are absolutely my type, Tilly. Curvaceous, clever, crinkly-eyed . . . did I mention curvaceous? Won't you give me a second chance? We were young. I was a hot-blooded male.' He twinkled. 'Can I help it if women fall at my feet?'

'Only when you get them drunk first . . . You led me on and lied to me.'

'I was just pandering to the macho, immature lad-culture of the time.'

'Hang on a moment while Jack Cassidy passes the buck. You are a World-class Champion Buck-passer, you really are. Why are you staring at me like that?'

Jack was giving me a curious look – a look I couldn't quite read. Could it be a look of remorse, I wondered, astounded.

'I'm just remembering you naked . . .'

'And I'm remembering you with scruples. I suppose a scruple would be out of the question, Jack Cassidy? By the way, here are your eyeballs. I found them in my cleavage.'

'You're judging me so harshly that you're starting to look

underdressed without a guillotine and some Madame Defarge knitting needles. I'm not a bad person, Tilly. I give to charity. I help old ladies across the street. I open doors for women . . .'

'It may have escaped your notice, Jack, but women no longer want men to give us their seats on the bus. We want them to give us their seats on the board. We want positions of authority.'

'I seem to remember your favourite position. Lying back against a satin pillow while I kiss you slowly from top to toe . . .'

'Do you know my favourite position, Jack?'

'Tell me. I'm intrigued . . .' he positively purred.

'Supreme Court Judge. I fully intend to make it to the top, you know.'

Jack couldn't disguise his amusement. He guffawed. The full throwback-of-the-head snort. 'If only that train of thought had an engine . . . You see? This is why I like you. You make me laugh so much. Which is why I think we could be so good together. I'm flying off to Dubai next week on a lucrative arbitration case. Why don't you come with me? You could act as my junior.'

'How tempting. A hot, sweltering city . . . standing on the edge of a cultural desert. What happened to you, Jack? You had so much potential. Yet you've ended up working for oil barons and despots.'

'Ambition is a poor excuse for not having enough sense to be lazy. Hard work pays off in the future. Laziness pays off right now. I'm still good at deal-making, though. Join my Chambers and I'll lend you as much money as you need. Let's finish what we began all those years ago.' The hand he placed over mine was warm. The air between us crackled.

I shook him off. The best way to deal with him was to

channel my inner Roxy. 'Did I mention the kick in the balls you're going to get if you look at my breasts one more time?'

'You don't just bite the hand that feeds you, you rip off the whole arm at the shoulder. How do you think you're going to survive in the big, bad world, Matilda? I also hear you have a daughter to take care of – which means school fees. And a mortgage. Mind you, I like dating a homeless woman – it's so much easier to get her to sleep over.'

'I'm going to set up a practice with my mother.' The words were out of my mouth before I'd fully formed the thought in my brain.

'Don't be ridiculous. Your mother's a solicitor. That would be like having a GP and a surgeon in the same office.'

'Yes. And imagine how time-saving that would be.'

'But it's not the done thing.'

'Once we do it, it's done, so then it is the "done thing",' I heard myself say.

'You'll be the laughing stock of the Bar.'

'I'm tired of trying to fit in when I was born to stand out.'

'Oh, well, I suppose it doesn't really matter.' Jack creased up. 'I mean, it's only your career.'

'We're going to champion women's causes and nail the knobheads who have blighted their lives.'

He was really laughing now – big, rich, rolling belly laughs.

'Do you know what, Jack? There is so much less to you than meets the eye. Just watch this space. Devine and Devine. So heavenly, they named us twice. The world's first two-person, mother–daughter, solicitor–barrister, boutique feminist law firm. We are going to make legal history. And we're going to make a hell of a success of it.'

Twenty minutes later I was climbing the warped stairs to my mother's Camden office.

'Where's Roxy?' I asked the gaggle of clients in the small waiting room.

'She just took off for a nooner with the local butcher,' said an Aussie guy on crutches nonchalantly.

I gasped. Not because she'd left complete strangers here in her workplace unattended, but because I knew it was a distinct possibility.

I power-walked the two blocks to my mother's house and leant on the bell till she answered, all dishevelled, lipstick smeared and smelling slightly of pork.

' "Pandora's",' I announced. ' "Thinking outside the box".'

'Pandora's! I love it!' she shrieked, crushing me into a bear-hug.

We laughed and embraced there on the step, our breath sending up smoke signals in the icy air. My mouth had signed me up to Britain's first two-person, mother–daughter, solicitor–barrister boutique feminist law firm . . . and the rest of me was now forced to follow. But it felt good. It felt exciting. Mother and daughter setting up a law practice together. I mean, how hard could it be?

3

United We Stand, Divided We are Screwed

So, how hard could it be? Harder than getting chocolate to go straight to your boobs, that's for sure. Four months into our joint venture and I discovered that the true meaning of 'stress' is when you wake up screaming, only to realize that you're not actually asleep.

You'd have thought someone would have warned me at law school that starting a small women's-rights practice with your mother during a time of legal-aid cuts was so tortuous. If it was adventure I was looking for, I could have flown a lawn chair over the Atlantic ocean propelled by party balloons. If I'd desired to dedicate myself to humanity, I could have raised war orphans in a camp in the Congo.

Pandora's had many cases. It was just that none of them was lucrative. One of our most time-consuming occupations was the tracking-down of dead-beat dads who weren't paying their child maintenance. Roxy reckons that the Child Support Agency should be renamed 'The Stupid Excuse Bureau'. One feckless father, eight months late with his payments, argued that, as he'd undergone a sex-change operation and was, therefore, no longer a man, he shouldn't have to pay. Another argued that, as he was now in a witness-protection programme, he didn't have to pay any more as, officially, he no longer existed.

Through Pandora's first Christmas and New Year I also spent a lot of time trying to find my own wayward husband. I sent constant texts and emails: 'The car is dying. It gets two blocks to the gallon and I think the tailpipe is backing up noxious fumes because I find I get very sleepy at the wheel, but hey, don't worry, I'm sure your *teeny, tiny, defenceless daughter* and I will manage somehow.' But they bounced back, unanswered. Meanwhile, the only bouncy things about me were my cheques. Portia received the odd postcard from exotic locations saying 'Wish you were here', which he clearly didn't, as there was never any return address.

Mum helped me with babysitting, housework and home-work, which gave me more time to work, but it was so hard to invoice anybody. Every woman who came to Pandora's had a sob story. Half an hour there was like hanging out with Eeyore ... if Eeyore had a toothache, a migraine and a throbbing big toe upon which he'd just dropped a hammer. My mother and I were kept constantly busy trying to get legal aid to bring to justice reckless cosmetic surgeons who performed botched liposuction, Botox and boob jobs. We'd successfully sued a male gigolo who knowingly infected several trusting and vulnerable women with hepatitis. 'I just wanted to get into someone's pants and not have to launder them later,' explained the lonely working mother who came to us to punish the man who'd given her Hep C. We also won compensation for a widow the gigolo had infected. She'd sobbed in our office that she'd hired a male escort only as 'a long way round to getting a hug'.

We defended a naive teenage girl tricked into working as a drug mule by an abusive boyfriend. He flew her from Jamaica with packs of cocaine in her luggage stuffed inside twenty-four boxes of cake mix. The girl turned eighteen shortly after her arrest, so had been charged as an adult to ensure she'd receive a heavier sentence. It was soon discovered that she was also carrying excess baggage in the shape of her abuser's child in her belly. This was surely punishment enough, I argued, in a successful bid to have her put on probation rather than in prison.

Pandora's also sued an Evangelical Christian preacher who'd told his credulous followers that prayer could cure cancer. His ideas killed two worshippers who stopped taking their life-saving drugs on the advice of this pseudo pastor. And wasn't it curious how the preacher had been written into all the women's wills . . . ? Where there's a will, this ratbag really liked to be in it.

We also represented a woman who attacked her lover with a vibrator and was arrested, much to our amusement, on an aggravated battery charge.

To subsidize the work we did for free, Roxy and I needed a lot of paying cases to survive. But solicitors who'd previously instructed me as a barrister were so hostile to our two-person, mother–daughter, solicitor–barrister boutique feminist law firm, they refused to send me any cases now that I was co-habiting with a rival solicitor. Sets of commercial Chambers, inhabited by the three-piece-pinstripe, dust-on-the-shoulders mainly male brigade, were willing us to fail. At the merest mention of 'Pandora's', not just their lips, but their whole faces pursed.

'Don't worry about it, possum.' My mother would laugh off the disdain of our colleagues. 'Being popular in the British legal world is like sitting at the cool table in the cafeteria of a mental hospital.'

The only lawyer who showed any interest in me was Jack Cassidy. At least once a week he sent an email inviting me to join his Chambers. I deleted them, unanswered. Finally he turned up at Pandora's. I was happily munching a chocolate eclair when he strode into our humble little waiting room in his bespoke suit and shiny Armani shoes, gold cufflinks flashing. He looked decidedly out of place amidst the nylon tracksuits, tattoos, lip piercings and scuffed trainers of our clientele. I tucked a wayward frond of hair behind my ear but found a pen already there. A pen that was leaking.

'How does a man know he's in Camden? When he's suddenly thigh deep in dogshit. As for the legendary Camden markets? I never knew there was so much crap I didn't want,' he said by way of greeting, kicking my office door closed behind him.

'I do hope the fact that I'm eating lunch isn't spoiling your cigar?' I said as he drew on his Cohiba.

'As you're eating a chocolate eclair for lunch, you're clearly not on a health kick, so excuse me if I puff away . . . I seem to remember that you only eat chocolate when you're stressed, which leads me to wonder just how this innovative practice of yours is going.' He cast a disparaging eye at the stacks of papers waiting to be filed, the boxes not yet unpacked and the piles of unwashed coffee cups.

I dabbed the crumbs from my lips and the ink from my ear and surreptitiously kicked a mousetrap under the desk. 'Success is in the eye of the beholder,' I said.

'Then I obviously need glasses . . . I've been waiting for you to take up the offer to join my Chambers.' He exhaled a fug of smoke. 'But you haven't communicated a word to me.'

'Well, maybe I'm trying to tell you something,' I said. 'And could you please put out that cigar. The Health Act of 2006 makes smoking in the workplace a criminal offence . . . should I choose to bring a prosecution.'

He sauntered to my side and planted a lingering kiss on my mouth. 'I find that people who don't smoke have such a hard time finding something polite to do with their lips,' he said.

I felt the skin tingle and jump where his lips had brushed mine, but turned my head away. 'Well, let me spell it out more clearly, Jack,' I said sternly. 'If you were a magazine, I would not be renewing my subscription.' I wiped his kiss away with a paper napkin. 'Although perhaps it's time you did a little light reading – say "Sexual Harassment in the Workplace, What To Do When You're Sued".'

Jack reluctantly stubbed out his cigar, then leant over my shoulder to see what I was working on. 'Chasing down-and-out dads, 'eh? Just write them off. The Child Support Agency has spent 12 million chasing payments through the courts but has only recouped around 8 mill. It's a complete waste of your time, Matilda.'

'That's not the point. Irresponsible men should be pursued,' I insisted.

'Wouldn't it be better just to suggest to the women concerned that it might be a good idea not to drop their knickers for feckless imbeciles?'

'Then how would you ever get laid?' I fired back.

Jack eyed me for a beat. 'Did you know that your own errant spouse was last seen disappearing into a yurt on a mountain in Kathmandu to "find himself" . . . At least *he's* found himself, even if *you* can't.'

I frowned. He'd touched a nerve. My husband's departure still pained me. A pulse in my temple started throbbing.

'How much child maintenance does the creep owe you? He's no doubt spending it all pampering Petronella. How are you managing to look after your little girl?'

My stomach knotted. Jack was pushing so many of my buttons I was lighting up like a pinball machine. When Steve ran off with the Piranha in Prada, I'd taken Portia to see a shrink. He'd called our session 'free association', but it seemed very expensive to me. She'd refused to go again. In truth, Portia didn't seem to miss her workaholic dad. My daughter's well-adjusted nature and even temper meant my shrink husband had never taken much of an interest in her. Tragic, but true. What would a shrink make of *me*, I wondered. In my case, marriage was not the answer – it was the beginning of a million questions, like '*What the hell did you ever see in that shmuck?*' Clearly, any woman who marries a psychiatrist needs to have her head examined. Although my darling girl was coping well emotionally, financially I was struggling to give her everything she deserved. I'd already had to take her out of her cosy and cosseting little private school and enrol her in the huge local state school. Money worries were giving me excess baggage on a one-way guilt trip. Realizing he'd disarmed me, Jack pushed his advantage.

'You'd be so much better off joining a successful, thriving Chambers where I could guarantee you work that pays.' Jack nonchalantly slid his arms out of the satin lining of his bespoke suit. He sat down gingerly on our brown office sofa, which had the look of a yak that had been dead for some time. 'All you have to do in exchange is go out with me. Just once.'

'Um, how can I put this? I'd rather gnaw my own ovaries out of my body. Now, if you'll excuse me . . .'

'You believe in redemption, yet you won't give me a second chance. Look on it as relationship parole. I realize not telling you that I was also seeing a few other females is the most atrocious, appalling behaviour . . . right behind clubbing baby seals or invading the Crimea. But we were young. I've changed. Give me a second chance to rekindle our romance.'

'Romance? It wasn't a romance, Jack! I just slipped and accidentally fell on you, erotically speaking.'

He glanced around my office in the manner of a feudal lord visiting the home of one of his indentured servants. 'You're smart, clever, original. You got a first at Oxford, for God's sake. You're wasting your time and talent here. You'll never make any money in legal-aided criminal and family law.'

I levelled a steely gaze in his direction. 'Jack, why did you and I spend all those years studying? Because we both wanted a socially relevant working life in which we could devote ourselves utterly to our clients. If money is now your prime motivation, why don't you just go off and become something more suited to the "new" you – say, a body-organ harvester.'

'Socially relevant? I saw your waiting room. This practice is nothing more than fly-paper for freaks. So think about my offer. Otherwise, obscurity knocks, kid.'

Two bounds and he was down the wonky stairs, out of the door and into the weak February sunshine, his jacket flung casually over one broad shoulder. My skin was still radiating warmth where he'd planted his lips. To regain my equilibrium, I dashed off an email: 'I think it wise never to smoke a cigar larger than your penis, Jack. It will only invite acerbic asides from ex-lovers.'

But, in truth, his offer was tempting. And I might have succumbed, to be honest, if Countess Flirtalotsky hadn't stepped in to keep Pandora's open by paying us a small monthly retainer because, in her words, 'a lawyer is the person you hire when you've killed your lover or accountant and you want it explained to the jury in the best possible light. And with me, dah-lings, either of those options is a distinct possibility.'

The Countess is my mother's best friend. In the eighties, they'd linked arms around airbases to stop nuclear weapons being unloaded on British soil. They'd fought to ban the bomb and stormed the Miss World contest, demanding that women not be seen as pieces of meat. They'd thrown eggs at newspaper proprietors who ran photos of topless women on page three. 'No self-respecting ass would wipe itself on that newspaper,' my mother still maintained.

The Countess had been a model. Her jet-black bob, red lips, pale skin, tall, angular frame and tabloid notoriety had ensured she was a favourite of all the famous men of the time. She'd even been seen crawling out from under a Rolling Stone. As her looks faded, her fondness for rich Russians increased, earning her the nickname Countess Flirtalotsky. She finally married an aged oligarch and disappeared for ten years into a five-star gilded gulag.

When she laughs, Countess Flirtalotsky's pretty, pleasing face is upstaged by teeth and gums, which is clearly why she developed the smouldering look which first made her modelling career and then attracted her brooding Russian. When he collapsed with a heart attack in Harrods, however, she couldn't stop smiling . . . which wasn't such a good look in the funeral photos. 'Oh, the relief, dah-ling!' she told us in the funeral parlour. 'His Viagra-popping meant I got lockjaw, working away on him.' Having been housed and fed and caged like some expensive pet, she was now back in our lives as a very merry widow indeed. This was one trophy wife who'd got off the shelf – and only slightly tarnished.

The oligarch had left $200,000 for an elaborate funeral. She told us she spent all of it on a memorial stone.

'Jesus! What kind of stone is it? The *Rosetta*?' Roxy wanted to know.

And that's when the Countess flashed something closely

resembling the Hope diamond which now resided on her middle finger. My mother cackled like a kookaburra.

But it was through her Russian connections that, six months into our joint venture, the Countess secured us a lucrative gig – maintaining a gagging order for one of her infamous oligarch friends. 'Trial by media is the act of putting a public figure on a spit and then getting the public to turn him, slowly roasting him alive. Unthinkable,' she'd shuddered.

The information we were gagging was so hilariously funny that my mother and I would often laugh ourselves hoarse as we discussed its finer details. Obviously, as there's a gagging order, I can't reveal any more details. But, suffice to say, there's whipped cream, a lactating female, goldfish and champagne enemas involved.

But, even after the Countess's intervention, I was struggling. With no financial input from my ex, I just couldn't meet my mortgage payments. I decided that it was prudent to rent the house and move in with my mother.

'Coming to live with me is a divine idea for the Devine family!' my mother enthused when I broached the subject. 'If only because I'm a much better cook, aren't I, Portia, possum?'

My daughter nodded eagerly.

'I can cook!' I piped up defensively.

'Darl, you cook the same meal over and over – "tuna surprise". Well, there's no bloody surprise in that "tuna surprise", Tilly, I'm telling you. By combining resources we can all live like royalty. And we'll be together all day! And we'll make cupcakes! And plant a rose garden!' Roxy enthused. 'And I will be taller!!! Yes, somehow, I will be taller . . .'

Portia was giggling delightedly, but I was slightly worried

about the Grand Canyonesque chasm between fantasy and reality. My doubts were assuaged by the fact that it would be good for Portia to have two full-time parents. Whereas my husband's betrayal hurt me like a nerve exposed to air every time I remembered it, Portia was so happy in the company of her mischievous gran that she didn't seem to give her absentee father a moment's thought. Her blonde, layered hair fell in a big cloudy curtain around her smiling, elfin face. She was developing into the most original, independent girl. At school, her new geography teacher had asked the class to give an example of a natural disaster, and she'd replied, 'The Kardashians'. And when my mother enquired about the rules of *The X Factor*, I heard her explain, 'Contestants must check out of the judges' hotel rooms by 9 a.m.'

'United we stand because, divided, we're screwed,' my mother declared the day we moved into her Camden cottage, lock, stock and pet tortoise, Sheldon (so named because clearly he rarely came out of his).

The Countess frowned on the move. 'Human beings are the only creatures on God's earth who move back in with their parents after they've left the nest. It's just not natural.' The woman had the maternal instincts of a guppy fish. Despite the fact that I was her god-daughter, she'd always been slightly jealous of my relationship with my mother. 'I hate children,' I remember her replying to Roxy's request for her to babysit when I was about eight. 'How can you not detest people who can eat sweets all day without getting fat?'

But there were nice aspects about moving back in with my mother after fifteen years' absence. Your mother is the person who can look in the bathroom cabinet and find the toenail clippers which aren't there, cooks the best Thai curries, lets you win at Scrabble and thinks you're wonderful, no matter what.

But other aspects were not so palatable. Roxy's taste, for one thing. Notwithstanding her turquoise Le Creuset casserole dish, her Italian-style espresso-maker and her 'Make Tea Not War' tea towels, my mother's idea of interior decoration is to drape everything in leopardskin. I had to do a lot of renovation and spent what felt like two and a half months in IKEA looking at bedrooms and bathrooms and wondering how my first from Oxford had led me to setting up shop with my deranged mother. If I never see another FAKTAG UPSLUG and IKBUND OBUNSTIK it will be too FRIKIN soon. I also had the embarrassment of dialling 999 after getting trapped in a flat-pack wardrobe I was assembling.

The other area of contention was our approach to romance. Basically, while I believe in love, my mother's idea of commitment is a meaningful one-night stand with a toy boy or ten. When I complained that Roxy was sleeping with men younger than her own daughter, my mother replied, 'Can I help it if I have voracious appetites? At least there's no cholesterol in toy boys. Which practically makes them a health snack!'

'How the hell does she do it?' marvelled the Countess one day when Roxy disappeared for another 'nooner', this time with the local baker. 'I think your mother must have beer-flavoured nipples. I mean, her carnal dance card is constantly full.'

When bored with stalking elks in Scotland or yachting on the Aegean, the Countess appointed herself our unofficial receptionist – which meant she then got to annoy me during office hours. 'You, on the other hand, Tilly . . .'

I felt my face go clammy. I didn't even *have* a carnal dance card. In the last month alone, my mother had bedded a Frenchman she called her 'Louvre God' (ho hum) and some businessman from the Middle East she conceded was more than likely 'a wolf in sheik's clothing'. I, meanwhile, had been on two blind dates in the space of six months, one with a physics teacher and the other with an accountant, which added up to exactly – nothing.

'The men you go out with are so boring, Matilda, dah-ling. It seems as though the maths teachers are multiplying . . . Which is what they're good at, I suppose,' the Countess said, perching on one bony buttock on the edge of my office desk.

In truth, I just couldn't subject men to my mother. The trouble was, in the past, if I brought home a man whom Roxy didn't like, she would parade about the place in her lime-green thong, which was usually enough to put off my more reserved suitors. If she really disliked him, she would play her Rolling Stones, Sex Pistols and Grateful Dead albums at full volume after hiding the remote.

Still, even though I was as devoted as Roxy to bringing to justice the men who'd used and abused women, I remained at heart a closet Jane Austen-addled romantic optimist. What my mother called 'a pathetic heroine addict'.

'I don't want to find the perfect man,' Roxy protested, 'I just want to be able to eat pudding without getting podgy. Besides, I found Mr Right once, remember?' My biological father's betrayal had left her opinion of men so minusculely low you'd need a microscope to find it.

The Countess had given up on men, both perfect and imperfect.

'Oh, the relief of no longer having to fake orgasms,' she admitted one day, breaking off from her haphazard document-filing.

'I don't fake orgasms,' my mother confided. 'I'm faking being six foot one and seven stone.'

'Really?' From her lofty six-foot height, the Countess

peered down at my mother, who was squashed into a lurex miniskirt, the buttons of which were bursting across her broad stomach. Then she deadpanned, 'And how's that working out for you?'

They chortled like two schoolgirls. The once-sought-after model was now said to be a 'handsome' woman. 'That's ugly with money,' the Countess had explained to me, self-deprecatingly. Not only did she own a race horse, but, as her long, elegant face lost collagen with age, she'd started to resemble one. However, around Roxy, she never stopped smiling.

While I often wondered what the world would be like if God had had a daughter, I most definitely had not gone off men. Unfortunately, only one man pursued me with any enthusiasm – the one man I didn't want. 'Your silence is causing me stress,' Jack Cassidy emailed. 'And stress could give me a heart attack.'

'Don't worry,' I pinged back. 'If you have a heart attack, I'll send for an ambulance . . . by carrier pigeon.'

But decor and dating aside, my mother and I were united in one thing – making Pandora's a success so that we could help women who'd been handed the hard cheese from fate's *fromage* trolley.

We hoped to go far. Of course, the Establishment thought the further away we went, the better. But the case that was about to change our fortunes was headed straight for us like a giant boomerang. I was just thinking, 'Why is that boomerang getting bigger?' and then, ladies and gentlemen of the jury, it hit me.

4

The Big Bang Theory

It was one of those days when I wanted to swap my life
for what was behind door number 1. Not only had I endured
a date with a man who spoke for an hour about his fossil
collection, but then I'd been flashed by a raincoat-wearing perv
in the park on the way home. (I just pointed at his groin and
said, 'What do you want me to do with it . . . *floss*?') In other
words, the whole night had been a total waste of waxing. I
flumped into an armchair and broke open a block of dark
organic chocolate to keep me awake while I waited for Portia to
come home from her best friend Amelia's birthday party.
Suddenly, my mother burst through the door with a pensioner
who was toting a rifle. Both of them were covered in blood.

There was a time when my mother bursting through the
door with an armed, blood-soaked septuagenarian would
have kicked me into cardiac arrest. But bursting in with a
gore-splattered fugitive just seemed kind of normal after
working at Pandora's for over a year.

'Let me guess,' I said. 'Your Amish prayer meeting got a
little out of hand?'

But then I saw my mother's strained face and realized it was not a prank. 'This is Phyllis,' she said. 'She's just shot her granddaughter's rapists in the testicles.'

I looked at the little woman before me. Then I looked at the gun in her hand.

What's fascinating about staring down a gun barrel is how small the hole is where the bullet comes out, yet what a big hole it would make in your social life. I looked back at the diminutive grandma. She was in her early seventies, with a face as warm and round as a muffin. In her floral dress and patterned cardigan, she did not look like a psychopath. She looked more like something that had fallen off the side of a ceramic Cornish teapot.

'I think you should have a stiff drink, Phyllis,' my mother advised the gun-toter. 'Vodka?' she asked, pouring a glass for herself and downing it in one gulp.

'I only drink water, Roxy, pet,' Granny Phyllis said, her voice as sweet as her soft, even features.

'Vodka is just water with attitude,' my mother advised, thrusting a drink at her with one hand, while gently prising free the gun with the other. My mother's nod indicated that I was to distract Phyllis while she stowed the firearm in the hallway broom cupboard.

'I do suggest you slug it down, Phyllis. It's medicinal . . . So what exactly happened?' I asked, steering the small woman across our living room and into an armchair. When she sat back, her dainty feet in their scuffed slip-ons didn't even reach the carpet. Blue veins, like lumpy knitting, ran from chubby ankle to dimpled knee. What poor tiny feet, I thought, to carry such a heavy load.

'Chantelle. My darlin' little granddaughter. She was raped. In a stairwell. By two gang members. Off the estate. She was on 'er way out to celebrate 'er birthday. Her sixteenth birthday. She wouldn't give 'em a "shiner". That's what all the girls are expected to do,' she said matter-of-factly.

'Blow job,' my worldly mother translated. 'Go on, Phyllis,' she urged, sitting by her side and taking her wrinkled hand. They were the hands of a labourer, the hands of a woman who'd spent her life cleaning other people's toilets. Provocation or mental impairment, I calculated: three years – max. Plus great mitigating circumstances . . .

'Uppity, they called 'er. Snobby an' that. So she was targeted and punished. She called me on 'er mobile, Chanty did. I went straight there. 'Er mother's in prison. Drugs.' She waved her hand in a weary way. 'I've raised 'er. My darlin' Chanty. She's the most sweet and lovin' angel. And there she was. Lyin' on the ground, beaten, sobbin', broken.'

She faltered, pausing to retrieve a hankie from inside her cardigan sleeve to wipe her red-rimmed eyes. She then took a ragged breath and gulped down the vodka, flinching at its bite. 'She gave me a description of them, Chanty did – leather jackets, tatts, the lot. I got me car and got 'er to the 'ospital, then drove back to their end of the estate. I followed those rats to see where they lived. Took photos on Chanty's phone. Then went back to the 'ospital to show 'er. She identified 'em. So I took me 'usband's old gun – he used to shoot rabbits, back 'ome in Derry, before the emphysema got 'im – then went round to their flat and knocked on the door. When one of 'em opened it, I shot 'im in the gonads. The other one I only grazed, I think. But I doubt he'll be playin' Hide the Sausage any time shortly. Then I came straight to Roxy.'

My mother and I exchanged wide-eyed, raised-brow glances.

'You took photos of them before the attack?' I asked, my

heart sinking. This was premeditation. The prosecution would put her away. Ten years minimum.

Phyllis extracted her granddaughter's mobile phone from her cardigan pocket. She patted the side of the armchair as an indicator that I should perch beside her. She scrolled through the photos she'd surreptitiously snapped of her grand-daughter's attackers. The two men, in their late twenties or early thirties, were pictured swigging from beer bottles outside the local pub. In their regulation leather jackets and huge biker boots, they looked as though they'd just popped in from the Hun/Goth-infested Dark Ages of evolution. The tall, bulky one had the body of a stegosaurus, with a brain to match, no doubt. He had pale, acned skin and his dirty brown hair seemed to have been styled with a whisk. The shorter one was Asian – wiry, brittle and mean-looking, like a half-starved, malicious ferret.

My mother and I stared at the photos for a while in silence, contemplating the veracity of Darwin's evolutionary hypothesis.

'Honestly, Phyllis, I too have a beautiful granddaughter,' my mother finally sighed. 'I would have done the same thing myself. The low-life, cowardly scum.'

'Mother!' I reprimanded her. 'We're not in downtown Mogadishu. We don't go around blasting the balls off rape suspects.' I turned my attention back to our visiting pensioner. 'So, what did he say, when he opened the door – the first man – and saw you aiming below his belt?' I probed.

'He said, "Don't shoot me in the nuts! What if I wanna have babies?"'

'And what did you say?'

'I said, "You? A father? I'm doin' the world a bleedin' favour."'

'Too right,' Roxy agreed, patting Phyllis's hand, which, I

now noticed, had started shaking uncontrollably. 'Clearly, his gene pool's as shallow as a mud puddle. It was really just an impromptu vasectomy. Saved him the trouble.'

'Roxy!' I looked at my mother, wondering if it was too late to put myself up for adoption. 'It's grievous bodily harm is what it is. Attempted murder. You must plead guilty, Phyllis. With extenuating circumstances . . . We must also call the police immediately.'

'We will,' Roxy said. 'I'm just getting the story straight. So, what did the other guy say? The second rapist?'

' "Gimme a chance, lady." '

'And what did you say?' I prompted.

' "Okay, swing 'em." '

Roxy snorted out a laugh.

'Then I recocked the rifle . . .'

'Unfortunate terminology, under the circs,' my mother commented wryly.

I levelled another disapproving glance in her direction. Parents can be such a disappointment. It's such a shame when they don't fulfil the potential of their early years. 'Roxy, what are you thinking!' I scolded. 'Two men have been maimed here.'

'What I'm thinking is what a good shot you are, Phyllis. I mean, what was the angle of the dangle?'

I took aim, too, and shot my mother another scalding look. 'Technically, you'll be under arrest for attempted murder, as the victims might die,' I sombrely informed the distressed gran. Her face was suddenly as rumpled as an unmade bed.

'But you didn't want to hurt them, did you, Phyllis?' my mother coaxed. 'No . . . Your granddaughter was raped. A fog came over you. You felt enraged. You decided to go door to door to find the culprits. You took the gun to arm yourself because that end of the council estate is very rough . . . You saw the men and felt overcome with rage and, before you knew what had happened, you'd shot them.'

Phyllis shook her head. 'No. Those poxy bastards raped my darlin' granddaughter. I wanted to take their balls off so they could never do anythin' like this to any other girl.'

'No,' my mother reiterated patiently. 'What I understand you to mean is that you took the gun around to wave at them, to frighten them. To warn them not to say anything that would degrade your lovely girl. That she was asking for it, or some such rubbish . . .'

'Um . . . Mother, do you really think you should be coaching the defendant?'

Roxy darted a crafty look my way. 'Coaching is contrary to the rules of practice, Tilly. I am merely assisting Phyllis to recall her confused emotions.' She turned back towards the old lady. 'Surely you just wanted to warn them not to say anything bad and untrue about your granddaughter, calling her a slut or a slag . . .' Roxy shushed me with her hand. 'You only took the gun to give them a scare . . . and to protect yourself.' She was speaking in the calm, steady, authoritative tone of an air-traffic controller who has to instruct an untrained flyer how to land the plane after the pilot has lost consciousness. 'And then, when they answered the door, terrorized by such frightening scum, before you knew it, you'd fired the rifle. That's what happened, isn't it?'

'I'm not listening to this, Roxy.' My mother's legal ethics were proving harder to find than a supermodel's pantry. 'Lawyers are not supposed to put words in a defendant's mouth and create a defence,' I explained to Phyllis.

'I'm not – absolutely not – creating Phyllis's defence . . . I'm merely helping her to articulate, in a more effective way, what happened, aren't I, love?'

I fired off another censorious glare in Roxy's direction. That was the biggest understatement since the captain of the *Titanic* said to his crew, 'Did you chaps just feel a bump?' If it was found out that she had fabricated evidence, my mother would be banged up faster than you could say 'pepper spray'. I took her aside, rather forcefully.

'Our practice is not exactly thriving, Roxy. The male-dominated Bar is dying to see us fail. We have to be above reproach. If you keep up this unethical behaviour, I'll have you incarcerated in a maximum-security old persons' home. I'm not kidding. As your only child, don't forget that your fate falls to me!'

'Matilda, I think you're confusing what happens in law school with what happens in real life. Women who've been traumatized can't accurately articulate what happened. They go into a post-traumatic-stress stupor. It's why we try not to put the victims of domestic abuse into the witness box – they're so beaten down, they're like robots. I'm just helping Phyllis to remember the events. Of course part of her wanted to kill them, but she's not daft. She went around there in a mad, confused muddle. She wanted to stop them destroying her granddaughter's life any more by slagging her off, but was scared out of her wits and—'

I left my mother illegally coaching her client and dialled the police. After giving a brief account of the facts, I hung up and returned to the grieving gran. She sat staring at her shoe with forensic absorption while Roxy topped up her drink. 'Are you okay, Phyllis?'

'Call me Phizz. That's what my friends call me. I have to remain strong, 'cause that's what a mother has to be. My daughter, she was the best dancer in school. Had all the main parts in the plays an' that. Then she got in with a bad crowd. Left school. Worked in a club in Soho. She couldn't catch the Tube without dancin'. She'd see that pole and off she'd go . . .

But then came the drugs. Her "medicine", she called it.'
Phyllis suddenly dry-retched. I moved back hastily from the
line of fire. But then she stopped gagging and slumped in
the chair, stricken. 'I came straight to you, Roxy 'cause you
know 'ow to give little people a voice.'

Roxy poured her another slug of vodka and patted her
hand consolingly.

'Once, I used to be frightened to question the head-
mistress,' Phyllis went on. 'Now, I would stand up to the
queen. When it involves yer kids, you'd stand up to anyone.
If yer child is hurt, it hurts more than someone hurtin' you.
Any mother can tell you that. Or any grandma.'

There was such dignity about her, it struck me that she
could have been the queen of some remote European princi-
pality, and not a cleaning lady living on a council estate.
Phyllis's small green eyes, buried in her cabbage-round face,
filled with tears.

'I swore to protect my darlin' granddaughter.' Her
shoulders drew together and her body twisted in a spasm of
grief. As she cried, something cracked open in her and I could
see straight through to her heart. It was a good heart. It had
worked hard and been kind to strays, and fed pigeons, and
scrimped and gone without for her girls.

As we waited for the police, my mother said, 'Phyllis is
going to plead not guilty. And I'd like to instruct you in this
case, Matilda.'

'I'm not free.'

'Yes, you are. I checked your diary.'

This is the downside of working and living in the same
house as your instructing solicitor. 'Does Phyllis have any
other convictions?'

'She has one conviction, yes, for non-traditional shopping.'

'You mean shoplifting.'

'Well, yes ... But times were tough. She had mouths to feed.'

'We're not in *Les Misérables*, Mother,' I boomed. 'We do have benefits here in Britain, you know.'

'Shhh.' Roxy moved me out of earshot of the traumatized gran and whispered sarcastically, 'Tell me, Tilly, with your diplomacy skills, have you ever considered a career in hostage negotiations? Will you just come and meet the little girl? She's still in the hospital.'

'This is exactly what I mean about you getting too close to the client. I can't take the case if she pleads not guilty. Phyllis has just told us she shot these men in cold blood.'

'So would I, if they did that to my granddaughter.'

'But you can't just take the law into your own hands. That makes you no better than Ku Klux Klan lynch mobs ... It's spine-chilling. Think of Anne Boleyn, Joan of Arc and the women of Salem, all executed after trials consisting of hysterical accusations of witchcraft. Just think of all that and it will make you respect the order of things – the slow taking of statements, the boxes of evidence, which are turned into documents, then the documents into a case and a case into a conviction ... and justice is done. It's the birthright of every British citizen to have a fair trial. It's the centre of my moral compass. It's the foundation of my love of the law.'

'Jesus wept. Have you taken a Pollyanna pill or something? I didn't realize I'd given birth to Atticus friggin' Finch.'

'They might not even be the right blokes. Then what?' I turned my attention back to the pocket-sized pensioner lost in our big leather armchair. She looked paler than the snow which had started falling outside the window. 'Is there anything I can get you, Phyllis, before the police arrive?'

Her lips were quivering with the effort to stop crying. 'Well ... I could do with a little lippy.'

Roxy extracted a peach-coloured lipstick from her handbag and handed it to her. A few minutes later, I heard the car tyres hit the kerb as the squad car jerked to a halt outside. I peeked through the curtain to see two uniformed policemen getting out.

'Now, Phizz,' my mother instructed, 'when the police arrive, as your solicitor, let me do the talking. Don't say anything.'

'But I wanna tell 'em what 'appened.'

'No, you don't. Let me handle it,' I heard Roxy stress as I moved down the hall to open the door. 'Okay?'

I ushered the officers into the living room. 'The scumbags raped my granddaughter,' Phyllis immediately blurted.

'Say no more,' Roxy admonished. 'My client doesn't want to speak.'

'Yes, I do!'

'No. You. Don't.'

'Two poxy druggie gang members raped my darlin' grand-daughter in a stairwell on the estate. On her sixteenth birthday. So I took me 'usband's old huntin' gun and I ended up shootin' them in the goolies. At least it means that they can't do it to any other little girl.'

The radio strapped to the policeman's shoulder made a sudden, violent sound, like the cough of a dying man. With end-of-shift weariness, he spoke into it to ask for a firearms officer to come and make the gun safe. The other policeman, who had the twitchy alertness of a small rodent, began his spiel. 'You do not have to say anything, but it may harm your defence if you do not mention when questioned something which you later rely on in court, and anything you do say may be given in evidence.'

Phyllis sat in numb silence as one of the policemen dusted her fingertips for gunshot residue. The firearms officer arrived next. 'Where's the gun?' he demanded. I pointed to the broom cupboard.

The uniformed policemen now cuffed Phyllis and led her outside. She looked up at us with the bewildered, frightened, shiny eyes of a small marsupial, disturbed in the dark.

'I'll come with you to the station to see what time you're being interviewed in the morning,' Roxy said soothingly. 'Then there'll be a bail hearing and we'll get you out.'

'Please go to the 'ospital and tell Chanty where I am. She's got nobody else to watch out for 'er . . . My one prayer for my granddaughter was to keep her safe from rape and drugs and violence. And I failed 'er . . .' Phyllis's voice cracked.

It was then, while I was standing shivering in our doorway, flanked by uniformed officers, a handcuffed, blood-soaked potential murderess sobbing in my arms, that Portia was dropped home from the birthday party by her best friend's prissy mother. I had an inkling this would pretty much ensure that I wouldn't be awarded any Advanced Parenting Proficiency Certificates at the next PTA meeting.

As Portia bounded towards me, I looked at my cherished child. She was a fair-skinned, bow-lipped girl with dancing eyebrows which seemed to lead a gymnastic life of their own above her sparkling eyes. She smiled at me, her eyes full of life and laughter – a young, happy, hearty girl on the brink of womanhood. With a sickening thud, I thought of Chantelle in the hospital. My only prayer for my daughter was this: 'Dear Lord: no tattoos. May neither a Sanskrit symbol for eternal love nor a dolphin leaping over a rainbow ever stain her tender haunches.'

What a charmed life we led compared to Phyllis and Chantelle. I felt a sudden stab of protective love for my daughter, which caught me completely off guard.

'Roxy,' I called out after my mother, who was escorting the grieving gran down to the police car. 'First thing in the morning, we'll leave for the hospital.'

My daughter took in the scene. 'Hi Mum, another quiet night at Pandora's then?'

5

A Good Bollocking

If jumping to conclusions were an Olympic category, I would be a gold medallist. The conclusion I jumped to the morning after Phyllis's arrest was that there was no way on God's earth that the old woman was going to get bail. Roxy called me from the police station to give me an update, or a 'Bollock Bulletin', as she called it. A 29-year-old man who went by the name of 'Stretch' because of his six-foot-two height had lost one testicle. Thirty-year-old Basharat Kureishi, nicknamed 'Bash', had suffered only a genital graze. But both had spent a painful night getting needlepoint in their nether regions. After interviewing the hospitalized victims, the police had charged Phyllis with attempted murder. The paperwork had been emailed to the Crown Prosecution Service and the hearing was fixed for the following morning.

As soon as my mother's Midget sports car mounted the kerb outside our house – her preferred parking manoeuvre – we headed straight for the hospital to honour our promise to Phyllis to check on her poor granddaughter.

Phyllis's girl lay pale as paper on her hospital bed. She

looked like a thing made of skin and bones pretending to be a teenager. Her back, a xylophone of spine and ribs, was visible through the thin white gown. A worm of blood inched up the tube from her wrist. Her head was bandaged, as were her hands. She had a bruise the size of a man's hand around her throat and a bad, bloodless look to her face.

Her long body lay awkwardly, as though not used to solid ground. Poor panting little fish, I thought. Presuming she was sleeping, I scooted a chair up to the bed, but as I did so her eyelids fluttered open. Her luminous orbs fleetingly held mine. They were bare and round as lightbulbs. She blinked in bewilderment, as if she'd just stumbled out of some remote jungle and was perplexed by the world she discovered around her. She drew a shuddering breath and started making a whimpering, squeaking noise, like a stuck drawer.

'It's okay, love. We're friends of your gran's. I'm Roxy, and this is my daughter, Matilda. We just came by to tell you that your gran is not going to be around for a few days. When she saw what happened to you she went after those scumbags. And, well, she's with the police right now . . . helping with their enquiries.'

'Water,' the girl asked quietly.

I noted there was no water jug on the side table and crossed to the door to accost a passing medic. 'Nurse?'

'And I wanna clean my teeth,' Chantelle's voice rasped behind me.

''Fraid not,' the nurse said matter-of-factly.

I was so shocked by her brusque reply that I turned to appraise the woman more closely. She was in her late twenties, with pale skin – pre-Raphaelite pale – with auburn tendrils of hair escaping her nurse's cap – a look that seemed far too delicate for the wards of an inner-city London hospital.

'Not till after forensics.' The nurse's harsh, nasal Estuary accent belied her exotic looks. If she'd been born in the 1850s, she'd have been 'discovered' by Dante Gabriel Rossetti and made to pose for hours in a medieval dress, fingering a lute, for a series of languorous portraits. Yet here she was, dealing with vaginal swabs, stale ejaculate and genital diseases which she couldn't quite put her finger on . . . and would much rather not, judging by her off-handedness.

Her voice was prodding, metallic, cold as a gynaecologist's speculum. 'It's protocol. No interfering with forensics till after the physical exam.'

'But why's it taking so long?' I asked the nurse. 'And shouldn't she be in a specialist rape suite?'

Lethargy clung to the nurse like satin in summer. She greeted my query with all the enthusiasm with which you'd welcome a yeast infection. 'Medical emergency comes first. The girl got smacked over the head. We have to make sure there's no concussion before a rape specialist can examine her. Plus, there're internal injuries, too. And bruising around her throat. And cracked ribs.'

'But the poor kid's been here since last night!' I protested.

'Yeah, well, so have I,' the redhead snarled.

'Listen up, Nursey. I'm Chantelle's lawyer,' my mother growled. 'So I suggest you get the rape specialist here right now. Otherwise, all you'll be putting a dressing on is a salad – in your waitressing job after I get you fired.'

One of my mother's attributes which I most admire is her breezy ability to cut through protocol like a scalpel through the epidermis. Ten minutes later, in a flurry of white coats and stethoscopes, a rape specialist arrived. A screen was propped up around the bed. Roxy and I were to wait outside. 'They have to take swabs,' my mother explained. 'Vagina and mouth. They'll take samples from under her fingernails, plus other scrapings and cuttings, and pubic-hair combings.'

Happy sixteenth birthday, Chantelle.

Roxy introduced me to the sexual offences liaison officer who had also just miraculously arrived. While we waited she talked us through what Chantelle had told her. The officer had established that there were two men and that it was a Section 1 rape.

'That's penetration of any orifice without consent,' my mother clarified.

The officer's description of Chantelle's harrowing ordeal was interrupted by raised voices inside the room – the teenager was too shy and traumatized to take off her hospital gown. We could hear the doctor explaining that she needed to take a vaginal swab. That she'd be really gentle and would use a cotton bud. That it would be a bit uncomfortable and may sting a little, but would be over quickly, as would the injection for a blood sample.

'I want my gran!'

My mother and I exchanged pained, wretched glances.

When the doctor finally emerged, she told us that the perpetrators had scrawled an inked message across Chantelle's abdomen in felt-tip pen. 'They've drawn an arrow pointing towards her pudenda with the message "Wash this". And "Dirty bitch".'

My toes curled up like dead leaves in my shoes.

'How can you not take this case, Matilda?' Roxy insisted.

When Roxy and I came back into the room, we immediately offered Chantelle the glass of water and toothbrush the pre-Raphaelite nurse had now, finally, fetched. The teenager drained the glass, then drew herself in against Roxy like a small animal in need of a place to hide, her hands clutching at my mother's sleeve. She started weeping. I looked down at her face pityingly. The nurse came back to administer a sedative.

'Don't fret, pet,' my mother said soothingly, stroking the girl's lank hair. 'I'm going to get the mongrels who did this.'

'Is . . . is Gran . . . in . . . trouble?' Chantelle whimpered.

'Not if we can help it, possum,' Roxy said. 'Isn't that right, Tilly?'

'Chantelle,' I probed gently, 'are you sure your grandma attacked the right men?'

The young woman nodded. As she turned her head towards me, I saw the necklace of bruises, dark as an aubergine, ringing her throat.

'Are you one hundred per cent sure the photos she took were of the perpetrators?'

'I know 'em. From round the estate. They load the girls up with alcohol and drugs an' that. They make all the girls do stuff they don't wanna do. I told my friends not to get treated like pieces of meat. They attacked me 'cause I didn't want nuffink to do with 'em. They trapped me. They threatened to burn my gran alive if I refused to give 'em a shiner. That scared me. I thought to meself "Don't be a baby. Just get on and do it, to save Gran." But I couldn't. I screamed and fought and then they ripped my top off and shoved my skirt up . . .'

A sorrow as black as night invaded me. I felt my throat clamping. The stairwell where she was attacked must have echoed like a cave. But nobody came.

Her eyes began to glaze over with the dull impassivity of medication. Soon the only hint that Chantelle was breathing at all was the relentless trembling of her legs beneath the sheet.

'If there's anything you need, you call me, all right?' My mother tore a piece of paper from her diary, scribbled down her number and left it on the nightstand. 'I'll be back tonight to check up on you.'

We closed the door softly and stood for a moment bathed in the harsh fluorescent light, staring at each other.

'That poor girl needs counselling. Can we get her some kind of help?'

Roxy trudged down the hospital corridor towards the lift. 'If a trial's coming up, then the police discourage counselling. If Chantelle says anything different to the counsellor than what she says to the police, the defence could use it against her.'

'But a trial may be six or nine months away. Besides, do you think she'll be strong enough to give evidence?'

My mother shrugged, stabbing the lift button. 'Right now she's in startled-deer mode. But if she's anything like her gran . . .'

The lift doors suddenly suctioned open and we were staring right into the face of one of Chantelle's attackers. It was the wiry, thin one we'd seen in Phyllis's photos. He had a diamond earring in his right lobe and prison-issue clothing – a navy sweatshirt, matching jogging bottoms and black plimsolls, and was handcuffed to an officer my mother knew.

'Jeez, Ray. Don't *you* get all the cushy jobs. Have you charged the bastard yet?'

'He'll be formally charged down at the station. They want forensics first.' He held up the accused's clothes, which had been bagged to prevent hair and fibres from falling off.

'Where's the other scuzzy dirtbag?' Roxy said, as we stepped into the lift.

'Surgery. Shot his ball right off.' The policeman winced. 'Nearly hit the femoral artery.'

'And this drongo?'

'Leg wound and slight graze on one nut. He'll live.'

'Unfortunately.' My mother glowered at the man in cuffs.

'Oy!' The rapist who went by the name of Bash thrust his head forward like a raptor. 'I neva done nuffink,' he said in a Norf London accent. 'Weez innocent, yeah.' Even at long range, his breath hit you like a solid block. It then melted and just slithered down your face, leaving a trail of nacho cheese and onion relish. 'Some mad hag comes and blasts us for no fuckin' reason. What's that about then?'

'Gee, I dunno . . . Possibly because you brutally gang-raped her granddaughter?' My mother's voice dripped angry sarcasm.

Bash reeked of malevolence. I could feel it coming off him in waves, as strong as aftershave.

'What do nine out of ten people enjoy?' the raptor rapist sneered. 'Gang rape.'

For a moment I saw my mother thinking about borrowing the policeman's gun and shooting him in his other testicle. She took aim with a verbal bullet instead. 'Just as well your dick isn't any bigger, or Phyllis might have actually hit you.'

I gave my mother a censorious look. Judges take a dim view of the defence team badgering prosecution witnesses. 'Um, Roxy, as Phyllis's solicitor, I suggest you make like a turtle and pull your head in,' I counselled.

'Of course,' she agreed. 'I never pass judgement on prosecution witnesses, and I'm not going to break the habit of a legal lifetime, for this piece of shit.'

'Anyways, it ain't rape if you yell "Surprise!" first.' The thug then leant right into my face, so I copped the full force of his sour breath. ' "*Surprise!*" ' His laugh was totally B-grade-movie satanic.

'Oy! Shut it,' the policeman told Bash. The lift doors whooshed open on the ground floor and he manhandled the raptor out of the hospital.

'Men like that need to be taught a lesson,' Roxy sighed as

we walked back to her car. 'This behaviour springs from cultures that fail to persecute rape. Men think they can get away with it, because they do. Phyllis's bail hearing's in the morning. Ah . . . if only I knew a good lawyer . . .'

My mother drives fast at the most relaxed of times. But today she was so furious she'd decided that amber lights were merely a device to get drivers to accelerate. She was so red-faced with anger that I was tempted to ask the guy at the traffic lights to forget the windscreen and just lean in and squeegee her forehead.

'On the surface, those rapists may seem like clichéd, brainless thugs straight out of central casting. But don't underestimate them. To my mind, those gangrenous polyps fit the mould of drug-gang members who treat girls like sperm spittoons. They have a Ph.D. in lying, misogyny and deception. It's time they were booted up the bum, right into maximum-security prison.'

I clutched the dashboard for dear life as the car caromed off a speed bump and we momentarily took flight.

'Look, what happened to Chantelle is unforgivable. But her grandma attacked in cold blood. All this eye-for-an-eye stuff, it's so Old Testament.'

'Sometimes it's the only way, Tilly. Phyllis knows that raped girls often end up too terrified and intimidated to testify.'

'But if you advocate the law of "jungle justice", society collapses into chaos. I specialize in civil not criminal law. I've spent my life cross-examining people who have acted unlawfully – dodgy doctors and dentists and such. I could only act for Phyllis if she pleads guilty. I could do a good plea in a mitigation to the judge for a lenient sentence.'

I was beginning to make Mother Teresa seem frolicsome, but it was the truth.

'Let me show you where it happened,' was Roxy's answer to that.

The Royal Free Hospital is on the edge of Hampstead Heath. Hampstead Village is a haven of arugula salad and Aga stoves and Cath Kidston cushions. But as you drive south towards Camden, the genteel Georgian properties quickly give way to council estates with a severe shortage of Montessori schools and yogalate classes. Roxy swung her car off the winding, picturesque road and into the mass of grim tower blocks that made up the Tony Benn Estate.

An inner-city-London council estate is like downtown Haiti, only without the glamour. At one end, an abandoned factory loomed out of the rain like a dark cathedral. It was surrounded by a tidal wave of concrete – cluttered, shabby tower blocks, their balconies strung with washing and their facades festooned with satellite dishes. Although there definitely was a rough poetry to the place. A second-hand-furniture shop on the corner boasted a wobbly hand-painted sign in its window which read 'Sofa King – Our prices are Sofa King low.'

Roxy's MG Midget swerved through upended green wheelie bins on to the ironically named Buttercup Road, where the shrubs bloomed with discarded crisp packets and plastic bags. Only the weeds seemed to keep growing, like the toenails on a corpse. The whole place looked ready for a Quentin Tarantino remake.

A cluster of adolescent boys wearing black hoodies sat on their haunches, like a row of crows, on the carcass of a rusted car. They seemed suspicious and furtive, like urban foxes, ready to scavenge.

Roxy nosed her car into a kerb and cut the engine. The rain had stopped and the sky was a curdled grey, with lumps of clouds. A film of grit and despondency lay an inch thick on everything and the atmosphere reeked of sewage and petrol fumes. I had little doubt that my mother and I were wearing the only natural fibres for quite a few miles in any direction.

Before us a dank stairwell led up to darkness. The lift was not working and hadn't been for years, judging by the arbour of cobwebs inside. The stairwell exuded a clammy odour, like the breath of a stray, half-starved dog.

Oblivious, Roxy bounded up the stairs in her leopardskin boots. As I panted along behind her, one thing became clear – there was little chance of me representing Britain in the next Olympics. On each landing there was a tiny window that had once let in light but was now so grey with grime that it might as well have been night outside. When I'd finally wheezed my way to the top floor, my mother was taking pictures of the routes to and from the stairwell. In the gloom, I picked out the mould-flecked walls and bare, broken lightbulbs. Visions of the little girl trapped and assaulted here turned my stomach. Torn fragments of crime-scene tape festooned the area. This bleak bunting marked the spot that had been cordoned off by scene of crime officers that morning. All physical evidence – condoms, weapons, cigarette ends, discarded bottles, cans and tissues – would have been photographed by the SOCO and bagged.

I was bending over, catching my breath, when a footfall alerted me to company. In the darkness, I heard low, heavy breathing, then a figure loomed out of the shadows and made a lunge for my handbag. I thought about running, but who was I kidding? The closest I ever get to an accelerated heart-beat is when the shoe sale is on at Selfridges. At school I was always the last to be picked for the hockey team. (It usually came down to me or the bench.)

My mother always boasts that she's a member of Athletics

Anonymous – 'Whenever I feel like doing some exercise, I call an anonymous friend who talks me out of it.' But despite this, she's strong as an ox and can outrun and out-wrestle most men. And so, in my usual heroic way, I just hid behind my mother.

'Gimme it,' a male voice snarled. It was then I saw the knife. He jabbed the serrated, evil tooth towards my abdomen.

I'm a lawyer. The only wound I've ever received is the odd paper cut. Which is why I was about to hand over my handbag when my mother roared, 'Oy! That's a hundred per cent genuine imitation Dolce and Gabbana!' then kicked the man so hard in the shin with her leopardskin heel that he dropped the knife. Next, she stomped on his instep and twisted his arm. 'Judo, the handshake that bites back,' I thought to myself. As she spun his arm up behind his body, she ripped off his hooded jacket. With his head and face now exposed, all menace evaporated. Our assailant was a boy of no more than fourteen, his face lightly frosted with acne. He actually looked like Justin Bieber, but the version that had been made to steal beer for his dad at the age of nine and watch his mum get high on crack.

'Gimme back me hoodie,' the boy whined. 'I'll catch cold. See? I'm snifflin' already.'

My mother kicked the knife into the light, where she could see it. 'Oh, good God. It's a friggin' butter knife. What were you going to do? Slather me to death with marmalade? What kind of hardened criminal *are* you?' Roxy scoffed. She then dipped into her pocket and retrieved a fistful of jellybeans which she thrust out at him on her open palm before relaxing her grip on him. The kid snatched up some sweets, then scuttled away.

'Jellybeans?' I asked, as we descended the reeking staircase.

'You bring your only daughter on to a crime-riddled estate armed with a packet of 9-calibre candy?'

'My secret weapon,' she explained. 'I always carry a supply in my pocket. It soothes the raucous. Most of these kids are just misguided and disadvantaged. They wouldn't know happiness if it jumped up and bit them in the bum. At school, they write essays entitled "What I'm Going to Be *If* I Grow Up",' she called out as she catapulted down the last flight. By the time I caught up with her at the car, a crowd of girls in stack heels the size of mill chimneys had gathered around it, lounging on a patch of threadbare grass in the feeble sunshine.

'Maybe the locals are planning a little barbecue,' my mother suggested.

'Oh, well, that's nice . . .'

My mother gave me one of her condescending if-only-my-daughter-specialized-in-criminal-instead-of-civil-law looks. '"Barbecue" is the local terminology for burning a body in a petrol-doused car. Possibly ours. Estates are made up of decent, hard-working people, Tilly. But flats become vacant, the council does nothing, the rats move in first, then the drug dealers, who also thrive in dark corners. Pretty soon it's a no-go area.' She pointed to the shabby, squalid block opposite us, which was throbbing with heavy metal bass and drums. 'If you're surrounded by crime, no matter how hard you try to protect your family, some of them will be sucked into the underworld. Especially when there's no work.'

She glanced back warily at the girls gathered by our car. But we soon saw why they were there.

In huge scarlet dripping letters on the stairwell's outer wall was emblazoned the still-wet graffiti 'Chantelle's a dirty slut'.

My mother went barrelling towards the gang, her face

fierce. 'Who did this?' she demanded. The wind made a comedy of her beehive, which now listed precariously to the left, a pale pagoda of toppling curls.

The girls collectively gave us the finger, their nails long enough to fight off a porcupine.

Roxy marched to the corner shop to buy turps and two scrubbing brushes. I trailed after her. A sign on the shop counter read 'No pork products sold here.'

'Shame there's no ban on chauvinist pigs then,' Roxy fumed. As she scoured and scratched at the graffiti, she mumbled, 'As I keep saying – *if only I knew a good lawyer*.'

I picked up the other brush and also attacked the scarlet lettering. An icy wind had sprung up. It moaned around the sharp corners of buildings, slapped my face and thwacked the backs of my stockinged legs. Bemused onlookers watched us work, our hands numb and red raw with cold. A clump of males in hooded puffa jackets and black chinos swaggered into view. The group of girls suddenly resembled a shoal of petrified fish as sharks slowly circle. I thought of Chantelle, terrified and cornered. I thought of my own darling daughter, just a few years younger.

'Okay, Roxy,' I told my mother, 'I'll take the case.'

6

Designer Genes

Before you eat anything in prison, just remember that every morsel of food about to pass your lips was supplied by the lowest bidder. That was my mother's advice to Phyllis when she was carted off to Holloway – a hotel where the guest is always wrong – after bail was refused by the local magistrate, just as I'd predicted.

Both of Chantelle's assailants had denied the charges of rape, conspiracy to rape, grievous bodily harm and aggravated assault. Roxy swept back into the office bearing these bad tidings. She plonked herself on the couch and immediately cracked open two things – the spine of a legal notebook for her and a chocolate block for me.

'Right. Plan of attack. As both scumbag rapists are pleading their innocence, and conviction rates for rape trials are lower than Lady Ga Ga's bikini line, it's imperative that our gran goes on trial first.'

'Why?' Countess Flirtalotsky wanted to know, leaning in excitedly. When paying us a visit from her stately pile in the country, the Countess likes to feel part of the action, even though the only law she really understands fully is pre-nup proceedings.

'If the Crown Prosecution Service doesn't get a conviction in Chantelle's rape trial, then the jury will lose sympathy with our ball-blasting gran. She will just be a deranged, vengeful old bat who shot two innocent blokes in their precious gonads in cold blood and will spend the rest of her life monitoring due dates in a prison library.'

The Countess shuddered. 'That just can't happen.' I glanced at her, surprised at this uncharacteristic show of compassion. 'I mean, prison libraries have such terrible book selections. And absolutely no Pushkin.'

'The point is' – Roxy got us back on conversational course – 'if we want to get Phyllis out of prison, then someone has got to talk to the Senior Treasury Counsel. The case is so newsworthy it's been kicked up to him.'

'Who is he?' If the Countess had been a cat, her whiskers would have been twitching.

'It's the senior prosecutor at the Old Bailey. He has the power to persuade the chief clerk to list our granny's case first, before the rape trial.'

'You should talk to him, Roxy. You can talk anyone into anything,' I said, dwelling for a moment on the potentially lucrative legal career I had swapped at Jack's commercial Chambers, where our exorbitant fees would be sufficient punishment for any wrongdoer, for the pandemonium of life as a criminal legal-aid lawyer on Planet Pandora.

'No, I think this job's a cert for you, Tilly.'

'Me? Why me?' I asked, surprised.

'Well, I think in this case, only *you* have the right powers of persuasion. The new Senior Treasury Counsel has just been announced. It's a name you know well. One Jack Cassidy.'

I made the face of someone undergoing a surprise enema.

'Mother, Jack won't do something for nothing. And the something he'll want is for me to go on a date with him and, basically . . . I'd rather eat my own pedicure shavings.'

'Who's Jack Cassidy?' the Countess called from the office kitchen, where she was searching for wine.

'He was once my lover-in-law.' My mother was clicking away on her laptop.

'Jack Cassidy was not my lover, Mother! He was just the guy who tricked me out of my virginity.'

'Oh, you misery-guts. Why can't you stop acting as though you're in a Spencer Tracy / Katharine Hepburn movie, admit that you're still attracted to the bloke and just go on a bloody date?'

'Yes, I could date Jack . . . or I could stay home and rearrange my own internal organs with a chainsaw. A much more enjoyable experience.'

Jack's chiselled face blinked on to Roxy's computer screen, along with various press reports of the eligible barrister helicoptering into Ascot on the arm of a Hollywood movie actress he was 'linked to romantically', limousining out of Annabel's nightclub in the company of George Clooney and lying supine on the yacht of some movie mogul in Cannes in swimming trunks so tight you could detect the man's religion.

A blog called 'Male Lawyers Hottie List' flashed up, and my mother clicked on the link. The Countess read his winning entry aloud:

'*Phwoar!* Jack Cassidy ticks so many boxes, we're going to need new boxes!! With his strong jaw, waves of luscious dark hair and suave man-of-the-world Cary Grant-charm, including a dimpled chin and naughty twinkle, the man would look more at home nursing a Martini in Monte Carlo than a case file in The Temple. Jack, cutting a fine figure in his smart suits, apparently works his abs like he works his briefs. Girls, there's some really hot flesh on this skeleton argument!

A 6'1" hunk who played rugby, tennis and cricket for Oxford Uni, he knows he's *da bomb*, not only because of his undeniable sexiness but also because of his impeccable academic record, topping his year with a starred first and a cornucopia of prizes.

Jack took his smarts straight to the piggybank, joining Regal Helm Chambers. Yes, legal ladies, Jack Cassidy as *numero uno* Lawyer Lust Object of the Year is a no-brainer! Being Jack's girlfriend could be tough, though, as you have to keep all those pesky paparazzi at bay. Can't a couple go to Elton John's white tie and tiara summer ball in peace?!'

'Strange how those bloggers see Jack as top barrister tottie . . . while I see him more as a lapsed satanist,' I said coolly.

'Really? My own hotness committee confirms that Jack Cassidy could have a very lucrative jockey-underwear endorsement deal,' the Countess purred, peering over my mother's shoulder.

'What the man has is a giant "To Let" sign on his brain. It's empty and up for grabs to anybody.' I snapped shut the laptop lid so forcefully, I nearly severed Roxy's fingertips.

The Countess's eyebrows are tweezed into pencil-thin arcs which give her a slightly surprised expression, even in her sleep. But she really did seem surprised at my reluctance to date the Senior Treasury Counsel. 'Of course you'll go and sweet-talk him . . . But you may have to borrow some of my clothes.' She cast a disparaging eye over my bobbled jumper and frayed jeans.

I am five foot seven, with green eyes and red hair, parted, like my politics, on the left, but still have a figure which can sashay down a Barcelona beach and get wolf whistles – at least if I'm holding my stomach in so hard my neck gets thicker. But when it comes to sartorial expertise, well, whoever makes my clothes is too embarrassed to sign them.

'Yeah, sure, I could borrow some of your clothes . . . as long as I wasn't planning to eat more than a twig for two weeks,' I mocked. 'Besides, I'm not going to talk to Jack Cassidy. The man is just not my cup of slime.'

Roxy gave me a stern, levelling look. 'Tilly, I didn't go through thirty-six hours of labour to give birth to a limp bit of lettuce. I have nipples down to my knees because of you.'

'Mother, the man has no moral code. Barristers like Jack believe a man is innocent until proven destitute.'

'Just think about all the sacrifices I have made for you, Matilda! Those perfectly straight teeth in your lovely mouth; that law degree on your wall . . . they represent my holiday home in the Dordogne, a bespoke Versace suit, the BMW sports car of my dreams . . . and all the other things I don't bloody well have.'

'You forgot the best gift you've given me. Guilt. The gift that just keeps on giving.'

'If you don't go to see Jack, I'll take terrible revenge. I'll buy Portia a descant recorder.'

Ignoring this truly horrendous threat, I retreated behind a magazine left by a client and immersed myself in the travails of Rihanna, a profoundly misunderstood young woman. (Apparently, wealth and fame are okay, but true spiritual happiness is the source of all enlightenment and still seems to be eluding the poor poppet.)

'Let me paint you a picture,' Roxy persevered. 'Prison is a place where you get *promoted* to cleaning toilets. With your own toothbrush. Right now, our poor, beleaguered, scared old gran is being taken from the court cells in a prison escort van known as a "sweat box". Once the prison gates slam shut, she'll be frogmarched to a holding pen to be photographed and fingerprinted and given a pat-down search by staff . . . And I mean the kind of intimate pat-down that's usually only associated with childbirth. But nobody will hear her weeping above the drug-withdrawal screams of other inmates. Although, in Britain's overcrowded jails, it's easier to get hold of drugs than underwear, which is rationed to two pairs of knickers a week. So it's probably preferable to be off your face actually, when locked in your cell for twenty hours a day – just you, a psycho, sex-addict cellmate with gastroenteritis and your communal dunny. Wardens will take away all Phyllis's property – watches, jewellery, self-esteem. She'll then undergo a risk analysis to see whether she's likely to self-harm during the critical early days of her imprisonment. That's when most suicides occur. If we don't get Phyllis's trial on first, she could be on remand for a year, having poo put in her porridge and boiling water "accidentally" spilt over her. If she's not pulverized into granny gruel by any prison cooks who are on the payroll of those rapists' drug bosses.'

'How fascinating,' I commented casually, glancing up from the magazine page I was reading. 'Jordan's undergone five breast implant operations. Boob jobs are like TV evangelists. You know they're fake, but you can't stop looking at them,' I commented conversationally.

'Matilda, if those rapists intimidate Chantelle into not giving evidence, our gran is going down. You might as well just shove her out of an aeroplane with a cast-iron parachute.'

'Do you really think Chantelle will go to water in the witness box?' the Countess asked, reappearing from the tiny kitchen with three wine glasses.

'Courts are bloody scary places,' Roxy sighed. 'The defence barrister will portray the poor kid as "delinquent" and '"manipulative". He'll say that it was consensual sex that got a little rough. He'll suggest Chantelle's not a victim but merely a naughty girl doing grown-up things. Or a bunny-boiler type who had a vendetta against these two innocent blokes because they wouldn't go out with her.'

'So Chantelle bit, punched, urinated and graffitied on herself then, did she?' the Countess asked, appalled.

'Just last week I heard a leading London lawyer ask a rape victim whether her so-called screams for help were really cries of pleasure.'

'May his wig shit on his head,' the Countess seethed succinctly.

'I heard another boofhead defence barrister describe a child as "sexualized" and "dangerous". He said she was "glowing with hormones" and "very confident about her body's power and movement" when she "seduced" a fifty-year-old bloke. He said she "played the game well" and was, he claimed, a danger to men. He was describing a girl who was eleven.'

The Countess narrowed her dark eyes. 'Let's just hope Satan has something special planned for that particular gentleman.' She sashayed back into the office kitchen to fetch the wine.

'Chantelle will be branded a fantasist or an attention seeker,' Roxy explained. 'She'll be repeatedly called a liar in front of a court room full of strangers, which will leave her feeling raped all over again . . . And which is also why eighty to ninety per cent of attacks are not reported. And why rapists are likely to attack again . . . And why Matilda is likely to see Jack later today and get the granny's trial on first.'

'Mother, I know Jack Cassidy won't help unless I go out with him. And that's as *likely* as, I dunno, the Pope pole-dancing.'

'I just hope the poor girl gets a female judge,' the Countess said, uncorking the wine.

'Not bloody likely. The police and the judiciary are paler, maler and staler than ever. The only country in Europe to have fewer female judges is Azerbaijan.'

'Save your breath, Roxy. I refuse to be bribed by Jack Cassidy. The man's ego is so big it casts its own shadow.'

'But at least he doesn't pretend to be anything he's not. The reason I like Jack is because I don't trust good men. Your father was considerate, romantic, attentive . . . and look who he turned out to be,' Roxy said bitterly.

'Who? Who exactly did he turn out to be?' I asked. My father's betrayal was always with her – like a shadow on an X-ray. And yet she would never talk about him. 'How can I ever have a healthy relationship with a man when I know nothing about the man who made me?'

My sudden ability to hear the bloke in the flat next door trimming his nostril hairs suggested to me that we had come up against what is known as an 'awkward silence'.

'You know what? You're right. I think it's high time I told you the truth about your father, Matilda. The truth might help you rethink your attitude to Jack Cassidy. Your father should have come with a "Buyer Beware" sticker on his forehead. But what you see with Jack is what you get. There's no jiggery-pokery.'

'Roxy, dah-ling! . . . Are you sure you want to tell her the truth?'

'What truth?' I demanded of the Countess.

A few invisible tumbleweeds blew through the room before the Countess thrust a glass of wine at me. 'Jesus. I think you'll need a little vino collapso first, dah-ling.'

'It's 3 p.m.,' I remonstrated. 'On a workday.'

'Drink. You'll need it. I know *I* bloody do.' My mother downed her glass in one gulp, then held it out for more.

It was now so quiet I could practically hear the cockroaches fornicating in the High Street. I stood up. 'Do you think we might conclude this conversation any time in my lifespan, because I do actually have a court case to prepare.'

Roxy took another deep swig of fortifying alcohol. 'Your father told me I was his soulmate. That he loved me more than life itself . . .'

'Yes, yes, I know,' I said impatiently. 'I've heard all this before. But then he ran out on you. And you had no choice but to gird your leopardskin loins and just get on with it.'

'When I found out I was up the duff with you, I contacted the British Consulate in Spain and Greece. I phoned every bloody backpacker hostel in Europe . . .' Her voice petered out. What the hell was happening? My vibrant mother had suddenly developed the charisma of a crash dummy.

The Countess picked up the story. 'Your mother even hired a private investigator. But not even he could find any trace of the elusive Daniel Kincade, dah-ling.' She, too, took a nerve-steadying glug of wine.

'It was the start of a journey for the truth which ended with me knocking on the door of a Mr and Mrs Kincade of Middleton.'

I sat back down with a jolt. 'You never told me you'd met my grandparents.'

'That's because they're not really your grandparents.'

'What do you mean? Who were they?' No answer was forthcoming. 'Okay, the Sphinx is less of a riddle than you right now,' I sighed in irritation.

'Your father told me he was estranged from his parents. It was something we had in common, actually. Two orphans in the big, bad world. I thought the totally exciting news of your existence might broker a truce . . . and of course help me find your dad . . .' Roxy petered out once more.

'But when Roxy knocked on the door of what she thought

was the family home – oh, can you imagine how horrendous?'
The Countess put her head in her manicured hands.

'What was wrong with them? Were they scientologists?
Card-carrying Nazis? Or worse . . .' I said flippantly. '. . . Tory
Party voters?!'

But Roxy's tease-o-meter was turned off. 'The two people I
thought were going to be your grandparents started crying. It
totally freaked them out to have someone asking after a child
who had died aged eight.'

'What? You're not making any sense, Mother.'

'It didn't make any sense to me either, Tilly. I thought they
were just playing silly buggers. The town and the house and
everything looked exactly as Danny had described them to
me. I felt as though I was in some weird sci-fi movie. But then
these poor people showed me Danny's death certificate . . .'
My mother's voice broke off raggedly.

'The document confirmed the details Danny had always
given us.' The Countess took up the conversation. 'It named
the town where he was born in March 1955. It was the same
person. The same parents. The same address. But Dan
Kincade had died as a boy in a hit-and-run accident.'

'I chucked a mental,' Roxy continued. 'I refused to believe
them. I gave them the rough end of my tongue, believe me.
Eventually, the only way they could get me to shut my gob
was to take me to the graveside. I saw the sculpture of the boy
standing guard above the grave. "Safe in the arms of Jesus" –
that's what the engraving said. It was then that my world
turned upside down.'

The Countess nodded. 'It was only later, after some
serious in-depth sleuthing, that your mother found out the
truth.'

'What truth?' I asked urgently. 'Roxy?'

'That your father was an undercover cop.' My mother

coughed up this confession like a fur ball. 'Using the alias of Danny Kincade.'

It's a strange sensation when two people you know well suddenly start speaking to you in Swahili. 'What?' I said.

'It's like something out of a horror movie, I know. Your father belonged to a special unit in the police force. He stole this dead boy's identity so he could infiltrate protest movements. Of which I was a member.'

I only knew of my dad as a crude outline filled in with grey and black. And now here he was, in full, garish, ghoulish Technicolor. 'I don't believe you,' I said, as casually as a cardiac arrest would allow.

'It's true. Even though it sounds more like something that would happen in an old Communist Bloc country. Turns out it was common practice in the seventies and eighties for undercover British police to use the identity of dead babies who roughly matched their age and ethnicity. The cops issued their undercover agents with fake passports, drivers' licences and national insurance numbers in the name of these poor little boys who'd died,' the Countess confirmed.

'And it was me who unwittingly gave the bastard credibility. I fell in love with a bloke I thought was a gardener. He was so sympathetic to all my beliefs and causes – animal welfare, pro-abortion, anti-nuclear – that I welcomed him into my circle. Because of me, this "Danny" was able to get inside information on all the peace activists and other protesters. It was the complete dingo act. I fell in love with a fraud,' Roxy fumed, violently tossing back more vino.

'And, oh, he was bloody good at his job,' the Countess elaborated. 'We found out years later that Danny's skills of deception earned him legendary status in the elite ranks of the covert unit known as the Special Demonstration Squad.'

It also earned him legendary status as the Biggest Asshole Ever. I gazed at my mother in mortified astonishment. I'd always fantasized that my missing father was off in the Amazon, using his horticultural expertise to discover herbal cures for cancer that would win him the Nobel Prize for medicine ... Or that he'd died heroically rescuing blind orphan babies from a fire in a far-flung favela. 'Oh my God, Roxy. Why didn't you ever tell me this?'

'I'm only telling you now because I want you to rethink your attitude to Jack Cassidy. Yes, he's a rogue and a rascal. But he doesn't pretend to be what he's not. Yes, he was a bit of a sexual kleptomaniac at college, but you were both young. I'm sure he's mended his wicked ways.'

I looked at my mother the way you would look at a stranger on the Tube who had 50 pounds of plastic explosives strapped to his body. A wave of irritation overwhelmed me.

'Well, I hate to break up this little joy seminar of yours. And I'm sorry about my biological father's appalling behaviour. I'm sorry about Phyllis taking the law into her own hands. I'm sorry about the quality of the prison soap on remand. I'm sorry about the male dominance of the law ... But what I'm *not* sorry about is that Britain has a jury system which works – twelve good men and women and true who know that rape is a heinous crime and will convict those scumbags with or without the interference of Senior Treasury Counsel, Jack Hymen-stealing-Cassidy.'

My office door flew open and my daughter pirouetted into the room. Most pubescent girls are little more than a hormone upheaval; a sulk with fake tan on it. Their preferred position is horizontal on the couch, with the remote control, while lackeys bring delicacies. When vertical, they merely moan. My Portia is the opposite. When not at school, she learns tap dancing, volunteers at a nursery for underprivileged kids and organizes fun runs to raise money for cancer research. She has the ability to lift everyone two octaves up on the happiness scale and she doesn't even know it. Her personality's so bright, she could act as a beacon for sailors adrift in the ocean. But today her wattage was dimmed. She dropped her tap shoes and school bag on to the floor and flumped into a chair.

'All the kids at school are talking about Chantelle. Some of the girls reckon she's a slut – so raping her doesn't count. During lunchbreak this one girl Tamsin – well, she said that Chantelle's so ugly they could use her in prisons to cure sex offenders. Tamsin's boyfriend reckoned he called the Rape Advice Line but, unfortunately, it's only for victims ... Another one of the boys wanted to know if you raped a pregnant bitch could you then tell your friends you'd had a threesome? ... A prefect was on lunch duty. He overheard some of this and marched over to interrupt. He said, "Rape isn't funny. You should never rape anyone." I felt *sooo* relieved and the boys stopped laughing and were kinda worrying about detention. Then this prefect said, "Unless you have a really good reason ... like *they won't have sex with you or something.*" The boys killed themselves laughing. And then on the way home from school I noticed this new graffiti in the bus stop that says "Stop rape, say yes." What does it all mean, Mum?' My darling daughter turned her elfin face towards me and gave me her famous candid stare, her pale-blue eyes wide.

My mother's head was tilted like a bird's, in that hyper-alert way that says nothing will get past her. 'What it means is that to many people rape is not a heinous crime, but just a "struggle cuddle",' she said pointedly.

I kissed the tip of my daughter's perky nose, picked up my bag and headed for the door. What it *meant* was that I was off to the Old Bailey. To see Jack Cassidy.

7

Hear No Evil, See No Evil, Date No Evil

'Must you have the heating so low? It's freezing in here,' I said, sweeping into the office of my nemesis unannounced.

Unable to find Jack at the Old Bailey, I'd tracked him down to his Chambers. I inhaled the aroma of dusty furnishings pomaded with cigar smoke.

'I employ a company called "Stiff Nipples Air-conditioning". Excellent, isn't it?' Jack said, dropping his eyes to my chest. 'So, I hear you're representing the ball-blaster?' He smiled wryly. 'Why does that not surprise me? Your "practice", and I use that term loosely, does so meta-phorically, already. You're always giving men a bollocking.'

'The reason my mother and I set up Pandora's is because women make up 51 per cent of the population, do two-thirds of the work . . . earn 10 per cent of the money and own 1 per cent of the property. In other words, it's still a man's world. The only reason you blokes let women off sinking ships before you is so we'll check the strength of the bloody lifeboats.'

Jack laughed warmly. 'Let me just check . . .' He placed a

hand on his heart and cocked his head for a moment. 'Yes, I still avidly adore you. And not just because your nipples are on high beam.'

'Sorry, but I obviously left my spontaneous quips in my other handbag. Something to do with the fact that I've just been visiting a little girl in hospital who was brutally raped by two heartless thugs.'

'Allegedly.'

'Your chronic scepticism is the very reason why we need to try my client first, before their rape trial. If the poor girl doesn't give a good account of what happened – and who could, under the circumstances, she's just turned sixteen, for God's sake! – the rapists will get off and my gran will go down. In your position as Treasury Counsel, it's the only humane and just thing to do.'

'Ah, so you've come here to make a plea bargain.' Jack Cassidy's eyes narrowed with keen interest. 'I hear the plea. But what's the bargain?' He gave me a playful smirk. 'If I do this favour for *you*, what's in it for *me*?'

'Professional decency. Something you know nothing about, of course.'

'I'm having rather *in*decent thoughts about another professional right now actually . . .'

I wrapped my arms across my chest. 'So, enlighten me. Don't your Narcissists Anonymous meetings somewhat interfere with your dating life? Now, will you help me or not? Can we agree her case should be tried first?'

'Why don't you charm me into it?' Jack suggested. He gave a wide smile, which increased his resemblance to the Cheshire Cat. 'Use your feminine wiles.'

'Sorry. Can't. I whiled away my feminine wiles while dating complete assholes in my youth,' I said pointedly.

'I think it would be beneficial to discuss this dilemma over dinner, don't you? I could wine and dine you by candlelight. What would life be without the occasional swing from a chandelier?'

'A chandelier is just a lightbulb with a big ego,' I countered. 'Something you *do* know all about.'

'Then after dinner,' he went on, ignoring my comment, 'you could slip into something more comfortable . . .'

'Yes, like a coma.'

'Why are you always so defensive, Matilda? I could be the perfect boyfriend for you. I've improved since we were students, you know. I've learnt to be so much more considerate . . . When you're hungover, I will use only little words. When you fall over, I'll point and laugh for a while, but will always give you a hand up. When you've got the flu – stay the hell away from me if I have a case. But I will make chicken soup. Why won't you give me a second chance?'

'Because I am not your type.'

'You're not anyone's type. You're a total original. That's why I like you so much . . . You're the human version of a platypus.'

'I vowed when I went to the Bar never to date a lawyer. A male lawyer is in love with one thing – the sound of his own voice.'

'Really?' Jack gave a slow smile. 'I find that talking is excellent exercise for the mouth's all-important oral-sex muscles.'

'You really are delusional. We wouldn't make love, Jack. We'd make war.'

'Yes, but with two winning sides.'

I tried to ignore him, but his gaze was like the touch of a hand on my arm.

'Date me, or it's no deal,' he said simply, rocking back on

his chair. 'And your gran will have to contemplate a very long sentence—'

'At least she won't put a *proposition* at the end of it,' I cut in contemptuously. 'What happened to you, Jack? When we met, you wanted to work for Human Rights Watch.'

'Yes, but that was before I realized it would mean spending my days with gruff, bearded men poking their gun barrels through my car window to demand bribes before stringing me up by the testicles anyway and beating me senseless with copies of their misanthropic manifestos.'

'Really? For a chauvinist pig like you, I can see many upsides to spending time in the developing world. For one thing, sexual-harassment suits are an unknown luxury,' I said, switching off his air-conditioning unit.

'True. And it probably does take a lot off your mind when the average life expectancy is, oh, thirty-four minutes . . . making it pointless to give up cigars, Martinis and carbohydrates. All of which talk is making me hungry. So, where shall we dine on our date? The Fat Duck? The Ritz in Paris? . . . Or shall we catch a private plane to a tropical resort so exclusive not even the tide can get in?'

I shook my head at him. 'You didn't change the world, Jack, you bought it.'

'The way I see it, if I can't subtract from the planet's sum of suffering, do I have to add to it personally? It's one of the questions I mean to take up with God if I ever get religion. Some people worry about the difference between right and wrong. I worry about the difference between wrong and pleasure. And it would be very pleasurable to get to know you again, Matilda.'

'Come on, Jack. We'd claw each other's eyes out before the waiter could say "Do you want fries with that?"'

'I think the River Café . . . I'll make a reservation, shall I?'

Why had I wasted my time? Jack Cassidy doing something altruistic is as likely as a Taliban with a bar tab. 'How can I put this so that you'll understand it? Going out with you would be only slightly more enjoyable than abduction by multi-headed aliens hell bent on death by anal probing.'

'. . . Oh, well, I'm sure your client will find a few distractions in prison. She can always join a writing workshop full of lesbians reading poems about bleeding, death and endless rivers of Satan's semen.'

'When did you get so cynical? It's as though you found out as a child that there's no Santa and just never got over it. Unlike you, I have the guts to stand up to evil-doers.'

I employed a tone of crisp reprimand that effectively closed the conversation, along with the door to his office. Striding across the cobbled cul-de-sac of Gray's Inn and through the ornate iron gates on to a Holborn lane, I vowed from now on to be less like my cowardly father and more like my principled mother. Brave. Heroic. Stoic. I was no longer going to let life walk all over me!

Ironically, life was about to grant me an opportunity to prove my new Wonder Woman credentials. I had just got into my car and fired the engine when I noticed a man lurking suspiciously outside the mini-market. As I buckled my seat-belt, I watched a security guard walk out of the store swinging a case, evidently full of money, towards a Securicor van. The young bloke I was observing then pulled out a gun, seized the case and leapt on to the back of a getaway motor-bike driven by an accomplice. They veered off towards the main road, right past my car. Sensing a high point in my crime-fighting career, I threw my little orthopaedic shoe into reverse and backed into their path. The two villains were thrown on to the bonnet of a nearby car. They staggered, dazed, to their feet and stared at me, aghast.

Aghast also were the director, the sound man, the cameraman and everyone connected with *Crime Stoppers*, a hugely popular TV programme, who were reconstructing an earlier robbery in the hope of helping the police to solve it . . . Or so the director explained to me as he emerged from the bushes. He pointed to the signs I somehow hadn't seen, posted on all the lamp posts, stating that filming was taking place.

I glanced up over the old stone walls of Gray's Inn to the first-floor window of Regal Helm Chambers to see Jack Cassidy bent double with laughter, having watched me perform the least successful citizen's arrest known to humankind.

What more could I do to embarrass myself? Possibly cartwheel into court, yodelling. I turned the car towards Camden and skulked homeward . . . via the hospital to have my toes surgically uncurled.

8

The Courage of Your Convictions

The 20-stone prison officer eyed me as though I was lunch. She had a face like a bottled foetus that had escaped from its formaldehyde jar. 'Youse just have to wait, like all the uvers.' She emphasized her decision with a slam of the sliding window in front of her.

Roxy and I were standing outside Holloway women's prison with a scrum of shivering people waiting for visits with loved ones. The prison had been home to feminists like Christabel Pankhurst and fascists like Diana Mosley. Moors murderer Myra Hindley was once incarcerated here, and five women were executed, including Ruth Ellis, their bodies buried within the prison walls in unmarked graves. Oscar Wilde was also interned here, obviously perceived as a woman by the judiciary. It was now also the temporary home of our client, Phyllis O'Carroll, infamous testicle markswoman.

'But we are here for a legal visit,' I said to the bulletproof glass. 'We have priority.' The warden just hunched down lower over the food she was eating in order to quicken its journey between plate and mouth. When she did glance up, I noted a speck of gravy in her eyebrow.

'You've clearly never been to a prison before. Welcome to the wonderful world of legal aid. The prison staff are like snails with attitude,' my mother commented drily.

'It'd be faster to move things telekinetically.' I banged on the warden's window once more, to no avail.

'Clearly, she's not going to admit anybody until after lunch,' said Roxy. 'We might as well have a nosh as well.'

'We have an appointment!' I waved our authorization documentation at the officer, who showed me no more concern than she would a gnat.

Roxy checked her watch. 'With no mood swings at Security, it should only be about another, oh, hour and a half before we get in.'

'That's outrageous! It's freezing out here.' While I continued to thump the window and make blustery, barrister-type noises, my mother crossed the road to a greasy-spoon café, the sort of eatery that serves salmonella on toast. She returned shortly afterwards and thrust a cardboard container at me. 'Jellied eels. A North London delicacy. Would you like a bite?'

'Sure . . . If I wasn't worried about an imminent attack of death.'

'It was quite clean, actually, for a greasy spoon.'

'Oh, what? The cockroaches were wearing hair nets?' I whiffed the grey slime on offer.

'It's better than the food in prison,' Roxy said. 'Last week, an inmate got hit in the face with a piece of mincemeat. Some of it got in her mouth and she died instantly. The food's so bad, if there's dental floss in the cells, the mice hang themselves.' She plonked herself down on the grassy bank in a patch of watery January sunshine by the bustling Seven

Sisters Road, then pulled her miniskirt a little lower on her chubby thighs.

'Mother, now you're in your fifties, do you think it might be time to lower your hems just a little? I mean, just to ensure that whenever you sit down complete strangers don't cop an eyeful of your primary sex organs?'

'Well, at least mine are in use.' She patted a patch of grass next to her. 'There is life after marriage, you know, Tilly. Is there still no man on your hormonal horizon, hon?'

I would have said no, but I was concentrating on manoeuvring myself on to the grass next to my more agile mother – except the grass was slippery and wet and I was in heels ... which is why I heard his voice before I saw him. After I had slid rather spectacularly down the slimy slope as though I were wearing invisible skis, his calm, reassuring voice was asking me if I was okay. I opened my eyes to say hello – to his feet first (brown, scuffed biker boots), then his legs (strong, muscular, encased in faded blue denim), followed by a big hello to his bulge (he'd obviously thoughtfully packed lunch for two). My eyes then travelled upwards across a tight abdomen and then further up to a chest broad enough to be rented out for advertising space. And then on up into an amused face. The glint in his eye couldn't just be because of my comedic topple down the embankment, because his mouth was bracketed by deeply etched smile lines.

'S–s–sorry, I've been a little sleep deprived since the baby was born.'

'Sure. No problem.' He offered his hand to pull me up. 'How old is your baby?'

'Twelve,' I answered.

The tall, tousled stranger smiled at me and I felt as though I'd passed some kind of minor test. As he gently hauled me to my feet, I took note of the remnants of a summer tan which was so lightly toffee-coloured I felt the urge to lick it. As he held my shoulders to steady me, I caught an aroma of limes and salt and possibly cinnamon.

Now that I was face to face with him, I could see that he had inquisitive eyes, a mane of gold-flecked hair and an aquiline nose which gave him the look of a Roman god. I controlled an overwhelming urge to cry 'Take me to your palace, Apollo!' His caramel skin and hazel eyes fringed with curly eyelashes made him centrefold handsome, in a slightly bohemian, aristocratic, world-weary way.

'Why thank you, kind sir,' I said in my friendly, flirty voice, which sounded slightly false from disuse. It was a ridiculously Jane Austenesque comment, since my dress was covered in grass stains, my knees were smeared in dirt and I possibly had dog turd in my hair.

The stranger then did the most surprising thing. He kissed my hand. Or, rather, breathed hotly on to it, head slightly bowed. The Sir Lancelot gesture made me laugh out loud, but it was also irrationally pleasing.

'Sorry. But you don't often encounter behaviour like that on the capital's prison forecourts.' I laughed, a little flustered.

'Sometimes I forget to hide my dark secret – a private-school past. Bryanston . . . Alternative boarding school for pampered poshies,' he explained, in case I didn't know. 'I think I saw you the other day. On the Tony Benn Estate.' He looked me up and down, quite slowly. 'Not your natural habitat, I'd say.'

'Absolutely. My mother says that a London council estate is not a good place to go if you have money, jewellery or a vagina on you. Oops.' The man had so unnerved me that the words had just blurted out of my mouth. Why did I only ever feel in control in court? I needed my wig and gown urgently. Perhaps I could have them surgically attached? But the glance he gave me was amused and, if I wasn't mistaken, a little titillated.

The stranger then dusted off my knees – an activity which sent electric currents from my tonsils to my toes . . . and quite a few places in between. He next bent to pick up a motorcycle helmet, giving me a ringside view of his tightly muscled rear. I watched as he wiped grass off his hands on to the back of his jeans. Oh, lucky hands, I thought. He gave a warm smile, his whole face in it, especially his eyes. The smile made me want to touch his arm – or, better still, slide my hand over the delicious contours of his derrière.

He straddled a motorbike, which spluttered into life and vroomed away while he was still adjusting his helmet strap with one hand. As he was giving me an insouciant wave with the other hand, it could mean only one thing – he was steering with his genitalia.

'Yowzah!' my mother commented as the pulchritudinous Good Samaritan departed. 'At the very least, I'd like to pash that man until there was nothing left but his helmet. How hot was *he*?'

'Really? I didn't notice.'

My mother raised a dubious brow. 'Tilly, if you were a dog, you'd have been sitting on your hindquarters and hanging your tongue out.'

'Don't be ridiculous, Roxy. He saw me on the estate. He's obviously some drug-dealer pimp type visiting one of his upper-class hookers in Holloway.'

'Then why are you beaming?'

'I'm not beaming.'

'Darl, you're smiling so hard you look as though you've just had a B12 vitamin shot.'

'I am not!' But, in truth, the thought of the stranger's smile stayed in my mind for a long time . . . even while we were being fingerprinted, frisked and bustled through metal detectors. (Please note that if you can't afford a doctor, go on a prison visit. You'll get a free X-ray and breast exam and, if you mention drugs in any way, a complimentary cervical smear test, too.)

As we handed over our shoes, phones and ID, I took in my surroundings. Everything seemed to be made not just of polyester, but imitation polyester. The prison smelt sour, like stale daylight trapped for decades until it has gone rancid. It wafted over me like bad BO seeping out of armpits in summer on the Tube. As we moved from the holding pen deeper into the prison, the whole place reeked of mourning, ghosts and desperation.

Another gargantuan officer led us in silence to a large room partitioned off into glass cubicles. She adjusted her underwear with a thumb and a wiggle of her opulent backside, then pointed to one of the small rooms. Phyllis was wedged into a chair that was nailed to the floor. As was the table. She looked as though she'd been plunked down on a planet to which she was not native. Her grey hair was strangled into a tight ponytail. Her skin and lips were gravestone grey.

'So the food hasn't killed you yet?' My mother's voice was sympathetic but also robust and unpatronizing. 'What did you have for lunch? Cup o' Crap or sweet-and-sour stray cat?'

'Somethin' like it, pet!' Phyllis's forced good cheer was painful in its transparency. She was giving a very good impression of a duck's back.

'Phizz is a very good cook, you know,' my mother told me. 'She's addicted to those daytime-telly cookery shows. *MasterChef, The Great British Bake Off . . .*'

'I am a bit partial to a drizzle of balsamic,' Phyllis said. 'You gotta get me out of 'ere, for the sake of me tastebuds alone,' she bluffed, adding eagerly, ''Ave you seen my Chanty?'

'Yes,' my mother reassured her, in a voice as composed and calm as a hotel receptionist's. 'She's on the mend.'

And then Phyllis smiled. A genuine smile. This smile was like the front door of an old house opening, disused with rusty hinges.

'And I will reunite you very soon.' Roxy smoothed the old woman down as though she were a crumpled bedspread. 'But let's talk about your defence first, shall we?'

'The poxy scum deserved it.'

'I know,' Roxy agreed. 'Kill one man and you're a murderer. Kill a million and you're a conquering heroine . . . Boudi-bloody-cca.'

I eyeballed my mother. This did not seem the most promising strategical tack, so I took over.

'Like Roxy, you're a woman of many convictions, Phyllis. Let's just not make them all criminal. Okay?' My pathetic attempt at a little ice-breaking humour fell completely flat.

'An eye for an eye,' Phyllis stated grimly.

'Unfortunately, righteous indignation is not a defence,' I told her.

'Listen carefully, Phyllis,' Roxy interrupted. 'As I understand, you went around there with a firearm to protect yourself while you warned them not to say one denigrating word about your granddaughter. But you had no intention of using the firearm, did you?'

'Yeah I did—'

'Hold on. Let me finish . . . But when you got there, Stretch opened the door and yelled something abusive at you. Isn't it *then* that you felt under threat?' Roxy prompted.

Phyllis shook her head, bemused.

'Some threat was made to you, so you had to defend yourself. Did you feel under threat, Phyllis?'

Phyllis was looking intently at Roxy.

'You were so frightened you pulled the trigger—'

'They don't frighten me, those evil knobheads.'

Roxy and I exchanged exasperated glances. My mother extracted a cigarette packet secreted in some fold of her vast bra. Over the next hour, I wrung from Phyllis every minute detail of the night she shot the rapists: the exact time she drove her battered bomb of a car to the estate to snap photos of the culprits on Chantelle's mobile; the exact moment she showed the photos to Chantelle for verification; where she got the gun; how long it took her to get back to the council estate . . .

My mother smoked continuously throughout until I begged her to desist. 'Roxy, can you please stop dropping cigarette butts on the prison floor?'

My mother raised a puzzled brow, looking around the small, grimy room. 'You're worried about mess? In this cesspit?' she asked sarcastically.

'No, I'm worried the rats are getting cancer.' I coughed dramatically. 'You're asphyxiating me. You're not allowed to smoke. There's a sign.' I pointed to the huge printed instruction on the wall behind us.

My mother responded with a wink and a blast of smoke in my face. 'I'm shortsighted.'

After another half an hour of passive smoke-inhalation and frantic note-taking, the prison officer waddled over to announce that it was 3 p.m. and visiting time was up. 'But you kept us waiting outside for at least an hour,' I complained.

The prison officer's yawn was like that of a hippopotamus in a watering hole. 'And you kept me cravin' a smoke for the last hour,' she rasped.

My mother took the hint and gave the smuggled cigarette packet to the officer. People were shuffling out of their individual cubicles into the long, bare room. Some visitors were weeping, others swearing. The guards, oblivious, herded them all together. Inmates and their guards did have one thing in common though. Immense bottoms. It looked as though everyone in the place had stuffed two watermelons down their trousers.

The fluorescent light above us was intermittent, the bulb buzzing on and off like a trapped blowfly. Phyllis, who had been calm throughout the visit, seized my arm. 'The estate's bad enough, but I reckon the drugs in 'ere are worse. These girls need help. Coke is called medicine. "J'have my medicine?" they keep sayin'. You've gotta get me out. Those poxy rapists 'ave a lotta mates in 'ere. I don't feel safe.' The old lady had gone as limp as a perm in a sauna.

Whereas *my* biggest fear is being trapped in a lift with a Scientologist, poor Phyllis was at the mercy of vicious inmates and unpredictable wardens. Holloway Prison is clearly full of the kind of people Jerry Springer could build an entire series around.

As we rose to leave, Phyllis clutched Roxy's arm with a trembling, arthritic claw. 'I'm scared, Roxy. Please, please, in the name of Jesus, get me outta 'ere.' Her face was so drawn it seemed to be melting.

'What the hell's that on your arm, love?' Roxy pushed up the sleeves of the old lady's cardigan to reveal a bracelet of bruises on both forearms.

'Oh, this one woman, she keeps tauntin' me all the time. Shovin' me round an' that. I can take it, meself. But I won't let 'em say one bad word about my Chanty! I won't! . . . I won't!!'

I understood Phyllis's desire to have the last word. I just prayed it wouldn't be on her epitaph.

'The bail appeal hearing's scheduled for next week,' Roxy reassured her with a pat on her back. 'Everything's going to be fine, Phizz.'

Phyllis returned the ghost of a smile.

My mother and I walked in silence back towards the daylight. The steel prison gates wheezed open with a death rattle, then slammed shut again behind us. And still we said nothing, because both of us knew that everything was about as fine as the grey drizzle which had set low over London. Phyllis might as well have been swimming in shark-infested waters with a gaping leg wound. As usual, Roxy and I had ended up testing the depth of the legal waters – with both feet.

9

Captive Audience

The type of handbag you carry says a lot about you. For example, if you're carrying someone else's handbag, it says that you're a thief. But, from petty thieves to porn stars, Pandora's was open to all women in trouble. At the time of Phyllis's arrest, our little practice had three other cases on the legal boil. One involved a woman whose Arabic hubby had been watching a pornographic film for the first time and was shocked to discover he was married to the star. He was now divorcing her and claiming custody of their two children and half her earnings. The other case involved a fire-eating stripper whose flaming nipple tassels had set off the club's smoke alarms. The nightclub's owner was trying to sue her for water damage. And then there was the bigamist who targeted women who were financially stable but vulnerable. He ended up leaving a string of 'wives' in thousands of pounds of debt. Roxy explained wryly to Portia: 'Bigamy is having one husband too many. Monogamy's the same.'

A solicitor's job is to collate all the relevant documents and witness statements. As Roxy was snowed under preparing all these briefs for me, it was decided that day that she would head back to the office to toil at the case coalface while I visited Chantelle in the hospital.

Pushing into the overheated hospital was like opening an oven to check a roast. A wave of stale warmth hit me. I eased open the door to Chantelle's room to find the bed occupied by an old man.

What with eighty-hour working weeks, no sleep, financial cutbacks and waiting lists longer than the Great Wall of China, nurses are a curiously uncommunicative lot. Too busy to answer my frantic enquiries, staff passed me from one desk to another like an unwanted parcel – one possibly laced with ricin. Then I saw the pre-Raphaelite-pale, auburn-haired nurse who'd been taking care of Chantelle. I grabbed her arm, begging for information. She gruffly explained that the teenager had checked herself out.

My intestines macramed instantly. Rape victims are statistically vulnerable to self-harm and suicide. Heart in mouth, I rang the mobile number Phyllis had given me. When I heard Chantelle's voice, my sigh of relief was so loud it's a wonder passing paramedics didn't suspect I was having an asthma attack and order an oxygen tent. Chantelle explained that she couldn't bear all the people at the hospital knowing what had happened, so she had gone to stay with her best friend from school.

I turned the car down the hill from Hampstead towards Camden and on to the Tony Benn Estate. In my rush to find Chantelle, I forgot to take my armoured personnel carrier – otherwise known as Roxy – which is why, fifteen minutes later, I found myself surrounded by a group of hooded youths, poking at me and demanding money, iPhone, car keys . . .

Council estates are daunting for bookworms like me. The

rats here could use a woman my size as a chew toy. Using my famed streetwise skills, honed for survival in the urban jungle, I immediately fumbled for my mobile to call my mother. But as I reached into my inside jacket pocket, the tension ratcheted up. Two flick knives materialized. The hair stood up on the back of my head as though I were a cartoon character.

'I told you the council estate was not your natural environment.' It was the handsome, golden-haired Roman emperor from the prison forecourt. I recognized his clotted-cream consonants and statuesque build. Even through a thick jumper his flexed arms were so muscular, it looked as though he had packets of cement implanted under his biceps. 'The only firm rule on an inner-city estate having drug-turf wars is that those with rocket-grenade launchers have the right of way, isn't that correct, boys? . . . So, what are you guys carrying?'

With the same pride and enthusiasm as an Englishwoman showing off her camellias, the boys paraded their weaponry. Four flick knives, a machete, six knuckledusters and a revolver of some kind – basically, everything lethal bar a drone plane and a ton of napalm.

'Oh my God! It's like a war zone. All that's missing are piles of sandbags with jumpy eyes and gun barrels sticking over the top,' I said nervously.

The stranger then advised the gang to get rid of their weapons and drugs as a police raid was imminent – at least, I think that's what he said, as he imparted most of this information in rapid-fire, guttural street slang. I needed United Nations headphones to decode the conversation.

'It's considered good manners to convey information about impending raids from rival drug gangs or police,' the Roman emperor told me. 'This takes the place of weather reports in inner-city ghettos. News of stab victims takes the place of celebrity gossip.'

After a bit of high-fiving and back-slapping, the boys sauntered off.

'If teenagers were a radio, then you seem to have their frequency,' I marvelled.

'You just need to speak their lingo.'

'Really? What's the local lingo for "I'm unarmed and not dangerous and quite academic, really, so please don't let me suffer a lingering death and just point me to the nearest library"?'

He smiled. 'Sorry, there's no such phrase in the local vocabulary. It's just that reaching inside a jacket for your phone resembles the gesture of drawing a gun and makes trigger-happy, macho boys a little more jumpy than is entirely prudent. They're not bad kids, really.'

'Really? I dunno . . . The way they clean under their nails with the blades of their flick knives kinda makes me suspect they failed their Health and Safety badges in the Boy Scouts.'

This time the stranger laughed. 'They've just been thrown on society's rubbish heap. They're in that weird no man's land between school and—'

'Jail?' I interrupted.

'Well, yes, sadly. Most graduate from school with certificates in how to make kerosene bombs out of plastic milk bottles. Where are you going, by the way? Would you like me to escort you?'

'I want you to know that I'm a feminist – totally independent and self-sufficient in all things . . . But, yes please.' I fumbled through my handbag for the scrap of paper on which I'd scribbled down the tower block and flat number Chantelle had given me over the phone. The stranger pushed up the sleeves of his jumper, threw his leather jacket over one shoulder, took me gently by the elbow and steered me through the buildings with no effort or disorientation.

'People presume those kids' only vocation is crushing beer cans against their foreheads. They're demonized as "chavs" by the press. But these boys have grown up amid poverty, family breakdown and the lure of easy money from dealing. What you have to understand is that, since Britain lost its manufacturing base, the drug industry's the only factory still open.'

I was trying to pay attention but was completely distracted by the man's muscled forearms, which flexed deliciously with each swing of his arms. 'In my line of work I see kids as young as eight or nine employed as lookouts and couriers.'

'And what is that, exactly? Your line of work?' I asked, thinking, Mr Universe? Hugh Jackman's body double? Number-one female masturbation fantasy as voted by *Moist* magazine?

'Nathaniel Cavendish.' He extended his hand. 'Ex-banker turned do-gooder.'

'I thought the only bank we could rely on since the Global Financial Crash was the sperm bank?' I bantered, thinking how much I'd like to make a withdrawal.

'You're right.' He laughed. 'As an investment banker, I was an expert at extracting money from people's pockets . . . only without the traditional method of resorting to violence. So I left the Swiss bank I worked for in the City and I now run a charity helping young offenders go straight.'

'Wait,' I said, intrigued. 'You gave up a life of luxury to work with the disadvantaged? I think *you're* the one on drugs.' But I was secretly impressed. This was the kind of man I thought Jack Cassidy would turn into.

'The whole GFC was caused by wanker bankers ripping off the system. It hit me that we were no better than these kids being sent down for dealing. If I hadn't been born with a whole canteen of silver spoons in my mouth and had grown up here' – he gestured around us, at the underbelly of the estate – 'I'd have been one of those boys you just encountered. They're not bad. They're just angry at their situation, at society, at themselves . . .'

Nathaniel Cavendish had a soulful, elegant quality that reminded me of a young Marcel Proust before he took to his bed to write *À la recherche du temps perdu* – if Proust had been in possession of rock-hard abs and perfect pectorals, that is.

'The worlds of investment banking and drug dealing are so similar. It's all alpha men, danger, deals, adrenalin, quick money, fast cars and sexy women. If you're in investment, you're managing a portfolio. Guys on the estate, they're the CEOs of drug businesses. They understand how to market, how to distribute . . .'

I was listening, but also awestruck by the man's caffè-latte skin tone, which was nearly as smooth as his style.

'Drug dealing's like a corporation, you see. It's a pyramid structure. Drugs from Afghanistan or Turkey are driven across Europe by young Bulgarians and Lithuanians, stuffed into every orifice of their cars. The heroin gets taken from them at Dover and hidden in the back of lorries. Once the drugs are in London, they're passed down through the distributors. In banking and drug dealing, cash is so easy to come by it becomes like Monopoly money.'

'Yeah, until you get the "Go to jail. Do not pass Go" card.'

'Exactly. But the worst that can happen to a banker is that your bonus is docked. I try to show these kids a different possibility. The charity I run gets young offenders work experience at banks and businesses.'

Nathaniel Cavendish seemed to have just popped in from the age of Enlightenment. All he needed was a frock coat and a pair of breeches. Even though I'd only just met the man, I could already see myself sitting by the fireside of his ancestral home, running my hand soothingly through his lovely locks as he told me about the hard day he'd had, saving ragamuffins and urchins from chimneys and coalmines.

'So how exactly do you wave this magic philanthropic wand of yours?'

'While they're inside, I have a captive audience. Literally. I get kids reading about the stock market and property investment. Then, when they leave prison, I ask friends to mentor them and give them work and show them how to invest in shares and make money from legal trading.'

My heart did a fast fandango. Nathaniel seemed mail-ordered – he was just the type of male I would write away for.

'Drug dealers are good at maths. I just show them the mathematical equations. For someone making money through drugs, if you add up the time they're going to spend in prison, the money for lawyers, et cetera, it's always going to work out better going straight. Even working at McDonald's is going to be a better bet in the end.'

'But what about you? Don't you miss the high life at all?' I asked, thoroughly captivated.

'Not really. After all, the best things in life are free – walking, talking, laughing, oxygen and orgasms.'

I swallowed hard. Oxygen might be free, but I didn't seem to be getting enough of it all of a sudden, as my head was spinning.

'I'm sorry. That was very forward of me! . . . But when tragedy waits to check your coat and jeopardy's mixing the drinks, there's no doubt that it adds a certain piquancy to the daily pleasures of life,' he said, in his mellifluous melted-chocolate tones. 'It makes wine taste better but also makes kissing a beautiful woman all the more poignantly appreciated.'

I would have swallowed again, but I didn't seem to have any saliva left after drooling throughout our entire walk across the estate.

Nathaniel stopped in front of a tower block with smeared-glass doors leading into a drab landing. 'Here you are.' He glanced back at my crumpled bit of paper, still in his hand. 'Floor 12, flat 49. Hawthorn House, Buttercup Road ... Hawthorn, Buttercup ...?' He looked around sadly at the sea of grey asphalt. 'England has become a place where they tear down the trees ... and then name buildings after them. But, oh, do forgive me. Here I am, blathering on. Just as well you found out how boring I am now, and not on a walking tour of the Cotswolds.'

Was he suggesting a walk in the Cotswolds? I'd rather he took me for a walk on the wild side ... Although, in my scuffed shoes and dowdy pencil skirt, I was clearly not dressed for a date, I thought, wishing I'd spruced up a little more that morning. Since joining Pandora's, my only sartorial motto seemed to be – if the shoe fits, it's ugly.

Nathaniel turned to face me, full on. 'But you haven't said a word about yourself. Why are *you* here, if you don't mind me asking?'

'Interviewing a witness. I'm a lawyer.' I gave him my 'Pandora's – Thinking outside the Box' card.

He cast his eye over it. 'Matilda Devine ... divine by name and divine by nature.' He slipped it into his back jeans pocket then kissed my hand in his gallant way. 'I'm delighted by this propitious encounter. Our second. Seems it's meant to be.' He smiled, doffed an imaginary hat, then strode off to abolish slavery or invent penicillin, or something equally noble.

Riding up in the rackety lift and walking along the dank corridor, all I could think about was Nathaniel Cavendish's general perfection. I would have dwelt longer on his aristocratic loveliness, but I'd found the right door, knocked and was now being appraised through a cyclopean spyhole. The perfectly coiffeured and made-up child who opened the door to me was lap-dance ready and wet-T-shirt glamorous ... if you like your fifteen-year-olds that way. Once I'd given my name, she let me into a tiny handkerchief square of a flat.

Chantelle was curled up on the couch next to an imitation Tiffany lamp. The stained glass reminded me of the delicate wings of a butterfly.

'How are you, Chantelle?'

'I ain't been able to cry yet ... Though I seem to be able to cry in my dreams,' she said. 'How's Gran? When can I see 'er?'

I didn't have the heart to tell her that her gran was currently claustrophobically ensconced in a psychotic boot camp otherwise known as remand prison, so said instead, 'Your grandma's well. She sent you all her love.'

'She's still in jail, ain't she?'

'Her bail hearing appeal is scheduled for next week. Meanwhile, I can take you to see her when you're feeling stronger.'

'I'm strong!' Chantelle's body may have been frail, but her voice was pure steel. 'I've already enrolled online for kick-boxin' and karate at the YMCA. I ain't gonna be a victim. I'm gonna fight back. To protect my gran.'

'That's so good, Chantelle. Because that's what I need to ask you.' I sat beside her and took her limp little hand in mine. 'Do you want the Crown Prosecution Service to go ahead with the prosecution? You *can* ask to withdraw your evidence. Being in the witness box in court can be really scary and intimidating. Nobody would judge you if you didn't want to go ahead, Chantelle. Nobody at all.'

She snatched her hand from mine and leapt up off the weathered settee. 'I hope their ears turn to assholes and shit on their shoulders! I want 'em locked up for ever! So they can never ever do this to any other girl! J'hear me!?'

Roxy was right. Chantelle did have her grandmother's fighting spirit. 'Are you sure?'

She gave a strained smile full of endearingly crooked teeth. 'Yeah, I'm sure.'

I relaxed for the first time in days.

Later, after a quiet supper with Portia, going over the most tedious multiple-choice maths homework (Q. Why did the maths student's mother throw her watch out of the window? A. Because she wanted to watch time fly), I went to bed that night and slept soundly, totally confident that justice would triumph and the rapists would be convicted – and all without the intervention of the Senior Treasury Counsel Jack bloody Cassidy.

I only wish I'd reminded myself that, if everything seems to be coming your way, you're probably going the wrong direction up a one-way street . . .

I awoke at dawn with the distinct feeling that I was being watched. I sat bolt upright in bed and switched on the light. As my eyes and mind adjusted, I realized that there was a parcel on the end of my bed. I picked it up with hesitant, pincered fingers. It was a box of handmade, crystallized rose-petal chocolates from the Burlington Arcade – the most expensive chocolates in London. Plus a note. Typed. No signature.

WARNING. YOUR GRAN'S NOT TELLING THE WHOLE TRUTH AND NOTHING BUT THE TRUTH. THE GRANDDAUGHTER LEFT THE HOSPITAL AFTER SHE WAS ADMITTED. SHE WAS MISSING FOR AN HOUR – THE EXACT SAME TIME THE RAPISTS WERE SHOT. SUSPECT THE KID POINTED OUT THE CULPRITS TO HER GRAN AND WATCHED THEM GET THEIR PUNISHMENT. THEN WENT BACK TO THE HOSPITAL. HERE'S THE HOSPITAL REPORT – THE ONLY ONE. WHICH I'VE NICKED TO HELP YOUR CASE.

A FRIEND.

P.S. HOPE I GOT THE RIGHT CHOCCIES

Enclosed in the envelope was the original hospital record, which clearly showed that Chantelle had been missing and unaccounted for between the hours of 9 and 10 p.m. Her rapists had been shot at nine thirty exactly.

I turned the letter over and over. There was no indication of who had sent it. Was it a hoax? If not, then Phyllis and Chantelle had lied to me. But, more worryingly, who had left this mysterious package? How had they got into my bedroom? I looked around, panic-stricken. I tried the window – locked. I break out into a sweat even *thinking* about jogging, but now found myself sprinting from room to room, flinging open cupboards and peering beneath beds. How could Chantelle have left the hospital when she was so battered and bruised? But there it was, in black and white – the official hospital record.

I rang Chantelle's mobile and confronted her. She maintained that, after the police had interviewed her, she'd staggered outside for a 'ciggy'. The kid's pants were so badly on fire I expected an automatic water-sprinkling system to kick in.

After briefing Roxy, we dropped Portia at school then headed straight back to Holloway Prison. On the drive there, my mother was smoking so much I was tempted to give her a tracheotomy so she could smoke two cigarettes simultaneously.

Then came the interminable wait at the gate to gain entry, followed by the mandatory free medical exam. As the officer gave my mother an intimate pat down, she feigned disappointment. 'What? Not even a movie and dinner first?' A surly half-hour later, we were finally granted access to the prison. Even on a sunny day there was an air of twilight and deliquescence to the place. It was hard to think of anywhere less appealing. Put it this way, if the prison officer had told me to go to hell, compared to my current surroundings, I would positively look forward to the trip.

'Kiss my left flap, you dog-fingerin' twat' were the charming first words I heard upon entering the remand wing – and it was downhill from there.

'Did Chantelle leave the hospital with you to point out the rapists?' I asked as soon as we were ensconced in our glass aquarium of a cubicle, wardens circling like sharks.

Phyllis put her hands to her head and covered her face for a moment. 'I can't remember. It's all a blur.'

'You can't remember if your bruised and battered granddaughter limped out of the hospital, went in the car with you to the estate then stalked two rapists?'

Phyllis shrugged, her plump triceps swinging like sodden washing in the wind.

'Phyllis, I have the hospital record here, saying that Chantelle was missing from her bed between nine and ten.'

Phyllis's cheeks hung slack as ancient breasts. Her silver hair was now a horror of Gorgon-like dreads from lack of brushing. Her few days in prison had not just been unkind to her face – they'd stomped on it with hobnailed boots.

'She was worried I'd shoot the wrong blokes . . .' She

trailed off nervously, sending us sidelong glances in sudden embarrassment. She gripped her hands together convulsively. 'Me eyesight's not that grand.'

'Forget your eyesight.' Roxy sighed. 'Do you have any idea how bad this makes you look in the eyes of the law?'

'Chantelle no longer looks like a victim, but a cold-hearted, calculating killer. She could be charged as an accomplice. Aiding and abetting attempted murder when her trigger-happy gran went for some testicular target practice. Didn't you think of that, Phyllis?'

The colourless dough of Phyllis's face was suddenly highlighted by the blotches of angry red which now rose in her cheeks.

'J'know the attitude of men to girls on the estate? These are throw-away girls. Worth less than a lollipop tossed down on the ground. Men are predators. Girls are prey. From the age of eleven they get raped. Those men told Chantelle they'd burn her alive if she told anybody. They threatened to cut my 'ead off with an axe. I just wanted Chanty to see *them* in pain. What would you 'ave done if it was your daughter?' she asked me desolately. 'Well? Answer me! *What would you 'ave done?!*'

Phyllis gave a brittle sob of exhaustion. Roxy patted her arm until she was ready to go on.

'Chantelle's mum, she was raped. She used to be teacher's pet. But these older men. They started buyin' her gifts – cigarettes and vodka, then crack cocaine and heroin. Then the rapin', the beatin'. When she got pregnant with Chanty, they threatened to murder the baby if she didn't start recruitin' younger girls for 'em. They said they'd chop Chantelle's head off and put it in a suitcase, then kill me, too, real slow and painful like. So, she smuggled in drugs for 'em, from Europe. Only she got caught and sent down. For workin' as a drug mule.' Her face was knotted in pain. 'I vowed on me ma's grave never to let anythin' like that happen to my darlin' Chanty . . . And I failed. I failed!' She buried her face in her chapped hands.

Roxy and I sat in sad silence for a moment, then my mother turned to me. 'My hearing's mucking up. I can't put any of that stuff about Chantelle leaving the hospital in the statement, as it just wasn't audible.'

'We're supposed to tell the truth, the whole truth, remember – not the varnished untruth. Besides, the prosecution are bound to find out,' I warned.

'Then we'll claim mental myasthenia gravix.'

'Christ, what's that when it's at home?' asked Phyllis, alarmed.

'It's Latin for memory loss in the mental muscle,' I explained to her.

'So, how does it affect yer memory?'

'I forget,' said my mother, winking. 'Besides, how can the prosecution find out that Chantelle left the hospital when we have the original documentation?'

'You're trusting an anonymous tip-off?'

'Well, whoever nicked it is obviously on our side. We can easily keep this as our little secret . . . Phyllis, you and Chantelle must not mention this to anyone else, okay? Otherwise, Chantelle could be charged as an accomplice and you'll both go down.'

Phyllis nodded furiously.

'So, let's talk about your defence again, shall we?' Roxy continued. 'You went around there with a firearm to protect yourself. Because it was the only way they'd listen to you and not denigrate your granddaughter. You had no intention of using the firearm. But it was when he pulled the knife out that you felt under threat and accidentally squeezed the trigger.'

I looked at my mother. There had been many times in my life when I'd wished that parents would be seen but not heard, but the predominant question on my mind right now was How could I ever have agreed to set up practice with a person who proved on a daily basis that the term 'criminal solicitor' is a tautology? Professionally, my mother and I had as much in common as a Las Vegas stripper and an Amish butter-churner.

'Um, Roxy, need I remind you that lawyers can't present a case in a way that is false to their knowledge.'

'If opportunity doesn't knock, get a doorbell. That's my motto.'

'You can't expect Phyllis to lie under oath. Oh, I can't believe what I'm seeing!'

'Then look away, kid. After all.' She winked again. 'Justice is blind.'

'Yes, and perjury is a real eye-opener.'

'Hon, the law is nothing more than a legal lottery.'

I looked at my mother, aghast. 'Sure . . . and Stonehenge is just a rock,' I shot back. 'The rule of law is the only rule I live by. It's practically a religion to me. I know I sound like the Julie Andrews of the judiciary, but Phyllis will get a fair trial, without having to lie.'

It was my mother's turn to eye me as though *I* were the one with a few kangaroos loose in my top paddock. 'Matilda, if life was fair, Elvis would be alive and all the impersonators would be dead . . . Did you feel under threat, Phyllis?' Roxy probed, more vociferously this time.

Phyllis thought for a moment. 'Yeah. It was when he pulled out the knife. I felt under threat. The big, tall one,' she improvised. 'I was so frightened that I must have accidentally squeezed the trigger. I can't remember doing it.'

Roxy patted her hand. 'Thank you, Phizz.'

Our visiting time was up and we were being bustled out of the prison. There was no point arguing with my maverick mother – I would just have to jump off that bridge when I came to it.

Leaving Holloway, Roxy and I drove straight back to the estate to counsel Chantelle. It was vital that she didn't talk to anyone about her moonlit flit from her hospital bed.

Whenever I ventured on to the estate, I felt as though I were wearing pork-chop jeans in a dog pound – a little something to do with the fact that parts of it are populated by people in ski masks who aren't necessarily Olympic tobogganists. But Roxy was totally unperturbed. She stomped about as though she owned the joint. I led my mother to flat 49 on the twelfth floor of Hawthorn House.

It was a very different girl I encountered this time. Whereas on my previous visit Chantelle had been chippy and defiant, she now lay curled on the couch with her back to the room. She wouldn't respond to my entreaties to talk to us. A wash of weak afternoon sunlight lay over the sofa, pale as the flesh of a lemon.

'What's happened?' I asked her girlfriend, who was so tarted up I presumed she'd just got home from an audition for Britain's Next Top Model and not her geography class.

'Dunno. I just found her cryin' an' that. She neva said nuffin'. But that was tossed on the floor under the telly.' She handed me a DVD case. I scrutinized the typed label. It read 'Girls Just Wanna Get Stabbed'.

'Bugger it. The poor kid's been got at.' Roxy turned to the dolled-up teen and spoke harshly, like a foreigner. 'Did you tell anyone that Chantelle was staying here?'

The girl shook her head violently. 'Nobody knows nuffin'. Not even me mum. She works nights.'

My mother scowled, before entreating, 'Chantelle, darling, talk to me, love. For your gran's sake. Did someone come around here and intimidate you?'

When my mother rolled the teenager towards us, her eyes were red-rimmed crescents from hours of crying. Roxy scooped her up into a giant bear-hug. Chantelle lay limp in my mother's strong arms. She then emitted the kind of noise you make before your car collides with a stationary object.

'They filmed it. The attack. On their phone. It's just close-ups of . . . the way they've cut it . . . it makes it look as though I'm enjoyin' it. The note said they'll put it up on Facebook if I don't drop the charges. All my friends will see it.' She drew a shuddering breath, then collapsed into heart-wrenching sobbing.

I felt my colon corkscrew. I would never complain about anything ever again. I mean, cystitis, childbirth, divorce – these are the jewels in life's crown compared to the sheer horror of seeing your own rape recorded by your attackers. 'This is blackmail. We'll call the police.'

This only made Chantelle scream louder. She pushed Roxy away as though she were radioactive. 'No! No! I don't want no cops seein' me like that! I don't want anyone to see it, ever, *ever*, EVER!!'

Chantelle's little schoolpal now moved to stand pro-tectively between us and her friend. My mother and I locked eyes.

'The level of sexual violence in these gang-afflicted inner-city areas is comparable to a friggin' war zone,' Roxy sighed angrily. 'If I had my way, sexual abuse would be regarded as being as harmful as a gun or a knife. How can the poor kid testify now?'

But any person with an IQ – even a moderately sized amoeba – would know that, if Chantelle withdrew her rape allegations, Phyllis would be in serious danger of being convicted. It was imperative that we got her case on first. There was only one solution . . . and I was looking forward to it about as eagerly as I would root-canal surgery with a jackhammer.

10

Devil's Advocate

After Chantelle's ordeal, would it be insensitive to call Amnesty International to say that my human rights were being abused by having to date Jack Cassidy? It certainly was a cruel and unusual punishment. These were my thoughts as I made my way through Camden to Primrose Hill.

Jack lived in a pretty, petal-strewn cul-de-sac near the park. Although the Saturday-morning air was crisp, the sun was shining. I'd decided to drop in on him at his four-storey Edwardian home, just to ascertain that there were no undisclosed professors' wives or live-in gym junkies in residence. I walked up through the cobbled streets, past pastel-painted houses and into the village, with its cutesy baby and bridal boutiques, tea-cosy-twee bric-a-brac gift stores and quaint little cake shops. It was like walking through treacle. I grabbed the lion's-head knocker and banged loudly on Jack's door.

'Are you working?' I asked, noting the Montblanc pen in his hand when he answered my knock.

'Just busy converting my bar bills into legitimate legal expenses I can charge to the client.'

'Gee, you're really putting that starred First from Oxford to good use. Don't you worry about what people think?'

'Nope. After all, they don't do it very often.'

'Are you sure you're not busy seducing a client or pre-boarding a flight attendant or something?' Jack gave me a slight frown of annoyance. 'Okay, then. May I come in?'

'Do you have any blood-splattered fugitives with you?'

'No.'

'That's disappointing.' I could hear a laugh beginning to surface in his voice, which was beyond annoying. He stood back from the door and beckoned me inside with a courtier's bow. The high-ceilinged cream rooms with their dustless wooden floors warmed by rich rugs and shards of sunlight, the cool green air of the park opposite breathing fresh oxygen into the hall through the wide, open windows, the piles of hardback books on side tables, spines not yet cracked, the velvety sounds of a Bach cello suite wafting on air scented by the blossom of luxuriant flower displays – it was the opposite of my current abode, with its chaos, feral canines and curling carpet.

I followed him through the house, past an atrium and conservatory and into a luxurious sitting room.

'So, how's your testicle festival going?' Jack flung himself back into a leather armchair and crossed one sockless ankle nonchalantly over the opposite knee, preparing to be amused.

I sat primly opposite him on a hard-backed chair. 'That's why I'm here. I've decided that I will go out with you . . . in exchange for scheduling my granny's case before the rape trial.'

'Well, that's an interesting turn of events. I got the

impression that you would rather ride the Death-defying Space Mountain rollercoaster, followed by a quick spin in the Tower of Pain, than be seen with me in public. So, what changed your mind?'

'I'm sorry. Am I under oath? I don't remember agreeing to a cross-examination. Let's just decide where and when and what we are doing so I can get it over with.'

'Hmm. Good question . . .' He rubbed his chin thoughtfully. 'We'd better not sit side by side in a dark theatre, as an erection is so tricky to hide in the interval.'

I realized then that what I had thought was my mild disdain for Jack Cassidy had morphed into acute repugnance. I glared back, lips curled.

'Although a hard-on in the car home afterwards is considered very good manners in most social circles,' he teased.

'Really? I find saying to a man's face that he's an irritating fucking bastard is considered rude in most *social circles*.'

Jack Cassidy narrowed his eyes at me. If he and I *were* in a Spencer Tracy / Katharine Hepburn movie, as my mother had suggested, I'm pretty sure this would be the moment when he'd put me over his knee and spank me. 'Let's do dinner, then. I find dinner dates are a good time to talk over each other's sexual preferences.'

'My only preference is for men who want to make the world a better place.'

'Yes, you're so right. If only I worked at the UN. Then I could just tell nations like Belarus that they're grounded. Or maybe drive around Iran with a sign on my bumper: 'Honk if you still have hands.' . . . As fighting is clearly foreplay for you, why don't we just skip dinner and pick up where we left off?' he baited, extracting a slim cigar from his pocket. The man was enjoying playing with me – think cat, think mouse.

'Because I no longer find you remotely attractive. Not since you sold out and became a cigar-addicted corporate-cowboy cliché.'

'Cigar smoking is not remotely addictive. I should know. I've been doing it for years,' he said glibly, picking up a lighter.

'I recently met the man I thought you'd turn into, actually. He's given up working at a bank in the City to help disadvantaged kids.'

Jack put down the cigar, unlit. 'What do you mean "given up"? That's clearly a euphemism for "getting the sack". Probably from Lehman Brothers, or some other bank that crashed and burnt.'

'Actually, he was very high up at Credit Suisse. But he had an epiphany and left to give back to the world in some way.'

'Ah, the Swiss. While they were dipping fondue, Britain was – oh, wait. What were we doing again? . . . Oh yes, I remember. Waging war against the Nazis.'

'I don't know. I've always liked the idea of an army which carries corkscrews instead of machineguns.' I rose to my feet. 'Well, I'd better let you get back to your "work",' I said derisively, before moving back down the hallway.

Jack followed. 'Well, I'm sure we can discuss this further at dinner. Over the Swiss cheese course, perhaps?'

'Yes, let's have dinner. I find that having dinner before diving into bed gives a girl a chance to re-evaluate and maybe just flee home for a hot encounter with her vibrator . . . So, where are we going? Do I need to bring anything?'

'Not much . . . just your birthday suit and a large tub of mango love butter.'

'You disgust me. Were you always this sleazy? Or have you been taking lessons?'

'Would you have gone out with me otherwise? . . . I'll be in touch to discuss details.' Jack was positively gloating. The man would win the Gloat Vote at a Gloat Festival. And it was nipple-numbingly annoying.

'I knew you'd come to your senses eventually, Tilly.' He gave a cat-that-got-the-cream smile, then opened the door and leant against the wall so that I had to brush past him to escape.

Come to my senses? Going on a date with the misogynistic, amoral Jack Cassidy, I was clearly out of my mind.

11

The Full Nest

I'd moved in with my mother, for better or for worse – but not to share shower facilities with suspected murderers.

Court 15 at Snaresbrook Crown Court in North London was packed with press eager to catch sight of the ball-blasting grandma during her bail hearing. Her case had become a *petite cause célèbre*. I made my application to the judge, pointing out that my frail, pensioner client had never offended before, apart from a one-off bit of shoplifting, even managing to get in a judge-amusing little aside about how the only cure for kleptomania was to 'take something for it'. Having wrung a small chuckle out of the court, I then went on to explain that Phyllis was a woman of very good character. I laid it on so thick, Phyllis was starting to look long overdue for a halo-fitting.

The judge seemed sympathetic, until the barrister for the other side objected to bail on the grounds that it was for Phyllis's own good. He maintained that, having committed such a serious offence against two popular locals, my nut-crunching gran would fear for her own life on the estate and that she'd be safer in prison. The judge concurred. He sat back to weigh up his options. That was when my solicitor, who just also happened to be my mother and my landlord, tugged at my robes from her seated position on the bench behind me. I half turned to face her.

'Pssssst! Get the judge to release her into my custody,' Roxy whispered.

It's no exaggeration to say that the moment of silence between us was a tad tense.

'Did I mention the fact that Phyllis has been watching *Cordon Bleu* on the cooking channel while she's been on remand? She's already mastered coq au vin. Which I suppose is quite ironic, under the circumstances,' my mother chuckled.

More silence from me, but my brow was speaking volumes.

'Oh, and Chantelle must move in, too, of course. She can't face her friends, so she'll have to be home-schooled,' she added in a low-pitched postscript.

'Is that all?' I whispered back sarcastically. 'Really? No asylum seekers or deported opposition leaders you'd also like to invite into your teeny-weeny terrace?'

'No . . . That's all. Well, apart from Phyllis's ferret.'

It took a beat for this news to sink in. 'A ferret?'

'Well, yes, it belonged to her husband, when he used to go rabbit hunting. The dead hubby with the hunting rifle, remember?'

'How could I forget? It's the weapon in our attempted-murder trial, *remember*?' It was an effort to keep my voice down. 'The trial in which we are supposed to *stay objective and not get too involved with our clients*?'

'Phizz is more than a client. She's a friend now.'

'Um. Let me see. How can I put this? . . . No!' I swivelled back to face the bench, but Roxy tugged my robe more violently.

'Chantelle's in no fit state to testify to the CPS. We need to keep her safe and buoyant and build up her confidence before her rape case comes to court,' my mother insisted in hushed tones. 'If she's living with us, I can boost her energy levels with ginseng and get her reading Simone de Beauvoir.'

The press were straining forward from the gallery, trying to overhear our heated, sotto voce deliberations. I smiled up at them before hissing at my solicitor, 'Phyllis moves in with us over my dead body.'

'Really? I think I'll wear black. Black is dead classy at a funeral. Look, I don't particularly want the ferret either. The neighbours were looking after it, until it ate their cat.'

'How comforting,' I muttered.

'But it can't be left home alone. The RSPCA would be on to us in a heartbeat.'

'I'm calling the RSPCD – the Royal Society for the Prevention of Cruelty to Daughters.'

The judge, a genial man in his mid-sixties with a head as bald as a boiled egg, had started to harrumph a bit, a pompous noise taught to perfection at Judge School. I looked over at Phyllis, in the dock, and she turned her face upward and smiled hopefully, like something frozen and in need of warmth.

'You can't send that poor old granny back to prison. Her cell is so small, if she turns around too fast she'll sexually harass herself.'

'Miss Devine?' the judge pressed.

With time running out and no other options immediately leaping to mind, I heard myself putting forward Roxy's suggestion. The court was now satisfied that Phyllis could be placed on conditional bail. The judge ordered her to put forward surety amounting to £20,000. The Countess agreed to put up the money and Phyllis was released into Roxy's residential custody.

With a curious press corps massed outside, we huddled for a quick confab. It was decided that Phyllis would leave through the service exit with the Countess. They would collect the crumpled Chantelle from her friend's flat and ensconce her in our tiny spare room. Roxy and I, meanwhile, would act as decoys, leaving via the front of the court, then, after shaking off the reporters with some nifty Grand Prix-type manoeuvres in Roxy's MG Midget, drive to Phyllis's flat to pick up some of our impromptu house guests' belongings. We would all then meet at Roxy's house in an hour or so.

All the way to Camden, pinballing around narrow side streets in Roxy's sports car with the soft top stuck at half mast, my hair flying in my face as I clung on for dear life, I fumed at myself for allowing my mother to railroad me into this living arrangement. Steve had often complained that I could never take responsibility for anything, 'Yes, and I blame my mother for that!' I would joke back. But there was some truth in what he said.

'That went bloody well, Tilly. Excellent teamwork,' my mother pronounced happily once we were safely en route to the Tony Benn Estate, press successfully evaded. 'Our union at Pandora's is so solid because we have so much in common.'

'Yes,' I sulked. 'Ethical disagreement, polar-opposite views on everything and occasional mutual contempt.'

My mother hooted. 'That's why it's a good idea to love your enemies. Just in case your friends and family turn out to be unbelievably bloody annoying.'

Phyllis's flat was situated on the first floor of a low-rise block at the quieter, greener end of the estate. I reluctantly chugged up the stairs behind Roxy. On the landing, she stopped dead in her tracks, causing me to crash slap bang into her back. Just as well I wasn't marching with a fixed bayonet, I thought idly, peering over her shoulder. Then I saw what had caused her derailment. The word 'Slut' had been written into Chantelle's front door. But turps wouldn't aid us now. The word was graffitied in bullet holes – a kind of lead calligraphy.

'So tell me, Mother,' I finally squeaked, 'do you know whether our work insurance policy covers *gaping chest wounds*?'

'Scare tactics. Pathetic. We will not let those rapist thugs intimidate Chantelle into not giving evidence to the CPS.'

'Really? In general, I kinda find it best not to antagonize anyone better armed than me,' I said, trying to keep the edge of panic from my voice.

My mother whirled around to face me. 'Tilly, we have to try to encourage the poor girl to stand up to these pissants – whether they release their shitty phone footage or not. It's horrifying how rape has become part of the warp and weft of daily gang life. These girls don't complain, they don't go to the police. It becomes just what happens. If a girl is linked to a gang member and he meets her at the school gate and says "Go with me" – she goes. Saying no is not an option. If Chantelle doesn't stand up to them now, they will always have this over her. That's no way to live your life. We can't let them destroy her.'

'But we can't let them destroy our lives either! I have my own daughter to worry about.' I turned on my phone to call the police.

My mother put her hands on her formidable leopardskin-trousered hips. 'Those knuckle-draggers don't scare me. I can protect us.'

'With what? A pocketful of high-calibre jellybeans?'

Roxy turned the key in the lock. Phyllis's apartment was charity-shop chic, and threadbare but eat-off-the-floor spotless. Cutesy-pie knick-knacks lined every shelf – the kind you see in souvenir shops and wonder who'd ever buy them: big-eyed dogs in sombreros, ceramic dolphins in snowballs – an entire kitsch menagerie beamed at us. Roxy hurriedly packed some of Phyllis's things, while I took the stuff I thought Portia would need if it were my daughter going into hiding. The ferret was thrust at us by a furious neighbour. It growled from its cage all the way back to the car. I knew just how it felt. The police pulled up just as we were leaving. Before taking photos of the door, they lowered Roxy's soft top so we could at least drive home without gale-force-5 winds blow-drying our locks into crazy creations.

'Gee, now the roof's down, it's stuffy in here, isn't it?' I said facetiously, as we hit the road once more. 'Oh, but wait. No need to worry. Because any minute now, drug bosses will be *ventilating our car with bullet holes . . .*'

'Well, aren't *you* a little ray of sleet?' Roxy chided.

'Most mothers look a little sheepish because they ate all the chocolate. Or, I dunno . . . forgot to bring in the washing. You look sheepish when you can't remember the name of the toy boy who's strapped to your roof rack or because you moved a client who has just shot the testicles off two gang members into your house, making your whole family a target for trigger-happy psychos. Why, oh why, can't I have a normal mother?!' I moaned.

I was still fuming when we walked into the house some fifteen minutes later. But then my mother nodded towards the little box room off the hall which she'd converted into a spare room. She nudged open the door with a hip. Chantelle was sitting on the edge of the bed, hunched into herself, as if freezing cold despite the overheated room. Roxy called her name softly and she looked up, startled. Roxy offered her the ferret cage. Chantelle perked up momentarily, but then caught sight of herself in the mirror and flinched as if scalded. She then retreated back behind a veil of sad bewilderment.

Roxy closed the door quietly and sighed. 'It really doesn't matter where Chantelle is now. When a woman can't feel comfortable in her own body, she has no home,' she said bleakly. 'There's no emotion left in her. It sounds mean, but I'm desperate for her to start crying again just so that she lets go. With her living here, we can really help her.'

'Yes, because we really are such a functional family,' I mocked, as one of Roxy's more gassy foster dogs bounded by, farting loudly. I now had an idea what the mustard-gas attacks must have been like in the World War One trenches. It was while gagging and rolling my eyes to heaven that I noticed one of my mother's peek-a-boo leopardskin teddies dangling from the chandelier.

I was balanced precariously on a chair, stretching ceiling-ward to retrieve it when the Skype on my iPhone buzzed. Roxy answered it before passing the phone up to me. Jack's amused face came into view. He was ringing to arrange our date. When I explained to him why this wasn't the best time to talk, detailing my rather unusual afternoon and my present predicament, retrieving my mother's lingerie from a lightbulb, he roared with laughter.

'Ah, Matilda, I can always count on you to bring a little sunshine into my day,' he chortled. 'Call me when you're free.'

By the time I'd pocketed my mother's smalls and made it

to the kitchen, Roxy was dipping her varnished nail into a persimmon and white chocolate tart Phyllis had whipped up for dessert. 'Ah!' Roxy sighed. 'What every feminist has always wanted. A wife! At last!!'

I flared my nostrils. Warm and tangy aromas were wafting from the stove.

'One man's meat is another woman's Sunday gone,' Phyllis said, stirring some exotic-looking sauce. 'But I'm more than 'appy to cook for us girls.' She was positively luminous with joy to be out of jail.

'You see?' Roxy enthused. 'It's going to work out wonderfully. We'll lead a quiet, stable, normal life here all together until the court case.'

I chose this moment to hand back her leopardskin peek-aboo teddy. She surreptitiously slid the lacy ensemble into a kitchen drawer.

'It'll be so much fun! Just like those communal Greenham Common days all over again! We'll all look after each other while at the same time helping Phizz and Chantelle to stay stoic!'

But stoicism, I was about to discover, is the ability to keep on smiling when a guest stands at the open door and lets all the flies in . . . So much for leading a quiet and simple life. Half an hour later, the press were foaming out of their cars like suds from a sitcom washing machine and oozing towards our front door.

I typed an urgent text warning Portia to use the back lane. But before I could press 'send', I glimpsed her through the window. With fear rising in my chest, I saw her submerged in the sea of photographers. Like a toddler in big surf, she disappeared from view, only to resurface, then vanish again. By the time I'd raced down the hall and flung open the door, she'd been jostled so badly that she'd dropped her school bag, spilling books across the road, and a foot had come out of one shoe.

Phyllis made it to the door at the same time as me. 'Oy! You gobshites! Shut it, or I'll do youse!' she yelled, which I believe is Cockney for 'Warning! Brain pulverization imminent.' A blizzard of lightbulbs flashed as the press got their snap of the Deranged Gonad-shooting Gran waving her cooking knife about threateningly. I sighed. Phyllis may be a good cook, but we were tabloid toast.

Roxy charged past me to haul Phyllis back over the threshold, while I made a dive for my daughter. 'Are you okay, darling?'

'I'm fine, Mum,' Portia said, once we'd slammed the door shut on the buzzing hornets' nest of press. 'My sunnies didn't make it, though.' She held up her mangled heart-shaped shades. 'Oh hi, Chantelle. Look, I have a broken heart,' she said, her nose crinkling adorably.

We all rotated, to see Phyllis's granddaughter standing in the doorway of the spartan spare room.

'Mum says you're moving in for a while. I'm so glad. I've always wanted a big sister,' my daughter added kindly. 'How are you?'

'I hate myself. I just feel proper dirty and disgustin'. Like I'm worth nothin'.'

It was the first time she'd spoken since she'd told us about the footage of her rape, edited to hide the identity of her attackers and overdubbed with moans of pleasure. Roxy gave a flimsy smile. Phyllis, relieved, dabbed at her eyes with a hankie.

'Carrie Katrona set fire to Mr Gove's toupee today. I've got a photo on my phone.' And, with that, Portia shepherded Chantelle off upstairs into her bedroom. As ever, I found myself marvelling at my daughter's personality. She possessed a kind of radiance in which others liked to bask. If she got any more radiant, I would need some kind of personality sunblock, I thought fondly.

'Sorry 'bout that, pet. Me fuse just blew. Can we still stay?' Phyllis asked nervously, looking at me with cataract-clouded eyes.

I glanced out of the window. The press were now looking up at our house as though waiting for it to audition for *The X Factor*. I looked back at Phyllis, who was twisting her hankie anxiously between arthritic fingers.

And drew the blinds.

For the rest of the day, the nation's airwaves crackled with heated debate about taking the law into your own hands. Talk-show shock-jocks were ranting and televisual rent-a-voicers raving. Law makers mounted their moralistic high horses and galloped around various media outlets condemning Phyllis, while many mothers rang in to praise the lioness-type love of the outraged gran. Despite the law that banned prejudicial press reports before the verdict of the trial, the Countess, who'd volunteered to go back and 'woman' the office, reported that the phone was shrieking with requests from journalists for comments – or 'testicle testaments', as Roxy called them. We left them to interview Pandora's front door.

Still, having been totally ignored by the Bar, 'Pandora's – Thinking outside the Box', Britain's first two-person, mother–daughter, solicitor–barrister, boutique feminist law firm was now the talk of the town.

From that day on, whenever I came home from work I never knew who was going to be in the kitchen. It could be a visiting celebrity sympathizer, or one of Phyllis's ancient Cockney pals. The notoriety of the case meant that every vague acquaintance of my mother's, from her gay dentist (whom we called 'The Tooth Fairy') to her tax accountant (whom we called as little as possible), also decided that now was the time to drop in.

Just when I thought things couldn't get any more bonkers, a week later I trudged into my bedroom after work one night to find the Countess naked and fresh from the shower. My blow-dryer looked like a gun in her hands. She aimed it at me.

'Do you want this back, dah-ling? I forgot mine, so we'll have to share while I'm living here.' The blow-dryer ticked like a clock as it cooled.

'Living here? You've . . . you've moved in?' My voice had gone up two octaves into a petrified squeak. 'When did this happen?'

'I'm having knee surgery tomorrow. Makes me sound so old. If anyone asks, just say I fell off my shoes during curtsey practice for my damehood, dah-ling. But I'll need people to take care of me.'

I was suddenly going for gold in the Fixed-smile event. 'Wait here, will you? . . . Although feel free to put some clothes on.'

I was down the stairs faster than a bobsleigh on the winter Olympics vertical-drop track. I found my mother in the ramshackle garden at the rear of the house, wearing her full bee-keeping suit. Harking back to her hippy days, Roxy not only tended a small vegetable allotment in abandoned factory grounds in nearby Kentish Town but also kept an apiary hidden away behind a patch of wild flowers, lavender bushes and the lemon balm she grew for calming tea infusions. She maintained it was her honey that kept her looking so foxy.

'Bees are truly bloody remarkable,' she said, replacing the

top on the beehive. 'I mean, you don't see wasps making Worcestershire sauce or maggots making marmalade, now do you?'

'You let the Countess move in! Are you crazy? We're already overcrowded. A sardine would feel claustrophobic here.'

'She needs me,' Roxy said, removing her gauze bee-keeper's hat and heading back inside.

'Hasn't she got indentured peasants from the gulag to take care of her in her country mansion? . . . Hello! Serfs up!' I said, closing the kitchen door on the February chill.

'I'm her best friend, possum. The Countess and I will be friends until we're old and senile . . . And then we will be new friends, obviously,' she chuckled.

'I'm sorry, but the answer's got to be no, Mother.'

'She's just staying a week. Till she's recuperated from surgery.'

'But there won't be any chance of her recuperating, because if she *stays* here I'm going to perform an autopsy. On her still-live body.'

'Be kind, Tilly. It's not as though she's got any loving children to take care of her. Like I do.'

'Don't count on it.'

'We're her only family.'

'It's not too late to have IVF.'

'Don't be ridiculous, dar-ling. I don't want children.' I turned to watch the Countess waft down the hall in a long black kaftan, vodka tonic in hand. 'It's better to have loved and lost . . . than to get up for the 2 a.m. feed.'

'Well, I, for one, am looking forward to you moving in!' Roxy enthused. 'It'll be fun. We can all take up the instrument we gave up in our youth and have a really bad band. Sax for me, violin for you. Tilly?'

'Hmmm.' The Countess looked me up and down judgementally. 'Triangle? Or bongos? We'll need some percussion.'

'Surely we can just use our low-hanging labia to beat out a tune?' my mother suggested. 'Or the testicles of men who've annoyed us as maracas.'

'Yes. We'll send you out to shoot off a few for us,' the Countess said to Phyllis.

The three women cackled loudly. It was worrying me how much they were enjoying each other's company. 'People left in this house longer than sixty days must have a forwarding address and will be towed away at their own expense!' I threatened to deaf ears.

Over the next few days, I realized that I was of very little importance in this domestic set-up. I got the newspaper *after* it had lined Portia's pet tortoise's cage. I got the food rejected by Phyllis's ferret. It's hard to pinpoint the worst aspect of my new living arrangements, but I think it might have been the post-operative Countess, lying supine on the couch, ringing her little silver bell for alcoholic top ups.

'I'd like to have a vodka with a vodka, and a dash of vodka with that,' she ordered the moment she returned home from day surgery.

'You drink way too much, you know. You're practically an alcoholic.'

'I most certainly am not,' she snapped. 'Alcoholics go to meetings. I'm a drunk – *I* go to parties.'

Six people in the house plus endless visitors and three rescue dogs meant constant chaos, but my biggest worry was press intrusion. With straggling snappers camped outside, my mother's tendency to walk around naked took on a new horror. Roxy's pubic area is so forested, it looks as though she has one of the Jackson Five *circa* 1970 in a headlock. Portia and I were used to it, but I wasn't sure the *Daily Mail* readers would quite understand her Aussie laissez-faire attitude to forestation and nudity.

Lack of sleep wasn't helping the situation either. This was mainly due to the older women's tendency to chortle into the small hours. 'I do hope my sleeping isn't disturbing your loud and raucous partying,' I called down from the stairs every night, to no avail. When I did finally get to sleep, I'd be woken by the dulcet strains of Phyllis's snoring reverberating through the wall. The fugitive granny was sleeping on the pull-out bed in the study right next to my bedroom. When she snored, which was often, it sounded as though she were trying to suck her face into the back of her head through her nostrils.

The only truly serene member of the household was Sheldon, Portia's tortoise. Mind you, if he *had been* enduring inner conflict, it would have been quite hard to tell.

Another week of this bedlam and I started wriggling my eyebrows mutely towards the front door. 'Surely you'd be more comfortable in your own home, Countess?' I pleaded, only for her casually to announce her decision to have a chemical peel and a jowl-ectomy, which meant she would need to stay a little longer to recover.

'What?' I fretted. 'Why not employ Roxy's home-grown solution to double chins and just wear a turtleneck sweater?'

'Well, I may rethink the chin op. But I'm definitely going in for the chemical peel, to erase laugh lines around my eyes and mouth.'

'A simpler solution would be to move in with your mother. Believe me, you will never laugh, smile or feel happy ever again,' I said despondently, to nobody in particular.

When I complained, my mother jauntily replied, 'Darl, it's only *you* who's incompatible. The rest of us are getting along fabulously.'

Roxy tilted her head in the direction of Portia, who was bent over her homework at the kitchen table. The tip of her tongue innocently caressed her top lip as she puzzled over a mathematical equation, totally at ease in the happy chaos. The other house guests were sitting in companionable silence on the living-room couch, watching reruns of the old American staples favoured by Phyllis.

'If Mister Ed could really talk, why didn't he ever complain about standing in his own urine-drenched straw all day?' Portia called over to Chantelle. The shattered teen who'd been numbing her way through each day managed a feeble smile with one corner of her mouth. Since viewing the footage of her attack, the sixteen-year-old wanted to be cuddled and cradled like a baby. Phyllis was even cutting up her food. Only Portia seemed able to lift the darkness from her eyes.

When she wasn't cheering up Chantelle or completing assignments, Portia was organizing environmental campaigns. 'It's quite a good idea to save the planet, because we don't actually have anywhere else to go,' she explained to Phyllis, who instantly converted to recycling. The radicalized gran was soon spending all her time helping to paint anti-litter posters, which read 'Don't be a tosser.'

In the pursuit of domestic harmony, my diplomatic daughter hung up a 'Thank You for not Snoring' sign outside Phyllis's bedroom and cheered the Countess by suggesting she forego cosmetic surgery and simply embrace her status as an iconic seventies model by putting out a fragrance.

'Great idea! We'll call it "Better than that Crap Liza Minnelli is Flogging",' she hooted at the dinner table.

'Or maybe "Really Old Spice",' I grumbled to Sheldon and the ferret, who were the only members of the household who ever seemed to listen to me.

Just when I'd reached breaking point and started taking chocolate syrup intravenously, Phyllis's case was scheduled for June. I counted off the remaining months, like a prisoner crossing off days in her cell.

12

Having Your Beefcake and
Eating It, Too

If only doctors had a cure for the human condition. Why wasn't there a prescription available to alleviate all the misogyny suffered by the clients of Pandora's? This was the thought that preoccupied me as I prepared for Phyllis's trial and Roxy managed our practice's caseload.

According to my mother, if you gave a man a fish he would eat for a day. If you taught a man to fish, he would lie in a boat all day quaffing beers and dreaming of porn. She was busy organizing legal aid for a girl who had endured the worst first date ever with a bloke she met on Facebook. He asked her to give him a lift, claiming he needed to pick something up from a mate. She drove him to a shopping mall, where he left her for five minutes. He returned in a flap, yelling 'Go, go, go!' She then drove back to his house. They'd just settled down for a get-to-know-each-other beer when the police arrived and arrested them both. The young woman was astonished to find the police accusing him of robbing a betting shop at knifepoint and her of being his get-away-driving accomplice. 'She thought she'd be ending the night in his arms and instead she ended up in the long arms of the law,' Roxy explained, as she set off to the police cells.

Another client wanted us to bring a sexual harassment case against a crusty old perv who managed a local department store. He'd insisted all the girls sit on his lap – only he wasn't dressed as Santa and it wasn't Christmas.

Roxy was also organizing bail for a woman who had tried to overdose her violent husband by mixing pure, liquid, medical-strength morphine with chocolate body paint and coating her vagina before cunnilingus ... forgetting that pussies are porous. She survived her overdose, only to find herself on a trip of another kind, to the cop shop on a drugs charge.

And then, of course, there was Jack. The emails started a week after I'd promised to go out with him.

Dearest Tilly,
I've been waiting to hear from you. Are you in prison? If not,
I've been invited to dine with the Lord Chief Justice. Would
be a good career move for you to join me.
Love, Jack

Jack,
Legal dinners are so stiffly formal they make tea with the
Queen seem like a quick pint with a stripper down the pub.
So that's a no.
Matilda

Dear Disgruntled but Still-gorgeous Girl,
A client has given me two tickets to the opening night of
Hamlet at the National. I know how you love theatrics, Tilly.

Then we can go to the after-show party and mingle with the stars.
Love, Jack

Jack,
Opening nights are full of people introducing you to people who need no introduction. Opening show parties are where the hors d'oeuvres get speared in the middle and the guests in the back. So that's another no.
Matilda

When I rejected his next offer of a day at the races as being too elitist, he insisted with some irritation that 'It's just a bunch of horses hurtling around the track.'

'Yes,' I emailed back. 'And hell is just a sauna.'

Jack: 'Dinner atop London's highest building, the Shard? We'll drink *Shard*onnay.'

Me: 'Vertigo. I have no head for heights. I'd get a nosebleed from all that social climbing.'

Having given up on cultural and charity events, Jack then tried to tempt me into conquering the Great Outdoors, starting with a cycle along the Thames from Hampton Court to Richmond.

I declined: 'The hardest thing about cycling is trying not to spill your wine.'

He suggested waterskiing on Lake Como.

'The art of knocking down a jetty with your face and hence the mainstay of neurosurgeons worldwide,' I responded.

Jack (exasperated): 'Bungee jumping over the Victoria Falls?'

Me: 'Bungee jumping is just whoosh, then dangle upside down in acute agony for an hour, followed by death.'

When I'd rejected every conceivable sporting event from

windsailing to abseiling, he resorted in desperation to bowling: 'You can't possibly object to this most innocuous of sports.'

Me: 'Marbles for grown-ups.'

'Okay,' he electronically harrumphed, 'why don't *you* make a suggestion?'

What I wanted to say was that it was second on my list of priorities, right after a self-administered appendectomy, but replied instead, 'I will. Let me think on it.'

That bought me some breathing space. In truth, the only way I would ever spend any of my leisure time with Jack Cassidy was if we were both kidnapped by Somali pirates.

When I didn't get back to him for two weeks, he sought me out in person. I often escaped the chaos of my office life to work in the relative quiet of a nearby café. When I saw Jack, immaculately suited and booted, striding across the cobble-stoned square, I made a valiant leap towards my bicycle, but I wasn't quick enough.

He sat down, commandeered my macchiato, sugared it liberally, then downed it in one gulp. 'You must have been writing to me in invisible ink, as I don't seem to have received any date suggestions? It's not as if I'm asking you to solve the riddle of the Pyramids or find the Bermuda Triangle. We made a deal, you recall.'

'Sorry . . . I meant to get back to you, but I'm living with my mother, her aged model friend, the pensioner fugitive and her shell-shocked granddaughter, plus their ferret and a tortoise. Not to forget all my mother's foster dogs and regular visits from her "Save the Bumblebee" society, and deranged locals dropping in for her home-made herbal remedies . . . which means that I'm seriously considering a DIY lobotomy,' I ad-libbed.

'If it's driving you crazy, why don't you leave Pandora's?'

He rocked back in his chair. 'My offer still stands.' Jack's strong legs were invitingly splayed as he said this.

I tried to avert my eyes but had to admit that it was a tantalizing view. Noting the drift of my glance, he gave a wide smile which increased his resemblance to a Cheshire Cat.

'Roxy and I are staying together on account of our accountant. I don't think she could handle the stress if we broke up.'

Jack looked at the chocolate brownie I was halfway through devouring. 'Would you like the name of a good heart specialist to go with that?'

'A new study has revealed that women who carry a little extra weight live longer than the men who mention it. The thing is, Jack, I'm a typical British woman, with European teeth and real, uninflated lips, a hundred per cent organic, home-grown hair, a proper appetite and serious chocolate cravings. You really don't want to go out with a woman like me. The only reason you do is because I'm the only female in the world who doesn't want to. Why don't you just give up and go get yourself another trophy girlfriend? A supermodel or a double-jointed Olympic gymnast, or something?'

'I don't like a woman I can walk all over. Literally. Trophy girlfriends are so thin, they fall right through the pavement cracks.' He gave a rich chuckle. 'Pick you up on Friday night. At eight thirty. No plans. We'll do something spontaneous.'

'Oh, but . . .' I racked my brain for a spontaneous excuse to get out of doing anything spontaneous.

'I promise there'll be no sacrifice of nubile maidens or ritual animal slaughter of any kind. Kisses on your bicycle seat till then.' He blew a kiss in the direction of my push bike, which was propped on the wall behind me. With an insouciant wink, he sauntered off, like some clichéd Humphrey Bogart hero, got into his sleek, low-slung BMW sports car and barracudaed down the street with a roar.

There was no choice, I thought, pedalling furiously back to my office. The man had more nerve than an unfilled tooth. The only way I could avoid Jack Cassidy would be to move to a remote lesbian monastery and take up a little light whittling ... But avoiding all contact with men looked less appealing when I saw what was waiting for me at Pandora's.

The law of attraction states that the chance of bumping into the man you secretly have the hots for is directly proportional to how unattractively scruffy you are looking at the time.

Nathaniel Cavendish was leaning on a wall outside my office, casually scrolling through his iPhone messages. In faded jeans and those scuffed biker boots, fair hair fetchingly wind-tousled, I found myself wondering if the man could ever turn up anywhere looking just a little mediocre. I mean, did he have to look centrefold sensational at *all* times, especially when I was dressed like Iris Murdoch, in a grey cardigan, with flat shoes and even flatter hair. I was just contemplating diverting my bike down a side lane when he glanced up, saw me and stood to attention.

'Sorry to drop by your office unannounced' – his expression was sombre, 'but I've just found out that two of the men in my rehabilitation programme are prosecution witnesses in a case against a client of yours – the grandma from the Tony Benn Estate who took revenge on two supposed rapists.'

'Really?'

'Their names are Basharat Kureishi and Peter Simmons. I've been mentoring them. They're out on bail, but swear they're innocent of rape. They came to me for a character reference, which, of course, I declined. Bash, the short one, well, he described the female legal eagle defending the grandma as, and I quote, "a feminist who slipped through the ugly net". So I immediately figured it must be you.' He smiled then, a smile which lit up the whole street. 'Am I right?'

I'd never been insulted and complimented so confusingly in the same sentence. 'Oh. Um. Bash. Yes. I remember him. He was definitely the brains of the desperate duo. I mean, the tall, hulking one . . . Have you ever looked at someone and just known that the wheel was turning but the hamster was dead?'

Nathaniel laughed. 'Stretch. Yep. That about sums him up. Although, Christ. I thought I'd made such progress with those two. I try to monitor tension on the estate. That way I can predict violence and mediate disputes with my clients before they happen. But I totally dropped the ball with those two.' He ran his hand through his thick, tangled curls. As he raised his arm to do so, I smelt something spicy and astringent yet lemony in his sweat, reminiscent of the whiff of a tobacco pouch – and it seriously stirred me.

'I'm so sorry about the poor girl.' He looked at me with a shy, delicate glance which belied his strong physique. 'I read in the papers that the grandma's staying with her lawyer, but is the girl okay?'

'She's living with me, too, but never ventures outside . . . A little something to do with people writing the word "Slut" on her door – in bullets.'

'"Slut shaming".' He sighed. 'An odious attempt to humiliate any woman for having sex, enjoying sex or looking like she might enjoy sex.'

When he uttered the phrase 'enjoying sex', the smoky, burnt scent of him entered my mouth and made it water.

He paced around the pavement a bit, giving me a delectable view of him from various angles. 'I despair sometimes, I really do. In a year when sexual violence against women dominates the media, the endless rapes, gropings, grooming and trafficking of vulnerable girls, young women imprisoned as sex slaves in bunkers, Internet and Twitter trolls making death and rape threats against feminists . . . it makes me embarrassed to be a man. It really does. Why are members of my own gender doing so many vile things to members of yours?'

He put his hand on my arm and the warmth of his body radiated into mine. It struck me that I wanted him to do something vile to me, right then and there, involving much moaning and partial nudity.

'Women are always so self-critical – "Am I too fat?" "Am I too old?" "If I go back to work, will my child grow up to collect Nazi memorabilia?" . . . It's time *my* gender did a little soul searching. Eighty-five per cent of all crimes in Britain are committed by men. Why? I mean, what do you think about that?'

What I was thinking about was how whenever he touched me I just lit up all over like a pinball machine. *Ding! Ding!*

'Men's brutality's seen as a given, a byproduct of that dark Y chromosome and the rocket fuel of testosterone. But what turns innocent boys into dangerous men? I think modern man's lost in a post-industrial landscape, functionless, porn-addicted, racked with performance anxiety in a Viagra and Jack Daniel's culture, unable to articulate his feelings. Don't you?'

I nodded, unable to articulate my feelings at all, which were totally R-rated and purely animalistic.

'Yet men are leaving all the heavy lifting against gender bias to women. I mean, in the universal movement for human equality, there's a big gap where the men should be. In the great civil rights struggles fifty years ago, there were white faces as well as black. Men have to engage with contemporary feminism to make a change. Don't you agree?'

I wanted to agree, but I was feeling faint from holding my stomach in to look thinner.

'I'd like to set up an anti-porn project on the estate. Porn affects how men look at women and think about sex. Men need to take our notions of sexuality back from these predatory pornographers . . .'

Again, I wanted to agree, but I was feeling quite predatory and pornographic myself. Nathaniel smiled then, a smile with his whole face in it, like before, and especially his eyes. The sun rested on the back of my neck like a warm and friendly hand. An involuntary shiver shimmied up my thighs. I smiled back at him.

'Christ, I'm rabbiting on, aren't I? If I bore any more, I'll strike oil! But I'm just so angry! And I feel so guilty that two boys on my watch could do this terrible thing. Anyway, I just came around to apologize on behalf of all blokes.'

'Oh, well, gee thanks' seemed the only appropriate response, other than 'Let's run away to a tropical island, big boy, where you can lick the roe of virgin sturgeon from my navel 'neath a tropical palm.'

'Anyway, I'd like to take you out to dinner to apologize properly and so we can discuss the case. Maybe I can be of help? Friday? Eightish?'

I must have nodded my consent, because he was now straddling his motorbike and peeling off down the street. I felt a huge sense of relief as I finally stopped clenching my stomach muscles. I feel about Spanx the way some people feel about fox hunting – that they're a travesty and a disgusting example of the deceit and decay of contemporary life – unless I'm on a first date with a gorgeous bloke, that is, and then they're a miracle of modern engineering.

After Nathaniel had disappeared around the corner, I retraced my steps to the high street to buy some control underwear. It seemed the only thing in my life I could have any control over, these days.

Last time we'd met, Nathaniel had told me that the best things in life were free, like sex and oxygen. Well, what *I* was thinking is that sex actually is a lot like oxygen – no big deal unless you're not getting any.

13

Sex Bombs

The worst thing about a car bomb is the gaping hole it leaves in your social life. This was the thought that came to mind shortly after I woke the following Friday evening from a quick nap before my date with Nathaniel. I'd had an exhausting day, reading witness statements and affidavits for Phyllis's case, in between food shopping, bill paying and driving Portia to her doctor, dentist and dance-class appointments. You deliver your child once vaginally, and then forever after by car. I'd finally collapsed fully clothed on the bed about 7 p.m., only to be woken shortly after by the sound of waves breaking on shingle. I imagined for a moment that I was back in my mother's homeland, about to dive into the Bondi breakers, until I groggily realized it was the sound of glass shattering. A rock lay on the carpet, surrounded by glass shards. There was a note attached.

Slut protectors. That chantelle slag is a fuckin worthless waste of female flesh. gonna blow yer to fuckin bits unless youse bitches back off.

My befuddled brain rallied instantly. A cold dread hit me in the pit of my stomach. I lurched on to the landing outside my bedroom and stumbled over a pair of sprayed pink go-go boots. 'Roxy!' A trail of clothing led like a sartorial version of fairy-tale breadcrumbs up the stairs to my mother's room.

I banged on her door until a dishevelled head appeared. 'It's time we talked about protection.'

'At my age? Don't be silly. It's the only upside to the menopause.'

'Not *condoms*, Mother. Police protection.' I unscrunched the note which had been chucked through my bedroom window and held it up to her face.

Roxy drew her silk kimono about her body and took a step into the hall to scan it more clearly. 'Crikey. He's not exactly plagiarizing Shakespeare, now is he? Just ignore it. It's all bluster. I mean' – she shrugged – 'what kind of hopeless psychopath would let you know beforehand that he's going to kill you?'

'Um . . . I believe that the clue is in the term "psychopath". We're not talking logical here.'

The tousled head of a young man bobbed up behind Roxy and mumbled hello. My mother attracts unsuitable men like iron filings to a magnet. I noted the boy's tattoos and Rasta dreadlocks, set off so nicely by a light scattering of acne.

'So tell me, Mother, are you going to date him or adopt him?' I started picking up Roxy's discarded clothes. 'What kind of example are you setting Portia?'

'A bloody good one, I reckon. To live life to the full.' She illustrated this statement by taking a drag on his joint. I recognized him then. He grew dope on the allotments where my mother grew her veggies.

'Living life to the full might be a tad hard when you're, you know, *dead*.' I snatched the bomb threat back from her manicured talons. 'Just tell me the number of your favourite taxidermist so I can get your blown-up remains reassembled and stuffed. Then you can be mounted for eternity!' I wheeled around and made for the stairs. 'I'm calling the police.'

'You're overreacting, Matilda. I've had loads of death threats over the years. Hell, I used to have Scotland Yard on speed dial.' Roxy padded down the hall behind me, knotting her silk kimono cord. 'They'll just tell you to look for car bombs. And have you ever looked under a car? *Everything* under a car looks like a car bomb! So, chillax. Let me make you a camomile infusion.'

All my life, I'd been embarrassed when my mother said 'chillax' or borrowed my miniskirts or smoked dope with my mates or rocked up to my law graduation packed into lime-green stretch pants, a sequinned boob tube and ten-inch wedge sandals. In truth, there's many a time I've been tempted to become a Hindu, as there is really nothing in my life that reincarnation couldn't cure. Sadly, Roxy shows no sign of becoming more conventional or curbing her behaviour with age. Which is why I shouldn't have been remotely surprised to have found her in bed on a Friday afternoon with a dope grower not much older than her granddaughter. But I was.

'You know, Mum, it didn't matter when Portia was little, but she's hitting her teens. She needs good role models right now,' I said, clattering down the stairs. 'Meaning, she needs a normal grandmother, who shops and mops and bakes cupcakes and doesn't bring home toy boys. I'm sick of playing mother to your irresponsible teenager ... Which is why I'm grounding you for the foreseeable future.'

My mother honked her amusement behind me. 'Really? 'Cause I was thinking of opening a toy-boy shop. With shopper loyalty cards. And a boy buffet. We could also sell time-share husbands . . .'

'I don't know why anyone would want a husband,' the Countess piped up from her prone position on the living-room couch. Her face was red raw from the chemical peel, her neck swathed in bandages. 'They're so lazy. They're like "You start the foreplay and I'll come in and finish off." Oh, I lost count of the amount of orgasms I faked with the aged oligarch.' She sighed.

'Who cares about the orgasms being faked so long as the jewellery is real!' Roxy snorted.

And they were off, hooting with ribald merriment. I groaned in despair. I now had irresponsible role models in stereo. It's really saying something when the only other sensible adult member of your household is on trial for attempted murder. I glanced at Phyllis, who was in the kitchen stirring up something hale and hearty in the soup department.

'Did either of you see anyone suspicious lurking outside just now? Someone's just chucked a rock through my bedroom window.'

'No, but it's after seven. Waaayyy past wine o'clock.' The Countess checked her watch.

My mother crossed the open-plan living room into the kitchen area to pour them both a glass of wine.

'Yes, my oligarch was my worst shag ever, not counting the Trotsky dwarf,' the Countess called out after her. 'As I was saying, the trouble wasn't me faking orgasms but him faking foreplay. Who was your worst shag, Roxy, dear?'

'Hello?' I remonstrated, pointing at myself. 'Nauseated daughter in the room!' I picked up the landline in the kitchen and dialled the police. 'May I remind you that there are two teens in the house, so can you please stop discussing penises at full volume?' A voice crackled down the phone line. 'Oh, hello? No, sorry, I wasn't talking to you . . . Yes, may I speak to a detective, please . . .'

'My worst? . . . Do you remember that doctor I dated? He was so afraid of disease, he wore a condom while masturbating.' Roxy gave a guttural whoop.

I placed a reprimanding hand over the receiver. 'I'm reporting a death threat here. I'm not sure if the Metropolitan Police need to hear the intimate details of your vaginal déjà vu.'

As I waited on hold for a detective, radio pop music pumped forth from the earpiece which I held away from my head. It was a Chris Brown song and I wasn't taking particular comfort from the lyrics: 'All my ladies, put ya hands up if you got that bomb – bomb – ba – bomb – ba – bomb – bomb . . .'

'When I grow up, I want to be just like you, Grandma!' Portia had cat-footed down the hall on her soft little paws. She walked straight past me and hugged Roxy hard. 'You're oo much fun.'

My anger rose like boiling milk. 'I can be fun!' I insisted, busting a few moves circa 1989 around the kitchen while still umbilically attached to the phone.

Roxy, Phyllis, Portia and the Countess were gawping at my uncharacteristic performance. My daughter exploded with laughter. Her giggle is totally infectious – which is why Phyllis and the Countess were also rat-a-tat-tatting with machinegun rapid-fire chortles. It was while my daughter's eyes were squeezed tight with mirth that I noticed she was wearing make-up. Greasy-green sparkly eye shadow and thick coats of mascara. I then watched in astonishment as Portia sat down to strap on high heels before gingerly making her way to the fridge, wobbling like a stilt walker traversing volcanic terrain.

I was still on hold, my ear going numb. 'Darling, aren't you a bit overdressed for political activism? I thought you were meeting Amelia and the girls at the Shake Shack before heading off to put up your anti-litter posters?' I asked in a flap. High heels and make-up was just the beginning. Any day now she'd come home with a nipple piercing, tongue stud and a tattoo in Balinese for 'inner peace' which would later turn out to be an order for stir-fried bok choy. And it was all because of my mother's laissez-faire influence.

My mother and daughter exchanged a glance of condescending complicity, which infuriated me even more.

'Amelia's dad's dropping me home at ten thirty.' She smiled at me, her head at an awkward but absurdly touching angle that twanged my heartstrings.

'Sorry, darling, but you are not going out in high heels and make-up.'

Portia shrugged and obligingly changed shoes and wiped off her eye make-up. She bid us a happy farewell and bounced out through the door.

Roxy passed me a glass of wine. 'You're so overprotective, Tilly.'

'I'm not overprotective!'

'I once heard you explaining in excruciatingly painful detail what to do in case of a tsunami . . . We live in London, for Christ's sake. At Portia's age I was in a band called Kamikaze Fellatio.'

I scowled at my mother. 'I rest my case. And please don't give me lectures on mothering. You left me with the Countess half the time. Her babysitting technique was to play Hide and Seek. I would hide . . . and she would make herself a gin and tonic and watch television.'

'It wasn't easy, you know, after your father ran off. It was just you and me against the world. But wasn't I always your friend?'

'I didn't want a friend. I wanted a mum! Your idea of a lovely summer holiday was to join a female collective and stitch a patchwork quilt in a remote Scottish bothy, chanting runic love poems while renewing your friendship vows in a drumming circle before a druid.'

'Oh, mental cruelty,' Roxy mocked. 'You should have rung Childline.'

'You thought nothing of telling me all about your boyfriends. How good they were, or weren't, in bed. And you're still at it.'

'Oh, well, I'm sorry for treating you like an equal.'

'I wanted a mum in a pinny who made shepherd's pie! Which is why I want to raise Portia differently. I want a proper family meal, eaten around the table. In a clean and tidy, ordered house with no talk of multiple orgasms and Ben Wa balls or *rocks with death threats thrown through windows*! . . . Hello! Hello!' I yelled down the phone to Chris Brown. 'Luckily, Portia has taken after *me*, not you. She's interested in getting good marks. Not in teenage boys.'

'But she should be interested in boys at her age.'

'Teenage boys are basically just a grunt with grime. They bore her rigid.'

'Well, that shows how little you know about your daughter, Tilly. Portia's very keen on a boy at school.'

I stood stock still, looking at my mother. 'She told you that?'

'Yes. She told me about him because we're *friends*,' she said pointedly.

'When did she tell you?'

'When we were rollerblading.'

'You went rollerblading with my daughter? When?'

'Yesterday. When you were working.'

'You went rollerblading without me? I like rollerblading!'

'She wanted some advice about a hooch-smuggling bestie who got caught with a spliff at school.'

I felt winded. 'Why would Portia come to you for advice? Your only previous advice to my daughter was to make sure her future tattoos are spelt correctly. But, fortunately, my daughter's not like that. Which is why she's out this evening, putting up her anti-litter posters to make the world a better place.'

'Um . . . I don't think Portia's out puttin' up posters.' The timid voice belonged to Chantelle, who, I now noticed, was in a corner of the adjoining living room, sitting in the near-dark like a nervous cat.

'What?'

'She's been meetin' some old dude. Every afternoon. After school. On Parliament Hill.'

My mother and I dropped our animosity to each other immediately.

'An old dude? What old dude?' we said simultaneously.

I was suddenly pitching and rolling in a wild sea, though there was only carpet beneath my feet. 'How do you know?'

'When I have nightmares an' that, Portia lets me sleep in 'er room, on the futon. I hear 'er talkin' to him on 'er phone, makin' arrangements an' that. I asked 'er about him but she wouldn't say nuffink. I don't want it to 'appen to Portia . . . Yer know, what 'appened to me,' she said in a small voice.

I felt panic rear up like a tidal wave. Here I was worrying about boys while my daughter was meeting some *man*. What man? The thrower of the rock? Some nasty predator, spinning his evil, sticky web as he groomed her for abduction? The papers were full of paedophiles pied-pipering teenage girls away . . . I imagined this horror for a sickening second before banishing it, appalled, from my mind.

Chris Brown finally gave way to a female voice. 'Detective Denise Phillips speaking.'

But there was no longer any time to report bomb threats – a bigger explosion had just been detonated in my life. I dropped the phone as if it had burnt me at the same moment my mother snatched up her car keys. With the synchronicity of Olympic swimmers, Roxy and I were down the hall and out the door. Roxy gripped my hand. I squeezed hers back as we bolted, terrified, for her car. At the bottom of the stairs we collided into two men who were arriving from opposite directions. In all the mayhem, I'd forgotten about my romantic rendezvous with Nathaniel – let alone my dating commitment with Jack.

Jack was looking sardonic and amused – a facial expression he really should copyright. 'You have way too much energy for someone without a crystal-meth addiction, do you know that, Tilly?'

'Am I too early?' Nathaniel asked, extending an artful bouquet of exotic flowers.

'Planning a *ménage à trois*, are we, Tilly?' Jack asked, eyebrow cocked, voice low and smoky.

'Oh God! Sorry. Just introduce yourselves,' I babbled, rushing by. Nathaniel called something out after me, but we were already in Roxy's car, careering around the corner on two wheels, nearly taking out a letterbox and a street sign in our race in the dark to the park.

How could I lose my daughter? There I was criticizing Roxy's maternal techniques when, obviously, I made Medea look like good mother material. One thing was clear, poor Portia needed a Mother Disability Allowance . . . if she lived long enough to claim it.

14

A Stranger in the Dark in the Park

The beam of Roxy's torch picked out Portia sitting with a stranger on a park bench on top of Parliament Hill which looked down over London. Her face was vivid with excitement. A bedraggled fox streaked through the bushes in the gloaming. It shivered through the trees, like a phantom.

My startled cry alerted the man, who looked up. He was a ravaged, Indiana Jones type with scruffy hair and haunted eyes. Before either of them could say anything, Roxy lunged, tackling him off the bench to the ground, delivering a quick kick to his gonads for good measure.

'Grandma! No! Stop it!' Portia cried.

I hugged my daughter with a relief so intense it was almost painful. I rocked her soothingly, inhaling her sweet smell of soap and chewing gum. I clung to her, paralysed by love. But my daughter pushed me away. Her wind-tangled hair blurred wildly around her face. 'Leave him alone! Both of you.'

'Christ Almighty,' the man said. 'Is that any way to greet me after all these years?'

'Who the hell are you?' I demanded, but he was looking at Roxy.

'The chiselled features don't give it away? The rakish charm? The green eyes and impish dimple? . . . Christ, Roxy, you look better than ever . . . Which I would tell you in a deep and manly voice, if you'd just get your stiletto out of my balls.'

My mother gave the man a measuring, suspicious look. Then her mouth opened wide in pantomime astonishment. Now, my irrepressible mother is famously garrulous. She can talk to anyone. The woman could exchange mobile numbers with a corpse. But she was now lost for words.

The mystery man rose to his feet and turned his attention to me. 'Wow! You have my eyes.' He grabbed my hand. It was a wrestler's handshake.

Roxy took a swing at his jaw and knocked him sideways.

'Gran! Behave!' Portia squealed, leaping between Roxy and the winded bloke.

'No, love, your gran is right. I deserved that.'

'Who the hell are you?' I reiterated.

'Just call me Dad.'

Now it was my turn to imitate a hyperventilating goldfish. For the next few minutes, all I could hear was the whumping sound of my blood in my temples. I felt like some traveller who for years has read of the existence of snow leopards or poltergeists but never expected to be this near to one. Gradually, my breath slowed down, my heart stopped knocking about in my chest and I began to regain my senses. So, here he was. Dark as a secret, bright as joy, my mother's first and last and only love. I shone my torch into my father's face and examined him with forensic attention to detail.

His hard, strong body was contoured and sinewy, with a light mahogany tan. There was a hint of grey amid his glossy fair curls, which were lassoed back in a ponytail. He had twinkly, world-weary eyes and an affable, gap-toothed smile. His broken nose gave him the look of a Greek god who'd been recarved by a tipsy sculptor, the features slightly misaligned. What's more, his genetic echo whispered in my daughter's veins – the high-winged collar bones, the blue eyes, blond hair and strong athletic frame.

'You're really my . . . my father?' I said warily.

'I believe so. And I've come to offer you an unreserved apology.'

'Oh' was all I could manage to say.

'And an explanation. So . . .' He spread his hands open, 'what do you know about me? If anything.'

A stridency of questions and exclamations exploded in my head. Where to begin? 'Well, I know you were an undercover policeman.'

'Who stole the identity of a dead child!' my shell-shocked mother seethed beside me, having finally found her vocal cords.

'So you know about that?' The man winced. 'Yeah, well, I'm not proud of it. At first I thought the tactic was justified because we had this mission to accomplish . . . The monitoring of political activists was in the greater good, and all that. Your choice of undercover name was of fundamental importance because on that would rest your whole sense of security, confidence and ability to do the job . . .'

'A dead boy!' my mother repeated, appalled.

'It's true. I was given a fake passport, driving licence and a national insurance number in his name, to make my persona more credible, you know, in case the protesters ever became suspicious and investigated me . . . But then, each year, I celebrated the birthday of that dead kid, realizing his parents were at that point thinking about their son and missing him like mad, and I'd get this really shitty feeling. It was almost like dancing on his grave. And then I fell in love with this kooky, funny Aussie girl . . .'

He smiled up at Roxy, flashing one gold tooth. 'Falling in love with you, Roxy, was kinda outside police guidelines for undercover operations . . . So I had to leave. Even though I loved you like crazy, I knew you'd be better off without me. So I told you I had to go on the run. But the whole experience totally nauseated me. I quit the force soon after. Joined the army. Went on tours of duty. Africa, Iraq, Afghanistan . . . I've been knocked down, locked up, shot, bitten, kicked and almost drowned, yet I'm pretty robust and largely intact, apart from half a thumb lost from a crocodile bite.'

He was trying so hard, it felt as though he was doing a one-man show at the Edinburgh Festival.

'But the one thing I missed was you, Roxy. My daily share of the wonderful here and now. And all the love that nourishes us through the appalling mystery of what the hell we're doing on this big hunk of rock spinning through the universe . . . Sure, there were other women. Hey, I'm no angel. But I could never settle. Just kept moving on. And then I started asking around about you. That's when I found out you had a baby. My baby. And that you'd been looking for me to tell me all those years ago. I was gutted. Blown away. Once I knew about Matilda and Portia, I just had to come back. And so, here I am. Hoping you can find it in your heart to forgive me and let me be part of your family.'

A tangible silence fell like dust over all of us. Finally, Roxy spoke.

'Really? You disappear for thirty-four years and you think you're going to waltz back into our lives and sit around and exchange pleasantries about the wallpaper and the weather . . . ? You used me, you bastard!'

My mother tried to swat him like a fly, despite the fact that he was six foot to her five.

'I loved you so much, you mongrel! But then I had to accept that you never existed. You lied from go to whoa. Yes, we imagined that our phones might be tapped or that some asshole might look at our post . . . but to find out that there was a spy in your bed! Jesus!'

'I just can't believe I'm seeing you again, Roxy,' my father – Danny – said. 'And that you're even more beautiful than ever.'

'Well, I'm sorry I can't say the same for you, you prick.'

Danny's smile seeped away.

'You told me you were a gardener, doing cash-in-hand jobs in well-heeled Hampstead, but that politics was really "your thing". You just used me as your girlfriend so you could portray yourself as this fully rounded person and get access to the protesters. People trusted me, so they welcomed you, too. Jesus, Danny! After the police busts there was a big crisis. The animal rights campaigners suspected there was an informer in our midst. Special Branch even raided our place, saying they "were looking for Danny" . . . Of course, you weren't there. Why? Because you'd orchestrated the bloody raids by your police mates to bolster your bloody cover story! Then you began to tell me that you had to go on the run abroad to escape the cops. I wanted to go with you, but you said it was too dangerous. You promised to contact me so I could join you. Then I found out I was up the duff . . . but didn't know how to reach you. I was so worried about you. So I just waited and waited and fretted for your friggin' call that never came.'

Portia was looking confused and a little frightened. I took her gently by the shoulders. 'Your amazing grandma raised me on my own while working full time as a barmaid *and* getting a law degree.'

'Yeah, and all the time I blamed myself for the fact that my daughter didn't have a dad. If only I'd been braver and gone on the run with you! If only I'd been more supportive! . . . I didn't date anyone else. I just stayed loyal to you, my Robin Hood . . . my Ned Kelly . . . And all the time you were in cahoots with the cops!'

Big, tough Danny wilted under her reproachful glare. 'Yeah, well, you have every reason to hate me, I know that.'

'Hate you? That doesn't even start to cover it. When I found out about your alias and how you'd lied and tricked me . . . well, it made it impossible for me ever to trust another bloke. I'm going to ring the police and report a theft – my lost youth. The police stole it from me. I don't know what I'm supposed to have done to have been chosen by the State to be treated like this.' Roxy was almost shouting.

'Roxy was part of Greenpeace. She was no threat to national security,' I admonished him. 'Plus she had nothing to hide. Her answering machine said, "Hi, I can't come to the phone right now as I'm out plotting the downfall of the capitalist state!"'

'And what was Matilda?' Roxy demanded. 'Collateral damage? And now you honestly think that coming here and confessing will miraculously absolve you of all lies and duplicity?'

'No.' His voice was metallic with regret.

'In fact, how did you find us? Christ! . . . Have you been spying on me?'

'I asked around . . .'

'Oh my God. You've been spying on us!'

'And you look so much better in real life than through binoculars,' Danny joshed 'I'm joking!' he added, seeing my stricken face.

'And you expect me to believe that you've bloody well

changed?' Roxy fumed. 'You're as underhanded as ever. Get out of our lives!'

'One of the Countess's new chauffeur bodyguards. He was with me in the Special Demonstration Squad all those years back. He remembered you and told me.'

'That two-faced shit weasel's so sacked! As are you! We don't want you anywhere near us.'

'Is that how you feel, too, Matilda?' Danny asked me flatly.

I took my emotional temperature. With the unexpected impact of meeting my father for the first time, I'd needed an airbag installed in my brain. But after hearing my mother's tirade, my shock had mutated into disdain. What was this man to me? Roxy had been both mother and father. 'You mean nothing to me,' I told him bluntly.

Roxy gave a sigh of relief. 'Right then. That's settled. Let's go home. If I look at this pathetic spectacle too much longer my retinas will detach with disgust.' Roxy put a protective arm around Portia. But my daughter eeled out of her grasp.

'He means something to *me*!' Portia exclaimed. 'We've been secretly meeting and talking for weeks. He's told me all about his past and how sorry he is for what he did to you, Gran. He didn't even know you'd had a baby! As soon as he found out he came back to say sorry.'

'Sweet Jesus! You've been secretly meeting up with my granddaughter for weeks?' The words flew from Roxy's mouth like bullets. 'Is there no end to your duplicity? And why here? In the dark, in a park?'

'He's been teaching me to navigate by the stars.'

Danny's broad shoulders were now up around his ears. 'I should've come to you first, Roxy. But I kinda lost my nerve. Weird, an old soldier like me. But I just wanted to see my darling granddaughter, who is more exquisite than words

173

can say . . . And to meet my beautiful daughter . . .' He smiled up at me.

'You have to give him another chance.' Portia's expression was polite but sullen, her eyes bright and defiant beneath an overlong fringe.

Roxy and I looked at each other, suddenly united, our differences forgotten.

'You're obviously keen to be orphaned, Portia,' Roxy told her. 'I mean, you're clearly trying to kill your mother and me.'

Portia gave us a look which said 'Raising parents isn't as easy as it's cracked up to be.' 'My dad's disappeared. But my granddad's turned up. It's meant to be, can't you see?' My daughter's dark-blond eyebrows were drawn up as tight as an archer's bow. She had such a serious face, yet there was hope all over her – she was positively perfumed by it.

'I'm sorry he left you,' Danny said to me. 'Your old man. Portia told me he buggered off.'

This rocked me. My husband had just disappeared, like a snowman melting, until all that was left of him was a pool of blue water – arctic cold and sorrow coloured. Portia never spoke to me of her dad's departure – yet here she was, opening up to this complete stranger.

'Where is he now? . . . Do you want me to find him for a little "chat"?' Danny adopted a military stance and cracked his knuckles menacingly.

'You'd have to go to Tibet, where I believe he is currently "finding himself". Not that it's any of your business.'

'How could he leave you three fabulous females? I'm over my wild ways – living off the land, sky-diving out of airplanes behind enemy lines . . . all that James Bond shit. I don't need all that excitement any more. All I need is you, Roxy. You and my girls.'

'You need me? But where were *you* when *I* needed *you*?

Where were you when I had to rush Matilda to the hospital at two in the morning? Or fix the hole in the roof when the rain came through? Or bash the cat burglar over the head with the bread board? Where were you then, you mangy bastard?'

'I'm sorry, Rox,' Danny said. I could smell the regret on him, a sour tang like earth and mildew. 'Let me make it up to you. And you, too, Tilly. I'd do anything to make it up to you both.'

His voice was full of remorse. If he were a medieval monk, he'd be flagellating himself before bed every night.

'The way you can make it up to us is to stay out of our lives.' Roxy pulled Portia down the hill towards the car.

'How can you be so cruel!' Portia cried, digging in her heels. 'Mum!?'

'I agree with Roxy. Let's go.'

'I'm never speaking to either of you again!' she cried out, running for the gate.

Roxy glowered darkly at the man she'd once loved. 'Chaos, panic, disorder . . . your work here is clearly done, Danny.'

15

Acute Lust in the Third Degree

Attempting to keep both my mother and my daughter happy made me feel like a gymnast trying to balance on a beam. Roxy forbade me from making any contact with my biological father, while Portia forbade me to ignore him. Which left me no time to fathom how I felt about suddenly having a father. I was a minestrone of emotions.

'He's my grandfather. The only grandfather I've got. Why can't we give him another chance?' my daughter beseeched me over supper later that evening.

My mother made the kind of facial expression last worn by a slug upon finding itself stuck on a pesticide pellet.

'Maybe we could give him another hearing, Mum? He seems genuine.'

'I'd rather spend time with a cockroach. Although they're rather alike. Both scavenge off others and know how to empty a room.'

I laughed, which only infuriated my daughter all the more.

'You're impossible! Both of you!' she shouted, stomping

back to her room without finishing her meal, her narrow hips swishing.

'Remember how excited we were when she learnt to talk?' Roxy said plaintively.

All I heard from Portia for the rest of the weekend was the 'Tss, tss, tss' of her earphones. When I tried to talk to her, she'd punish me by turning up the volume on bands with names like 'Phlegm', 'Nappy Contents' or 'Regurgitated Sick'. The only inhabitants in the house she would talk to were Chantelle, Phyllis and her ferret – oh, and Sheldon, the introverted tortoise.

Occasionally, she'd emerge from her lair to throw open the refrigerator door and declare, 'There's nothing to eat in this house.' The following week, she took to skulking in a battered second-hand leather jacket. Actually, it looked as though the jacket was wearing her rather than the other way round. I had no doubt it was Danny's. Brooding, eye-rolling, refusing to eat with the family – it would seem that clichéd terrible-teen behaviour had seriously set in.

When I checked my emails before bed, there were two or three from Jack, wondering if I'd been abducted by aliens. I deleted them, unanswered, and went to bed, as I had enough trauma to deal with, without tossing Jack into the psychological mix.

By 8 a.m. Monday morning I was on the train to Birmingham to attend a Crown Court case involving a self-taught hypnotist and part-time astrologist who was suing my client for unpaid bills. My client, a married mum of three who had been seeking help for weight loss, maintained that the hypnotist had put her into a trance and told her that she was his sex slave. She awoke during one session covered in ejaculate, to find him fondling her breasts, his pants around his ankles. 'Now that's what I call a "happy medium",' Roxy had quipped.

After a long day in court trying to charm the jury with bad jokes about hypnotists ('All those who believe in psychokinesis, raise my hand') or astrology ('I don't believe in star signs. I'm Cancerian and we're naturally mistrustful'), I was standing on the rain-sodden, windswept train platform at 6 p.m., shivering, tired and already contemplating my warm pyjamas and hot chocolate, when an announcement came over the public address system that there'd been a storm and there were leaves on the line. Passengers exchanged nervous glances. Oh no. Were they the kind of leaves Network Rail liked or not? I rang Roxy. 'I don't know when I'll be home. Apparently, there are leaves on the line, which you'd think would only be a problem if they were still attached to a tree.'

'How can a country which stopped an entire blitzkrieging Nazi invasion armed with only a tea cosy and a couple of kippers be regularly brought to a standstill if the wrong leaves fall on the line? As an Aussie, I'll never understand it.'

The only news from home was that Phyllis's ferret had escaped and was growling nearly as much as Portia, who was threatening to auction herself off on eBay to the highest bidder with maternal instincts if we didn't allow Danny into our lives.

When the stationmaster then announced that the train was indeed delayed, for an hour, I slumped down on to the cold, metal bench. I'd just cracked open the emergency block of Cadbury's Whirl secreted in the side pocket of my handbag when I felt a hot breath in my ear.

'Why don't you just buy a cocoa plantation and cut out the middle man?' It was the melodious voice of Jack Cassidy.

'God, you're like some creature from the Black Lagoon which just won't die.'

'Nice to see you, too. What are you doing up here . . .? I've been on the northern circuit all week. I cannot eat one more pasty. Or hear one more person say "Yer don't get nowt for nowt these days." I've already rung a car company. A warm, comfortable, chauffeur-driven saloon should be here in five minutes to whisk me back to London in style. Would you like a ride?'

He loaded that phrase with so much sexual innuendo I immediately felt the urge to reach for a post-coital cigarette. I thought about the freezing-cold wait on the desolate platform. I thought about the nice warm car. I thought about enduring Jack's snide comments and smugness all the way back to London. But at least it would be snug smug. In the end, warmth and comfort won out.

Once we'd settled down into the silver Mercedes, Jack raised the partition which separated us from the driver, then leant back against the plush leather seat and swivelled towards me. 'So, what's the latest instalment in the soap opera that is Pandora's? . . . Has your mother come out as a card-carrying lesbian? Has Countess Flirtalotsky undergone a sex change? And, more importantly, have you decided on our date yet? . . . I await with bated everythings.'

'Are you any good at ferret-taming?' I side stepped. 'Apparently, there's an escaped ferret gnawing its way through my legal robes as we speak.'

'Ah, sorry. I'm sad to report that's not my area of expertise.'

'What exactly is your area of expertise these days, Cassidy?' I asked him.

He gave me a wicked grin.

'Besides that,' I said. 'I mean, what have you been doing up here in Birmingham? Banning abortions? Inventing new gun laws so that students can machinegun each other on a regular basis? . . . Sacrificing the odd virgin in a volcano?'

'Matilda, the modern world is a vicious and vulgar place. The human race is hell bent on hurtling itself into the abyss.

All you can do is live your life in a way that makes you look urbane and well dressed on the way ... That's my only philosophy. Oh, and never to lick a steak knife ... Or kiss a girl before removing the lit cigar in your mouth ... Or an e-cigarette.' He produced one from his pocket and took a drag. 'You see? We cigar-addicted, corporate-cowboy clichés do listen occasionally.'

I levelled a curious gaze at him. 'Okay, where is the real Jack Cassidy? And who is this pod person?'

'But how are things really?' he asked, changing the subject.

'Great. Fine. Fabulous ... But that's mainly because I have a nitroglycerin tablet ready to slip under my tongue at a moment's notice. Which could be *any* moment. As you know, the testicle-shooting granny moved in, lock, stock, shell-shocked grandchild and irascible ferret. I'm now getting death threats. My ex-husband is still in no man's land. I'm paying a solicitor friend who specializes in dead-beat dads to hunt him down for some child maintenance. And my long-lost father, who, apparently, changed his name to become a spy for the Special Forces, and disappeared before I was born, has turned up out of the blue, causing my mother to go into meltdown if I speak to him – while my daughter refuses to speak to me, if I *don't*. In fact, I'm beginning to think I need combat pay.'

Jack took all this in for a beat, then grinned. 'There was a time when I'd be alarmed by that monologue, but having known you for so many years now, Matilda, it just seems sort of par for the Devine course ... But what's this about a death threat?' His brow creased in consternation.

'It came attached to a rock. Through my bedroom window. ... You look genuinely concerned. Thanks. My mother just laughed it off.'

'Concerned?' His defences went back up immediately. He

took another puff of his electronic cigarette to compose himself. 'No. Not at all. Just think of the good points. You can now have a bumper sticker which reads "Don't tailgate. Car bomb on board" . . . You'll get through traffic in no time!'

I felt a smile welling up in me. I looked at him, not sure what we were, if we weren't adversaries. I broke the spell by rummaging in my handbag for a lipstick.

'Do you remember our first date in Oxford? . . . A student production of *Hamlet*. As the lights went down and the audience hushed in expectation, someone shouted out "Knock knock"! . . .'

I looked at him blankly, lipstick uncased and poised in my hand.

'I'm sure I don't need to remind you, Tilly, that the first words of *Hamlet* are . . . "Who's there?" . . .'

My laughter caused the lipstick to etch a calligraphic stroke across my cheek. 'And do you remember that poncey, stuck-up Etonian reprimanding us for laughing? He called us fucking chavs. And you said—'

' "Knock, knock." '

' "Who's there?" '

' "Fuck." '

' "Fuck who?" '

' "No, fuck *whom*." '

We were both laughing now. We stared at each other for a moment across the abyss that divided us. And it suddenly didn't look so wide.

'God, when I first got to Oxford, those posh people seemed as exotic to me as animals in a zoo. I'd never seen anything like them,' Jack admitted. 'I wasn't sure whether I wanted to be one of them or simply live among them taking anthropological notes. But when you arrived a few years later, they didn't faze you at all. You were always so passionate about the law ... The first night we had dinner you told me how furious you were about Eve getting the blame for the whole Garden of Eden eviction. You maintained she was framed. You wanted to put the snake on trial for entrapment.'

'Yes, I remember. But, to be honest, the main reason I'd always wanted to become a lawyer was because I'd grown up watching all my mum's barrister pals with those little suit-cases on wheels, going *clackity clackity clack* over the cobblestones of the Inns of Court. I thought lawyers were always going away on holiday. I had no idea that their little wheelie bags held only masses and masses of the most tedious tomes.'

Jack laughed. 'Ironically, I went to the Bar to save the world ... only I soon realized that I didn't have what it takes.'

I'd expected to be scaling Mount Smug all the way back to London. So it was a shock to find Jack so humble, humorous and low key. 'That's not true, Jack. You pretend to have no more substance than the froth on a cappuccino. But there's so much more to you than that.'

'Not enough to interest you, though. A man would have to get himself taken hostage or tortured by a military junta before you'd even notice him. But, Tilly, there's more to life than racing from one Third World death-row prison to another ... You should at least stop occasionally to smell the goats and hand grenades.'

My palm was resting on the leather console between us. He placed his hand over mine. His warm fingers on my skin sent a chemical chain reaction zinging through my erogenous zones. I could tell by the light in his eyes that he could feel it, too. An alarm bell sounded in my psyche. Uh-oh. I was starting to find Jack Cassidy attractive again. How could this be? I obviously belonged in one of those Oliver Sacks books, because it was becoming increasingly clear that I had some kind of a rare head injury.

'You're not like the other women I meet, Tilly. All hard stares, high heels and droopy handshakes. I've reached the age at which a man can no longer face one more date with a legal secretary who secretly wants to be an actress.'

He was looking at me in the same way you'd eye a fillet steak after a ten-day fast. He leant towards me to wipe the lipstick smudge from my cheek with his fingertip. I saw his eyes flick almost imperceptibly to my breasts and then down to my legs. I could smell the musky, spicy scent of his skin. He pulled me towards him and bunched my hair into his hands. It made the nerves on the back of my neck tingle. Nothing this thrilling had happened to my nape, ever. I wanted to tell him that this was ridiculous and that I didn't even like him but felt the words float away. My resistance was like butter, and he was a warm knife, slicing through it.

'I've waited over a decade to kiss you again and I'm not going to let you get away so easily this time.' He folded the console back up into the seat and leant in to kiss me. He put his mouth on mine. His breath was sweet as caramelized toffee. He pulled me into the whole length of him. I felt a burst of sensation. I kissed him back, all yearning and heat. Lawyers like nothing more than the sound of their own voices, but there was no need for words now. Just 'yes'. And 'yes'. And 'yes, now'.

I don't know how many miles we kissed for, but I was pretty sure I'd need to put my lips in a cast and my tongue in a splint. Everywhere he touched, my nerves fluttered as though there were moths trapped beneath my skin.

It had been so long since a man had touched me, I was convinced that not even medical science wanted my body. By the outskirts of London, I could stand it no longer. The glass partition separating us from the driver was conveniently fogged, so I said, 'That's a mighty impressive suit, Jack, but it would look so much better crumpled up on the floor of this car.' I began to unbutton my blouse.

Jack's voice felt as though he were pouring treacle into my ear. 'Wait.' He took hold of me by the wrists. 'Let's not make the same mistake as last time. I want us to get to know each other better first . . .'

I pulled back to take a proper look at him, amazed by this uncharacteristic declaration.

'I told you, Tilly. I'm a changed man.'

It was taking an enormous effort not to tear off his trousers with my teeth.

'You mean it?'

'Yes. I was too young to truly appreciate you. It was like giving fine wine to a football hooligan. In those days, it was all about quantity, not quality . . . Let's start with dinner tomorrow. I'll pick you up at eight. And,' he twinkled, 'could you try not to double book this time?'

'Jeez. You sleep with a man once and, before you know it, he wants to take you to dinner,' I said, but I was smiling as I manoeuvred myself back into my seat and realigned my clothes. 'But then why have you been behaving in such a predatory way?'

'You rise to the bait so beautifully. It's just too much fun not to tease you,' he grinned. Jack stroked my arm, and kept on stroking it as we drove on in silence, night filling the car. Rain was pattering on the windowpane and the windscreen wipers swished rhythmically. All I could hear was the strangled vowels of the satnav which sounded as though the driver had Helen Mirren locked in the boot.

The car purred to a halt outside my mother's modest Camden abode. I alighted with my briefcase. 'Thanks for the ride.' A skittish wind pulled at my clothes, as if trying to undress me. 'Well, the almost-ride.'

Jack looked longingly at my legs and beamed at me. 'Think practically nothing of it,' he said.

And then he was gone.

I stood there, astounded for a moment, his touch whispering away on my skin. Maybe the man really had changed? Occasionally, a ratbag could make the transition into human being, I rationalized. Shakespeare's Henry V, Jean Valjean in *Les Mis*, the prodigal son . . . I raised my face up to the starless night. The liquid, fluent notes of a jazz solo seeped down from my mother's bedroom window. I had just turned to waft happily up the stairs when a flash of movement in my peripheral vision snagged my attention.

The death threat. It had slipped my mind, but it crashed into my consciousness with a vengeance now. Startled, I gasped and stepped back. A shadowy figure loomed there in the darkness. 'Who is it? Step out into the light, or I'll . . .' I rummaged desperately in my bag for my pepper spray – but emerged with only a tampon. Great. Maybe I could shove it up his nose and give him Toxic Snot Syndrome. Where were my mother's jellybeans when I needed them?

My nerves were on high alert, a scream on the tip of my tonsils.

But the man who stepped out of the shadows shot me a bashful look.

'Sorry. I didn't mean to scare you, kid. I'm just makin' sure you gals are okay.'

'I'm thirty-four, Dad.' Did I just call him 'Dad'? I wasn't sure what the hell to call him, as Danny wasn't even his real name. 'Shouldn't you be off spying on some international terrorist of ambiguous nationality or something? I don't need a bodyguard! I know exactly what I'm doing.'

'Ah-huh.' He glanced down at my blouse, which was buttoned unevenly. It started to drizzle again, so I hoofed it up my front steps to stand under the iron portico. He squelched along beside me in the rain, like a large, orphaned dog.

'The past is only visible to me in painful flashes of memory. It's mostly just a gloomy cloud of shapes and noises. Apart from your mother. She's always in vivid Technicolor . . . I want to do everything I can to make it up to you and your mum. I will pick you up from airports, watch Portia in every bad school production of *Annie*, I will dog-sit, shower grout . . .'

I was about to dismiss him out of hand, when he added:

'. . . *steal incriminating documents from hospitals proving that your client left her bed at exactly the same time her granny was shooting the rapists' gonads.*'

I reappraised the man who had ruined my mother's life but had also been our anonymous helper. That was one mystery solved. And he'd bought exactly the right chocolates. 'We have a ferret, too,' I finally acquiesced. 'So you'll also have to ferret-sit.'

Danny smiled gratefully. His world-weary, craggy face creased up into a smile. Maybe Portia was right? She always maintained that, in life, anything is possible – except for mountaineering in stilettos and moon landing in a ballgown. Perhaps I needed a support group for recovering pessimists? I mean, Danny was acting like a hero and Jack like a human. It was very confusing. Overwhelmed by the night's revelations (what was it? Global Blokes Behaving Nicely Day?), I went inside, shut the door and headed straight to the fridge for a fortifying bowl of chocolate mint ice cream.

'Be careful what you wish for' is one of life's greatest lies. Like all women, I wished for James Bond, naked, telling me how much he liked wrinkles and crinkles on a woman. And there'd be nothing better than getting that wish fulfilled . . . except for getting my other wish – for things to turn out for me and Jack Cassidy.

The window of opportunity seemed to have opened . . . and, this time, I was not going to draw the blinds.

16

Dinner with a Side Order of Sarcasm

In the list of the worst things men say on dates, like giving details of their prostate difficulties or revealing a recent gender-reassignment operation – this topped them all.

Everything had been going so well – champagne at the Beaufort Bar in the Savoy, followed by dinner at the Delaunay restaurant on the Strand, a place where the human menu is so delectable the chef should advertise the 'Celeb du jour'. Jack and I were gossiping about the famous faces around us – who had recently taken out a gagging order, sued for libel over sex allegations or settled out of court over compromising behaviour involving drugs, rent boys or reasonably domesticated tethered livestock. We were bantering and quipping, just as we had when we first met. When I mentioned that the air-conditioning was too cold, he draped his satin-lined suit jacket across my shoulders, resting his hands on me for a moment. I remembered then how much I loved the shape and strength of his arms, how safe I had once felt wrapped up in them. When I showed curiosity about his main meal, he leant over and kissed me so that I could taste the truffle oil.

At first our lips just brushed, but it turned into a kiss. He kissed me as though he was trying to erase all the many women who had gone before. When the waiter offered us more wine, it was with great reluctance that I pulled away from his delicious mouth. I had a feeling that, when we did finally go to bed, we were going to make John and Yoko look like amateurs. When the waiter took pudding orders, I knew that all I really wanted for dessert was Jack Cassidy, naked, on a bed of meringue. It was then that Nathaniel walked past our table.

'Hello, Matilda! What a charming surprise.' He leant in for the regulation air kiss, then nodded to Jack and extended his hand. 'Nathaniel Cavendish. I think we bumped into each other, quite literally. Outside Matilda's place.'

'Jack Cassidy.' When Jack stood up to shake Nathaniel's hand, I glanced from one man to the other. Jack's look is minimal, svelte, sophisticated – all in a monotone, moody palette. I suspected that if his shirt ever looked less than perfect, it'd be taken out and shot. Nathaniel, in his leather jacket, brightly patterned shirt and biker boots, sported a tough Metro look of grit and devil-may-care dishevelment.

'I'm so sorry about standing you up. I hope you got my message? But what are you doing here? Delaunay's doesn't seem your "natural habitat", Nathaniel,' I joshed, recalling his remark when he'd found me on the council estate.

'Putting the hard word on some banker mates to cough up some cash for my mentoring charity. But' – he looked from me to Jack – 'how great that you two already know each other. I guess it makes squaring off in the court room all that much easier.'

'We try not to make a habit of that . . . Mainly because I could eat a whole bowl of alphabet soup and regurgitate a better argument than anything Jack could ever come up with,' I teased.

'Oh, really? I could win any case from you, Matilda, and you know it. You couldn't talk a nudist into wearing sunblock in the Sahara,' Jack parried.

'Well, I guess in a few weeks we'll have the perfect opportunity to find out which of you really is the better lawyer,' Nathaniel added conversationally.

'What do you mean?' I asked, puzzled, putting down my wine glass.

'I work with rehabilitating offenders,' Nathaniel explained to Jack, 'and I believe you are prosecuting the woman who shot two of my clients. They go by the unedifying sobriquets of Bash and Stretch . . . Didn't you know?' he asked me, surprised.

My head spun to look at my dinner date. 'You're prosecuting my client? A poor gran who simply sought revenge on two scumbag rapists?'

'Alleged rapists. Both men deny the charges, by the way.' Jack's napkin clung absurdly to his waist like a loincloth. 'The barrister who took the case is from Regal Helm Chambers. He's fallen ill suddenly. So I've had to step into the breach. I'm Senior Treasury Counsel and this case has attracted a lot of lurid media interest. Which is why the DPP's insisted I take it. He says he wants a safe pair of hands to prosecute it fairly.'

'Oh, and what, it somehow slipped your mind to tell me?' Why had I allowed myself to be taken in by him again? Why hadn't sirens gone off and SWAT teams set up a security cordon?

'I was going to tell you. I was just waiting for the right time.'

'Right after you pumped me for information on my case strategy, perhaps? How conniving! How underhand!'

Nathaniel looked longingly towards his table. 'Look, I'm so sorry. I didn't mean to throw a spanner into the works.' He clung to the conversational cliché like a drowning man to a buoy.

Jack ignored him. He reached over to touch my arm. 'I was hoping we could have a civilized discussion about it, lawyer to lawyer.'

'Civilized!' I recoiled. 'You make the head-hunting, missionary-munching tribes of the Irian Jaya jungle look civilized. How could you call those two low-lifes as witnesses of truth?'

'Need I remind you, Matilda, that the most important principle in English law is the presumption that the accused is innocent until proven guilty.'

'You seriously can't believe those minging A-list ratbags are innocent.'

'May I also remind you that the witnesses are not on trial here. Your client's on trial for taking the law into her own hands. Which I know you abhor as much as I do, Matilda,' Jack said sternly.

'I'd like to take the law into my own hands right now, actually, and skewer you on the end of this dessert fork.'

'If your grandma changes her plea to guilty, I'm sure the judge would be lenient. We could do a plea bargain and save the State – and us – so much time and trouble. You'd be well paid by legal aid for a mitigation plea, instead of getting a daily pittance for a two-week trial.'

'Gosh, you really are a devil's advocate, aren't you?' Nathaniel interjected, unwisely allowing himself to be drawn into our argument.

Jack appraised Nathaniel for a moment. 'Don't tell me. You're that banker Tilly mentioned. The one who's hell bent on downward mobility. No wonder you left Credit Suisse. Swiss people routinely get into fistfights over the correct time. Matilda has no doubt only befriended you for your connection to chocolate. It's her biggest weakness, you know.'

No, Jack Cassidy's my biggest weakness, I thought to

myself. He regularly made me feel so at sea I needed a distress flare. 'Nathaniel is a man with backbone. You, on the other hand, are obviously still waiting for that spine donor. I mean, you couldn't even get up the courage to tell me that you'd decided to prosecute my poor grandma.'

'Actually, I was planning to tell you tonight that I'd taken the case to make sure it was prosecuted fairly and compassionately.'

'Oh, really? Before or after you'd taken me to bed? I don't think you would have told me at all if Nathaniel hadn't accidentally blown your cover.' I squeezed Nathaniel's hand. 'Thank you, Nathaniel. May I have the bill, please?' I asked the passing waiter.

Jack eyed Nathaniel with cool disdain. 'And you help those witnesses of mine, how exactly?' He was using his cross-examination voice.

'I mentor drug addicts and dealers who are coming out of prison on how to use their business acumen in the banking world, where wheeling and dealing are legal.'

'Really? I'm totally pro drugs, actually,' Jack said flippantly. 'Drugs have taught an entire generation of British kids the metric system. Plus, an overdose of ecstasy tabs can be a polite way to get rid of someone you can't stand – sancti-monious, holier-than-thou do-gooders who look down their noses for a living, for instance.'

I remembered now what I loathed about Jack: the self-satisfaction, the condescension, the amorality, the chip on his shoulder big enough to fuel a barbecue.

It was Nathaniel's turn to bristle. 'I'm just trying to help kids from the estate find an alternative to crime.'

'Oh, shame. Life has let them down! There's a support group for that. It's called "humanity". We meet regularly at the pub,' Jack taunted.

Nathaniel gave Jack a look so hard it could deflect small-arms fire. 'These kids are not intrinsically bad. They're victims of society.'

'Yes, yes, there's such dignity in being poor . . . as long as they stay downwind.'

Nathaniel was now clearly wondering why I'd opted to have dinner with the captain of HMS *Cynicism*. In fact, the captain of the Exxon tanker would have made a preferable dinner date – even the captain of the *Costa Concordia*. Oh, where the hell was that waiter? I just wanted to pay my share and get the hell out of there.

'Though he pretends otherwise,' I intervened, 'Jack grew up on an estate. Slum landlords, gang warfare, race riots, two rooms in a tenement declared unfit for habitation.'

'Yes. The whole Dickensian cliché.' Jack turned his laser eyes on Nathaniel. 'You, though, probably went to Eton and can only get turned on if you're touched on the gonads with a velvet opera glove . . . Although, wait.' Jack reappraised him. 'I bet you went to a wanky, liberal, bisexual school. Do I mean that? . . . No, I mean co-ed. Sorry.' He gave an insinuating smile.

'I went to Bryanston, actually,' Nathaniel replied stonily. 'And yes, the female pupils played a big role in civilizing us.'

'I knew it. Ha. You're probably a feminist, too, am I right? Who needs Sisters to Do It for Themselves when Nathaniel is on hand!'

'I'll have you know that Nathaniel has dedicated his life to helping people who are less advantaged than himself.'

'Oh, well, I don't want to keep you then. I'm sure it must be time to go and fell a few trees to make your cross.' Jack turned his back on Nathaniel and said to me, 'I only agreed yesterday to take the case. I was going to tell you straight away, but I've waited so long for this date and it was going so well that I kept putting it off . . . Can't you at least try to see it from my point of view?'

'I'd like to, Jack, I really would. Only I just can't stick my head that far up my own backside.' I pushed up to my feet.

'Why don't you come and join my table, Matilda. It would be a pleasure to introduce you to my friends. And then I'll see you home safely.'

I dumped Jack's coat from my shoulders as though it were toxic. 'See you in court, where you will take a heavy beating from me.'

'While the thought of being exquisitely birched by you is obviously quite exciting to our upper-class friend, I would prefer to whip your arse in the traditional legal way, by winning the case, hands down.'

'Well, that's never going to happen. Last time I saw you in court, I yawned so much I got lockjaw.'

'Really? You're such a hopeless lawyer, you couldn't convince a jury of anything. Hell, I doubt you could sell crack to Charlie Sheen.'

'We'll let the jury decide, shall we?'

Jack slammed some money down on the table with such violence it made the hinges wince. Jack Cassidy, I marvelled, showing real emotion – that was a first.

I watched him disappear out into the night. A storm had blown up, full of thunder and lightning – which I was trying hard not to match with a torrential downpour of angry tears. Jack and I parted in that cloudy, electrically charged atmosphere. The court case now lay between us, as solid as a mountain – a huge granite geographical feature, impassable. Jack Cassidy had lied to me and let me down. It was déjà vu all over again.

17

Textual Harassment

There has been a little confusion of late over the definition of a troll. One is short-tempered, ugly and lives under a bridge. The other is a warped, lonely male probably still living in his mother's basement, with stale ejaculate in the cracks of his computer keys.

'@rapehernow disgusting bitch ... should have been aborted with a clothes hanger' and 'SHUT YOUR WHORE MOUTH ... OR ILL SHUT IT FOR YOU AND CHOKE IT WITH MY DICK' were probably not the ideal greetings first thing in the morning. But, as Phyllis's court case came closer, the abuse on social media became more cretinously cacophonous.

Every time I turned on my iPhone there'd be a twisted message on Twitter. 'Nine Nos and one Yes is still a Yes, bitch.' 'Raping a prostitute's not rape. It's shoplifting, slag.'

Chantelle's Facebook, Snapchat, Whatsapp and AskFM sites were clogged with equally delightful messages from strangers announcing that she'd 'seen more pricks than a second-hand dartboard'. Or telling her to drink bleach, hang herself or cut off her vagina, as she was a 'diseased slut'. Cyber-bullies created a Facebook page, posting Chantelle's obituary. A fake profile in her name offered abusive comments about men and how to frame them with rape claims. We closed her accounts and reported the abuse to the police but were told it would take weeks to investigate.

Television offered no respite. It seemed that whenever we gathered on the sofa after supper and tuned in, some chippy 'comedian' would be thrusting his testosteroned misogyny down our throats.

'The cops said "Men who rape will be named" . . . Cool, can I have "Nightstriker" or has that already been taken?' bantered some weedy bloke on a comedy panel.

'The only girl in the room said, "I've often wondered if I'm strong enough to stop someone trying to rape me" . . . Turns out she's not,' leered another, as the studio audience roared with hilarity.

Flicking on the radio one morning, I heard a politician pontificating that a woman being sexually assaulted while she's drunk 'is akin to falling over when inebriated'.

'Except, of course, the pavement doesn't choose to insert itself into your vagina,' I grumbled back.

Even when shopping for new trainers with Portia at the shopping centre, the lyrics of rap songs seared into my psyche. 'Mad cases of manslaughter, I rape this man's daughter, then put the shit on camcorder,' I was charmingly serenaded in the shoe shop, along with other songs about 'ho's and 'slapping my bitch up'.

I tried to make a joke out of my discomfort by covering my daughter's ears, but she shrugged me off. Since my mother and I had forbidden contact with her grandfather, my once effusive, ebullient child would utter only a few grunts in our direction. In a supermarket queue we stood behind an old codger who was holding the hand of a little girl. 'Why can't I get to know *my* grandfather? I mean, it's not like I have a dad any more,' Portia implored. It was the most she'd said in weeks. Even the traumatized, shell-shocked Chantelle was more verbal than Portia these days.

'Your father, who has the loving and affectionate nature of volcanic rock, is otherwise occupied in his role of emotionally constipated shagger of my ex-friends' is what I wanted to say, but I bit my tongue, replying instead, 'Your daddy loves you very much, but had to go away on a research trip.' Which sounded like the crap it was. Portia marched off towards the car, her eyes rolling. Since the arguments about Danny had begun, she had been doing so much eye-rolling, passers-by must be wondering if epilepsy ran in the family.

But, even though Roxy had banned us from having anything to do with Danny, Danny was obviously determined to have a lot to do with us. With 'Shoemaker and the Elves' fairy-tale magic, we'd wake in the morning to find the front door painted or the garden weeded. The gate no longer squeaked and the hedge was pruned. There were suddenly flower boxes on the outside sills and no leaves in the guttering. Not only were our cars waxed and polished, but Roxy's MG Midget could now reverse and the soft top opened and closed with ease. Roxy was reluctant to believe this was all Danny's doing until the parking officer who was about to tow her car was found hanging from a tree branch by his pants.

'Okay, now *that's* classic Danny,' Roxy drawled, with the tiniest hint of begrudging appreciation.

Nathaniel was also paying us a lot of attention. He'd discovered that my mother kept bees, as did he. 'Bees are endangered, just like beautiful, smart, feminist women,' he'd said. It gave him the perfect excuse to drop in with jars from his own hive. Then he'd linger and stall over coffee and tea, which often turned into joining us for dinner, followed by wine and nightcaps. Whenever Nathaniel was around, the Countess laughed flirtatiously and made many extravagant, comical gestures with her arms. Roxy would always turn up in her tightest leopardskin trousers. The downside to this intestine-constricting sartorial pant choice was that one night she ate a cupcake too many and they split at the crotch.

'That cake was the straw that broke the camel-toe's back,' the Countess quipped, and they both fell about, killing themselves laughing. If the death threats didn't get them, their own riotous cackling surely would. Or perhaps 'toy-boy-itis' would be the cause of my mother's demise? Roxy was currently dating a 24-year-old gym instructor. I'd had to give her new partner a safe-sex talk, as in, what to do if my mother has a heart attack.

Eventually, his addiction to computer games tried her patience. She kicked him out and joined us for a celebratory helping of Phyllis's scrumptious Beef Wellington.

'I simply can't believe you're over fifty, Roxy,' Nathaniel flattered.

'It's all those age-preserving chemicals found only in champagne,' I said a little censoriously, as I watched my mother down her third glass in a gulp. 'You really shouldn't encourage her, Nathaniel. She's quite bad enough already.'

'The badder the woman, the better, in my view,' he flirted. 'I so enjoy coming around to your house. It's like entering a comedic coven. But where's Portia's father, if you don't mind me asking? What happened to him?'

'The glass slipper didn't fit Tilly any more,' Roxy volunteered, mid-munch.

'Yeah. It's on another woman's foot,' the Countess added.

'Okay! No need to blab my entire life history to all and sundry.'

'I hope you consider me to be a little more than "sundry",' Nathaniel said, placing his hand over mine.

Roxy and the Countess signalled astonished delight through ocular semaphore.

Portia always says that a smirk is a thought that appears on your face. And I did a lot of smirking that night, as Nathaniel kept finding any excuse to brush up against me, take my arm or touch my leg. Now that he'd ascertained my single status, a date could not be far off.

As Nathaniel's interest in me became more obvious, the only thing that could wipe the smile off my face was my deteriorating relationship with my daughter. Not only was Portia communicating exclusively by grunt, but her school marks were dropping. Her religious studies teacher sent me a copy of her essay on Buddhism, which started, 'Buddha is something you spread on bread.' Her economics teacher said that her essay on globalization had been a paragraph-long rant about the Western world getting too fat, which Portia described as 'globulization'. The teacher wanted to know if anything was going on at home.

Of course, these were small border wars compared to Phyllis's predicament, but I was starting to wonder if it was too late to reconsider rigorous boarding schools and arranged marriages. But, finally, one Saturday afternoon, I heard Portia's voice fire with enthusiasm, 'Wow! Oh, wow!' She was peering through the living-room curtain. A scallop of sunlight fell across her face, reminding me of her delicate beauty. She bounded for the door. Curiosity meant I wasn't far behind her.

It was the first time I'd seen my father in daylight. I stood for a moment, peering at him. My daughter's high forehead and long limbs, the dimple we both shared – these obviously came directly from him. He was battle-scarred but handsome, strongly built, with bulging muscles. His eyebrows resembled worn toothbrush bristles. He didn't look like the demon of my nightmares but more like an amiable, fighting-fit, slim-line Santa: a man who should be in a big chair in Harrods, as kids wriggled in his lap, whispering action-figure names in his ear.

I was still taking stock of him when I heard my mother's footfall in the hall behind me. 'Don't tell me, it must be National Asshole Day.'

'Peace offering.' Danny held a bottle of wine out to my mother. 'A nice Aussie drop of red. I think the label reads, "Because we're fussy bastards".'

Roxy pushed past Portia and me to slam the door. Danny put out a muscular arm to prop it ajar. And so we stood there, three generations of the Devine clan, facing our phantom patriarch.

'The law of machoness prohibits men from admitting that we're ever wrong. But you're right, Roxy. I have been the world's biggest asshole and I want to spend the rest of my days making it up to you. And getting to know my daughter.' He patted me gingerly on the back, as if I were an unknown dog which might bite his hand off. 'And, of course, my darling granddaughter. Can you find it in your hearts to forgive me?'

'Can't you see he's sorry, Gran?' Portia chirped. 'He has such a puppy-dog look.'

'Then get him wormed,' Roxy scowled.

'The thing is, when I was born ... way back in, oh, about 1533, we didn't question authority. I was only twenty when I joined the force. I thought I was just doing my job ... But when I found out we were using the names of dead babies . . .' Danny looked down at his feet, totally dejected. 'Well, it turned my stomach. And then I fell for you, Rox . . . Which meant I had to leave Special Branch and get out of your life. Because how could I confess the truth to you? You would have hated my guts anyway. The police force used and abused me, too, you know,' he said bitterly. 'But I would never have scarpered if I'd known you were expecting. On that, you have my word.'

'Gee, let me add that to my list of things I don't give a fuck about.'

'You're as beautiful as ever, Rox. I have a face which would launch a thousand dredgers, barges, tugs . . . I know that. But I do have a big and loyal heart. And I want to give it to you.'

I sensed genuine contrition and melted a little towards him, but Roxy answered by slamming the door on his arm. He leapt back, yelping. Portia made a move towards the door. My mother blocked her, arms folded.

'I'm sorry, possum. But this is for your own good. You just don't understand the male of the species, darling.'

'That's because you never let me meet any!' Portia retorted mulishly, before executing another exaggerated eyeroll.

'If you keep doing that, darl, you're definitely going to shake loose a few brain cells. And then all those Montessori pre-school fees and maths tutoring will have been for nothing.'

My daughter looked to me for help, her eyes large and pleading.

'Danny does seem genuinely sorry, Mum. He says he really loves you,' I ventured.

'Yeah, he loves me kinda like an Aztec high priest loves the still-throbbing heart of his human sacrifice.'

'My grandpa's not the type to give up, you know,' Portia said rebelliously.

'That's because the man's not normal. If he was a normal man, I would hit him repeatedly over the head with copies of *The Female Eunuch* until he bled to death, repenting.'

'I agree with Portia, Mum. Somehow, I don't think killing Danny would entirely eliminate his desire to befriend us. I suspect he would just come back and haunt us.'

A note came through the letterbox, followed by a dis-embodied male voice. 'This is where I'm living, temporarily. The lift seems to be powered by oxen and I have to share a communal laundry with several Baltic republics. But you're all welcome, any time.'

I picked up the folded piece of paper from the mat and scanned the address. It was a flat on the canal near King's Cross. Portia snatched the note and memorized it, too, before Roxy grabbed it back and tore it up.

Half an hour before my daughter went missing again, I was sitting up in bed with a coffee and a Sunday newspaper, vaguely wondering what gift to give Portia for her thirteenth birthday while also concerned about a world in which Saudi women can be electronically chipped so that an alarm goes off if they try to escape, when a phone call came from Portia's best friend, Amelia, informing me that my daughter hadn't turned up to dance class. A Saudi-type electronic chip was starting to look like a pretty attractive birthday gift all of a sudden . . .

My mother and I drove straight to the address Danny had given us. The whole harrowing trip, I experienced once more that cold, nauseous shock of dread all parents feel when a child goes missing. We parked half on the pavement and, the car wheels still spinning, shot up the stairs. I banged on Danny's door while my mother took aim with her capsicum spray.

'What kept you?' Danny said, motioning us inside. He had opened a bottle of wine and put out three glasses on the coffee table. Portia was curled up on her grandfather's couch, eating birthday cake. She looked so happy it was as though she were being tickled from the inside with a feather.

Even though I hadn't had breakfast, I immediately took a big, nerve-soothing swig of vino. 'Some day, Portia, when you have your own children, you'll understand why I drink.' What with dating, InterRailing, sex talks and driving tests to come, I needed Valium even to contemplate the years ahead. When women I meet at work tell me how stressed they are with their small children, I think to myself – Just you wait!

'Don't give the kid a hard time. Portia's supposed to be rebellious. I mean, she's practically a teenager – the period when your offspring are certain they'll never be as bloody stupid as their parents. When she's having a teen tantrum, I suggest you just keep eye contact, back off slowly and sleep on the nature strip,' Danny joked in an attempt to ease tensions.

Roxy turned her capsicum spray in Danny's direction. 'What the hell would you know about raising a kid?'

'Nothing, worse luck,' Danny admitted. 'But I want to learn. I know you don't believe me,' he entreated earnestly, 'but I've changed. *You* changed me. You changed my world view on everything. Nuclear weapons. Animal testing. Even page-three topless models . . . Jesus, do you remember the time we stormed the Miss World contest and flour-bombed the judges?' He gave a crinkle-eyed smile.

'Who could forget?' my mother said. 'Those Miss Worlds couldn't spell their country's name without looking at their sash.'

'And you suggested to the press that it was only fair that women who'd had cosmetic enhancement assure the judges that at least 75 per cent of their body parts came from their country of origin.'

'Oh God, I do remember that. Then you got hold of the loudhailer and announced that the beauty contestants from countries with military dictatorships must vow not to topple duly elected winners.'

Danny grinned. 'Yeah, that's right. Just before you got arrested.'

'Christ, don't remind me. I was wearing a sash that read "Fuck You!"'

A momentary truce ensued. My mother holstered her capsicum spray back into her leopardskin handbag and sat down at the small kitchen table.

'You got arrested?' Portia asked, enthralled, all big eyes and ears.

'Hon, why don't you get along to dance class now and leave the grown-ups to talk for a bit, there's a good girl.' The dance studio was only a block or two from here, in Bloomsbury. She could walk quite safely and join in the last hour of her class. 'Your mum and I will pick you up afterwards and go shopping for birthday presents, okay?'

'Okay, Gran.' My daughter beamed. Her job here was done. All the people she most cared about were sitting in the same room, talking things through, and there were no visible lethal weapons, obvious body wounds or signs of bloodshed. As soon as Portia skipped down the stairs, Roxy turned towards Danny.

'If I changed you so much, why did you bugger off?'

'I didn't want to shatter your illusions. How you would have hated me had you known the truth – that I was working undercover.'

'People trusted me, Danny! People believed you were who you said you were because I had welcomed you into my life.'

'Yeah. I know. Doesn't exactly win me Boyfriend of the Year, right?'

'And why now? Why come back after all this time?'

'Do you really want to know?' Danny sat down opposite Roxy.

'Yes.'

'Well, I've always had this inclination to small, invigorating bursts of danger. Jesus. I've got so many bullet scars and wounds after my Special Services mission in Afghanistan, my chest X-rays look like the national grid. But then I really nearly did die. I was bodysurfing. In Sierra Leone. Got dragged out by a rip. It was a remote, ugly place. I can only remember the floppiness of my arms and that feeling of shifting apart from everything. I lay on my back, I cried, swore, said things like "Oh God!" a lot.'

'There's no such thing as an atheist in a big surf,' Roxy interjected flippantly.

'And then all I could think about was you, Roxy . . . Okay, I've had a lot of women. Sure. But I never felt the same connection. I couldn't settle . . . Anyways, my next memory is of touching a sandbank with my foot. By giving up trying to swim, I'd drifted free of the rip and washed ashore like an old bit of driftwood. I crawled up the beach, threw up, then lay on the warm sand, waiting for the loneliness to go away. Only it didn't . . . and I realized for the first time that I won't be here for ever. And that there's only ever been one person I've ever given a damn about.'

'A woman would have to have a heart of stone to listen to that story . . . and not guffaw hysterically,' Roxy scoffed.

'Fair enough. I don't blame you for being sceptical. But actions speak louder than words. Your line of work is dangerous, Roxy. You ruffle a lot of feathers. And, well, with my training and skills, I just figured there could be times when I could be useful. Protection, phone tapping, breaking and entering, surveillance, some persuasive conversations with wife beaters in which they're dangled by the scrotum from the odd windowledge . . . Is there anything I could do for you right now, for example?' When Roxy ignored him, he turned to me. 'Matilda?'

'Well,' I sighed, 'I have been feeling the need to wear a bulletproof bra of late . . . what with all these abusive tweets.'

'Abusive? How abusive?'

'Let's just say that the word "pussy" is being used in a non-feline context.'

Danny flinched and his jaw muscles flexed.

'It's just some scrote of a troll.' Roxy waved a dismissive arm. 'Just tweet back suggesting he try not to use words that are bigger than his dick.'

'Roxy doesn't take death threats seriously. When she got a Twitter message recently from some maniac, warning that he was going to hunt her down and kill her, she tweeted back "I'm in Boots on Camden High Street, buying haemorrhoid cream. See you there!"'

Danny's face went granite hard. 'This isn't funny, Roxanne.'

I looked at my mother, amazed. I'd never heard anybody use her full name.

'Trolls hate women because they're so repulsive they never get laid. If a troll went to a prostitute, she'd get a headache.'

'Roxy's blasé, but I'm terrified. Portia's safety's my only priority. One guy is threatening to throw battery acid over us, like some crazed Muslims did to those poor English girls in Zanzibar. "Do you like to eat?" he tweeted. "Coz acid likes to eat you."'

'Show me,' Danny said stonily, putting his hand out for my mobile.

I helped him click on to my Twitter feed and let the abuse scroll down the screen:

'I'm gonna be the first thing u c when u wake up, man-hating bitch.'
'Drink bleach and die, fuckface.'
'Silence is golden, but duck tape is silver.'
'You carpet-munching cunts needs to get raped.'
'RAPE RAPE RAPE RAPE.' #hopeyougetraped.
'A car bomb will go off outside your house at midnight. I will be watching you to make sure you burn.'
'Hi again slut!! It took twitter 30 minutes to ban me before. I am here again to tell you I will rape you tomorrow at 6.pm.'

'Do these assholes know where you live?' Danny asked quietly.

'Well, I did get a rock through my window. And, I don't know if it's related, but my bike was chained up outside the house the other night and it got mangled.'

I clicked on to my iPhone camera icon and showed Danny a photo of my twisted bicycle. 'As you can see, I think it might be time to buy a new bike.'

'What kind? Armoured? Steel-plated? Or perhaps a stealth bicycle with long-range missiles and a couple of drones aboard?'

'For God's sake, calm down, both of you.' Roxy sighed. 'Truth is, if you're possessed of breasts and an opinion, you attract trolls quicker than the three Billy Goats Gruff. It's all bluster and bullshit.'

'You don't know that, Rox. You need protection. Call the cops again. Or let me hassle them for you. I've still got some good mates on the force.'

'We're big girls. Phyllis's case will be over in two weeks and then things will go back to normal.'

'Roxanne, this is serious. You need help.'

'Don't tell me what I do and don't need!' She wagged a chastening finger.

'You can't be expected to cope with this kind of threat on your own.'

'Well, I've coped very well on my own so far. Where the hell were you when I *did* need you, 'eh? To do the midnight feeds and go to parent–teacher night? If I can cope with *that* on my own, I can cope with these filth-breathing fleabags.'

'I have all the gadgets and gizmos of the PI trade. Let me help you. I'll do surveillance on your house. I have GPS trackers that can be deployed magnetically anywhere on a vehicle. Anyone acting suspiciously, I can track him and see exactly where he lives, then, thanks to Google Earth, focus on his kitchen and see what he's having for fucking breakfast.'

'Maybe we should take up Danny's offer of help, Mum? If only for Portia's sake. The police aren't doing much. And so many of the Twitter accounts are bogus anyway, set up on stolen phones with aliases . . .'

'Let's just compromise and say I'm right, shall we?' Roxy said curtly. 'After the court case, this will all blow over.'

'Maybe so, but it would make me feel safer to have a little protection,' I countered.

My mother took a beat. 'Really? And who do you think has been protecting this family all these years? The whole reason we started Pandora's, Tilly, was to protect women from men like *him*.' She pointed at Danny.

Danny's face drooped. 'The trouble with you, Roxy, is that you can't see a belt without wanting to kick below it.'

'And who do you think made me that way?' Anger was bubbling beneath the surface of her words. 'I brought up

Matilda as a single parent. I blamed myself for the fact that my daughter had lost her father . . . When all the time you were probably working undercover a few friggin' miles away.'

Whatever brief camaraderie had flared between my parents was now extinguished.

'Yes, Danny's a submarine dad,' I agreed. 'I mean, the man just sank without trace. But now that he's surfaced un-expectedly, why don't we let him make amends by helping us?' I suggested.

'Absolutely not.' She rounded on Danny, her mouth a thin slit. 'You see the mess you're making? You're already dividing me from my daughter and granddaughter. No wonder you made a good fighter. You're a born soldier. You just go around lobbing hand grenades into people's lives.'

Danny shook his head emphatically. 'When I nearly drowned, Christ, all I could think about was how I'd wasted my life . . . The sour taste of that. It changed me, Roxy.'

'You say you've changed, but the point is, who the hell *are* "you"? Cop? Crusader? Masquerader? . . . "Hi, I'm Danny. Allow me to introduce my selves." You should hire a detective and have yourself followed!'

'I want to make up for all the deceit, Roxy.'

'You can never make up for it. Don't you get it? I don't know how else to say it without a police restraining order. We don't need men. And we most certainly don't need you. Come on, Matilda.'

My mother clomped out of the apartment and down the rickety stairs. I followed reluctantly. Halfway down, I turned to look back up at my father. He had the look of a drowning man.

After a tense afternoon we ate dinner in uncustomary silence. Even though it was Portia's thirteenth birthday, and she was heaped high with presents, the mood remained muted. Despondency had set in. Chantelle spent so much time crying, I expected volunteers to start stacking sandbags around her. She was also making noises about leaving the country rather than testifying in any rape trial. She told us she'd even called the police officer in charge of the case, who'd informed her that the evidence was pretty shaky already – the defendants had denied rape, claiming consent. There were no witnesses. Whether the case went on at all depended on her testimony. But dropping the rape charge would seriously imperil Phyllis's defence . . . Which was no doubt why Phyllis was now making noises, too – about skipping bail. This in turn made the Countess, who'd stood £20,000 bail, decidedly jittery and she doubled her alcohol intake. Portia, after half-heartedly thanking us for her presents, maintained that the best gift of all would be if she could move out and live with her BFF, Amelia, in a 'normal' family for a while. She was giving us the cold shoulder for not inviting Danny to her birthday party. Only 'cold' was an understatement. Put it this way, if we were at a funeral, she'd be confused with the deceased.

After dinner, I found myself scanning the Employment pages of the *Guardian*. Nathaniel was away at a conference, so I didn't even have the delicious distraction of his visits. At a low ebb, we all retired early to toss and turn the night away.

It was after 1 a.m. when I heard the thud – the unmistakable thud of an intruder. I flicked on my side-table lamp. My mother was already on the landing, wearing her alarmingly short, frilly pink nightie covered in pictures of cupcakes – not the most ideal crime-fighting ensemble. Her beehive was listing to the left in full leaning-tower-of-hirsute-Pisa mode. She had Portia's hockey stick in one hand and her capsicum spray in the other. I picked up an umbrella. Thus brilliantly armed, we rattled down the staircase in tandem. I am normally cowed and cowardly, but Portia's presence in the house lent me strength and resolution. Besides which, I had my formidable mother as a human shield.

Roxy called out 'Oy! Who's there?! I've rung the cops, dirtbag.' From the living room came a wailing sound which might have been feral or human. Or both.

My mother leapt down the last remaining stairs, bellowing obscenities. I followed behind, prepared to face whatever acid-throwing, bomb-planting, bike-mangling rapist troll lay in wait.

When my mother flicked on the light switch, the man in our living room looked ill-defined and blurry at the edges, like a watercolour smudged by rain. His hands were jammed deeply into his pockets, his mouth tightly drawn, his eyes puffy from drinking. At his feet lay the chair he'd tripped over.

'See? If *I* can get in so easily, so can a killer. You never would have known I was here if this chair had only taken evasive action . . . But that's not the real reason I popped by.' He dropped to one knee. 'Roxy, will you marry me? Marrying at our age, well, there's not so much p–p–pressure on the happy-ever-after c–c–clause, right?'

Roxy slowly lowered her hockey stick but, by her stance – legs planted firmly apart, face like thunder – I knew that she hadn't yet abandoned the idea of clobbering the intruder into a coma.

'You're looking at me as though I've p–p–pissed on your s–s–shoes.'

'I'd forgotten how eloquent you are when you're drunk,' Roxy finally said.

'Kiss me, Roxy, darlin'.' And with that, all six rugged foot of Danny Kincade lunged towards my mother, his mouth puckered.

'Ugh,' she said, side-stepping, 'that's what I also remember about you. You always want sex when you're hammered.'

'That's not true ... Sometimes I want a kebab,' Danny replied from his prone position, where he'd crash-landed on the carpet.

After Roxy had thrown him out, my mother assembled the sleepy female inhabitants of our house into the living room, including a yawning Portia.

'So, Tilly, what led us to branch out, together, into an alien world of surveillance and sleuthing by starting Pandora's?' I looked at her blankly. 'It can be summed up in one word.'

'Desperation?' I suggested.

'Equality. So, let me say this once and for all. We are not going to be intimidated by any bloke. Now, Chantelle, the Crown Prosecution Service will soon bring charges against your rapists based on your evidence. And yes, there's a very good chance that the vile footage of your attack, disgustingly overdubbed with moans of pleasure, will be posted online. If you want to back out, nobody would judge you ... But do you really want those blackmailing bastards to get away with it? And for them to have this power over you for the rest of your life? I do *not* want to let you become nothing more than a sad statistic. I say we fight back! I say we don't take rape lying down! I say we nail those amoral monsters so they can never do this to any other woman! I say we fight for Phyllis's acquittal! Then help Chantelle get those misogynistic ratbags put away in prison, where they'll hopefully be buggered against their will on a regular basis by twenty-stone, syphilitic psychopaths! Are you with me, girls? What do you say, Phizz?'

Phyllis drew herself up to her full five-foot-nothing height.

'I say . . . let's go through 'em for a short cut. Shall we nail 'em . . . Chanty?'

'I will do it for you, Gran. As long as I can change schools,' she whispered.

'Excellent! No woman in this house will ever just lie back and think of England . . . or of Canberra!' Roxy concluded.

Buoyed up by Roxy's indomitable spirit – and real spirits, in the form of half a glass of nerve-steadying whiskey – we hugged, a group hug: Chantelle, Phyllis, Portia, Roxy, the Countess and me. My mother then took another husky slug of Glenfiddich and proposed a toast.

'To Chantelle – the bravest girl I know. To Phyllis, who taught her everything she knows. To victory, because we are bloody well going to win this. To my brilliant barrister daughter, Tilly, who is going to win it for us . . . To Portia – who will one day follow in the family's high-heeled footsteps and become a legal eagle. To the Countess, who pays for the grog and chocolates which fuel our feminist enterprise . . . And to Pandora's – where we think outside the bloody box!'

18

Bewigged, Bothered and Bewildered

The night before the court case, I was so nervous I slept for about one minute, during which I woke up at least three times. Roxy suggested I take tranquillizers, but I was too worried about the effect of tranquillizers to take any. If only there were a tranquillizer I could take to make me calm enough to take tranquillizers, I told her.

On the morning of Phyllis's trial, as our minicab crossed London, the vast Victorian mausoleum of the Old Bailey loomed up before me. The Old Bailey is one of the best known buildings in London. Its infamous trials have included Oscar Wilde's tragic criminal libel debacle and, from the sublime to the vicious, a Who's Who of psychopathic murderers from Dr Crippen and John Christie to the Yorkshire Ripper and the Kray twins ... And yet it seems carelessly to shrug off its own importance. The scrappy streets around the building twist their way up towards the pudding dome of St Paul's Cathedral, which is itself dwarfed by the skyscrapers of the financial district rising up like jagged teeth behind it.

Roxy, Phyllis and I alighted from the minicab outside the court. I looked up at the imposing golden statue of Lady Justice, with her sword in her right hand and the scales in the other, and noticed that she was sensibly barefoot. I, however, was strapped into my highest heels, even higher than usual, because one of Roxy's rescue dogs, a German shepherd she claimed was merely 'fun-loving' but looked as though it could drag you down into the underworld, had chewed through my favourite black court shoes. I'd seen him, ten minutes before I was due to leave home, disappearing outside with my footwear between his foaming incisors. I was now wearing my only other good, black pair, shoes which were so vertiginous I reserved them for first dates only. Those extra five inches meant I was practically en pointe. Which rather imperilled the impression I was trying to create for my first appearance at the Old Bailey of a cool, suave, legal-eagle sophisticate.

As Roxy and Phyllis slalomed ahead through the crowd, I gingerly negotiated the pavement behind them like a toddler taking to the ice. The area was jammed with braying reporters, which meant the ground was crawling with the electrical snakes of TV cables – yellow, black, poison-green – any one of which could trip me up.

'*L'atmosphère est très primitive,*' surmised Countess Flirtalotsky when I finally made it through the barriers of the metal detector. Despite the brightness outside, it felt cold in the court building, as though sunlight had never entered here. Roxy and I exchanged a glance before we parted. My mother's look was full of confidence and pride. Mine was the opposite.

'I don't look like a big ball of anxiety to you, do I?'

'Darl, if you were any more unwound I'd have to mop you up. But I have every faith in you, Tilly.' She took out a flask and gave me one of her home-made energy-boosting ginseng drinks – although I suspected a kilo of cocaine might prove more beneficial. 'Most barristers are either brilliant brainiacs, versed in clause-this and sub-clause that ... or people-pleasing jury charmers. You have a most unusual combination of both skills. Which is why this will be Pandora's finest moment.'

She squeezed my hand before escorting Phyllis across the baroque Grand Hall towards the court room, where she would be placed into custody then seated in the dock between two prison officers. Phyllis walked towards her fate as if against a tide, dragging her limbs. I watched as she crumpled on to a bench, head in hands, quietly sobbing. Roxy leant down to speak soothing words. If I lost the case, the old lady would be led into the labyrinth of dark, eerie tunnels below, first to a cell, then straight to prison for a ten-year stretch ... No pressure then.

A court usher derailed my train of thought to ask if I was nervous about appearing against Jack Cassidy, who had never lost a case here ... I replied no, but was thinking – nerves? What nerves? ... I always spray my hair with a deodorant that protects for eighteen hours, spritz my pits with breath freshener, floss my toes and put my tights on backwards.

I wandered off through a warren of hallways, along which eccentric-looking persons hurried past wearing White Rabbit expressions and stiff horsehair wigs. With twenty courts in operation, there were so many barristers it was like following a flock of crows, the black wings of their gowns flying out behind them.

I took the lift up to the fourth floor. Barristers streamed towards the robing room. But there was no sign of Jack in the throng. In the women's changing room I adjusted my wig, shrugged on my robes and tried not to throw up my breakfast.

Court room number twelve had a church feeling. It was full of oppressive, heavy nineteenth-century mahogany, ornately carved and imperious. I took my seat at the bench assigned to the defence team, to the immediate right of the jury box and facing the judge's bench, and pretended to be busy with my papers.

The more conventional lawyers at the Bar had always looked at me the way one might study a bizarre decorative item at someone's house bought as a 'talking piece'. But that reaction was tame compared to the frisson of disapproval which rippled around the room when my solicitor burst into the court in her leopardskin miniskirt and matching wedges with a crumpled Phyllis in tow. Roxy was as out of place as an iridescent parakeet schooled in profanities holding forth in a prayer meeting.

But the hushed reverence in the room was only truly disturbed when Jack Cassidy strode into view. As he swept past me, robes billowing, wig rakishly askew, the attention of the entire court room shifted to him like flowers turning to the sun. The man was perfumed with success.

'Good morning, Ms Devine.' He paused and looked down on me, as I sat at the defence bench. '. . . What? No barbed jibe at my expense? Obviously, you're not quite yourself today . . . I noticed the improvement immediately.' Jack gave me a sly smile, full of cocksure confidence and devilment.

I passed him the tissue tucked up my sleeve. 'Wipe your mouth, Jack. There's still a little bit of bullshit on your lips. Or, better still, why don't you travel light and leave your sarcasm at home.'

He answered my query by leaning across my bench and stealing my emergency bar of Green and Black's dark organic, half hidden on the seat beside me.

Before I could remonstrate, the usher called the court to

order as the judge lumbered in and sat at his bench, plump as a cushion. Oh no. My heart sank to Jules Verne depths. If only I'd thought to pack some cyanide tablets, now would have been the perfect time to take them, I ruminated, as the dreaded Judge Jaggers, newly promoted to the Old Bailey, arranged his black robes around him then peered sanctimoniously at me over his half-moon specs. If only my desk had an emergency airbag to cushion the blow so I could thump my head on the table in despair. That, or an eject button.

I tried to calm my hyperventilation by looking around the court room. Phyllis was now in the dock at the back of the court, flanked by guards. Roxy was seated directly behind me in order to fire brilliant ideas at my back, while the judge would no doubt fire destructive comments at my face. Jack took his seat at the prosecution bench on my right. When we were all settled, the judge gave the nod and the jury usher brought in twenty potential jurors. They blinked like newborn fieldmice under the harsh fluorescents. Twelve names were drawn from a box by the clerk of the court. The other potential jurors were dismissed. After taking an oath and swearing to tell the truth, the whole truth and nothing but the truth, the selected jurors, nine women and three men, sat in overawed silence on their wooden pews, peering up at the judge's bench as though it were a pulpit.

'Will the defendant please stand.' Phyllis was helped to her feet by the officers as the first charge was read out: attempted murder.

'How do you plead?' the clerk of the court asked. 'Guilty or not guilty?'

Phyllis mumbled.

'Speak up!' Judge Jaggers boomed. His voice was as sonorous as Big Ben, ringing out across the capital.

Despite the potential of a full ass-over-tit high-heel tumble,

I pushed up from my seat and tottered unsteadily to the dock to hold her hand. 'Phyllis?' I said in an encouraging tone, as though offering her a slice of sponge cake.

'Not guilty,' she muttered.

'Speak up!' the judge grumbled. He was clearly going for first place in the Mr Caring and Sharing Compassion Championships.

I gave her a heartening nod and her arthritic fingers a gentle squeeze.

'Not guilty,' she sniffled. The further charges of causing grievous bodily harm and discharging a firearm to endanger life were also read out, and Phyllis duly repeated her not-guilty pleas.

After I'd taken my seat, the judge reminded the members of the jury of their grave responsibilities. He glowered at me once more before nodding approvingly at my nemesis. Jack rose to his feet and began to speak in his velvety, honeyed vowels.

'Let me start by saying to you, members of the jury, this case comes before us against a background where rape is alleged. Let me say to you that this matter is still to be resolved by the courts. But you must firmly have in your mind that, even if a rape did take place, it does not justify the taking of a firearm and exacting revenge. There is no place for revenge in our system of justice. The reason we have police and courts is precisely so that people do not go off and seek vengeance for perceived wrongs.'

The timbre of his voice was mesmerizing and the female members of the jury were following him with rapt attention. They'd clearly already found Jack guilty – guilty of being totally adorable. 'Hold me in contempt,' their eyes seemed to say, 'or just hold me.'

'In this case, I, on behalf of the Crown, allege, and will

prove to you, that Phyllis O'Carroll, hearing an account from her granddaughter, rather than engaging the authorities and the police, took the law into her own hands and tried to kill two people.'

Even at this distance, I could catch his scent, a scent that still had the power to intoxicate and unnerve. I clung to my cloak lapels like a caricature of an overly confident lawyer from an old *Punch* cartoon and stared straight ahead, in an attempt to give the impression of a barrister not on the brink of a complete coronary embolism.

'Taking the law into your own hands, ladies and gentlemen, is a recipe for chaos and social disorder. And so, I remind you, as a jury, of your responsibility to society as a whole. We are not here trying the allegation of rape. We are trying the conduct of Phyllis O'Carroll, who took the law into her own hands in the most serious way possible. I call my first witness, Peter Simmons.'

The man I knew as 'Stretch' hobbled into court with an exaggerated limp, wincing with each overacted step. Gone were the leather jacket, biker boots and Hun/Goth-infested Dark Ages barbarian look. His frizzy hair had been straightened into a wiry halo, his tall, muscular frame squeezed into an incongruous and ill-fitting suit. He was still gargoyle-ugly but groomed to within an inch of his lowly life.

Having set the scene, Jack asked him to tell the court what the angry grandmother had done to him. As he began, with difficulty, to describe the experience of being shot in the testicle, I saw the men on the jury grimace and cross their legs in such flinching unison it could have been choreographed.

The judge, looking squeamish, addressed the witness gently 'Mr Simmons. I know these are matters about which any man would find it difficult to speak. But you are going to have to talk about these sensitive concerns. Which is why I just want you to know that the court understands the . . . delicacy involved.'

'She shot me fuckin' ball off!' Stretch cried out, not so delicately. 'The old bag turned up rantin' that we'd raped her granddaughter and just shot at me gonads. The crown jewels of the family! She knocks on the f-ing door. Next fing I know, she blows me ball off. Thank me lucky stars I've still got me tonsil tickler.'

The judge raised a brow. 'Your what, Mr Simmons??'

'Me meat popsicle . . . Me beef thermometer . . .' When the judge looked no wiser, he continued: 'Me stinky pickle . . . Me baloney pony . . . Me pork sword . . . Me . . .'

'Yes, thank you, Mr Simmons. Your manhood, I think you're referring to,' Jack clarified. His very use of the term had the female jurors swooning. I, too, was preoccupied by thoughts of Jack's big, throbbing organ – the one between his ears. In this court case, that was the only place where size would count.

'Would you like to take a break to compose yourself?' Judge Jaggers asked solicitously, tilting his head towards the witness with compassion.

The judge's obvious sympathy prompted Jack to glance across at me with one of his trademark smug smiles, then break off a piece of my chocolate bar and surreptitiously eat it with lip-licking pleasure. I kept my poker face intact but turned slightly to catch Roxy's eye. My mother has never learnt to school her features into impassivity. Seeing the judge favouring the prosecutor and Chantelle's rapist meant that angry emotions were chasing each other across her face.

I was more determined than ever to ensure that Stretch had the words 'long' and 'prison' precede his name but, when it was my turn to cross-examine, I was sweating more than a Colombian at Customs. I rose and, high heels pinching, tiptoed towards the one-balled warrior. What I wanted to ask Stretch was 'So, tell me, how long have you known about your third chromosome?' but I said instead – 'You're quite a big fish on the estate, aren't you, Mr Simmons, or Stretch, as I think you prefer to be known. Is that right?'

'Well, yeah,' he peacocked. 'I get about a bit.'

'You're cock of the walk, so to speak.'

'Yeah . . . I'm well respected an' that. I know how to handle meself,' he preened.

'Wouldn't it be fair to say that people are scared of you?'

'I don't take no crap, if that's what you mean.' His huge chest puffed outwards until I thought the buttons might ping off his shirt and hit jury members in the eye.

'And you wouldn't take any rubbish, especially from an old lady, would you? I mean, how would that look on the estate? So, anyone coming around to see you is going to be scared and probably armed, isn't that fair to say? Because of your fierce reputation.'

'P'robly. Yeah.' The thug's mind was clearly wandering – and it really was too small to be allowed out on its own – which meant that now was my moment.

'But isn't it true that this frightened, frail old grandma just came around to tell you not to trash her granddaughter's reputation? That it would be unacceptable to belittle the girl by calling her a slut or a slag?'

It was then that Jack tried his best to distract me. He gave me a mischievously gloating wink before devouring most of my purloined chocolate bar in one great gulp. I felt an over-whelming urge to teach the man a lesson. What I was about to do wasn't fair. But then, neither is life. As Roxy said, if life was fair, then Elvis would still be alive and all the im-personators would be dead. Vacillating for a moment, I glanced quickly at the jury.

On the one hand, I totally believe in the jury system and the ability of ordinary men and women to discern the truth . . . On the other hand, it's also true that a significant proportion of the population believe that the moon landing was faked. Which is why I next heard myself say—

'Wasn't your favourite weapon close at hand?'

'What weapon?'

'You are a man who carries a knife, aren't you, Mr Simmons?'

I hadn't intended to take the Roxy route but, when the odds are against you, a female barrister's just gotta get even.

'Knife? What fuckin' knife. I never pulled no knife!'

'Why are you mentioning pulling a knife, Mr Simmons? I made no mention of you pulling a knife? . . . Did you pull a knife?'

'Fuck, no!'

'My client saw you reach for your pocket and in her terror cannot recall the next seconds. Was it your knife that frightened the poor old lady?'

'Objection, My Lord.' Jack uncoiled to his feet with languorous disdain. 'A suggestion is being made that there was a knife. There is no evidence of a knife.' Gone were his velvet vowels. The prosecutor's words were crisp, clipped and precise. Jack is a master of insouciant understatement, but when roused, you'd rather be pinned down by mortar fire in the middle of a war zone than endure one of his verbal volleys.

'My Lord, I was asking the witness whether he's a habitual carrier of a knife.' I sent out my own salvo. 'It was the witness who then insisted he had not used any knife – rather precipitously, the jury might think. His own answers raise the question. It is my case that he reached for his pocket and, in terror of what he was about to produce, my client shot him.'

The judge harrumphed, as if to belittle my defence, but allowed me to continue.

'After the shot was fired, there were – what? – thirty or so people crowded around you, correct? Friends. Allies. Gangland compatriots ... Any knife would disappear very quickly, wouldn't it?'

Jack took the moral high ground with his eyebrows then leapt up. 'It's mere conjecture, My Lord.'

Prompted by Jack, the judge disdainfully dismissed my line of questioning. But the doubt had been sown in the minds of the jury. I felt a bit squeamish – but I hadn't *lied*. Lying in court would get me struck off. This was just a little bit of gamesmanship, and, after all, life is full of games – games which women usually lose.

Jack shot me a withering look before bringing in his second witness, the more sinister thug nicknamed, appropriately, 'Bash'. His wild hair was now perfectly smooth, like plastic. His shoes were shined, jaw cleanshaven, his suit expensive and immaculate, except for a tie that looked too tight. It wasn't the only noose I'd like to see around his neck, I thought, as he spun an identical story to the court.

During my cross-examination, despite Bash's polished appearance, I soon sensed that the jury disliked his monosyllabic hard-man attitude, especially the way he looked at me with the slow lizard blink of a top-order predator. The man had all the charm of a drug baron's hitman – possibly because he was one. I asked in a very loaded way whether he had seen a knife that night. His shifty look and diffident 'Nope' was greeted with scepticism by the jury.

I knew he had prior convictions – basically, the piece of pond scum had been in so many police line-ups he could just wave at the witnesses and say 'Remember me?!' So when he foolishly denied that he had any 'previous', I pressed him.

'Are you absolutely clear on that point?' When he gave a haughty nod, I continued, 'Well, let me make it clear that the point I'm suggesting is that you have invented your account because you are a complete stranger to the truth.' I put his previous-convictions sheet under his nose and got him to read it out to the jury, making him repeat his GBH and sexual assault offences. Mistrust rippled through the jury box.

After the officer in charge of the case confirmed that these were indeed Bash's previous convictions, Jack concluded with a standard 'My Lord, this is the case for the prosecution.' His conclusion may have been standard, but the gravitas and charm he oozed was definitely not. I wouldn't have been surprised if the female jurors committed a joint crime right then and there, just on the off chance that he might represent them, preferably after a strip search.

The judge announced an adjournment, and Phyllis, looking bewildered and terrified, was handcuffed to a police officer then led down to the cells. I spent the nail-gnawing recess going over my choices. I had thought about opening with a speech to the jury outlining the defence case. But sometimes it's more powerful and authentic to let the defendant go into the witness box straight away to tell their side of the story. But I wasn't confident that Phyllis wouldn't wobble on the detail; so I decided to woo the jury first.

When court resumed, I utilized every sympathetic adjective in my linguistic armoury to paint Phyllis as a doting, docile grandma. I conjured up so many cosy, nostalgic images of the jurors' own grannies that the aroma of home-baked biscuits was practically wafting through the air. By the time I concluded my opening address the jury were so sweet on my dear old gran, I worried I'd given them all diabetes.

I now turned to Phyllis, who sat rigid on her stiff-backed chair in the dock, still flanked by uniformed prison officers.

In a loud, clear voice, I said, 'I now call Phyllis O'Carroll.' The trembling gran was escorted to the witness box, where she took an oath. She was holding on to the railing in front of her as if trying to squeeze blood from it. I took Phyllis through her evidence, as carefully as a trainee in a minefield, guiding her to the safety of the right answers without setting off any unexpected explosions. But when asked to explain to the jury what had happened on the night in question, Phyllis suddenly employed a weird Reading Aloud to a Classroom Full of Children voice. Her delivery was so wooden, she was practically a fire hazard. Overawed by the surroundings, the poor woman was trying hard to enunciate, which strangled her natural oratorical flow and struck a false note with the jury, who shifted uncomfortably, instinctively dubious of her sincerity. When I asked if she had heard rumours that Bash always carried a knife, Jack objected, saying that I was inviting hearsay evidence. I insisted that if my client knew Bash was a local knife wielder as well as a rapist, it would explain her frame of mind as she courageously set off to see him.

Phyllis's head was swivelling so fast from one side of the court room to the other that she resembled a meerkat watching tennis. Jack objected once more, but this time Judge Jaggers reluctantly, almost apologetically, allowed my point. 'Well, Mr Cassidy, it may be speculation but Miss' – he made a theatrical scramble to find my name on the court papers, thus signalling to the jury that I was so insignificant as a barrister that judges had never heard of me, even though Jaggers knew my name so well he'd once got me sacked – 'Miss . . . Miss . . . Devine's defendant is entitled to put her case to the court.'

I then asked Phyllis if she saw a knife. She hesitated. My toes were plaited in dread, as I waited for her answer. Then she replied hesitantly that she wasn't certain . . . but she did see him put his hand to his pocket.

'Yer Majesty, I was quakin'. I reckoned that I was about to be ripped from me gullet to me fanny. An' that's when the gun went off.'

When it was Jack's turn to cross-examine the defendant, he smirked condescendingly at me before turning a sympathetic smile in my client's direction. Jack Cassidy's great skill as a cross-examiner is never to examine crossly. He treated Phyllis with the utmost care and kindness. He was respectful and gracious as he led her towards the suggestion that, driven mad by grief, she'd picked up a gun, a gun she just happened to have in her cupboard, and gone around there to teach those boys a lesson they wouldn't forget. Lulled by his lovely, deep, lilting voice, it was hard not to agree with all of his utterances, just to keep him talking. 'You went around there to kill them,' Jack insisted. 'Because you were full of outrage about what you thought they'd done, isn't that right?'

Behind me, Roxy gave a derisive snort which, to her mind, was probably quiet but, to normal people in the stillness of a court room, sounded a lot like a hippo in the final stages of labour.

The judge glowered in my mother's direction, while respectfully apologizing to Jack for the interruption. 'I'm terribly sorry, Mr Cassidy. Please continue.'

'Thank you, m'Lord . . . You've been a mother to that grandchild of yours. Your own child is in prison for drugs-related crimes, yes?' Phyllis nodded and hung her head. 'You felt you'd failed one child and then, oh, what torture, to feel you'd failed another. You went around there to kill them for what you thought they'd done to your granddaughter. And I ask you to tell the truth to this court. You went around there to shoot the men who you thought had attacked your beloved grandchild. That was your intention, yes?'

There was a pause. All eyes were now on the wilted grandmother. 'Yes,' said Phyllis softly.

There was a theatrical gasp in the court room as people mumbled their surprise. Judge Jaggers scowled once more, ensuring silence immediately swooped down and tightened its grip on the court. Jack sneaked another tiny victorious smile in my direction and licked his chocolatey fingertips. A sweat patch the size of Devon had appeared under each of my armpits. What was she thinking? How could I interrupt Phyllis's journey into the centre of self-annihilation?

Out of the corner of my eye, I saw Roxy's leopardskin wedge jacking up and down, as if she were working an invisible bicycle pump. Stretch and Bash were now sitting beside Jack. They wore cocksure grins that flickered on and off like faulty lightbulbs.

'Please continue,' Jack coaxed Phyllis kindly. 'I know it's hard for you, my good woman.'

I looked at Phyllis, willing her not to give in to Jack's persuasive charms. Fat chance, I thought bitterly. The female jurors could toast marshmallows on their faces, they were so hot and bothered by the debonair presence of prosecutor Jack Cassidy.

'My first instinct, when I saw that child of mine, all beaten up and bruised an' that, was to kill 'em . . .' The regions beneath my armpits now expanded to include all of mainland Britain. A tense hush fell over the court room like a fog. 'But, well, I ain't no fool. You don't get to be seventy-odd and have lived the life I've lived . . . and not know the consequences of doing somethin' as feckin' crazy as that.'

I felt myself unclench. I tried to devise a facial expression to cover up my glee. I furrowed my brow in a learned, weighty way, as though calculating mc^2. But I couldn't help sending a surreptitiously smug smile of my own back in Jack's sanctimonious direction.

'. . . But I also know what bastards those blokes are. I went round there with a gun so those animals would listen to me. Then he' – she pointed at Stretch – 'pulled a knife on me. Or so I thought. An old granny. I was that terrified that I don't even remember pullin' the trigger.'

Phyllis swayed as though she were being buffeted by the fiercest winds, despite the fact we were safely indoors. An Oscar nomination could not be far off for the wily old woman. As the day's proceedings came to a close, I felt the jury lean ever so slightly in Phyllis's direction.

On day two, I was feeling much more confident. Put it this way, I'd only had about four heart attacks during breakfast, down from ten per minute during the previous day's trial. But I also hadn't forgotten that the rapist thugs did have a powerful secret weapon – Jack Cassidy. And the judge. As the morning wore on and Judge Jaggers denied all my objections and indulged Jack's every line of questioning, I wondered if it would be inappropriate to ask him if he only enjoyed being a judge so he could wear a wig to hide the horrible alien life form sprouting from his head, otherwise known as the world's worst comb-over?

For Jack's closing argument, my nemesis utilized every ounce of his captivating magnetism. He was more disarming than a UN peacekeeping force. Jack's arguments sneaked up on the jury so stealthily they might as well have been dressed in camouflage combat fatigues. By the time Jack delivered his passionate, damning closing speech, in which he accused the septuagenarian grandma of the premeditated attempted murder of two innocent men who were attacked, in cold blood, in their own home, Phyllis had crumpled in the dock, hiding her face in her hands, and every one of the women on the jury had not just fallen for his act but seemed totally ready to leave their husbands, run off with him and live orgasmically ever after.

After Jack had sat back down, flicking his robes back with toreador flamboyance, the judge called on me to address the jury. I took a sip of water so that I could be doing something else with my lips besides trembling. It was tepid and stale. I swallowed hard, reminding myself that the closing speech is the part of the trial I most relish. I like knitting all the threads of the case together: drawing the jury in, until they're in the palm of my metaphorical hand. I steeled my nerves, then stood to face the jury.

'You've heard from Mr Cassidy, and he's told you that you have to be the guardians of the system: that you can't take the law into your own hands. But ask yourself' – I was careful to make eye contact with each and every one of the jurors as I spoke – 'who *are* the people taking the law into their own hands? Phyllis has never broken the law. But these men?' Phyllis's minor shoplifting charge was so long ago it had been erased by the Rehabilitation of Offenders Act. But I spared no grizzly detail of the witnesses' past crimes. The vivid pictures I painted were so vile that the jurors were clearly wondering how these men could hide their cloven hooves in their shoes.

A barrister's most effective ploy in emotive cases like this one is to pluck at the heartstrings of the jury. I strummed each juror individually as though they were the most precious lyres and lutes, harping on the grandma's horror and subsequent rage, making them all feel that it was their own child who had been violated that day. I noted the body language of each juror and particularly eyeballed the more dubious ones. 'If your child was raped, beaten and grossly abused, would you sit on your hands?' I reminded them that the dear old gran had only wanted to tackle the men verbally. She went armed simply for self-protection. 'But on confronting the men she was so distressed that she had no control over her aged arthritic fingers. Presented with these wicked, gloating men, she feared even for her own safety – she was so fearful that, driven mad with terror and grief, she pulled the trigger on a reflex.'

My next tactic was to flatter their intelligence. 'As you know, for a crime to be committed, in law, there has to be *mens rea* – an intention to kill or cause serious harm. This poor, gentle gran had no such intention. You may think the Fates took a hand in putting her finger on the trigger, but that was never her conscious intention.'

I then addressed the three male jurors directly, intent on ego massage and mild manipulation.

'Of course, most of the men in this world are decent. It's so hard for kind, law-abiding, gentle men like you to understand how other males could behave in this violent, malicious way. But they do. And Phyllis believed that these two men had.'

As men, in general, prefer facts, I then resorted to lists and statistics.

'I want you to imagine also what life is like for women on Britain's council estates. Two women die a week in Britain at the hands of their partners. Violence is a bigger threat to the health of European women than cancer.'

I could have gone on for hours, listing man's inhumanity to woman, but I didn't want to overwhelm them. There's nothing worse than a lawyer who talks for so long that the usher's snores wake up the jurors. But I managed to weave in some stats without inducing collective narcolepsy. I let them know that in the last year, in England and Wales alone, 69,000 women were raped. Over 400,000 were sexually assaulted; 1.2 million suffered domestic abuse. Then I detailed the shamefully low rate of conviction.

Jack muttered a sarcastic aside which only I could hear. 'So, tell me, does Oprah know you're available?'

Ignoring him, I utilized all my rhetorical powers, speaking in cadences not unlike a charismatic preacher's, in sentences that built and rolled and rallied in a great rhythmic refrain. I rammed home the point that failure of governments to protect the rights of women continues to hinder gender equality all over the globe. 'It's a grave injustice which holds us back as a society. A conviction in this case will only empower men like this.'

It was time to lay it on with a trowel – or not just a trowel; a steamroller.

'The prosecution maintains that my poor, traumatized grandma took the law into her own hands. But how often does the law wash its hands of unimportant women like this doting, downtrodden pensioner and her darling innocent little granddaughter? Put yourself in Phyllis's shoes – cheap, vinyl, worn down at the heel. The shoes of a decent, hardworking, law-abiding cleaning woman who is always walked over . . . Members of the jury, don't let them walk all over her today.'

Good advocacy is the ability to keep the jury from coughing. By the time I sat down, I realized that there hadn't even been a little throat-clearing during my summing-up – the court room was a total cough- and snore-free zone. What's more, Jack knew it, too. He sat with folded arms and a bolted-on expression. Glancing up at the public gallery, my eyes snagged with amazement on to Nathaniel. I didn't know he was back from his conference and he hadn't told me he was coming to watch the trial. His eyes were resting on me with keen admiration.

Judge Jaggers, who was of the I Sentence You to Prison until Such Time as You're Found Innocent school of justice, began his summing-up. The judge is supposed to be impartial, but while he'd greeted every one of Jack's quips with appreciative bonhomie, whenever I'd spoken he'd displayed the relaxed, friendly demeanour of a CIA operative. And he reinforced his disapproval by practically instructing the jury to convict.

'The defendant decided that these men were rapists, which put them outside the law, then felt entitled to take the law into her own hands. What you must ask yourself, members of the jury, is whether this vicious act of revenge had anything to do with the law or justice. I think not. Look deep into your conscience and ask yourself this question: are we citizens or savages?'

He sent the jury out to make their deliberations. As they filed from the court, Jack winked victoriously at me before strolling out, his witnesses in surly tow. I turned to face my mother with a heavy heart.

'Let's call David Attenborough urgently. Judge Jaggers has just proven that dinosaurs definitely do still roam the earth,' Roxy said, trying to make light of it.

Women who've given birth are better equipped to deal with the vicissitudes of life. After all, we've been stitched up and experienced acute pain. But, looking at Phyllis's stricken face, how I longed for an anaesthetic.

19

A Brief Encounter

While the jury deliberated, Phyllis, Roxy, the Countess and I sat in the cafeteria. The scratched modern plastic furniture clashed with the paint-clogged Victorian woodwork. Seconds plodded by, each separated from the next by an eternity.

'This law malarkey is too soul-destroying. I want a new career,' Roxy said conversationally. 'There's a woman who breaks in the Queen's shoes. Not a chauffeur but a shoe-ffer. That would be perfect for me.'

But nobody was in the mood to banter. We said little and ate less. Roxy squirted Bach's Rescue Remedy down our throats to calm our nerves, but it had about as much effect as a parasol in a gale-force hurricane. The fluorescent light above buzzed and crackled and bathed us all in its sickly yellow, almost furry glow. As time dragged on the atmosphere grew heavy, almost solid. The London traffic made a distant, surging sound, like a flooded, angry river. Visiting jail is like taking a trip through a sewer in a glass-bottomed boat. If I lost the case, Phyllis would be treading water there for the next ten years. She would probably die of old age in prison, if some maniac didn't kill her first. My stomach turned at the thought.

Across the canteen from us slumped the two witnesses, wiping up the gravy on their plates with slabs of bread. Bash – the wiry, thin one with the ferret face – gave me a smirking salute. In his mouth bobbed an unlit cigarette. He removed it to wriggle his tongue at me lewdly.

I looked away, unable to describe my feelings about either of them without recourse to slang terms for faeces.

When the clerk called us back into court I couldn't tell if it was a good or a bad sign that the jury's deliberations had taken only one and a half hours. Bash bounced by on the balls of his feet. 'Why did the feminist cross the road?' he said to Stretch, for our benefit. 'To suck my cock.'

Building down our hopes, we set out like prisoners off to our execution. Back in court, Stretch and Bash sat with the police. Bash balanced himself on the edge of his seat, as though ready to leap up with jubilation. He jigged his knee up and down and thrummed his fingers on the desk in time to some jangled rhythm in his head. Stretch flexed his muscular arms and gazed up distractedly at the ceiling as though High Command on Planet Neptune were telling him it was time to start Phase Two.

Phyllis sat in the dock, bent almost double, head angled towards her knees, arms wrapped around her flabby mid-section. All I could think about was not giving Jaggers or Jack the pleasure of seeing me cry in front of them. It was an impossible case to win. We might as well have opened a glassware shop in downtown Baghdad. The tension was nerve-twanging . . . But not for Jack. He strolled back into court, pausing by my table to look me up and down.

'I like the shoes . . . they show off your legs so nicely. Especially when your robes gape and I can see your short skirt. I'm going to talk to the judge about having you arrested for persistent inner-thigh exposure, as it's really quite distracting.'

His cockiness was infuriating, but there was no time to retort because the usher was issuing the command 'All rise.'

I jumped up out of my chair with an alacrity my body hadn't seen since I accidentally electrocuted myself on a hair-dryer in my mother's bathroom. Jack's dodgy clients rose simultaneously, too, as though doing callisthenics. We all turned to face the jury forewoman, who was looking straight at me. I couldn't tell if she was sympathetic because we'd lost the case or just possessed a face which had a gravitational pull towards melancholy.

'Do you have your verdict?' Judge Jaggers asked, doing his over-the-top-of-his-spectacles peering routine, no doubt practised before many mirrors.

Devon had moistened again beneath my armpits. I looked at Phyllis in trepidation. Negative thoughts looped through my mind. Why had she entrusted her life into my hands? I mean, I was clearly out of luck. If I won a car in a raffle, it was bound to be a Skoda.

In the list of the most terrible words anyone could ever utter, besides 'Incontinence hotline. Please hold', 'Your client is guilty' is by far the worst. On the other hand, there's no doubt that the most beautiful words in the English language, besides 'You've won the lottery,' 'Peace has come to Syria' and 'Brad Pitt would like your hand in marriage' are 'not' and 'guilty'. Especially when uttered in the same sentence.

When the forewoman uttered the words which saved my client from prison and trounced my enemy, it took a moment for the reality to sink in, especially when I looked up to see Phyllis crying steadily. She was making proper wa-wa-waaaaahs, with gulping and coughing and hiccuping, which is why I thought we'd lost. But then I heard Roxy. The noise of her victory hoot rivalled, in decibel levels, a Harrier Jump Jet.

When I'd regained my senses, I strolled across to reclaim my one remaining square of purloined chocolate from the prosecution. 'Like the Great Wall of China, your ego is visible from outer space. I think I'll suggest *you* are arrested for persistent inflated-ego exposure, as it's really quite distracting,' I said. Revenge tasted even sweeter than the stolen chocolate which I reclaimed and devoured in one greedy gulp.

A gridlock of journalists were scrumming for position on the court steps. For days, the press had been crawling over Phyllis's case like African ants over a corpse. The verdict was not what they had expected. The press now scuttled towards us like insects, microphones thrust forward. Roxy took centre stage, Phyllis at her side. As the crowd crushed in, an aggressive reporter mosquitoed around me, demanding comment. I glanced about wildly, desperate for a way out. Cameras flashed. I saw stars, like a cartoon character. Blinded, I lost my footing in my vertiginous heels, wobbled and lurched face forward into the mob. I was saved from a humiliating front-page nose-dive by a warm hand on my upper arm.

'Elbowing you in the ribs as you pass is paparazzi speak for "Excuse me".' It was Nathaniel's voice. He pulled me into his body, and the warmth of his skin radiated into mine. 'Motorcycle escort, m'lady?'

Nathaniel's height and musculature meant the crowd unclotted to let him pass. On the corner of the street, he unchained his motorbike and patted the seat behind him. I straddled the bike and curled into his strong back.

An hour later, I was on my third Martini and about two drinks away from suggesting we find a whipped-cream orgy for like-minded singles. Phyllis, the Countess and a few select supporters had come back to our little home for a drink.

As the afternoon wore on, Roxy, as impetuous as ever, decided that the best way to celebrate Phyllis's freedom was to whisk her away to a music festival in Dorset. Portia and Chantelle were invited, too. My mother, who was still a mung-bean-munching Bohemian at heart, immediately got busy packing rainbow-coloured jumpers, Joni Mitchell CDs, tofu and tempeh.

'Tilly, you must come!' she enthused. 'What a way to celebrate our feminist victory!'

I shuddered at the memory of my many childhood music-festival excursions. 'Mum, I'm too exhausted. Eight people in a two-man tent will mean no chance of rest, and not just because some venomous insect will be constantly blinking its 9,000,623,002 eyes at me in the dark . . .'

Roxy recruited the Countess instead. Now, the Countess will sleep in any bed – providing it's a four-poster Marie Antoinette-type antique or a heated waterbed filled with Perrier. She consequently set about booking a luxury camper van, driven by her new bodyguard, having sacked Danny's old undercover pal.

'I really should stay 'ere and cook yer somethin' nice to say thanks,' Phyllis offered, grasping my hand gratefully.

I had to admit, it was tempting. Burning the midnight oil preparing for Phyllis's case, I'd lived on so much tea and toast I'd given myself a toaster tan. But then I looked at the fatigued face of my now-infamous gran. It was hard to spoil Phyllis O'Carroll. She had been shaped by resistance and had no concept of the joys of trust, of letting go and frivolous hedonism. I could see how excited she was by the thought of getting out of London with her granddaughter.

'Don't worry!' Nathaniel placated the old lady. 'I'll concoct some culinary delight for our learned counsel,' he said, smiling at me.

As the house drained of people, I thanked him for the offer. 'My cuisine starts with broad categories such as "mineral" or "linoleum". When I cook dinner, my call to come to the table acts as a cue for people to go shopping, disappear into the loo with the *Encyclopaedia Britannica* or take their passports and leave for an extended holiday.'

'Well, you're in luck. I take great delight in cooking. It will be my pleasure to pamper you.' Nathaniel steered me to the living-room couch. 'But let me freshen up your drink first. After that stunning win, you are now officially excused on Saturday and Sunday, and I doubt whether Monday and Tuesday will be all that productive either.'

Handing me another Martini, Nathaniel's hand touched mine. He didn't pull it away, but stroked my wrist. I made a vague purring noise as his gentle brush strokes progressed up my arm. It was as though he were laying fine silk threads all over my skin. A few minutes later, I was nothing more than currents and impulses. He smelt like coconut oil. Coconut ice and all things nice. As his fingertips brushed across my leg, I felt an instinctive sexual quickening within me. My purring must have gone up a few decibels as he then nuzzled my neck while slowly moving his thigh across my body. Forget food. This was exactly what I craved – weight, bulk, muscle, strength: something bigger than me and Phyllis's court case. And yet, I pulled back from his embrace. It wasn't as though we'd even had a date yet. There was no need to rush . . . But then Nathaniel pulled his shirt over his head and I saw the ridges of muscle on his stomach. They rose under his skin exactly like the divisions on a slab of chocolate. Tangy, sweet, nuggety chocolate with a twist of caramel toffee and roasted coffee. And that was it. I felt a volt of excitement through my body, a deep and desperate hunger. I simply had to devour him, whole.

Nathaniel pulled my hips towards his, to let me know how much he wanted me. I would have cleared my throat to say something appreciative, except his tongue was already down there. As he lay me on the carpet, he didn't leave my mouth, not for a second. Everything became a blur of buttons, zips, hooks, carpet grazes, head bumps on lounge-chair legs, followed by moaning and amazement. And then all I was conscious of was life collapsing around me in panting, grainy pieces.

20

Is That a Gavel in Your Pocket or Are You Just Pleased to See Me?

I woke feeling sick and hungover. By the poison-green light of the digital alarm clock I read that it was 1 p.m. I had never slept this late in my life. My stomach felt as if I'd swallowed barbed wire. How many Martinis had I drunk? The slow thick drip of nausea made it hard to sit up in bed. I rolled over to find Nathaniel propped up on his elbow beaming at me, his wheat-blond hair seductively tousled.

'Were you faking it last night?' he teased.

'No, I really was asleep.' I had no memory of what had happened at all, although the bed did smell deliciously briny and I could feel the lingering afterburn of sex between my legs, plus there was an undeniable carpet burn on my left elbow. It also gradually dawned on me that I was naked. I quickly wrapped the sheet around me like some raddled Greek goddess who'd lost her footing on her plinth. Embarrassment washed over me in waves which were even more unnerving than the queasiness.

'You weren't asleep, my sweet. You made love like a crazy

gypsy, with your hair flying around. It was really exception-
ally exhilarating! Though I'm totally knackered.'

'*Ohmygod*. Those Cosmopolitans are lethal! I have no
memory of it at all.'

'Really? Because I have enough memories to last a lifetime.'
He smiled, stroking my hair.

'Well, Nathaniel, we've had some excellent meals and some
wonderful conversations, won a court case and had a night of
unbridled passion . . . but I think I'm going to go stagger off
into the wilderness now to die.' I tried to get out of bed but
fell back on to the pillow. 'Ohhh. My head!'

He laughed. 'Let me make you breakfast in bed to say
thank you for being the most sexy and scintillating woman
I've ever met.'

Who could he be talking about? That did not sound like
me. I gingerly sat up and orientated myself. Watching the
muscled Adonis padding out of my bedroom in his boxer
shorts made me think that perhaps I was still drunk and
having a hallucination. A throbbing head made dressing too
arduous. I slowly leant over and leadenly pulled on
Nathaniel's T-shirt. 'Coffee' was the only word rattling
around my ravaged cranium. I made my way downstairs at
the pace of a convalescing geriatric. I had just tentatively
navigated the bottom step when the doorbell rang, cleaving
my cranium almost in two. I eased open the door but was so
blinded by the light of day that it took me a moment to focus
on who was standing there.

'Beaten fair and square . . . and by a woman. I awoke this
morning, thinking, "Hmmm, which South American country
should I flee to?" But, before I go, I wanted to let you know
that you are a brilliant advocate, even without your
emergency court-room chocolate bar. I know I once laughed
at the concept, but you really could become a High Court

judge if you wanted. Anyway, please accept this gift as recompense. You deserve all the chocolate the world can offer.'

Jack then presented me with a booming bouquet of chocolate boxes in a basket. 'I got fresh truffles from a stall at Stoke Newington Farmers' Market. Then dashed to Peckham for slabs of chocolate made by this famous Parisian chocolatier Isabelle somebody or other. I think you'll like the flavours. They range from cumin and mint to coriander and grapefruit. I've added in some Prestat too – they're the chocolate truffles favoured by *Charlie and the Chocolate Factory*'s Roald Dahl. That particular purchase entailed a drive to Ealing, by the way. Yes! Halfway to Heathrow. But Dahl loved them so much he made them central to his novel *My Uncle Oswald*, as you no doubt recall, so I figured they'd be worth the trek . . . Oh, this may amuse you. Look, cocoa pasta and cocoa pesto . . . I also procured for you the most delicious chocolate on the planet – pale-lemon and sea-salt chocolate which is a palate orgasm, apparently. The experts say that replacing cheap chocolate with high-quality stuff helps in losing weight, too . . . Not that you need to, of course,' he added, hastily. 'As I like you just the curvy way you are.' He looked up from the basket at me expectantly.

'Christ. I think I'm going to throw up.'

'Not quite the thank you I'd envisaged,' he said, stepping out of the line of fire, 'but, actually, there's no way to make vomiting polite. All you can do is vomit in such a way that the anecdote you tell about it later will be entertaining. Do you want me to hold back your hair?'

I ran my hand through my tousled mane, which felt like a horror of Gorgon-like dreads. 'Oh God, don't come any closer. I think you could use my breath to scour an oven.'

'It only makes you more lovable, Tilly. In fact, I also thought I might ring Amnesty International and say that my human rights have been abused. Because I've fallen in love with a feminist lawyer ... It's Cruel and Unusual Punishment, as she's interested only in saving the world. I suppose what I'm saying is this – you love the whole world. And all the world obviously loves you. But do you think you could make a little room for me?' He ran a hand through his own luxuriant, black locks.

I was staring at him, astounded, struck dumb by this un-expected volte-face and romantic revelation.

It was then that Nathaniel, naked bar his boxers, strode up behind me with a mug of hot coffee in one hand. The other hand he used to wrap around my waist.

Jack's face was quizzical at first. Then it fell floorward. It took him a moment to relocate his vocal cords. 'Oh. Look who's here. The passionate champion of the common man. I didn't recognize you without your cross.' The words seemed torn from his throat like pieces of rough skin, causing him physical pain. 'Right. Okay ... I'll be off then. I just came to say that you beat me fair and square, Matilda.' His voice was now clipped and precise, like that of a wing commander in a British war movie. 'So, job well done. Is there anything you want to say to me, before I skulk back to my lair?'

There were a million things I wanted to say, but what came out of my mouth was 'Well ... now you know what it feels like.'

'Touché.' He turned, then disappeared around the corner in long, urgent strides.

'What did that Tory twat want?' Nathaniel asked, leading me to the kitchen, where plates of creamy scrambled eggs laced in truffle oil and thick slices of grainy toast and salty bacon lay waiting. 'How do you know him anyway?'

'We met at Oxford. We were both studying law.'

'So, what was he like? When you met him?'

'Cocksure, self-centred, ruthless, dishonourable, manipulative, lusty and ambitious.'

'So what happened?'

'What do you think? . . . I fell truly, madly, deeply in love with him. He was quite radical then, believe it or not. At the barricades and all that . . .'

But Nathaniel had lost interest. He was now dissecting yesterday's trial, eagerly enquiring when the CPS would bring their case against the two rapists. But I was finding it hard to absorb his words. Mainly, because Jack's words were still whirling around my addled brain and only now really registering. My heart flopped like a fish . . . The commitment-phobic Jack Cassidy had just told me he was in love with me . . . And it suddenly began to dawn on my few remaining unsozzled neurons that part of me was still in love with him. This extraordinary revelation struck me in lightning-bolt fashion. It literally fused me to the spot. Just catching sight of Jack there at the door had sent my alcohol-poisoned blood singing in my veins. His rich voice, his smell, the silk lining of his ludicrously bespoke suits, which did, indeed, speak volumes, his ribald banter, his tendency to tease me until my toes curled, his twinkle-eyed rascality . . . the fact that he would be able to tell me if 'rascality' was even a real word. And to tell me in Latin. The man was a force of nature, which is why it was appropriate that it now hit me, with the full force of a tsunami, that I wanted him still.

It had taken a lot for Jack to come here and open up and I had slammed the emotional door shut in his face. Nathaniel was still talking, but all I could think about was showering, dressing and pounding the pavement as fast as I could to my car. Jack's blinking, roguish wit was like a lighthouse, guiding me back to him.

In reality, it took me much longer to act on my impulse. After breakfast (which I was too nauseated to eat), I sent Nathaniel home while I took a nap. I woke an astounding five hours later, which meant that I didn't make it to Jack's place in Primrose Hill until that evening. When he answered the door, I pushed past him into his living room and launched into my prepared speech, a speech aimed to win over this one-man judge and jury.

'Do you know how an oyster makes a pearl? It's all the little irritations. Grain by grain, they rub and rub and then finally you realize what you have – a gem. You've rubbed me up the wrong way for so long, Jack, that it now feels right.' I laughed.

'I think you should go' was all he said. His face was granite hard in the half-light.

When I stood my ground, he took me by the shoulders and started to steer me forcibly towards the front door. And so I did the only thing I knew would convince him I was serious. Slowly, silently, I, Matilda Devine, body-shy and birthday-suit-averse, surrendered my clothes, piece by piece, until I was standing stark naked before him.

Jack's eyes travelled the length of my body and back up again. Nervous, I blurted, 'I hope you appreciate this. I haven't been completely naked, without strategic sheet draping, in front of anyone for thirteen years. I haven't even gone sleeveless in ten. I've not even worn open-toed sandals.'

Then he smiled, a slow burn which lit up his whole face. He gazed down at me, his lips wet. 'Tilly,' he sighed. And then his mouth was on mine as his hands ran over my flesh. When his fingertips brushed lightly a little south of my navel, I quivered, pierced by desire. Pleasure extended in concentric waves across my body, lower, deeper, more intense. My mind was electric, filled with the present.

'Jack,' I whispered.

'. . . *Jack?*' It was a female voice, echoing mine.

Disorientated, I prised myself free of his embrace and opened my eyes. A petite woman wearing fishnet tights and peek-a-boo La Perla underwear was mincing across the carpet towards us in skyscraper heels. I couldn't believe it was possible to take such small steps and remain standing. The woman had smoky eyes, red lips and the most striking red hair.

I felt as though I'd been in some kind of nuclear explosion. My head was pounding. My first reaction was to beat Jack senseless with his brass fire poker but I felt pretty sure this activity would be misunderstood in a manner that might lead to an encounter with the judiciary.

'Come back and parrrrtyyy,' the woman purred, slurring her words. I had a vague feeling I'd met her before. I recognized something about that harsh, nasal Estuary accent which felt like having your eardrums shredded on a cheese grater.

I shielded my nether regions with both hands. Standing there in the exact pose of Eve leaving the Garden of Eden, I scrutinized Jack's face. 'Twinkle' suddenly seemed completely the wrong word to describe his eyes. 'Twinkle' was a word with crinkled, happy edges. This was a glitter. A cold glitter of wolfish mischief. For a moment I fell into a trance of despair. What the hell was wrong with me? I obviously suffered from Stockholm syndrome. Otherwise, why did I keep on empathizing with my tormentor? I scrambled back into my clothes, then followed the sound of staccato laughter down the stairs into the basement living room. The redhead was dancing and undulating to soft, low music, swigging from a champagne glass in between tipsy giggles. I felt a knot of remorse in my gut like an acid reflux. What had I been thinking, getting naked in his house? Sex was no more personal to Jack Cassidy than algebra.

'Meet my new friend, a nurse from the Royal Free,' Jack said, following me. 'We met at a pop-up bar near Hampstead Heath at lunchtime,' he slurred. 'When I told her I had a broken heart, she said she knew the cure. So, I'm taking my medicine.' He gestured to the gyrating nurse. Then I remembered where I'd seen her. The pale skin – pre-Raphaelite pale – and the auburn hair ... It was the nurse I'd imagined posing for a Dante Gabriel Rossetti portrait in a medieval dress, fingering a lute.

I now noticed just how sozzled Jack was. I'd never seen him drunk before. 'Look at yourself, Jack. Nearly forty and still acting like a student ... Is this really what you most want in the world?'

'No.'

For a fleeting moment, I thought he was going to say something heartfelt and recapture the emotion of the morning.

'What I really want is a limber lingerie model who owns a vineyard and has an open-minded sister, who likes to wrestle in jelly ... No. Make that *two* sisters.'

'You're so much smarter than this. Why, when it comes to women, do you always take an IQ test and fail?'

'I think the brain is an overrated organ,' he drawled. 'It's not only all spongy and inert, but grey. Why should it wield power over other parts of the body which provide so much more pleasure?'

'You know what?' I spoke in a strained BBC announcer's accent 'I'm the one who has failed her IQ test ever to have thought that you could change.'

I rushed out into the night, furious with myself. The rain

washed the tears from my face. But not the taste of Jack Cassidy from my lips. There was nothing the rain could do about that.

Experience is a wonderful thing, I realized. It allows you to recognize a mistake when you make it all over again.

21

Courtus Interruptus

A pretty good indication that your life has gone to hell is when you find yourself eating the cooking chocolate at three in the morning. Although our court victory did afford us a day or two's grace, post win, offers of work came pouring in. After eighteen months of feeling ostracized by our profession, Roxy and I now adopted the brace position for legal stardom. Not only had we been approached by a sultana – no, not a dried fruit but the genuine wife of a sultan, who needed defending after cutting up her philandering husband's Savile Row suits – but there was also a female politician claiming duress after her circuit judge husband forced her to take his driving points. Both cases would be very high profile. From overseas, we had a money-bags Malaysian actress who'd been caught, um, with her mouth full, and wanted to pay us a small fortune to write an opinion challenging her government's absurd sexual-offence laws banning oral sex. 'Do you think we're biting off more than we can chew?' Roxy tee-heed.

Another wealthy woman wanted us to sue her ex-husband

for emotional distress. During their acrimonious divorce, he'd told the judge that he had no intention of getting married ever again and cut off his wedding-ring finger right there and then, before presenting it to our client. 'Well, it's one way of sticking your finger up at the British divorce laws,' my mother commented wryly.

With prosperous, paying clients for the first time, Roxy's holiday home in the Dordogne, bespoke Versace suit and BMW sports car of her dreams were tantalizingly within reach . . . Finally, Pandora's would be able to prop itself open without the patronage of the Countess. She had already announced that she intended to spend the money she'd save on a diving school in Cuba, just so she could say to people, 'I'm off to scuba in Cuba.'

Roxy and I had decided that Phyllis and Chantelle should keep living with us while the council found them a new flat on another estate. Yes, it was for their protection, but also because it would take a little time to wean ourselves off Phyllis's excellent cooking.

Five days after her trial victory, Phyllis received a letter from the Crown Prosecution Service. Roxy and I brought it home from the office after work. We presumed it was the CPS's formal notification to Phyllis, as Chantelle's guardian, about the upcoming rape-trial date.

Our gourmet gran was busy concocting something complicated from her advanced cordon-bleu book. I called her culinary concoctions 'quiz-uine' as I was never one hundred per cent sure what went into them, but they were so mouthwateringly wonderful that I had been about to invite Nathaniel over for a celebratory supper, when Phyllis finally opened the envelope.

The letter from the CPS wasn't so much a 'to do' list as a 'to don't' one.

The formal notification, which Roxy read aloud, stated that the CPS was not proceeding with the rape charges, which would now be dropped. 'We've applied our test as to whether to prosecute and we consider there is no realistic prospect of conviction.' The letter went on to cite the reluctance of the alleged victim to testify, cataloguing the panic-stricken calls Chantelle had made to the police voicing her intention of perhaps withdrawing her evidence. 'The CPS has to be robust when quality-assuring cases to maximize CPS efficiency.'

'What does it mean?' Phyllis asked, befuddled, leaving her boiling pots to hiss and rattle on the stove behind her.

I could feel Roxy going limp next to me. 'What it means is that a woman's word is worth less than a man's.' She was deflating faster than a pool-side Lilo at the end of summer.

'What it *means* is that Jack Cassidy is a bad loser,' I clarified. I could definitely see his hand in this. Appointing Jack as Senior Treasury Counsel was like putting Dracula in charge of the blood bank. Sore at losing the case against Phyllis, and also his carnal conquest, he'd obviously advised the CPS to drop the case against the two alleged rapists.

Roxy was now fuming more than the abandoned pans. She lit up a cigarette and opened the kitchen door. She spent the next few minutes pacing the garden as she incorporated every obscene term for the male reproductive organ into her explanation of events.

'What are you sayin'?' Phyllis reiterated, unable to fathom the nuances and undercurrents of legalese.

'What those drongos don't understand,' Roxy bellowed from somewhere near the herbaceous border, 'is that victims vacillate and are inconsistent because they're traumatized.'

I tried to clarify. 'It's all to do with cutbacks in police and CPS resources. Despite a big increase in reported rapes, the number of people charged with rape by the CPS has fallen by 14 per cent.'

Roxy shook her head in disbelief.

'You mean, Chantelle's rapists will get away with it?' asked Phyllis, in an annihilated voice.

'Yes,' Roxy said.

Phyllis dropped a baking tray with a cymballic crash and let out a wounded sob. Her hand chilled my arm in a death grip. She looked at me with pitiful, pleading eyes. 'Is it true?'

'No,' I heard myself saying. 'It doesn't mean we can't bring a private prosecution. I will waive my fees.'

'As will Pandora's,' Roxy rallied, stubbing out her fag and barging back inside, reinvigorated. 'But' – she hesitated – 'what about our big-paying cases?' Her voice was wistful as she watched her new sports car purring off into the Dordogne sunset . . .

'They'll have to wait,' I said, putting my arm around Phyllis's hunched shoulders. 'We have more important work to do.'

'But Tilly, if we lose, we'll have to pay defence costs, which could run into £30,000 or £40,000,' Roxy fretted.

'So we'll obviously need a financial backer . . .'

A tinkling sound drew our attention to the living room. The Countess was ringing the little bell she'd used to summon us while recovering from surgery. The black-clad woman had become such a permanent fixture in our lives, either slumped into one of the bulbous office armchairs or lying supine on our Camden couch, that I'd forgotten she was there. She was starting to make those stick insects whose camouflage trademark is that they haven't moved since the Stone Age look like hyperactive fidgets.

The Countess took a slug of her vodka tonic. 'I used to be an advocate of Murphy's Law – if anything can go wrong, it will. But after hearing that pathetic letter, my new view on Murphy's Law is that Murphy was a fucking optimist . . . So, to hell with it, girls.' She raised her glass in salute. 'Count me in.'

'What about your scuba in Cuba?' Roxy asked.

'Hey, if God had meant us to scuba dive in the ocean, we would have been born wearing shark-proof metal cages.'

Once the press reported news of our private prosecution, the abuse and death threats directed at Pandora's tripled. To every complaint, my indomitable mother sent the same reply – 'If you have a problem with me or my daughter or our practice, please write it nicely on a piece of paper, put it in an envelope, fold it neatly . . . then shove it up your arse.' But, despite Roxy's casual dismissal of danger, I took extra precautions with Portia, driving her everywhere and monitoring her whereabouts. I also notified the police of anything I deemed suspicious or scary. I wanted to call on Danny's bodyguard and surveillance services, but had no doubt that my mother would drop me off at the nearest orphanage with a note pinned to my pyjamas if I did. Still, I secretly hoped he was out there in the shadows, watching over us . . .

It was an unusually hot summer. The private prosecution was scheduled for the first week of September. A court case is a mental decathlon. I trained for the case day and night by slaving over a hot case file. The sun outside my office window was like treacle dripping off a sluggish spoon. As tempting as it was to frolic, I turned down all Nathaniel's invitations to open-air concerts, summer fairs and river regattas.

Matters were hotting up on social media as well. The closer we got to the rape-trial date, the more sinister the abuse oozing through the airwaves. A week before the trial, Chantelle received a message on her new Snapchat account saying that, unless the private prosecution against the two men was dropped, the sex tape, in which the footage had been edited and overdubbed to suggest pleasure and the identities of the men obscured – would be posted on the Internet.

Chantelle's little mouth gaped wide below two saucer-shaped eyes that looked like they hadn't blinked in weeks. But she strapped a shock absorber to her brain and held fast.

A week later, as threatened, her attack was posted online and began turning up on endless illegal websites. The police were involved, but would have little luck outwitting highly skilled cyberstalkers who knew how to stay one click ahead of the law.

'Twitter trolls are like some weird thought experiment that has broken out of the lab and infected millions,' I explained to Phyllis. 'As yet, there's no known cure for this electronic pandemic, except to ignore it.'

But how do you ignore a bomb exploding in your life, embedding shrapnel in everyone you love? Phyllis ground her jaw and heaved with sobs. Chantelle lay in a foetal ball in her bed, shell-shocked, back in startled-deer mode. The next body blow came in the form of a Twitter message on her new account warning that, if she didn't withdraw her evidence, a bomb would be detonated outside our house at precisely 9.30 that very night.

'In the middle of *Downton Abbey*? . . . Has this person no heart?' Roxy flippantly responded . . . until she saw the name of the Tweeter's site. It was called @killchantellenow. The accompanying profile photo was of a man in a vampire mask, blood dripping from black, feral fangs. Sickened, I immediately blocked his account. But he had another account up and running moments later with the message 'It's great to be back after 30 seconds. Lol.' Followed by 'After strangulation, which organ in the female body remains warm after death? My cock.'

An involuntary shiver shimmied through my frame. The bomb threat was restated, too. This time with our exact street address. While Roxy called the police, I blocked the man once more. Seconds later, the same vampire mask loomed up on the screen again. 'Drop the case or you die . . . slowly . . .' he said, his voice scrambled into a metallic, unidentifiable buzz. Two drops of blood fell from his fangs and sizzled before the screen went blank.

Chantelle began rocking. She moaned in pain. Then she threw up, right across the kitchen table. Phyllis's skin was the colour of an overcooked roast – completely grey. She started palpitating and I made her lie down immediately. The police soon confirmed that the accounts were bogus, the culprits untraceable.

We evacuated the house while the police combed the premises. Roxy called a round-table conference at the outdoor table of a café in Regent's Park so she could smoke. A summer storm was brooding and the air was sullen and oppressive.

'Chantelle, we can cancel the private prosecution right now. It's your choice,' I told her gently.

'But let me just remind you that it's always darkest just before the dawn . . . If you're going to steal your neighbour's newspaper, then that's the time to do it.' Roxy gave a hearty laugh, then added, between cigarette puffs, 'Public shame constantly stops girls from pursuing rape cases. Today, it's tweets. Yesterday, it was scarlet letters branded on to their foreheads. But my profound view on the subject is . . . *Bugger those bastards!'*

'Mother, you're chainsmoking. Slow down,' I chastised her. 'I doubt the nurse will be all that understanding when you tell her you didn't realize you were in a non-smoking lung-cancer unit.'

'The thing is,' she puffed away, ignoring me, 'why should those vile shits get away with it? They have the sexual compassion of a praying mantis.'

'Chanty?' Phyllis coaxed, resting her pikelet pile of chins on her hand and looking into the terrified eyes of her granddaughter. 'It's up to you, pet. I'll stand by you whatever, for ever. You know that.'

The once-pretty girl was now so pale, thin and bedraggled with worry that if she went into the House of Horrors she'd come out with a job offer. 'What more can they do to me?' the teenager said desolately.

The summer storm broke. Pelting rain slammed into the soil, ploughing it up like a volley of wet gunfire. The trees became a snarled wall of limbs and leaves. We sat, sheltered beneath an awning, watching the downpour. Something about the weather steeled Chantelle, and she drew herself up in her chair, adding, in a perfect imitation of my mother's Aussie accent, *'Bugger those bastards.'*

Roxy looked as though she wanted to run down the road doing the click-heeled dance from *The Wizard of Oz*. 'That's the spirit! And you don't have to face your attackers in court. We can have screens. Or you can testify by video link, which is just like watching the telly . . .'

'Only it's not as effective,' I explained, my invisible lawyer's wig already jammed on to my head. 'The jury thinks it looks shifty. It's much more effective if you can look the jury in the eye. If you feel up to it?'

'The police have already proved that the phone footage of your rape has been doctored and is therefore inadmissible, so it can't be shown in court. Which is one less humiliation to endure,' Roxy added.

'I wanna stand up to 'em. Face to face. I'm no coward!' Chantelle uttered these fighting words in a childish lilt, all big eyes and innocent expression.

'We have all the evidence – the forensics, your testimony, the prior records of the thugs who attacked you . . . And we have you, Tilly . . .' Roxy rallied. 'As everyone knows, a jury is a group of twelve people summoned at random to decide who has the better barrister. And we have the best barrister in London. What could possibly go wrong?'

My indomitable mother believes there are no fiascos, only opportunities. I, on the other hand, tend to believe there are only opportunities for fresh fiascos. Her sentiments about me were so honeysweet they could be poured on a crumpet. But I knew that the case would be hard and that I would need to draw on all my strengths to win it. Which is why I went to bed with the only confectionery left in the house – a packet of cooking chocolate. And why I was sitting up beyond the witching hour, silently devouring it.

22

The Scales of Injustice

'Oh, hello.' The female lawyer who stole my husband had a voice like cold water and breath like peppermint. With her pale skin, blonde hair and icy expression, Petronella resembled a warrior princess in an Icelandic saga. Today, her golden mane was strangled back into a tight bun. The flesh of her face was pumped up with fillers, which made her cheekbones look high and prominent but also pulled her mouth upwards into a mirthless smile. She was alighting from my husband's purloined Porsche outside Southwark Crown Court.

'Terribly hot, isn't it,' she said, through lips that were a slash of glossy pink. 'No air-conditioning in court either, can you believe it? At least it won't be a long trial. Rape trials usually collapse. At least they do if I'm defending,' she added, with a smug note of certainty.

When I realized Petronella was representing the two rapists, I tried to keep my gaze absolutely neutral and unperturbed. September had turned into an Indian summer. The wind was blowing like a hair-dryer on high and my temper was running hotter. I followed her into the crusty, dusty Crown Court building without speaking. It was only when we reached the robing room that I managed to say, through lips that didn't feel like my own, 'So, how is my husband?'

Her tight, serrated smile was like an oyster, milky-white and sharp as a razor, made for making cutting remarks. 'Oh, he pampers me like a princess. Although you know what? It's tiring sometimes, being beautiful. Not Stephen of course, but other people presume I'm too pretty to be intelligent. I wish I could make myself less attractive . . . So tell me' – she looked me up and down – 'how do *you* do it, Matilda?'

I stared at my old college rival as she adjusted her robes. Steve always said that I didn't 'make the most of myself'. Which is true. I invariably do my make-up in the rear-vision mirror at traffic lights or bumping along on the Tube, a technique which takes fifteen seconds tops. A swipe of rouge, a lick of mascara, a dab of lippy and, if I really want to impress and the lights are red for long enough for me not to take my eye out, a line of kohl pencil. I did go the extra make-up mile on my wedding day, with a little foundation and eye shadow. But I usually get by on a winning smile and charisma.

The perfectly coiffured and coutured Petronella, however, made me feel I should get my mirrors insured. She swept from the robing room. I trailed, flabbergasted, behind her. When Roxy bumped into the Piranha in Prada walking into the court room, my mother's bouffant puffed up around her head like a cobra's hood.

'How can a woman defend a rapist?' Roxy said to me, loud enough to be heard on the Mir space station. 'So much for sisterly solidarity, eh? A case of Hear No Feminism, See No Feminism, Speak No Feminism.'

'She's hungry for success at any cost. Mind you, it's the only thing she is hungry for,' I marvelled, holding my stomach in. 'Have you seen how thin she is?' Yes, I'm a feminist, but I would have killed there and then for some support hose.

'Are you sure she's actually human?' I asked my mother.

'Apart from the drinking blood, hanging upside down to go to sleep and sucking the souls out of newborn babies, you mean?' My mother poured me a lemon-balm-and-camomile-infused tea made from home-grown flowers which she'd brought in a hipflask. But not even a medically induced coma could calm my nerves now.

The usher brought the court to order and the judge entered.

The judge was old – Galapagos Island-turtle old. His lips, surrounding lettuce-green teeth, looked like two slugs copulating. When he spoke, his worm-white jowls quivered and the way he sat at the bench, all straight-backed and aloof, reminded me of a recently installed dictator. After the jury was sworn in, he clasped his hands together and nodded towards me. Silence erupted. A deafening silence. Giving evidence in a criminal trial is daunting. When the witness is a teenager asked to provide graphic detail in public about sexual offences committed against her by numerous men in front of a room full of strangers, it's the equivalent of entering a lion's den. It was my job to make sure Chantelle wasn't torn limb from limb and eaten alive.

I glanced at Phyllis in the public gallery. In the weeks leading up to the case, Phyllis had become a woman who subsisted on a diet of anxiety, unleavened by the smallest crumb of joy. She sat perched on the edge of her seat, her hands clenching and unclenching. Only Roxy appeared unperturbed. She blew me a big, juicy kiss which was the sign to launch into proceedings.

Despite the fact that my anxieties were so enormous they

could be awarded National Park status, I made a strong opening address to the jury, outlining the facts of Chantelle's brutal rape. I then called the sixteen-year-old to the witness box, where I proceeded to draw the story out from her as gently and discreetly as possible. Chantelle's fidgeting hands reminded me of the terrified beating of an insect's wing.

The rape tableau had played ceaselessly in my mind for months, on a spool. When I asked Chantelle whether she knew the men who'd raped her, she described them perfectly, without a glance in the direction of her assailants, stating in a clear voice their names as Stretch and Bash, and adding that they were well known on the estate.

The accused, sitting rigid in the dock, registered a look of innocence that was so contrived it was hilariously parodic. The jury seemed less critical, possibly because this was the new and improved version of the men I'd first met. Bash, the lean and mean one, was still muscled like a fighting dog but had cropped his hair into a buzz cut, as though on day release from a Mormon prayer meeting. Stretch had removed his suit jacket in the heat. His chest appeared to have been covered in superglue and rolled in black hairs. Nestling there, amid the foliage – in fact, highlighted by the darkness of the undergrowth – was a large Christian cross. This ploy was as subtle as a fart in a space suit, but could possibly sway one or two of the more gullible Catholic jurors.

When it was Petronella's turn to cross-examine Chantelle, she started softly. In an effort to charm the jury and disarm the teenager, her voice, which normally held the hauteur of a sequestered duchess, all rounded vowels and clipped 't's, was suddenly as cloying and tangy as clear honey. I could sense the jurors warming to her, totally unaware that Petronella was the type of person who would make steak tartare out of endangered species.

As I'd predicted, it wasn't long before she began to ask Chantelle about how she'd been dressed on the night in question, leading the girl into accepting that perhaps she dressed 'older than her age' and wore make-up and fashions 'more appropriate to a woman in her twenties'.

I immediately interjected. 'Can't you smell that whiff of brimstone, people?' is what I wanted to shout to the jury, but I said instead, 'What bearing does this have on the case? Should all girls lock themselves away and wear chastity belts because males are not expected to monitor and control their behaviour?'

'Your Honour,' Petronella purred, 'Wearing provocative clothing is like a bank storing all its cash by the door.' She went on to draw a parallel between foolish people who leave their laptops on the back seats of their car.

'I'm sorry, Your Honour, but that infers that Chantelle wanted to be raped. That she "asked for it" . . . Let's compare that to murder, shall we? No one ever thinks "Maybe the murder victim wanted to die. Perhaps it was a consensual death."'

The jury tittered and the judge tightened up the gristle that passed for his lips. He tsked his tongue and sighed at my interruption, but reluctantly asked Petronella to desist in her line of questioning on the plaintiff's attire.

'Rape isn't always rape, though, is it, Chantelle? Consensual sex that gets out of hand is a long way off being snatched off the street or systematically violated. Did you lead them on? Not make yourself clear? Change your mind too late? Are you a victim, or just a naughty girl doing grown-up things you bitterly regret?'

'No!' Chantelle gasped.

I glared at Petronella, disgusted. Clearly, the woman needed to go to the vet to get her claws trimmed. Why wasn't the judge stopping this barrage of commentary? The man must be wearing headphones under his wig. I tried to inter-ject once more, but he silenced me with his hand.

'Go on,' he encouraged the Piranha in Prada. What a shame it wasn't an American court, I thought, so I could make rude remarks about his tiny gavel . . . or preferably use it as a meat tenderizer and pulverize him into pâté.

'Yes, there was sexual activity, but it was not of my clients' doing, was it, Chantelle? Despite them being older and stronger than you, you might say it was forced upon *them*, wasn't it? Because you are not a Little Miss Muffet, are you? Indeed, you have quite a lot of experience, haven't you? Isn't it true that you and your friends refer to each other as SB1 and SB2 and SB3, etc. Would you mind telling the jury what that stands for?'

Chantelle looked horrified. 'It's a joke,' she spluttered. 'We call each other that for a laugh.'

'Call each other what, Miss O'Carroll?'

Chantelle's face flickered and tensed. 'Slut Bag 1, Slut Bag 2,' she whispered.

And I was up on my feet again. 'Rape is the crime, not facetious texting to friends.' My angry words clanged around the court room like traffic. But Petronella insisted on her line of attack.

'And would you be so kind, Chantelle, as to clarify for the jury if this is you, twerking?'

I'd had enough. I demanded the court be cleared while I made a legal argument to the judge to prevent this brutal line of questioning. But pouting Petronella, whose eyelash-batting average would rival Donald Bradman's, effortlessly smoothed all her requests past the drooling lech. Why couldn't the old fool see that Petronella is good at flirting, the way a shark is good at being predatory?

After the jury filed back in, he permitted the defence to show the grainy phone footage of Chantelle in teeny shorts and a bra top, performing a Miley Cyrus-type dance involving rump-shaking gyrations during which she rubbed her posterior up against boys on some dancefloor. The judge, bushy eyebrows bristling, asked for clarification.

'Twerking, Your Honour, is a sexually suggestive dance move from Jamaican dance-hall culture. I put it to you, Chantelle, that this tongue-flashing twerker we see before us in this phone footage is not the innocent your lawyer is leading us to believe you to be. Dressing older than your age, dancing provocatively, calling yourself a "slut" ... isn't it true that you were in as much control of the situation as the men? You were like a spider – predatory in all your actions, totally sexually experienced and older than your chrono-logical age.'

Chantelle's blue eyes blinked and blinked.

I made yet another gazelle-like leap to my feet. 'Objection, Your Honour. It sounds as though the defence is describing a voracious temptress. Jessica Rabbit perhaps? Samantha from *Sex and the City*? We are talking about a sixteen-year-old girl who was raped. Dancing is not against the law, I believe, unless living under the Taliban.'

Once more, the jury gave a little sympathetic titter, but Petronella continued to attack Chantelle like a wasp eats a fallen peach. She revealed medical, school and social services records. The judge glanced through the sensitive material and, showing the compassion of a piece of petrified wood, decided it was relevant. I seethed silently. As for Petronella, the woman was clearly so evil I began to wonder if she offered a 15 per cent discount to clients who'd trade in their souls.

'Is it true you approached the school nurse to ask about contraception?'

This time I leapt up so quickly I made a gazelle look sluggish. 'I object to this line of questioning! It doesn't matter if you are a sixteen-year-old virgin, a practising prostitute, or paralytic and lying naked on a bench. The blame lies with the perpetrators of rape, not with the victim. If a man takes it upon himself to rape a woman, he is guilty of breaking the law,' I clarified, restraining myself from adding that, clearly, Petronella's vile personality was her own chief contraceptive method.

The judge silenced me once more with his gnarled hand. He peered at the world beneath veined saggy eyelids, then addressed Petronella in the lock-jawed diction practised only by the Queen and a couple of inbred lords. 'Miss Willets, I don't think some of these questions are necessary. The sexual experience of the plaintiff is not relevant.'

I ground my teeth, thinking 'you old bastard'. Yes, *I* know, *you* know, and *Petronella* knows the questions aren't relevant, but now the jury has heard them they'll imagine that the wickedly wanton and experienced Chantelle has seen more ceilings than Michelangelo. Having already compared Chantelle to a sexy, grown-up, make-up-wearing spider, Petronella then posited the notion of revenge.

'You were obviously keen on having sex with these two men because they're held in high esteem on the estate. It would get you kudos with your friends. So you ran around in high heels and short skirts, trying to get their attention, positively gagging for it.'

'No.' Chantelle shook her head. In the glare of the court-room fluorescents, the tiny teenager was striving to become invisible. Her eyes flinched from everything.

'But, after having consensual sex with my clients, you were still denied membership of their posse and you wanted revenge, isn't that right? So you concocted this rape scenario.

266

I want to ask you straight out why are you telling lies?'

'I'm not telling lies.' Chantelle's frightened blue eyes filled with tears and her face twisted up in anguish.

'The truth is, you're a compulsive liar.'

'Was you there? Was you there?' Chantelle shouted back at her. The girl's raw misery and pain was apparent to all, except Petronella.

'You're telling lies.'

'No, I'm not! Shut up! Shut up!'

'You wanted the police to bring a prosecution in this matter, didn't you? So, take the jury into your confidence – why didn't they proceed?'

'I dunno why,' she whimpered.

'Even though you were lying in hospital, unable to move after this allegedly brutal attack – you were unable to move, yes?'

'Yes.'

'I suggest that you were play-acting. I suggest that they knew you were not a reliable witness. Because you're a lying little minx, aren't you?'

I was yo-yoing up and down, making so many objections the jurors must have thought I was auditioning for a fitness video. I demanded that the prosecution stop badgering the witness. The women on the jury were also uncomfortable with the attack. They shifted in their seats and looked away. But the judge remained robotic and inflexible – think German tank invading Poland. Petronella, sensing that she was losing sympathy, changed tack.

'Perhaps you're not lying. Perhaps you just can't remember the details because you were high on drugs. Your mother is a drug-addicted prostitute currently in prison for drug smuggling, is that right?'

Chantelle gave an almost imperceptible nod. Her face was

a blur of misery. I looked at the judge. I could not believe he was not going to reprimand Petronella. With his ancient-tortoise overbite and shoulder-length ear hair, he was clearly too old to be allowed to operate heavy machinery – like a law book.

'Your Honour, there's a matter of law.' I was up on my feet once more. This court case was becoming so aerobic I was practically hyperventilating. 'I'm afraid the jury will have to leave the court room again.'

I watched the jury file past me with Petronella's question still ringing in their ears. Once the court room was cleared, my oleaginous opponent immediately apologized.

'I'm so sorry, Your Honour. I got carried away,' she simpered, all moist pout and batting lash. 'I shouldn't have asked that question.' Petronella was putting on such a show for the judge, she might as well have done some jazz hands.

The 'impartial' judge, who made lip farts when he disagreed with anything I said – which was everything – responded by giving Petronella a verbal pat on the head. 'No harm done. The jury will be told to put that thought out of their minds,' he concluded, proving that he was the only living brain donor in world history, because the damage was already done. When the jury returned five minutes later, despite the judge's instruction to strike that comment from their collective consciousness, I could feel suspicious glances directed at this daughter of a convicted felon.

The defence continued its hackneyed attack. 'These young men are the real victims here,' Petronella asserted. 'Because isn't it true, young lady, that this was merely consensual sex that just got a bit rough?'

This time I jumped up as if I'd been bitten on the backside by a bullet. 'Are you seriously implying that this little girl egged on these two poor, vulnerable, grown men? Yes, because there's nothing a beautiful, bright young girl wants more than to be gang-banged by two thugs on a cold, dog-faeces-riddled stairwell.' I wanted to shout, *'Look at them! Both men are so ugly, when they were born the doctor slapped their parents'* – although this was a difficult concept to get across using only my eyebrows. But I could definitely feel a shifting of opinion in our direction. Despite the judge's bias, the majority of the laser-eyed jury were not wearing rat-bag filters on their glasses.

Still, a lawyer learns to be fluent in body language, and I intuited that, thanks to Petronella's insinuations, three or four jurors were clearly of the opinion that Chantelle possessed what Portia's male classmates called 'margarine legs', i.e. easily spread. And even though it shouldn't, it would cloud their judgement on her rape.

Finally, it was time for my re-examination. I breathed a sigh of relief. This was my chance to recoup.

I immediately got Chantelle to explain that, yes, she's a normal, fun-loving teenage girl who likes to wear high heels and short skirts but that she had never had sex prior to the attack. I took her through the grim and gruesome rape in all its heart-wrenching detail, providing medical evidence of her injuries.

Sometimes in court, it's best to eschew virtuoso verbal high-wire acts and keep it simple. 'Chantelle, were you raped?' I asked gently.

'Yes,' she bleated.

'And are you telling the truth?'

'Yes.'

By the time Chantelle, wrung out and shaking, was allowed to leave the witness box, a few of the female jury members were dabbing at their eyes. Despite all the bullying, the tiny teenager hadn't given up. There were still small corners of hope in her, like air pockets in a ship that was going down.

Petronella opened her case and called for the defendants. Roxy snickered loudly when both men promised to tell the truth. She laughed even louder when they continued to claim their innocence. The jury's body language had also turned hostile. Petronella set about dismissing Chantelle's injuries as the side effects of playfully rough sex, but her words were just running into each other like raindrops down a window-pane. I turned to see how Phyllis was coping. A glimmer of optimism had seeped into her eyes like a timid guest.

In my cross-examination of the pair, I took apart their characters before moving on to specifics. 'Rape has become a rite of passage for many gang members, hasn't it? I put it to you that you deliberately went after Chantelle because she refused to succumb to peer pressure. Because she wouldn't give you a "a shiner", which is the term your posse use for forced fellatio. Then you left her beaten and broken, with a bruised and bleeding vagina and the words "Dirty bitch" and "Wash this" scrawled, by you, on her abdomen. This was my client's welcome to womanhood. And you inflicted this upon her, didn't you?'

The icing on my argument was to enlist a handwriting expert to confirm the high probability that the words inked on to Chantelle's abdomen indicated the writing style of one of the defendants, a clever ploy Petronella hadn't anticipated.

By the time the brow-beaten defendants skulked out of the witness box, I was mentally tweaking my closing address, which would convince the jury to bring in a guilty verdict and send these rapists off to prison. Then, all of a sudden, Petronella announced that she'd like to call a final witness. I glanced up, surprised. As the redhead swept into the court room, my mind whirred and stopped and whirred and stopped like a broken clock. Where had I seen her before? It took me a moment to recognize the woman, because this time she had her clothes on. The last time I'd seen Nurse Baddington, she'd been cavorting around Jack's living room in her lingerie. After she had sworn on the bible and been introduced to the jury as the nurse attending Chantelle on the night of the alleged rape, Petronella asked if it was true that Chantelle had disappeared from the hospital between the hours of nine and ten.

'Yes,' she said.

Life had just dropped a saucepan lid on a hard-tiled kitchen floor. The impact rattled around my cranium, clanging. How could they know this when I had the hospital record? Jack must have quizzed the nurse during pillow talk, discovered that Chantelle had gone missing and slipped the information to the defence team. But I couldn't comprehend it. Could Jack really be so vengeful and malicious as to sabotage Chantelle's case? It was as though I were under-water in some old, heavy diving suit and the thought was being piped laboriously down to me, thoughts instead of oxygen. *Jack!*

'Is there a hospital record of this?' Petronella probed the nurse.

'No. The record went missing. Presumed stolen.'

The room pitched around me like a rolling ship. How could I ever have trusted the man? Beside me, Chantelle screwed up her eyes as if in pain.

The judge's grey, disordered eyebrows were working over-time to show his curiosity. 'Would you be so kind as to explain the relevance of this, please?' he asked Petronella courteously.

Petronella's black eyes glittered. She went on to explain how Chantelle's grandmother had been tried in an attempted-murder case, in which she admitted taking a firearm around to the residence of the two accused men and firing at their genitals, seriously injuring one and grazing the other. 'I put it to the court now that the alleged "victim", the alleged "beaten", "broken" and "bruised" *victim* in this case, got up off her alleged "sick bed" and trotted down to the estate with her grandmother to point out the men upon whom she wanted revenge.'

A murmur of disapproval ran through the jury. The tiny girl beside me was flushed and trembling. I turned to see Phyllis: her face was paralysed. After a few more perfunctory queries to the nurse, the judge called Chantelle back to the witness box. A faint shudder coursed through her etiolated frame.

'Do I have to?' she mewled.

My heart shrank like a raisin. I nodded.

Petronella gave my client a cold, hungry stare – the stare of a raptor about to seize a rabbit. Her voice was sinuous and exact; the richness of her tone oozed confidence. 'Did you leave the hospital on the night in question, to point out these two men to your grandmother?' She indicated her clients, who were the picture of outraged innocence. 'The men upon whom you wanted revenge, because, after having sex with them, they didn't let you join their posse and chilled you out?'

Chantelle's pale skin was so taut with tension it seemed stretched across her skull and nailed behind her ears.

'Let me remind you that you are under oath.' Petronella's voice set my teeth on edge. It was falsely cheery, her smile as sharp and sweet as icing. 'Did you leave the hospital with your granny?'

Chantelle's face froze and the words came out slowly and

haltingly. 'Yes,' she said quietly. 'I didn't want 'er to attack the wrong men.'

I suddenly felt as though I were walking on the moors, had lost my footing, and was sliding down towards the bog, clutching at tangles of gorse and weeds which came out of the chalky soil in my hands.

'So, you're not quite the innocent little victim portrayed by the prosecution, are you? Yes, you're playing innocent now. But you incited your grandma to assault these men upon whom you wanted revenge because they wouldn't accept you into their gang. When they blew you out, you got your grandma to blow off their testicles.'

'No! No! It weren't like that!'

Petronella, going in for the kill, was as excited as a barracuda in a shoal of fat fish. 'You are prepared to lie to this jury. I asked you quite specifically whether you were unable to move. You told this court you were unable to move, didn't you?'

'Gran! I want my gran!'

A male member of the jury who'd looked quite sympathetic earlier now lifted his eyebrows high in fastidious disdain. A female juror made a moue of disgust.

When it was my turn to re-examine, I tried to cast the event in a better light, but Chantelle was traumatized, dazed, a glazed look in her eye. 'When your grandmother, heart-broken and furious, told you she was determined to confront the men who had raped you and was taking your grandpa's old hunting gun with her for protection . . . how did you feel?'

Shattered, the pain-racked little girl said nothing.

'Did you know how your grandma was feeling?'

Chantelle stared at the floor, stonily.

'Was she scared?'

Silence.

'Were you frightened they would turn the gun on your grandma?' My words went crashing and rattling around the court room like trapped birds.

'You were still really hurt – bleeding and covered in bruises, when you staggered out of your hospital bed to protect your grandma, isn't that right?'

The judge barked a command down to me. 'Stop leading the witness.'

'Were you in pain when you left the hospital?'

Turning slightly, I noticed that Chantelle's attackers were now directly in her line of vision. Bash was twitching excitedly, like a spider. Chantelle had hung her head to avoid their gaze, but it was making her look shifty in the eyes of the jury. Then the poor girl began rocking. When she gave a high-pitched gulp, I knew that I had to let the child go. We would have to rely on my closing speech. It was all we had left.

As soon as Chantelle limped out of the witness box, I started talking. But I could feel the case slipping away from me, like thinning ice cracking beneath my feet. I talked faster, accelerating like mad to save us all from drowning. I described the men in the dock as wolves in a lambing shed, prowling the estate and preying on girls, exploiting them sexually, filming the abuse, then blackmailing them into working for their gangs as drug couriers or prostitutes. I explained that if the jury found the defendants not guilty, it would discourage other victims from coming forward and allow rapists to attack with impunity. I threw everything I could at the jury before the judge could stop me. I wove in the terrible murder and domestic-violence statistics which proved that women were runners up in the human race. I bemoaned the fact that rape had gone mainstream. How pub crawls and parties now have themes such as Rappers and Slappers or Geeks and Sluts.

Cases are tried before a live jury – at first. When I heard a juror yawn and saw another rest his face on his hand as though about to go to sleep, I realized I was losing them, but I ploughed on. Yes, it was heavy-handed, but my only option now was to club the jury into submission. I pleaded with the jury to take a stand against violence perpetrated on innocent women, concluding with a list of the defendants' prior misdemeanours – a list which made *War and Peace* look like a haiku . . . But then a couple of jurors coughed, and that was when I knew it was time to sit down and shut up.

In Petronella's final speech, she depicted Chantelle as a cold-blooded slattern, hell bent on premeditated revenge because the men she had seduced did not reward her with gang membership. 'Was Chantelle blameless? . . . Can one hand clap, ladies and gentlemen?' She painted the sixteen-year-old as an arch-manipulator, pressing her befuddled grandmother into committing a murderous revenge on her behalf. 'Ladies and gentlemen, you've heard from a young woman who we say is unstable and has not had the benefits of a proper upbringing.'

After this 'the apple doesn't fall far from the tree' innuendo, she ran the whole clichéd 'rape accusations ruining the lives of innocent men' line. She spoke as rapidly as a sewing machine, threading words together, stitching Chantelle up. She used the phrase 'cried rape' over and over, making Chantelle out to be a scheming harridan who used her sexuality as a weapon to hurt men. I was used to defending, not prosecuting. It was agonizing not to have the last word. I had to tie my tongue in knots to stop from interjecting. All I could do was grind my molars into a pulp.

'Members of the jury . . .' Petronella had the face of a news anchor trying to look serious while reading from the autocue about the death of someone they have never heard of. 'The two men accused here today may seem somewhat unsavoury, but no man should be put through the horror of a false rape allegation. You must be sure of guilt beyond any reasonable doubt. Also remember that you're dealing with a woman who's been found to be lying. She said under oath that she was raped and so hurt that she lay in hospital, unable to move. But in reality she left the hospital after coercing her poor, addled grandma into taking her to the estate to sort out the testicles of the men who had rejected her.'

Roxy's mouth twitched and then set into a grimace. That was when I understood that we were going to lose the case.

When the judge addressed the jury, my case became the legal equivalent of flying over the Atlantic, well known for not having anything solid you can actually land on, and the pilot announcing that he had a 'minor engine problem'. The judge instructed the jury that they could not convict unless they were sure that the sex was not consensual.

The light in Phyllis's eyes was slowly extinguished.

When the jury found the defendants not guilty, the two rapist thugs whooped. Bash gave me a sign with his finger which could not be mistaken for the Vulcan symbol for 'Peace and Prosperity'.

I looked at Phyllis's suffering face. I felt misery rise up from her like steam. The not-guilty verdict began to cling to me like a chill. The deadening weight of failure settled into my body. As the court room emptied, silence pressed down like a low ceiling. Supporters gathered around Phyllis and Chantelle as if at a graveside.

Chantelle was lost in her own private torment. She gazed at me out of huge blue eyes with the peculiarly helpless, agonized expression of someone who knew it had all gone wrong but didn't really know why. All her eye make-up was washed away with crying. The vile video of her rape had gone viral, for nothing. Zilch. Nada. Sweet FA.

'I'm sorry,' I told them.

'It wasn't your fault, Tilly. The conviction rate for rapists is limbo low. We knew the odds were against us going in.'

'I should have insisted Chantelle gave video evidence . . . I was the one who talked her out of sitting behind a screen . . .'

Roxy was working hard at turning up the corners of her mouth. 'We need to change the court culture. Judges need to stop that kind of aggressive cross-examination which leaves the victim in shreds.'

Countess Flirtalotsky was twanging with indignation and anger. Drawn up to her full six-foot-one, stick-thin height, she resembled a malignant tuning fork. I presumed she was angry about how much my defeat would cost her, but then she said, 'Raped by men, then raped again by the judicial system. You'd get a fairer trial in fucking Russia, dah-ling!'

Phyllis's face had slammed shut. Her eyes fixed on something I could not see. 'I'm more glad than ever that I shot those scum in the nuts now,' she said bitterly.

My heart felt full of sludge. 'Oh, Phyllis,' I said sadly. 'It's never right to take the law into your own hands. We would have won if that nurse hadn't turned up.' But Phyllis was no longer listening. Useless defiance is what remains after everything else has been scoured away. The last thing she wanted, I knew, was sympathy. And so I said no more. I had to get some fresh oxygen into my lungs. I left the court, fogged with gloom.

The day had darkened, with rainstorms gathering. The sun suddenly came out from behind a grey cloud. It flickered briefly, then retreated back under cover, dispirited by what it had glimpsed below. There was no breeze. I saw flags on a high building hanging limp against their poles. I knew just how they felt. I stared across a dirty road at brightly coloured advertisements of products I would never buy. A woman thrust a flyer at me. 'Jesus wants to know you,' she said.

'Yeah, well, I don't want to know him – not at the moment, thanks very much.'

Then I saw Nathaniel striding across the busy road towards me. 'Sorry to miss the trial. I had to help source bail for a re-offender. You look like hell,' he said.

'At this point, hell seems like a major improvement over a life in the law.'

'Oh, no.' He screwed up his eyes, as if in pain. 'What happened?'

The words I had to find felt heavy and sour in the back of my throat. 'I lost the case . . .'

'Oh, Matilda. It wasn't your fault.'

I silenced him with my hand. 'Nathaniel, thanks, but there really is nothing you can say right now to make me feel better.' In truth, my confidence level had sunk so low, you'd need a pressurized mini-sub to find it.

'Come home with me. I'll cook you some supper and rub your feet and pour you some wine. There are times when it is imperative not to stay sober. Funerals, weddings, and after losing a trial. Not to be drunk in these circumstances indicates you are either a Baptist, a Muslim or an alien.'

'No, thanks. I think I just need to use my body as a repository for chocolate for a while.'

'What went wrong?'

'Jack Cassidy, that's what went wrong. He ratted me out, as revenge for beating him in Phyllis's court case. He betrayed me to the defence team. Which allowed two violent rapists to walk free.' I thought back to the time the press had massed outside our house. I'd told Jack on the phone that Phyllis and

Chantelle were at my home. Had he leaked our address?

I clearly needed to ask my mother if she had drunk during pregnancy, because falling for a monster like Jack Cassidy in the first place had to prove that I was a few neurons short of a synapse . . . And explain why failure seemed to be the only thing I was a success at.

My brilliant and mature lawyering skills became even more strikingly evident when I burst out crying and sobbed into Nathaniel's shoulder.

23

The Underworld on Top

The trouble with the future is that it's not what it used to be. That was my first thought when I woke at lunchtime the day after losing Chantelle's trial. My second thought was not to neglect the present – not when you're lying in the warm arms of a man who has spent the night adding a few new chapters to the *Kama Sutra*.

A hazy vanilla light seeped into Nathaniel's bedroom. His tall, antique-filled house was on a small Georgian square which had miraculously survived the Blitz, unscathed, when London's docklands were flattened. With St Katharine Docks to the right and Canary Wharf further downriver, the house was an architectural gem, nestled in a crook of the twisting Thames. Through the bow window the river glistened as whipped-cream clouds sailed overhead and a plane embroidered the blue sky with vapour. Sighing contentedly, I shrugged myself deeper into his embrace, close against his chest, and inhaled his strong, heady scent. When I looked up into his face, Nathaniel's smile came out like the sun.

'Breakfast in bed, m'lady?'

I took a nibble of his earlobe. 'Um, actually, I think you are my breakfast in bed.' Corny, but allowable under the Post-orgasmic Cute Phrases Lovey-dovey Clause.

'I've got to go and check in on a client, so why don't I pick up some croissants en route? I'll be back in an hour, after which I'll spoil you rotten.' He nibbled my ear now.

'You're just too good to be true, Nate. Are you sure you're not a mirage or a hologram or something?'

Nathaniel's face took on a serious cast. 'I'm only good now to make up for being bad in the past. I did some truly un-ethical things as a banker. Things I'm not proud of. I'm just trying to make amends. Speaking of which, will you come with me tonight to a charity fundraiser for Reprieve? It would be such a delight to have you on my arm. Middle Temple Hall. Seven.'

He nipped a line of kisses down my neck and I felt a volt of excitement shoot up my thighs and pulse between my legs. I stayed silent as I watched him pull on his jeans, but only because I'd totally run out of superlatives. As he lifted his strong arms to shrug on a T-shirt, his muscled stomach sucked inwards and his broad ribcage rose. His face, neck and the V-shaped triangle at the base of his throat were honey-coloured and darker than the rest of his taut torso. After he'd bounded down the wooden stairs, his biker boots beating out a rhythm on the old and worn wood, I lay in bed and thought about the marvel that was Nathaniel Cavendish.

The first time we'd been to bed together, I'd jettisoned him out the door to get back to Jack. The stupidity of it made me groan aloud. What had I been thinking? Or rather, *not* thinking. Anyone would presume I'd spent a lifetime doing sit-ups underneath parked vehicles, because the man was so damn perfect he could star as the protagonist of a Hollywood rom com. He attended charity events, helped the less fortunate, made his own bread . . . the man harvested his own honey, for God's sake.

'Bumblebees, like feisty, funny feminists, are teetering on the verge of extinction. Your numbers have dwindled alarmingly in recent years. You need nurturing and protection,' he'd said to me while kissing my hand. Not only was he attentive and concerned, he was also practical – a Swiss Army man. Handy for everything, able to mend fuses, change car tyres, open bottles with his teeth and, oh! what nifty additional extras . . . One night with him had released me from the tinnitus buzz of self-reproach after losing Chantelle's court case. I was like the donkey that had finally caught up to the stick holding the carrot. And it was time I showed my appreciation.

I threw on one of Nate's T-shirts and padded down the stairs into the kitchen. The reason I don't cook is because I don't want to go down for manslaughter. I'd only ever once attempted anything more complicated than tuna surprise . . . and had nearly fallen into the blender and made a crudité of myself. My mother loves to tell people how I once went to the corner shop and asked for a 'pinch of nutmeg' and a 'clove of crushed garlic'.

I peeked into his fridge. The fridges of most of the bachelors I know contain a few petrified lumps which could once have been chorizo, some chutney bottled during the reign of Alfred the Great and some yoghurt whose expiry date reads 'When Tyrannosaurus Rex Roamed the Earth'. But Nathaniel's fridge was groaning with gourmet delicacies. There was really no excuse not to try to concoct something.

First, I'd chop the onions. Not wanting red eyes, I rummaged through his laundry looking for swimming goggles and found a mask and snorkel. Donning this aquatic apparatus, I diced away happily. I managed to brown the onions without any major disasters, thanks to the fact that, without watering eyes, I could see what I was doing. Then I threw in some bacon. As I cracked eggs into a saucepan, I began to wonder why everybody made such a fuss of Domestic Goddesses and Gourmet Love Gods. This wasn't so hard. I was getting on with Nathaniel's kitchen like a stove on fire . . . Except for the fact, that – um . . . it was.

Roxy always jokes that I use my smoke alarm as a timer. And, today, it proved terrifyingly true. Moments later, black smoke was billowing from the hob. The tea towel I'd left too near the flame had caught fire. As I dealt with the miniature inferno, the bacon spat fat in every direction. The fire alarm in the hall made sure everybody in a ten-mile radius would know about my gastronomic faux pas. It screeched into eardrum-grating life. The high-pitched shriek was cranium-piercingly loud and toe-curlingly constant. Turning off the gas rings, I scrambled up on to a chair to prod frantically at the alarm. When I failed to silence it, I tried to detach it from its base so I could smother it in cushions or hurl it out of the window. I tugged on the contraption with all my might . . . Which proved too much might, as I was immediately show-ered in ceiling plaster. It fell around me with the soft, snuffled thud of snowflakes. But that's not all that came tumbling earthward. The hall was now intriguingly carpeted in money. Great wads of ten-, twenty- and fifty-pound notes wafted carpet-ward amidst the ceiling plaster.

I stood, shrieking smoke alarm in hand, staring in bemused shock at the impromptu windfall. When Nathaniel walked in, the moment was frozen in time: me, wearing a snorkel and goggles, covered head to toe in plaster dust, him bug-eyed with bemused disbelief.

Nathaniel took the smoke alarm from my hand and gently squeezed out the battery. The sudden silence was equally deafening. 'You're obviously as good at DIY as you are at culinary pursuits, Tilly. I take it that you always cook in a snorkel in preparation for the high-pressure hoses of the fire brigade?'

I'd forgotten about the goggles. Through perspex sockets I watched Nathaniel kick at the cash on the carpet. 'What the hell's all this?' he asked, scooping up a bundle of money. His expression hardened, and he spoke gravely. 'Bloody idiot!' His voice sounded as though he'd eaten cut glass for breakfast.

'Who?' My own voice was now as nasal as my mother's Aussie twang. I pushed the scuba-diving goggles up on to my crinkled forehead and spoke normally. 'Who are you talking about?'

'Sorry. I'm house-sitting this place for a banking mate of mine, Christopher Grayling, who went to the dark side,' he said, brushing plaster dust off my legs. 'In fact, he's the one who needs goggles and snorkel, as he really has dived into the deep end.'

'How do you mean?'

'He started doing a lot of coke. Banking mates called this place "Antarctica" – or "Snowman's Land". I got suspicious that Chris had started dealing because of the amount of cash he carried. We went to the races once and he bet £20,000 on a horse without batting an eye. Twenty thousand!' Nathaniel took my hand and helped me down from the chair. 'The problem with dealing is that if you earn lots, you have to spend lots, too, otherwise, how do you explain it to the taxman? Anyway, he eventually got caught, of course, and sent down for three years. He sits in a cell twenty-three hours a day now. I can't even send him books. And all they have in the library is Jeffrey Archer. Now that really *is* punishment! Anyway, I think you just found his secret retirement fund.'

'At least it saved you from having to eat my cooking. We'd better call the police, though.'

'Yes.' Nathaniel reached for his iPhone, then paused. 'But we have to be careful. When Chris was arrested I did wonder why the undercover unit was targeting what they call "low-hanging fruit". Why did they nab my mate instead of the kingpins at the top of the criminal tree? Some covert operations become focused on getting "heads on sticks" which means "Let's bag as many people as possible for whatever offence we can."' He picked some plaster pieces out of my hair. 'But, other times, it's because the cops in the drug squad are in on the act and taking a cut. The drug squad's notoriously corrupt. This year alone, rogue cops have siphoned off more than £1.2 million worth of drugs seized in police raids and then sold them back on the streets. We're not talking about one bad apple, but rotten-to-the-core institutionalized corruption.'

'Roxy always says that you can tell an undercover cop . . . but you can't tell him much,' I agreed.

Nathaniel's face took on a cloudy cast. He scanned the room. 'I have to be really careful about getting framed, too. Through my work, I've put a lot of noses out of joint, and made a lot of enemies.'

'How?'

'By exposing various officers, on charges ranging from rape to drug dealing . . . Giving one cop away to another cop is very dicey. The blue brotherhood and all that . . . I think the best thing is if I take this load down to Scotland Yard myself this afternoon and speak to the chief . . . But let's keep it quiet. I don't want any addicts breaking in and ransacking the joint looking for contraband or quick cash. Jesus, what a hassle. But thank you for attempting to cook for me.' His eyes sought mine. 'Although I think what really set off the alarm is the fact that I have such a smoking-hot babe in my bed.'

He leant me back against the wall and kissed my mouth. His hands were on my haunches, pulling my hips against his. He scooped me up and lay me on the carpet, there among the piles of money, and breathed along the inside of my thigh, his lips brushing the skin, each place more delicate and electric than the last.

Later, when we finally stirred and got vertical, I looked at the mounds of money around us and grinned. 'I think you've over-tipped, Nate.'

'Really? I'd say you've undercharged.' He held my hand to his lips and kissed it softly.

'But, seriously, if you're worried about the drug squad being corrupt, why don't I ring my father? He has so many friends on the force. He'll know who to trust. God knows, he's desperate to help me.'

Nathaniel gazed at me with an expression that was both tender and perplexed. 'You'd trust a man who cheated on your mother? . . . Those undercover operations had a terrible impact on the lives of innocent women. After you'd told me about Danny, I did a bit of snooping on the snoop, actually. And do you know what I discovered? Your father won an award for the best undercover infiltration of a left-wing group . . . But what are you? An embarrassing little postscript? A doggy-bag daughter? No. Better not tell him anything. Officers from those elite covert operations units inside the Met, they don't shoot straight. Some of my clients, ex-dealers – well, the Special Branch guys give them class-A drugs as bribes. I'm told they often take the drugs themselves.'

'Not Danny. I know he did some bad things in the past, but I'm convinced he's changed. The man's not just turned over a new leaf but a whole new tree.'

'I don't want to upset you, Matilda, but the truth is I saw your old man buying coke from a dealer. On my estate. Right near my office.'

My facial features rearranged themselves into the look of someone who had just been handed a jar of warm sputum. 'What? Are you sure?'

He nodded sadly. 'Yep. And I have a rule about that. Law-makers cannot be law-breakers, even if they are washed-up hasbeens.'

'You're a hundred per cent sure that it was Danny? I mean, do you know what he looks like?'

'Portia showed me some photos of him, one night when I was at your place. That's why you have to be very careful about Danny's influence on your daughter . . . I suppose you know she's still sneaking off to see him? I saw them together a number of times through the summer, around Camden. I didn't tell you before because you were so stressed preparing Chantelle's case. I just kept an eye on her for you.'

I flew across the room as though propelled by a poltergeist. I grabbed my phone and punched in Portia's number. When there was no answer, I was dressed and off out the door within minutes. *See Mother run! Hear Mother talking to herself! See Mother get down the bottle of tranquillizers! . . .*

I hailed a taxi and offered the driver a big tip to put his foot down. Careering west along the river towards Blackfriars Bridge at breakneck speed, I tried to reassure myself that Portia was okay. But I had a feeling that if I filled in a magazine quiz to see whether I was a 'good mother', I'd fail. And that I'd fail even if I *cheated*.

24

Daddy Dearest

As far as I'm aware, no parenting manual has a chapter covering how to find a missing, disobedient daughter, most likely abducted by a drug-addled, duplicitous, absentee, ex-Special Branch biological granddad.

By the time the cab turned off Farringdon Road towards King's Cross, I was wound up tighter than a Joan Rivers facelift. The windscreen wipers made a half-hearted salute at the sheets of rain which suddenly deluged the taxi. We lurched on to Euston Road, smack bang into a traffic jam. The grey highway ahead ran with molten red and green, as traffic lights changed as far as the eye could see. I swore and cursed and banged the seat, begging the driver to find a faster route.

Finally arriving outside my father's flat, I leapt out before the cab had stopped moving. After ten minutes of banging on Danny's door, his neighbour popped her head out to say that Danny had taken his granddaughter – 'a grand lass' – to the British Library, next to the Gothic towers of St Pancras.

Even though I get winded licking stamps, I sprinted the few blocks there, cutting through the graveyard of St Pancras but not even stopping to pay my respects to my heroine, Mary Wollstonecraft, buried here beneath a crooked tombstone. When I got to the library, the sun had come out again. The forecourt was dotted with buskers and tourists. Portia was easy to spot in the fray, with her high-winged collarbones and strong athletic stride. She and Danny were walking towards the ice-cream queue. I waved to her histrionically. When she saw me, she brushed her silky hair from her eyes. 'Don't do a Chernobyl and go into meltdown, Mum.'

But my anger had already reached thermo-nuclear levels. 'You are *so* grounded! Roxy and I told you to stay away from this man and you directly disobeyed us.' I reached for my daughter, but she vaulted out of my arms to Danny's side.

'He's not this *man*,' she exploded back at me. 'He's my grandfather.' They both faced me now, side by side. At this close proximity, there was no denying their physical similarities – the blond features and lithe, wiry frames. 'Why can't I hang out with him? We get on great.'

Danny beamed at my daughter, who smiled back – which only infuriated me more. I was overwhelmed with conflicting emotions. On the one hand, here was the father I'd yearned for all my life. But, on the other hand, here was just one more man in my life whom I couldn't trust.

'Because he's a drug user, for one thing,' I spat out.

Danny whipped around to face me. 'What?' He spluttered into laughter. 'We're getting ice creams. I'm definitely addicted to those!'

'Don't try to fob me off, Danny. A good friend of mine works with offenders. He told me he saw some of his boys selling you coke on the Tony Benn Estate.'

'That's complete crap. Not only have I never set foot on that estate, I would never do drugs . . . Mainly because there's always a chance you'll miscalculate the dosage and just end up in a vegetative state ... or running for parliament.' He winked at Portia, who disintegrated into a squall of giggles. She was clearly already under his spell ... the same spell that had so beguiled my mother. I probed my feelings for this man, who called himself my father, in the same tentative way you poke your tongue into a loose tooth. All I felt was pain and irritation.

'I don't want you coming anywhere near Portia or me again, is that clear?'

'Matilda, I'm your father.' He gazed at me, hurt. 'I wouldn't lie to you about this.'

'You're no father to me. Why should I take any notice of you? You ran off before I was born, remember?'

Danny held on to my daughter with both hands, gripping her shoulders as if she were a human steering wheel. 'This little girl – and you, too, of course, Tilly – mean everything to me.' He sounded like a tyre going flat. 'My life was turned to shit by the police force, too, you know. My own happiness – straight down the plughole. I've been fighting the world for so long – skirmishes, wars, clandestine operations behind enemy lines ... bring it on! Yet all the time I've been on the run from my own shadow. Then to find out I have a family ... The pure and simple joy of that! All I want is to be a small, supportive part of it. As Portia's own dad's done a runner, it's important for her to have some male influence in her life, don't you reckon?'

I felt the body blow as his words impacted. Stephen had abandoned me, just as my father had. Was it any wonder that I was constantly in HMS relationships that hit icebergs only to realize too late that nobody had told me there was a BYO-lifeboat policy? A thought struck me then, like a giant gong. The psychology of the scenario was so obvious it could have been neon-lit with airport runway lights, but somehow I'd missed it until now.

'I would never have married Stephen if I hadn't been searching for a father figure,' I blurted. I gave Danny the kind of look usually reserved for a strangely vacant person you see sauntering into a fast-food restaurant wielding a chainsaw. 'But you don't have to worry about male role models for Portia. I'm going out with a good, decent man now. Nathaniel is honourable and dependable.' Drawing on my fine command of diplomacy, I then added, 'He's the one who told me not to trust you. We found a stash of drug money today. I wanted to call you to deal with it . . .'

'Huh? What drug money?' His eyes flashed on to high alert. 'Of course I'll deal with it for you.'

'Ah – I don't think so! Nathaniel reckons you've told enough white lies to ice a wedding cake. He's taken the drug money to Scotland Yard himself. You see, he's not a double dealer, like you. Nathaniel's exactly the sort of father figure Portia needs in her life . . . Come on, darling.'

Danny took hold of my arm. 'Matilda, I'm not the type to get gravel rash on the knees from grovelling. But I will if that's what it takes for you not to shut me out of your lives,' he said dejectedly.

I felt my resolve wavering but drew on my inner Roxy. 'I think it's best if you stay away from us. I don't know how else to say it – except with a stun gun. Now let's go.' I tried to grab my daughter's hand, but she squirmed out of my grasp.

Portia stormed ahead of me in the direction of Euston station. All the way back to Camden on the Tube, she refused to speak. The old teenage silent treatment frays a mother's nerves more than Chinese water torture. When we finally got home I told Roxy what had happened. She reiterated her orders that Portia was not to let Danny into her life.

'Really?' My thirteen-year-old daughter groaned, then looked from one to the other of us disparagingly. '*This* is my gene stock? Ugh!' She then executed the clichéd teen stomp up the stairs to her room and the requisite door slam. The way things were going my daughter would soon just disappear into her room and I wouldn't see her again until she got her driver's licence and needed to borrow my car.

'I'm just wondering how I gave birth to this soap opera?' Roxy sighed. 'Drink? I think we both could use one.'

I glanced at my watch. 'Oh, God, I'm so late. I promised to go with Nate to Middle Temple Hall. It's a charity fundraiser dinner for Reprieve, to get people off death row and out of Guantanamo Bay.'

'Gee, try not to have too much fun in one go, will you?' my mother commented drolly.

I threw on a black cocktail dress and did my make-up in my normal studied fashion – at traffic lights on the journey in, only nearly taking my eye out three or four times. I sweet-talked my way past the Middle Temple porters and drove through the ancient wooden gates, jerking to a halt outside the Temple Church. During my pupillage, I would often take quiet refuge here in the same place where the Knights Templar, a brotherhood of noblemen, met to organize protection for pilgrims travelling to the Holy Land in the twelfth century. But it was a quiet sanctuary no longer. The exquisite building, with its medieval choir, is the only Gothic church to have withstood both the 1666 Great Fire and the Blitz . . . but was now taking a beating from the boisterous onslaught of Dan Brown fans pursuing secret *Da Vinci Code* signs in baseball-capped packs.

I was so distracted by the noisy, exclaiming American tourists and my own heels clackety-clacking over the cobblestones towards the grand Middle Temple Hall that I didn't notice the figure lurking in the gloaming by the courtyard fountain until his voice looped out of the darkness in my direction.

'Hard to believe I'm at another fundraiser. Since taking the post of Senior Treasury Counsel, all I bloody well seem to do is attend charity functions so Third World people can learn to sauté tsetse flies or knit their own wells, or whatever. I can't imagine there's anything left to save . . . Except my love life, of course.'

It was quite a vertiginous experience, unexpectedly bumping into the man I had once thought I loved, leaning nonchalantly against a wall in an elegantly tailored tux.

Every time I thought of Jack's betrayal it was as if a slathering wolverine were trying to claw its way out of my abdomen via my oesophagus . . . Which is why it took me a moment to kickstart my vocal cords. 'How can you just stand there, bantering inanely, after what you did to me and my client? Why don't you listen to your conscience for once? But then again . . . why take advice from strangers?' I bristled.

Jack shrugged with his eyebrows and drew back on his cigar. 'I have no idea what you're talking about.'

'The only person who knew that Chantelle left the hospital to go with her granny to point out the rapists was that red-headed nurse . . . The one you were dating. The one I saw semi-naked in your house. She obviously told you – and you told the defence team.'

'The nurse with red hair? . . .' I could see him mentally flicking through his romantic Rolodex. 'From the Royal Free? That was nothing more than a fling. I was on the rebound from your rejection, as I recall.'

I had been hoping to conclude our conversation with a minimum of broken bones, but that was looking highly unlikely. 'Why should I ever believe anything you say to me,

Jack? You lied to me at uni and you're lying to me now.'

Jack looked at me as though I were a non-alcoholic organic beetroot juice instead of the pint of Guinness he'd ordered. 'Hey, I may sometimes sink low, but I'm not a complete snake.'

'You're lower than a snake's prostate!'

'I am not lying.' His stare bored into me like a drill.

'What I can't forgive is that you acted out of revenge. Revenge for me winning the case against you. To satisfy your pathetic male ego, you'd let two rapists go free. I mean, what kind of monster are you?'

Jack's fury was tight and monumental. 'The kind who doesn't have to stand here and be character assassinated.' He stubbed out his half-smoked cigar, but he was still smouldering. 'I know you so well, Matilda. And this is the side of you I like least. Don't bother talking to me again until you've taken off your spurs and dismounted from that ridiculous high horse of yours. Till then, it's probably best if you just gallop off into the sanctimonious sunset and leave me the hell alone.' He turned on his designer heels and strode into the Middle Temple Hall. I fumed silently for a moment. I then felt an overwhelming urge to demand a little R-E-S-P-E-C-T, Aretha Franklin style.

The ornately carved, cavernous banquet hall has seen a lot of drama. Literally. Shakespeare's *Twelfth Night* was first performed here and The War of the Roses kicked off in the pretty gardens below. The little theatrics which were about to unfold were minuscule by comparison, but massive to me. Following Jack into the grand hall, I watched him sidle up to a statuesque woman who was clearly waiting for him. She had honey-blond hair and no discernible underwear. Just as she was poised to take a nibble of her goat's cheese crostini and mainline a Caipirinha, I seized her arm.

'Be careful when he pats you on the back, lady, because he's actually drawing a bull's eye.'

A passing waiter with a rictus smile proffered a tray of wobbling drinks. Again channelling my inner Roxy, I took a full glass of red wine and hurled it at my nemesis. It stained Jack's white shirt like blood.

'You see? You obviously don't know me so well, otherwise you would have seen that coming.'

I obviously held the World Indoor Record for Bad Bloke Selection. But those days were over. I hurried to find Nathaniel in the tuxedoed throng. As Roxy always said, the only way to find heaven is to back as fast as you can away from hell.

25

The Senile Delinquent

'Do you ever wonder why people take an instant dislike to you, Danny? . . . Because it saves time.' This is what I said to my biological father when I found him loitering outside Portia's school the following afternoon. 'What the hell are you doing here?'

'Apparently, your ex-wanker-banker mate Nathaniel's not all he seems.' Danny said this gravely, as though he were disclosing that he had a brain tumour and two weeks to live.

'Oh, like *you*, you mean?' An awkward membrane had grown between us. He looked at his feet and clenched his jaw.

Much to Portia's fury, I'd decided to collect her from school every day, to make sure she came straight home and didn't end up on an unscheduled Danny detour. Portia called this arrangement 'house arrest'. She'd threatened to contact Human Rights Watch to complain of inhumane treatment. Needless to say, since Danny had come on the scene, mother–daughter relations were rivalling the hostilities of two Balkan republics.

'I've been checking up on this Nathaniel of yours. He got

the sack from his bank over suspicions of insider trading. Did he tell you that?'

'Wait. You're spying on my boyfriend?!' I asked, aghast. 'Tell me, with a lobotomy, is there pain afterwards?' Sarcasm seemed the only appropriate response – or perhaps beating him senseless with a tome entitled 'Privacy Law for Dummies'.

'There's more . . . I fed his licence-plate information to a cop mate. He ran a country-wide computer check and found one – and only one – sea-green Ducati Desmosedici motorbike.'

'How do you know what kind of bike Nathaniel rides? Oh my God! You've been stalking him as well? . . . I've got a good idea. Why don't you go and test the resilience of his motor-bike wheel *with your head*! Roxy was so right about you.'

'The bike belongs to some jerk who's doing time for drug dealing.'

'His name's Chris Grayling. Nathaniel's told me all about him,' I replied coldly. 'He's an ex-colleague. Nate's minding his house while he's inside. Not that it's any of your business. A lot of his banking friends went to the dark side. That's what triggered Nathaniel's epiphany.'

'An unexplained lavish lifestyle is the key to identifying criminality, kiddo. Yachts, Porsches, holiday houses . . . coupled with no legitimate source of income. Where does your lover boy's money come from, do you reckon? How does he have enough dosh to set up this charity of his? I've done a bit of snooping and—'

'Snooping?! You have no right to snoop on me or any of my friends! Um, I don't know how to break it to you, but you're not an undercover agent any more, remember? What you *are* is a senile delinquent!'

'We're talking exotic holidays, a home in the Caribbean, expensive artworks, a luxury car . . . How does he afford all that, this do-gooder of yours?' Danny produced an iPad and tried to show me the pictures and photos he'd sourced and filed.

'Listen, Sherlock, you can put away your Holmes hat. Nathaniel worked in the city, for a decade. Have you heard of banker bonuses? Not just that, but his family's wealthy.'

'Yeah, well, his accent does make him a cut above your average criminal. At least he'll say "excuse me" before he mugs you. And "thank you" when he steals all your bling.'

'Okay, I've had enough of your innuendos. I've got to pick up my daughter now. And stop harassing us. Or I'll call the police. The *real* police.'

'. . . Oh, yeah. Which reminds me. I checked with my mates down at Scotland Yard. Lover boy didn't hand in any drug money.'

I remembered what Nathaniel had told me about police corruption and felt a swift shudder of revulsion. 'Really? Is that so? Nate warned me that his honesty has made him a lot of enemies. Enemies who are trying to set him up.'

Danny looked at me coyly. 'I – um – I also took the liberty of "borrowing" his house keys.' He dangled them in front of my face. 'He's getting a security alarm installed. The security engineer happens to be an ex-cop mate of mine.'

'Jesus! Is there anyone who *isn't*?'

'. . . So, I – ah – got the keys copied. I thought I'd go in today and take a look around . . . Just to be sure.'

I gawped at him in disgust. No wonder Nate didn't trust the police. 'I'm beginning to think it's time to have you sectioned under the Insane Fathers Act.'

'I know how you feel about taking the law into your own hands, Matilda. But there's something about that guy I just don't trust.'

'Funny, he said exactly the same thing about you. Can't you

hear yourself, Danny?' I snatched Nathaniel's keys from his hand and stomped off to find my daughter.

'I just felt like I had to speak my mind . . .' Danny called out after me.

'Why not?' I called back. 'It's not as though you've got anything to lose!'

26

A Hive of Activity

Nate's security firm was fraudulent and I was desperate to let him know. I attempted to call him so many times, I practically wore off a fingerprint. Concerned, I handed over Portia into Roxy's custody at the office, then drove through the congestion zone to his house on the river. I leant on the bell for a good ten minutes. The keys were too bulky to slide under the door, so I let myself in. I was simply intending to leave them on the table with a note to sack his alarm people and phone me immediately. But warm, enticing rays of afternoon sunlight were warming up the living room.

The light drew my eye outside through the double sliding glass doors into an emerald-green garden which led down to the Thames, twinkling and sparkling below. There was barely a cloud in the sky. The one cloud that was visible looked as if it had wandered off from the herd merely to emphasize how blue the sky was. Bees hummed vacuously in the fruity air. A few stunned themselves against the clear glass pane. I slid open the door. Perhaps I would wait for him? Especially as, for a change, I wasn't dressed like Iris Murdoch and was sporting a short, flowery frock and pretty pink heels. A giant bumblebee stooged through the wildflowers, its furry underbelly grazing leaves and petals. I followed it to the wooden apiary at the bottom of the garden. I knew quite a lot about beekeeping from my mother. I'd been helping her collect honey since I was young. September is the time bees are given sugary drinks for the oncoming winter. A small jar of syrup sat on the grass by the hive. On a whim, I lit the smoker and took the lid off the hive. After smoking the bees into a stupor, the way my mother had taught me, I raised the vertical grille to taste the honey with a finger. It was tangy and delicious. I then dripped some sugary syrup on to the grille, raising it higher for better access ... And that was when I saw the box.

Matters, like pimples, have a habit of coming to a head. And this was one of those moments. The box secreted at the bottom of the hive was black, metal and encased in plastic. Why would there be a box hidden in the bottom of a beehive? Curious, I lifted it out, placed it on the grass, peeled back the plastic covering and opened the lid. Disturbed, sleepy bees took flight, hitting the windowpane and falling to earth, fatly baffled.

But not as baffled as me. Because there, lying on top of a pile of DVDs was a disk with Chantelle's name on it. I rubbed my temples, dazed, as though I'd been in a car accident. Then I shook my head furiously, like a dog tormented by wasps. I rummaged deeper into the box and extracted a leather book. I flicked through it. It looked like some kind of ledger, meticulously detailing drop-offs and percentages paid to people who had nicknames and codes. There were references to 'little fellas' and 'ticket men'. Under the book were about twenty DVDs with girls' names felt-tipped across their covers. A sudden awakening of instinct strung my veins together.

And then, just when the ground was already buckling beneath my feet, I saw the mask. My mild fear morphed into something solid and terrifying. It was the vampire mask worn by the ghoulish tweeting troll @killchantellenow when sending us death threats. I stood rooted in disbelief, my mind rejecting what my eyes so plainly saw.

I attempted to assume the crash position, even though I was earthbound and nowhere near an airport. One thing became startlingly clear to me. I should never consider psychology as a career choice, because I had no bloody idea whatsoever about people. Was someone setting Nathaniel up? Or had I been duped by a man in the same way my mother had been duped? We obviously shared a dupe gene. The macabre image of the man in a mask flashed back into my psyche – it had been a constant screengrab in my mind. *'Drink bleach.' 'Go get cancer, slut.'* Yet whenever we blocked his Twitter profile, he'd reappear, like some indestructible cyborg.

'Drop the case or you die . . . slowly.'

'It's great to be back after 30 seconds. Lol.'

'After strangulation, which organ in the female body remains warm after death? My cock.'

No, no. It must be a set-up. A true honey-trap, I thought. But then pieces of a sinister jigsaw began to fall into place. I thought back to the time on the estate, when I'd 'bumped into' Nathaniel. Only *I* had known where Chantelle was hiding. Yet, later that very night, she'd mysteriously received the doctored DVD of her own rape. *'Would you like me to escort you?'* Nathaniel had said, and I'd given him the exact address. My mind snapper-clicked on to the night Nathaniel had slept at my house, after the court victory. That monumental hangover . . . The realization that Nathaniel was not who he appeared to be pierced my skull. I felt like one of those cruise-line passengers who has talked all the way through the 'muster drill' and now has no idea where her lifeboat station is. 'Woman overboard!'

I was deep in shocked reverie when I heard the front door slam. I felt my organs clench and thought my legs would buckle. My only instinct was to run. High heels are okay in a controlled environment – teamed with fishnet stockings while you're lying down on your lover's bed, perhaps. But not so ideal when you're say, scuba-diving, climbing the Himalayas or . . . fleeing from a ruthless criminal. This is what I realized as I lumbered towards Nathaniel's side gate, encumbered by six-inch pumps.

'Oy! Stop!' He was on me in a flash, his big, muscled arms around my waist. I went down to the ground with a painful thud. He flipped me over as effortlessly as he would a pancake. He pinned my shoulders to the ground. His brows hitched in amazement. 'Matilda?'

I saw something flash in his eyes. He had just noticed that I was clutching the mask. Everything suddenly crystallized.

'Well, fancy seeing you here.' He spoke to me as though addressing a cat that had strayed into his yard. 'Rather inventive place to hide things, don't you think? Most people are too scared of stings to go near an apiary. Not you, though, of course. Your mind is just a hive of activity, isn't it?' he jested blithely.

I was suddenly on a white-water raft in a category-five hurricane. The air seemed thin, insubstantial, and it was a conscious effort to breathe.

'Yes, I guess you could call it a sting operation,' he bantered on. His expressionless eyes bore into mine. 'Shame our fun is over, though. I was so enjoying myself.' He got to his feet. 'You've given me quite a ride,' he said salaciously, though his voice was thin and diffident.

Still winded, I sat up on the grass and spoke in my best, imperious barrister voice. 'Well, I suggest you start thinking about what kind of gang you're going to join in prison.' It was a bluff, attempted to hide my fear, even though my heart was a jackhammer in my chest and blood thudded in my ears.

'Prison? I don't think so. The colour of those drab uniforms would be a total nightmare for my skintone.' The man was unflappable and totally beyond the reach of insults.

My only thought was to keep him talking while I thought of a plan. 'You're right. You'll be locked away in a mental-health ward after the evidence I give against you.'

Nathaniel eyed me like a cobra rising up out of its basket. 'I don't think you'll be giving evidence against me, Matilda. ... Not after your whorish behaviour the other night.' Nathaniel's tone had changed. He now sounded ruthless, cold, plausible. 'Who'd have guessed that you, Little Miss Prim and Proper, would go off like a firecracker? I wouldn't have believed it ... if I didn't have evidence.'

Then he started laughing. Not a nice laugh. With a bitterly triumphant look on his face, he drew his mobile phone from his pocket, tossed it up into the air, then caught it again with casual mirthlessness. He thrust the phone towards me, pressing a button. I heard muffled groans and cries. Then a voice I recognized as my own. As my eyes adjusted to the footage, I realized it was me. Naked. Moaning. I felt the sickened sensation I sometimes did after seeing a dead squirrel on the pavement, or a leech dropping off my leg, gorged with blood.

'Quite an Academy Award-winning orgasm. You got really wild on me after I doctored your drink. You rode me so hard I nicknamed you Annie Oakley. You sang like a bird, too. Told me all about Chantelle leaving the hospital to go with her gran. That snippet of information was the exact "Get my boys out of jail free" card I needed.'

Each word he spoke was a bitter bullet. 'I – I – don't understand.'

He gave me a flat, measuring look. 'Basically, unless you forget everything you've seen here today, I'm going to put this footage of you up online.'

Every ragged breath I took felt as though I were inhaling fire. Sweat trickled down my face as I stared at myself gyrating and writhing on his iPhone screen.

'It's so simple. I just hack into your Facebook page and replace your profile picture with a naked, compromising photo of you and a link to the videos I filmed that night.'

A mixture of terror and revulsion struck me like a blow from some gargantuan hammer.

'After that, the photos and video will start popping up everywhere, with your name on them. You'll drive yourself crazy chasing images across the Net. You'll have to change your name. And, obviously, your career will be in tatters.'

His words pumped out like darts from a lethal blowpipe.

'Sure, you can employ "reputation restorers". But they charge thousands of pounds to stop Google links that lead to your family name, and the images will just keep popping up in other places. Then an anonymous source – namely me – will alert the Bar Standards Board to your secret life as a sex worker and you'll be defrocked, or whatever it is they do to you lot. De-wigged, I suppose. You'll probably end up killing yourself, from the shame. Especially *you*, Matilda, as you've told me how much you hate being seen naked.' His smile lines hardened into a leer. 'Oh, look. It's time for your close-up . . . Pandora's . . . box. Quite literally. The biggest opening night in London.'

The focus of the footage shifted from my face and body to

down between my legs. I stared at the screen in a funereal stupor. This was a tectonic-plate-shifting moment. Something in my stomach churned and twisted. 'I think I'm going to be sick.'

He threw me an icy glance. Gone was the affable, compassionate philanthropist, replaced by the coldest, smoothest man I'd ever met. It took the effort of every muscle in my body to stop myself from vomiting all over his biker boots.

'I put off screwing you at first, as you're really not my type – far too old and way too curvy. But I really did enjoy fucking you, you know. You're quite hot-to-trot.'

'But why?' I managed to mutter, dry-mouthed and nauseous.

Nathaniel shrugged. 'I'm an entrepreneur. Kids will always be addicted to something – designer clothes, boy bands, alcohol, danger . . . drugs. Someone might as well make money out of it.'

'But . . . but what of all your talk about being so passionately anti-drugs?'

'Drugs do less damage to the decor than guns and are quicker and quieter than other forms of self-destruction, such as going into banking to impress your father,' he said with light malice. The monster was finding himself so amusingly urbane. A smile was acid-etched on to his face.

I staggered to my feet. My incomprehension of what had transpired was so intense it made me dizzy. My mind was clattering – none of this made sense. 'What happened to your mantra, that the best things in life are free?'

His eyes suddenly became as sharp as sword points. 'Wealthy family members are renowned both for stinginess and long lifespans. And when they finally *do* become food for worms, imagine the distress when you discover that they've left their entire estate to their Cavalier King Charles spaniels.

What can I say? It embitters one.' His voice was chilly and self-absorbed. 'Just because of a small misunderstanding at my bank, my holier-than-thou papa said I'd "blackened the family name". That I'd never amount to anything. Well, if only the pompous prig could see me now, eh?'

His monologue was glutinous. Pushing through it was such an effort, like swimming underwater. 'What about your so-called epiphany?'

'The only epiphany I had was that I could make much more money dealing drugs than moving other people's money around. The international business I'm a part of is extremely lucrative. Which is why I couldn't let my boys go to prison. I need them. I've got a big shipment coming in. I've been working all year on this little project.'

I swallowed a sob. Was the man about to measure me for a body bag? I suddenly began to regret not filling out my organ-donor card. I mean, it couldn't be good that he was boasting to me about his crimes, now could it? 'So why . . . why are you telling me all this?' I asked in a tiny voice.

'Because no matter how clever one is, relying on others is unavoidable. All kingpins need minions. Loyal minions. Stretch is my chief recruitment officer and stand-over man. Bash is my money launderer. It's imperative I keep them on the streets. But ever since your insane granny shot at their testicles and dragged them into a ridiculous trial, I've had to develop numerous tedious tactics to avoid detection – failing to turn up for pre-booked flights, then taking different routes, always paying in cash . . . It's meant developing a totally new criminal shorthand, indecipherable to all but a few of my fellow conspirators.'

That explained the ledger. 'What's a "little fella"?'

'Ecstasy tablets.'

'A "ticket man"?'

'A courier. And a "quid" is a thousand pounds.'

'What are the DVDs with girls' names on them?'

'Films of their rapes,' he said nonchalantly. 'Stretch then blackmails the girls into working as couriers or granting sexual favours to clients.'

Despair and disgust was a heavy blackness that let no light in or out. Unfortunately, studying law hadn't prepared me for this kind of scenario. Of course, time is a great teacher but, sadly, it has a tendency to kill all its pupils. I found myself backing away, slowly. 'Are you planning on trying to . . . silence me?' What was left of my mind was racing. I contemplated jumping over the wall into the river. I'd no doubt be drowned in the treacherous undertows and found washed up in some Dutch dyke, but it would be better than relying on the kindness of a passing psychopath.

Nathaniel clicked his tongue in consternation. 'Don't be so melodramatic, Matilda. I'm telling you all this because I need a lawyer. Legal assistance is the one thing missing from my enterprise. But who to trust? . . . I took that naked video of you as an insurance policy. I now own you. Which means you and Roxy are on call. If you don't look after me and my interests, when required, I'll release that rather frank footage of your "Pandora's Box" . . . I'm moving all this evidence to a safety-deposit box to which Bash has the only other key. Go to the cops, and your vag goes viral.'

His voice coiled around me like a snake. I couldn't speak, in case my own betrayed the explosion of horror I was feeling inside.

'You've obviously fried your brain cells sampling your own drugs, because there's no way Roxy and I would ever represent you. Not ever! I don't care about your little porn movie! Do what you like with it!'

Nathaniel gave me a dismissive look with a hint of barely

suppressed animosity. 'Oh, well, yes, I suppose you could always take another name. Get cosmetic surgery. Find another profession ... But if only it were so easy for your darling daughter ... I've been grooming Portia for a while now. And I don't think she would get over a rape quite as easily as you have.'

The remarks hit me like a grenade at close range. I reeled. 'Portia?'

'Yes, I got her involved in my anti-drug campaign, through school. Didn't she tell you I've been giving talks to the pupils? She's agreed to be a fundraiser for my charity.'

She would have told me – if she'd been talking to me, that is.

'Yes, we've become quite close ... Gorgeous girl, and so bright. But ridiculously easy prey,' he said with an acidic chuckle. 'Boys would be queuing up to fuck her.'

His words were like a noxious gas, invisible, murderous, unstoppable.

'Once she's recruited and blackmailed, I could get a lot of money and favours by bartering that cute little morsel...' His face was a mask of pure malice. 'Especially to my Middle Eastern clients, because of her age, blond hair and blue eyes.'

I felt the colour drain from my face. My legs went cold and numb. Every particle of my body prickled with something more physical than loathing.

'Keep away from her!' Small beads of sweat studded my skin and ran down the recessed line of my spine. I've never had any self-defence classes, preferring just to rely on the fact that men tend to underestimate my sheer determination and anxiety. Which is why I simply lunged at his throat, took hold of his hair in my talons and yanked as hard as I could, screaming.

And that was when he punched me, hard, in the stomach.

I hit the ground with a bone-cracking whack and lay winded as he loomed above me. 'I need a lawyer on hand in case any of my boys ever gets arrested again. Then, if they're stopped by the cops and can't answer questions about why an apparently unemployed scrote is carrying hundreds of pounds in rolled-up cash, my boys can talk to their lawyers . . . you and Roxy. Two liberal, feminist Pollyannas. I mean, a Goody Two-shoes who would never take the law into her own hands. What could be better cover?' he sneered. 'I'd been cultivating you for a while but, once I saw you in court, I knew you'd be perfect, so I fucked and filmed you that very night. And you won't be a liability like my last legal eagle. He turned out to be more of a legal budgie.'

I ground my teeth in rage. 'Who was it? What happened?'

'His addiction to charlie, ket and rocks left him hopelessly compromised. The idiot was arrested after a police surveillance operation. He was found guilty on two counts of perverting the course of justice . . . Which rather left me in the lurch. When Bash was arrested, I had to take matters into my own hands. Hence the trolling. And intimidation. And videoing . . . Well, occasionally I do like to mix business with pleasure. Hey, every job has its perks . . . But tweeting threats and doctoring film footage is so time-consuming. A tame lawyer on tap is quicker, simpler and safer.'

I stared at him in a wide-eyed parody of disbelief.

'So' – he offered me a hand up – 'welcome to the team, Matilda.'

27

Crème de la Crim

Too shell-shocked to cry, I walked on automatic pilot back to my car. Once the doors were locked, I gripped the wheel and closed my eyes, but horror exploded on the screen of my eyelids. All I could see was my daughter in distress, running, hiding, dark shapes coalescing and blurring, until the world was black on black. I punched her number on my speed dial. Nothing. I rang the home line. When Roxy answered, I tried to speak, but I felt as though I had a lip full of novocaine.

'Where's Portia?' I blurted.

'Under house arrest upstairs. Doing homework. We're not long in, actually.'

'Check, will you?'

'Portia?!' my mother fog-horned. '. . . Possum?' I listened to Roxy's footfall on the stairs. I heard the bedroom door creak. 'Bloody hell. She's not here.'

I let out a strangled sob. My nerves were shredded.

My mother's voice went down a semitone. 'What is it, Tilly?'

'Ring around her friends. I'll check Danny's.'

'What the hell's going on?'

I tried to answer, but my tongue felt swollen and dry, my mouth taut with terror. I killed the call, then headed straight to my errant father's flat. Danny let me in and gave a quizzical look as I searched his apartment. When I'd ascertained that she definitely wasn't hiding there, I pressed my fingers to my temples and prayed the panic would pass, like a brief storm.

'I don't know what to do,' I said, in a voice more appropriate to a six-year-old.

'What's going on?'

This was a dizzying new sensation. I'd never had a daddy to turn to before – a rock and a soft landing simultaneously. It felt disorientating and strange, but there was also a sense of relief in being able to blurt out the whole sordid scenario. When I stopped talking, Danny pounded his fist on the wooden door so hard that the sound echoed in my head like an explosion. What happened next is hard to describe. My father went through some kind of Incredible Hulk transmogrification. He bulked up. Veins stood out on his neck. He did everything but turn green. When I then added that Nathaniel had threatened to groom my daughter, Danny's face contorted into a look of volcanic rage.

'Two questions. Where is the fucker? And how do you want me to kill him?' He was sparking with electric current. I could feel the heat coming off him.

'No!' I recoiled. 'I just want that humiliating footage destroyed. And Portia protected. And him punished. By the law . . .' I started pacing his living room now, wringing my hands. 'But he says if I contact the police the naked footage of me will be posted online.'

'I can make this go away, Tilly. There's only about nine people in Britain who can make a man disappear . . . Maybe three more that we don't know about, behind enemy lines in Afghanistan . . .'

'Don't you know me at all? When it comes to walking on the wild side, I prefer to tiptoe! The most dangerous thing I've ever done is to park in a bus lane! The odd overdue library book is my greatest crime.'

'So what? You think God's going to take some time off the Middle East to stagger over to the window and sort this out for you? It's up to you to change the bloody narrative.'

'If *I* were writing this narrative, Danny, Nathaniel would die a slow, grisly death, preferably with his nuts pegged out over an ants' nest . . . But I don't believe in vigilante vengeance. Who am I? A mafia don? Don friggin' Corleone? Should I just go put a horse's head in his bed?'

'You have the killer instinct of a chihuahua, do you know that? You have to toughen up, kid.'

'It's not about toughening up. You don't understand, Danny. I respect the law, not the law of the jungle. A group of maniacs up north just murdered a paediatrician, thinking the word meant paedophile.' I thought back to the rough justice meted out to Anne Boleyn, Joan of Arc and the Salem 'witches'. 'Respect for the law is the centre of my moral compass. It's the foundation of my love of the law. It's the rule I live by—'

'Yeah, well, that worked out so well for Chantelle, didn't it? Thank God her granny shot those bastard rapists' balls off. At least it's a victory of sorts. Now it's *your* daughter under threat . . . And *your* genitals about to be flashed to the nation on YouTube. So what the hell are you going to do about it?'

'I don't know!' In the list of Ten Things to Do before You Die, not date a psychopath probably came top.

I was staring, pole-axed, at the front door, when it suddenly whooshed open. A beehived Roxy came cantering into view like a hyperactive peroxide haystack, capsicum spray at the ready.

'What the hell's going on?' she demanded, legs planted, weapon extended. 'I told you never to come near us again!' she shouted, and squeezed the trigger.

A split second later, Danny hit the floor, moaning. The caustic capsicum particles were burning his eyes and skin, blistering his face and making every mucous membrane feel as though it was being injected by boiling-hot knitting needles.

'What the fuck!' he wailed.

'Mum! He's innocent . . . You see? You see?' I said, running to wet some tea towels. 'This is what happens when you take the law into your own hands. Mistakes are made! Oh God. Are you okay? How bad is it? What does it feel like?' I asked Danny, who was writhing around on the floor.

'Like I'm inhaling cut glass dipped in acid.'

I laid the cold towels on Danny's face, then disarmed my mother and sat her down.

As I detailed the terrifying events of the evening, Roxy's face moved into a rictus of incredulity. My fearless mother, who's prone to elation and never exhausts her wholehearted commitment to life, wilted visibly in her chair.

'Clearly, the man must die,' Danny growled. 'I'd riddle him with bullets right now if some psycho hadn't bloody well blinded me!' He squinted up at us through the red slits of his eyes. 'Does that Nathaniel asshole know what I look like?'

'Well, yes. He describes you to me as a washed-up has-been.'

Something in Danny shifted and tightened and squared off, making him into a compact knot. 'Washed up?' he snarled, struggling to his feet.

'Well, the man has a point, Danny. Look at you. You

couldn't even disarm a woman with a capsicum spray,' Roxy stated baldly.

'I am not bloody washed up!' Danny fumed, just as he fell head first over the coffee table, due to capsicum-induced blindness. 'Christ Almighty!'

'*I* should go and kill Nathaniel,' Roxy declared. 'I smoke, I drink, I sugar my tea . . . I'm already a prime candidate for sudden death. If something happens to *me*, it doesn't matter.' Roxy lifted up her lime-green leopardskin T-shirt and flashed her tattoo.

Danny blinked at her through inflamed orbs. 'Why the hell do you have "Do Not Resuscitate" tattooed across your chest?'

Roxy then showed him her flipside of 'PTO'. 'If anything happens, do *not* revive me!'

Danny rubbed his stinging eyes to take a better look. 'No friggin' way will I agree to that. I've only just found you again. I'll be buggered if I'm going to lose you. You'll be comatose, so you won't have any say.'

'It's not your choice! You'll keep me alive over my dead body . . . so to speak.'

'Would you both stop it! We are not killing or reviving anyone . . . Nor are we committing murder. I just don't have what it takes to be a criminal mastermind. I don't even know what size nylon stocking fits my head.'

'Well, what do you propose we do, Miss Abide-by-the-Rules? Write a letter of complaint to his Oxbridge alumni?' Danny mocked.

'Come on, Tilly. You're making Mahatma Gandhi look aggressive.'

Both my parents stood facing me.

'I don't *know* what to do! If we tell the police and Nathaniel is arrested, one of his accomplices will put that horrific footage of me up online . . . My spread-eagled, naked body

will end up on a hundred thousand websites overnight . . .
And then there's Portia . . .' My heart was pounding in my
chest louder than a drum soloist at Glastonbury. 'He could be
holding her somewhere, for all I know!'

'Let's keep calm. It's only five o'clock. She's probably
sneaked out to go shopping or to a friend's place. We *have*
been a bit hard on her lately, Tilly.'

'But the threats he made about her . . .' My blood curdled.
'It's too terrifying . . . But I can't just let you two loose on him.
I mean, what kind of person does that make me? A criminal,
that's who. Someone no better than he is—'

'It makes you a mother, Tilly,' Roxy said softly.

'If you go to the police, he'll post your sex DVD online and
you'll be the laughing stock of the Bar. Even if by some
miracle you can prove that he spiked your drink, raped and
blackmailed you, he'll just say you're framing him out of
revenge because he ended your love affair – meaning, the
fucker will get away with it,' Danny boiled. 'You just lost a
rape trial where the men were guilty as sin. Do you really
want to go through that ordeal yourself?'

'And just think how many other poor women the dirtbag
has blackmailed in this disgusting way. Women he's now
pimping to his drug clientele on a regular basis.'

'Let me fix this for you, Tilly,' Danny reiterated. 'I've just
got to persuade the arsewipe to tell us where he's stashed the
copies of the DVDs, and destroy them. A safety-deposit box,
you think?'

I nodded.

'I promise not to kill him . . . even though I bloody well
want to. I'll just rough him up a little. He's a pretty boy, so no
doubt his body is his friggin' temple . . .'

'At which he is the most fanatical worshipper,' I agreed
bitterly.

'If the bloke's most recent major relationship is with his own mirror, then he won't want to be disfigured.' Danny cracked his knuckles menacingly.

'The thing is,' I said, after a beat, 'abduction requires a cool head, a hard heart and, if he escapes and is armed, *Olympic sprinting* . . . God, oh God! I need to clear my head. Let me just find Portia, and then I'll think it through overnight,' I prevaricated.

'Never go to bed angry, Tilly – stay up and plot your revenge,' Roxy said. 'That's my philosophy.'

'Mine, too,' Danny agreed. 'We also need to get some insurance so that the toffee-nosed scumbag never attempts this stunt again. Which means getting some incriminating footage of *him* to post online.'

Roxy gave Danny an approving nod. 'Good thinking . . . Let's put a stop to this monster, in the name of all the other women he and his henchmen have raped, blackmailed, groomed, prostituted and pimped.'

'Let's do it for Chantelle,' Danny added.

'Let's do it for Phyllis,' Roxy agreed.

'Let's do it for Portia,' they said in unison.

'Portia's most probably sulking at a friend's place – but she's still missing. And he may know where she is,' Roxy urged.

'What do you say, Matilda?' added Danny.

'Tilly?' Roxy pleaded.

A curious numbness washed over me, the same numbness a woman might feel seconds after she's pulled her pushchair out of the way of a speeding car. I felt hot and cold all over. The nausea made me stagger a little. But, though I was unsteady on my feet, my brain was suddenly, miraculously clear. Anger welled up in me – an anger bitter enough to taste. Something altered in the air – and I knew what had to be done. My reflection in the mirror above Danny's couch was harshly alien. The knowledge that I was going to betray my beliefs and take revenge slid into me cleanly, like the sharp edge of a knife.

'Do it,' I said to my father.

'Go home, both of you. I'll call you when the deed is done.'

28

The Plot Sickens

I had practically gnawed my nails down to my elbows, worn
a path in the living-room shag-pile and dialled my finger to
the bone desperately calling my darling daughter when my
phone finally rang a few hours later.

'I was wondering if I could park something in your garage
for the night.'

'Something?'

'Yeah . . . A lying, rotten, drug-dealing rapist.'

That was when I realized that a truly loving dad doesn't
buy you a smiley card after a bad day. When you find yourself in trouble, a truly loving dad will kidnap the psychopath
who's ruined your life, string him up by the nipples and
await your instruction on his imminent destruction.

'What about Portia?' I gasped. 'Does he know anything?'

'I'm about to find out.'

'What happened? Where are you?'

'I tracked the weasel down. He wasn't all that pleased to
see me.'

'How did he react?'

'Let's just say that there were harsh words and a little gunplay. We're now in a shack on Roxy's allotment.'

The vegetable allotment in Kentish Town is a patchwork quilt of gardens on disused factory land stuck in legal limbo land with developers. As we turned the car into the deserted dirt cul-de-sac, the headlights cut twin funnels of light in the rain, illuminating a ramshackle little lean-to. Roxy silenced the engine. The surrounding woodland backing on to a disused railway line was pitch black except for the sliver of light seeping out from beneath the door of Roxy's gardening shack. The wild, overgrown grass was full of the whisper and scurry of small lives. We walked quietly to the shack and eased open the door. An aureole of light from a naked, bare bulb in a broken hurricane lamp illuminated Nathaniel, bound and clad only in boxer shorts, on a chair. My father, wearing some kind of camouflage outfit that looked as though it dated back to the Boer War, was pointing a gun at his chest.

'I know it's rude to point, Nathaniel. Please forgive me . . . but I didn't have the benefit of your posh upbringing.'

'Fuck off, you deranged lunatic!'

'Although it's not a strict rule of etiquette *not* to point a loaded gun at someone. A strict etiquette rule is never, ever to point an *unloaded* gun at anyone, don't you reckon, Roxy?'

'Ab-so-bloody-lutely.'

Tongue-tied with fury, it took me a moment to find my vocal cords. 'Where is my daughter?'

'Untie me, you unhinged maniac. Matilda, tell him to untie me right now, or you know what will happen. That Academy Award-winning footage of you will be up on every legal website . . .'

Danny shoved the gun into Nathaniel's mouth. 'Don't talk

with your mouth full, matey. You know it's bad manners. Did they teach you nothing at your uppity boarding school?'

'What's bad manners, actually, is that sartorial ensemble,' Roxy reprimanded Danny in a sotto voce aside. 'What the hell are you wearing?'

'Is that any way to speak to an international crime fighter?' Danny replied quietly. 'So, girls,' he now boomed, 'how would you like me to ... persuade posh boy here to tell us where he's stashed my darlin' granddaughter and the rape DVDs of you and his other victims.' When Nathaniel said nothing, he continued, '... What about we play a little bondage charades? ... That's where one person is tied up and the others guess what diabolical thing they'll do to him.'

'I still have my capsicum spray. What about if we just give him a very hot asshole,' Roxy suggested.

'Great idea!'

I looked from my mother to my father with a mix of horror and amazement. They were in perfect, diabolical harmony, as though they'd practised for the part. As Portia would say, *'This* is my gene stock?'

'Just find out if he knows where Portia is.' My nerves were in a blender turned to fine chop. I checked my phone for the millionth time. It was only 8 p.m. but, with every minute, my panic was mounting.

'Of course, you could avoid all this unpleasantness if you'd just tell us where Portia is,' Roxy cajoled.

Nathaniel's face distorted into a red gargoyle mask. 'I'm fucking freezing. Give me back my clothes. I could catch pneumonia.'

'You know, I don't think your long-term health is a major concern for you right now ...' Danny stated.

'Mind you. It's so thoughtful to die young enough to make

sure that the funeral crowd will be fashionable and good-looking,' Roxy mused.

I gawped at them both. I was a Jane Austen-reading, chocoholic pacifist. I was equipped to kill someone only one way – with kindness.

'Yeah.' Danny picked up Roxy's theme. 'I always think that, if you're going to die, you should try to be considerate about it, you know, and die in a manner that entertains people. A blind date with Hannibal Lecter or home lipo-suction with a vacuum cleaner or a violent inflatable-sex-doll explosion. Which is why I have something quite colourful in mind . . .'

Danny pointed his torch to a darkened corner of the shed. The beam illuminated a small children's paddling pool. 'A little something I pumped up earlier,' Danny clarified. I now noticed a garden hose draped over the pool edge, which ran in from outside. He disappeared for a moment to turn on the tap. As water gushed into the pool, Danny wheeled in a huge sealed bucket. He removed the plastic lid and peered inside.

'What is it?' I asked, sick with anxiety.

'A fish that could give the great white shark competition as the most terror-inspiring creature of the deep. On my travels around the world, this is the species that petrified me the most.'

'A fish? Really? Why?' Roxy asked, intrigued.

'Well, its appearance for one. Take a look . . .'

Roxy and I took a tentative peek into the bucket. A fish which could easily play the part of a sci-fi monster in a spoof-horror flick was thrashing about in the water. At three foot long and weighing four stone, it resembled a giant piranha, except for the fact that the teeth looked uncannily human.

'Ugly bugger, isn't it? But it's the diet of the pacu fish which makes it so horrifying,' Danny explained, tipping the creature from the bucket into the plastic pond, where it started snapping viciously. Roxy and I instinctively drew back from the pool's edge. 'You see, the pacu has a penchant for men's testicles.'

I winced, horrified. I'd obviously been secretly cast in some Mario Puzo *Godfather* remake in which people were dispatched to sleep with the fishes.

'Um, just one question. How did you find an Amazonian fish in North London?' Roxy marvelled.

'I just happen to have a friend who's a collector of exotic fish species. Ex-SAS.'

'Is there anyone you *don't* know?' I said. The man's Christmas-card list must be longer than Proust's seven-volume *Remembrance of Things Past.*

'They bite because they're hungry, and testicles sit nicely in their mouth. The big bugger hasn't been fed all week, so he's ravenous. Fishermen in South America attacked by the pacu usually bleed to death after losing their nuts in the fish's vicious fangs.'

The whole time Danny was speaking, he was rocking Nathaniel's chair towards the pool. Nathaniel's face had gone arctic white and, despite his protestations about the cold, his complexion now glistened with sweat.

I seized my mother's arm. 'Okay, this is getting seriously insane. My daughter is missing. Let's just call the police.' Not only did I not have a licence to kill, I didn't even have a learner's permit.

Roxy cupped her hand to my ear and whispered, 'Just play along.' She took a knife from Danny's belt and approached Nathaniel, who immediately started whimpering.

'Don't worry, mate. I've never castrated a man I didn't like.' In one deft movement, my mother sliced through his shorts.

I looked down at the bound man whom I'd so recently bedded. His manhood had shrunk to the size of a pea. As Danny tilted his chair towards the water, Nathaniel let out a scream normally associated with childbirth.

'Oh, grow a pair, mate . . . mind you – soon you might have to,' Danny chortled. He returned the chair back on to all four legs for a moment. 'I think it's time we put you into the pool, don't you? . . . Unless you're feeling more chatty.'

'Just tell us where Portia is and where you've hidden the DVDs. You mentioned something to Matilda about a safety-deposit box? . . .' Roxy waved the knife near his penis. 'You really don't want to mess with a woman who is all out of HRT and has a scalpel.'

'Okay, I think it's time our untalkative friend here went for a little dip, don't you?' Danny trained the gun on his captive. 'Untie him, Roxy.'

But, as soon as she did so, Nathaniel kicked out at Danny in an attempt to knock the gun from his hand. With a speed that belied his age, Danny floored the prisoner with a karate chop. Nathaniel slid into the plastic pool like a startled otter from a riverbank. 'Never hit anyone below the belt, bud, particularly a black one earned in ju-jitsu,' Danny quipped. 'Oh, and by the way, who exactly were you calling "washed up"?'

Nathaniel was now crouched in the centre of the paddling pool, his knees clasped to his chest. Danny had his gun trained at the man's head. Roxy aimed her knife at his heart. A comma of blood appeared on Nathaniel's grazed knee and started to drip into the water, exciting the fish, which circled closer and closer in the rising swirl. As the water level in the pool got higher, the frantic fish arced nearer and nearer to its human prey. The water inched upwards. When it lapped Nathaniel's testicles, the man made a weird grunting noise, which I imagine involved a quick conversion to religion.

'The last guy whose testicles I fed to this fish took longer to die than a friggin' opera singer. But the good thing about bleeding to death is that all your organs are still intact.'

'Exactly,' Roxy chorused. 'So, let's not think of it as murder but more as a kidney-transplant scheme.'

'All right! All right! You sick fucks!' Nathaniel yelped. 'Your daughter's volunteering for my mentoring charity. There's a fundraising karaoke night. St Mary's Church. She's selling tickets at the door.'

Danny kept him in the pool at gunpoint until a snivelling Nathaniel had confided the exact address of the church hall and the location and number of the safety-deposit box in Hatton Gardens where the DVDs were stashed. He also confirmed that the bastard rapist Bash was the only other person with a key.

My memory of the hours that followed is fuzzy. Anger as keen and cutting as a razor blade's edge kept terror at bay. I recall collecting Portia and being too thankful to be furious. Relief relaxed the skin around my temples, and my chest unknotted.

'I promised to help, Mummy. And I knew you wouldn't let me come,' she stammered, guilt-stricken.

'Shhhh. It's okay. We'll talk about it later.'

I remember ringing Amelia's mother and pleading with her to let my daughter sleep over, clearly maintaining my winning position of World's Worst Parent at the next school PTA meeting. I recall drinking plantations of coffee to stay awake, then driving in a wishy-washy rain to Hatton Gardens, where we accessed the safety-deposit box. I recall two half-moons of sweat appearing in Roxy's armpits as we extracted fifteen DVDs, one of which had my name on it, plus wads of money. The dosh we'd use to repay the Countess for her losses on Chantelle's private prosecution. The rest we'd donate to a rape crisis centre. The disks? Well, we were pretty sure no woman would ever want these watched by an office full of policemen, let alone a jury. As they'd all been edited and overdubbed to look consensual anyway, we snapped them in half and stomped on the memory stick with them. Roxy deleted all the footage from Nathaniel's phone, which she'd already confiscated and then we just clung together in an exhausted embrace, like boxers nearing the end of a bout.

It was midnight by the time we got back to the shed, to find Danny and Nathaniel sitting motionless in a bizarre private tableau. Nathaniel was wearing a silver tiara and a pink tutu, hoiked up around his waist. He had a Tinky Winky glove puppet on his hand, a hand with which he was half-heartedly masturbating to a *Teletubbies* episode which was showing on the iPad propped up beside him.

Danny had the gun in one hand and was filming the event with the other. 'Tug harder,' he instructed. 'Put some effort into it ... Christ. It feels disturbing even saying that! Welcome, ladies. We've had a very interesting time in your absence. After Nathaniel had a few oxygen-deprivation issues, he finally felt inclined to tell me all about his life. It's been most enlightening.'

One side of Nathaniel's face was shiny and swollen, testifying to an eventful few encounters in my absence.

'As Tilly told us, Nathaniel does indeed work for the kingpin of an international network of organized criminal gangs. They flood the UK with millions of pounds worth of illegal drugs. So, after he got disinherited by his obviously astute parents, and put under investigation by his bank, the fuckwad turned to drug trafficking and money laundering to fund his lavish lifestyle. In fact, there's a big drug delivery due tomorrow from Turkey – 57kg of heroin, 15,000 ecstasy tablets and a batch of pure MDMA powder. The heroin has a street value of almost £7 mill. The ecstasy tabs are worth half a mill ... the drugs come into the country labelled as legitimate products. He maintains a network of serviced virtual offices across the UK to which the drugs are delivered, and of van drivers, enforcers and dealers who then take the merchandise on to the estates. He gets his boys to rape girls so they can be blackmailed into running drugs, because girls don't get stopped and searched like boys do. And it's all under the guise of his charitable works. The man's a class act, as you can see.'

'Ah ... that's all fascinating, Danny. But would you mind talking me through this rather unusual scenario,' I asked tentatively. 'If it's not too much trouble.'

'Insurance. We need insurance to make sure this tosser never tries this shit again on any girl. And that he doesn't try to exact revenge on any of us. And to make sure, now that I've flipped him into an informer, that he can never go back on his word.'

'You flipped him?' Roxy asked, impressed.

'Yep. He's agreed to a deal. My mate on the drug squad's on his way over now. Nathaniel's gonna wear body wires to get electronic evidence so we can roll his bosses further up the line, who have no idea, as yet, that there's a chink in their armour.'

Roxy squeezed out a chuckle. 'Basically, we've got you by the short and curlies, matey. If you don't obey our orders, this little video of you goes all over the Internet,' she explained to our miserable captive. 'I think we'll call it "Reach Out and Touch Yourself".'

'I filmed his little confession, too. For the cops. I've now got so much incriminating footage, even friggin' Houdini couldn't get out of this one.'

'So, basically, we own you,' I said, tossing Nathaniel's words back at him.

'One false move and the whole of the estate will know you're a paedo who wanks over kiddie shows in a pink tutu,' Roxy warned. 'They'll be on you like a pack of half-starved hyenas.'

'You'll be begging to go to prison for safety . . . And you'll think you're safe . . . until the night you get ambushed by a lifer and knifed in the back for being a rock spider.'

I looked at Nathaniel in his ludicrously lurid pose. His face was puce with fury. The colour went quite well with his pink tutu, actually. 'Well, Nathaniel, you have to agree, there's a certain cinematic symmetry to it. The blackmailed black-mailing the blackmailer.'

'Poetic justice. The only true justice in the world.' Danny winked at me. 'And I say that, even though I'm the rather proud father of a very brilliant lawyer.'

29

Subpoena Envy

I squeezed open my eyes the following morning and, after a few minutes of disorientated incredulity, realized that I hadn't overindulged on the cheese platter and that I really had actually kidnapped, terrorized and blackmailed a drug baron.

I squinted at the clock. It was only 10 a.m. Still, I pondered, it must be happy hour *somewhere* on the planet. Surely I could have just one little drink to steady my nerves? Because, as I thought over the events of the previous day, the aftershock of my own behaviour reverberated through me. I heard a low, incoherent moaning and slowly realized that this strange disembodied sound was my own voice. Who had I become? I had compromised my core belief system and taken the law into my own hands. I was little better than a common thief. A vigilante. A desperado highwayman bandit-type bushranger. If I were writing an updated rap sheet for myself, it would now read:

Matilda Devine

35, mother of one gorgeous, if slightly disobedient girl, whom I'd put in serious danger . . . and daughter of a renegade mum with a heart of gold whom I often woefully underappreciated.

Previous convictions: that Jack Cassidy was an A-grade ratbag way back in law school when he took my virginity and he always would be.

Current convictions: that I'd convicted Jack Cassidy of leaking information to the defence without any hard evidence and with no chance of a fair trial.

Misdemeanours: taking the law into my own hands and betraying everything I believed in.

Future convictions: that clearly I was the one who should be on trial, for going for gold in the hypocrisy Olympics.

Crimes of the heart: yes, my relationships with Stephen and Nathaniel made me a pathetic hit-and-run-romance casualty. Yes, it was no wonder that my trust in men was now so minuscule it could only be located by X-ray But I, too, had been unfair, refusing redemption to my long-lost father. And, even worse, being totally judgemental and prejudiced against the one man who had ever really meant anything to me.

A conscience, I now discovered, is what hurts when all your other parts feel fine.

Still, one thing was startlingly clear. I was not cut out for life at Pandora's. I had to resign immediately and take a nice, quiet job in a nice, steady practice, handling nothing more stressful than parking infringements and jay-walking fines. I would spend the rest of my legal life grazing on the easiest of cases, like one long, bland buffet.

I dressed with the intention of walking to the office, to tell my mother I was quitting Britain's first two-person, mother–daughter, solicitor–barrister, boutique feminist law firm. But, halfway there, I lost my nerve. Could I really just leave my dear mum in the legal lurch? Roxy was evangelical about our purpose – liberating the world's female underdogs from their kennels. I detoured left to Regent's Park to think it through. It was a crisp morning. The air seemed freshly laundered, but everything about me felt stale. I lay on my back on a grassy bank, looking past the interlaced limbs of the trees, with their russet-red and gold leaves, into a sky where grey and white clouds sloshed about like jumbled washing. Black crows were like bullets in the blue sky. A vigilante's bullets . . . My stomach curdled once more. My mind was made up. I was going to leave Pandora's. From now on, I really was going to think outside the box, as I never, ever intended to set foot back inside it.

Roxy was on her mobile when I slunk into the office. She rang off and chortled. When Roxy laughed, she shook all over, as though a seismic tremor were coming up from her core. 'This would be funny if it weren't so tragically pathetic.' She slapped her knee, which was encased in a pair of lime-green lizard-print stretch pants which left nothing to the imagination. It was teamed, naturally, with a cobalt cashmere jumper and pink go-go boots.

'That call was from a British woman in Kuwait. Her husband and daughter drove over the border to Saudi Arabia in their British car to visit a mate. They were pulled over by the police, who presumed the daughter was driving, which, as you know, is illegal for women there. When the daughter pointed out that their car was a right-hand drive, she was accused of *driving without a steering wheel*. She's been bloody well arrested.'

'Roxy, I need to talk to you . . .'

'*Apparently*, one imam has declared that women can only drive wearing a full burka, which completely covers the face

– talk about the blind leading the blind.' My mother guffawed again.

'Mum . . . listen, I have something to say . . .'

'Plus, we have a poor woman who's being sued by her husband because she gave birth to an ugly baby.'

'*Roxy!* . . . Listen to me for a moment . . .'

'Wait, you'll love this. *Apparently*, the father fell in love with his wife because of her beautiful looks, not realizing that she'd paid for them. Nose, eyes, boobs, botox, lipo, collagen, fillers . . . When she squeezed out an ugly baby, he went snooping through her childhood photos. She had no choice but to confess to her enhancements, and now he's suing her for false advertising. Think of the bloody fun we're going to have with *this* one!'

'Roxanne!' Using my mother's full name, which I'd never, ever, done in my whole life, won her full attention. 'I think it's best if Portia and I move back to our old house and I find a job with a more . . . conventional clientele.'

'Don't be silly.' She waved away my comment with a flutter of pink varnished nails.

'I mean it, Mum. It's time I lived an independent life . . . just as soon as you wash my clothes so I can pack them,' I joshed, to soften the blow.

Roxy swivelled around to face me and peered over the tops of her diamante, cat's-eye specs. 'We've had an unusual few days. You're just shell-shocked, possum.'

'My God, Mum! We kidnapped and tortured a man. What we did was wrong.'

'Maybe, but it achieved the right result. Look.' My mother turned up the volume on the BBC lunchtime news. The screen was filled with the Darth Vader outfits of the riot police, who had launched a morning raid on Nathaniel's drug ring, and the reporter was saying:

Hundreds of Met police officers swooped on suspected drug dealers in a mass raid across London today. Nearly 100 people were arrested, 10 guns were recovered and more than 60 crack cocaine rocks and 57kg of heroin were seized, according to officers from the Serious Organized Crime Agency. More than 300 officers took part in the Operation Hawk initiative against street-level drug dealing, using tip-offs from the community.

'The "community"? That's Nathaniel the Nark to you and me, kid. And look who's there.' My mother vaulted from her seat with the speed of a teenage gymnast and jabbed a nail at the screen. A group of men were being hounded out of a block of council flats on the Tony Benn Estate. Amongst the hoodied throng I glimpsed Stretch and Bash being taken into custody.

'What's not to be happy about, darl? Your reputation's saved, those rapist bastards are going down and that posh, lying git is now a police informer. I'm so happy I feel I should – I don't know – dance a jig, or run naked through the streets, or slaughter a cow, or something.'

'Roxy, what we did was immoral.'

'Oh, Tilly, if you want a moral, go look in an Aesop's fable.'

'I've made my mind up. I'm leaving.'

'You can't resign. Especially not today. It's Pandora's anniversary party. Two years and still standing. Phyllis is coming over to help me cook up a feast.'

'I'm still resigning, though I'm not sure where I'll work. Jack always said he'd take me into his Chambers. But I haven't just burnt bridges with the man, I've kinda demolished both riverbanks.'

A Skype call buzzed insistently on Roxy's computer. She pressed the green phone icon and the Countess's lugubrious face came into full view.

'Shhh! I can't speak!'

'That's a first. Why?' Roxy asked.

'I'm at a Buddhist retreat,' she whispered. 'I took a vow of silence.'

'Gee, that's working well for you, possum.'

'Yes, it's killing me! Because guess who I ran into in the Indian Sweat Yert? . . . Stephen!'

'I hope he's got a third-eye infection,' I said, nonplussed. The man was so far off my radar he barely registered a blip.

'Apparently, Petronella caught him slathering his scalp in Regaine and popping Propecia pills to turn back the tide of hair loss and, repulsed, immediately hit the relationship ejector button. He told me to tell you that he's ready to come back home.'

Roxy gave a rich chuckle. 'The only way we want that bastard back is in a box.'

But the way I was feeling, it would be *me* not him, to turn up my toes. If I were in hospital, the wavy line on my terminal monitor would be fading to black. No doubt the French would have a name for this flattened, empty feeling of crushed expectations and self-loathing. But the best I could come up with in English was 'I mean it, Mum. I want out.'

Exhaustion suddenly overwhelmed me. I trudged home and collapsed into a coma. I was woken, hours later, by nostril-tickling aromas wafting up from the kitchen below. I hadn't eaten in what felt like days. Not even a chocolate bar – which proved how discombobulated I was. Hunger propelled me to pull on a pair of jeans and a T-shirt. I bunched my hair in an elastic band and padded barefoot down the stairs. Through the stained-glass panel of the front door I could see the outline of a person on the landing. Thinking it might be Portia, home from her enforced sleep-over at Amelia's, I opened the door.

The man leaning nonchalantly on the stair rail was immaculately dressed, a cashmere jumper casually knotted around his broad shoulders. He was all sanguine charm and sardonic eyebrows and was pulling decadently on a cigar.

'I don't want you to presume for one minute that I'm here for any other reason than your mother's cooking. In fact, I've only been pretending to like you all this time to get a taste of Roxy's legendary Thai curry – a curry so strong I'm told it would send a South American chilli chef screaming from the room with his tongue in flames.'

'Who invited you?' I asked, perplexed.

'You did,' he said, breezing inside, unasked and kicking the door shut behind him with a suede loafer.

'Well, I must have been writing in invisible ink again.'

Jack extracted his iPhone from a hip pocket and scrolled down through emails. He angled the phone screen towards my face.

Please come to dinner tonight. My mother's cooking her famous Thai curry. For those who don't like chilli, there's a gratin dauphinois and duck à l'orange in the oven too. My exonerated murderess prepared it, so if it's laced with poison, you can tell everyone that you were the very last person to hear from me and that I send them greetings. Love, Tilly.

'Well, yes, it does sound like me, but obviously I didn't write this. I have never ended a correspondence to you with the word "love".'

'I invited him this morning, after our little chat.' Roxy's voice thundered behind me. 'Ulterior motive. Once you spend time with each other, you'll realize that you couldn't possibly work together. One or other of you would be up on a murder charge by lunchtime.'

Jack hitched a brow and looked my way. 'Work together?'

The door rat-a-tatted before I could reply. This time, Roxy answered it.

'Thanks for asking me for dinner, Rox.'

'I didn't bloody well ask you,' Roxy snapped at Danny, who was all freshly showered and shaved and looking a little ill at ease in his ironed jeans and best shirt, from which his big, bulging muscles were trying hard to escape.

'No, I did. I texted him this morning. It's time you two made up,' I said.

The four of us stood in silence in the hall, absorbing the situation. Portia turned her key in the lock and entered. Seeing her grandfather, she vaulted into his arms and hugged him hard. Roxy couldn't eject Danny now, not after this display of granddaughterly devotion. When nobody took out a restraining order or rang the police, or even spoke, Portia immediately read the situation and threw us a conversational life raft.

'I'm sorry I worried you all. I have been acting a bit teenagery lately. But none of you has been behaving much better. So, may I suggest that the tableware-throwing resumes after a brief truce and a drink or two, because dinner does smell yummy,' she said, all poise and precocity.

In desperate need of alcoholic fortification, we four adults practically stampeded our way to the drinks trolley in the living room, steeplechasing over any furniture in our path. While Portia cleverly involved her grandparents in a complicated conversation to do with homework matters, I decided it was best to take the stand and make a full confession to Jack, and hope he showed me more clemency than I'd afforded him.

'At least we now know I'll never have to pen a long and

complicated speech after winning the Nobel Peace Prize . . .' I gulped at my drink.

Jack canted a mocking brow. 'Is that your way of saying sorry?'

'No. But this is. You'd better guzzle that down, then get another drink. You're going to need it by the time you hear the evidence in this immorality tale . . . I know *I* do.'

After Jack had topped up our champagne, he settled back on the couch while I explained how Nathaniel's mask had slipped, literally. His vampire mask.

When the whole gruesome story concluded, Jack feigned huge astonishment. Rising to refresh his drink, he said, 'Nathaniel turned out to be a lying, deceitful, grade-A arsehole?? No. I'm shocked.' He put his hand on his forehead and staggered backwards a few feet.

'What can I say? One of these days I'll be out of therapy.'

'I knew the toffee-nosed twit was a charlatan. I help a charity called Connect, which really does help ex-offenders go on the straight and narrow. I checked with them. They'd never heard of him.'

'You help a charity?' I marvelled.

'I'm on the board. But don't tell anyone. I don't ever want it to get around that I'm not as evil as you've led people to believe. You'll ruin my bad-boy reputation.'

He gave me a warm, wry, mischievous smile, which I reciprocated. The French would no doubt have a word for this, too – the secret kindness you don't want the world to see but which gives your ex-girlfriend the urge to lick you all over. 'This is worrying. The way things are going I'll soon have to remove the word "bastard" from your resumé.'

'So . . .' An amused but sceptical line furrowed his brow. 'Nathaniel told you all about the DVDs of the girls' rapes and the drug deal coming in from Turkey because he was intimidated by your moral indignation and superior reasoning powers?'

'Well, yes . . . and also Danny's Glock 500 . . .'

'Ah, I see.'

'Plus the added incentive of a testicle-devouring South American pacu fish and the blackmail potential of a mock-paedophilia photo shoot involving simulated masturbation to an episode of the *Teletubbies*.'

Jack, who was draining his second glass of champagne, spluttered so hard, Veuve Clicquot came out of his nostrils. He then gave me a look of profound, if baffled, admiration. 'The compromising film footage of Nathaniel in mock-paedophile pose does appeal from a karmic point of view . . . But couldn't you have just taken the traditional Pandora's approved route and shot him in the nuts? And . . . what happened to the fish?'

'We're eating it tonight. It's in the curry, apparently.'

Jack laughed. 'Well, I suppose it's wiser to eat *it* before it eats *you*. Dieting from the inside . . . But tell me, how did Nathaniel, um, cope with the stress of the evening?'

'The big hard man cried like a baby.'

Jack's smiling mouth stretched even wider. 'So is this private and confidential, or must I keep it to myself?' he teased.

'In fairness, Jack, who'd believe you?'

Jack reappraised me. 'Well, Miss Inhabiter of the Upper Slopes of the High Moral High Ground, what a turn-up. If this is your idea of law enforcement, it's just as well that you're friends with a top criminal-law practitioner.'

'So . . . are we friends?' I asked tentatively.

'I'm feeling quite friendly towards you right now actually,' Jack said. 'In fact, my offer still stands,' he entendre-ed, smirking flirtatiously. 'To join my Chambers.'

I swallowed hard. 'Really?'

'For the comedic value alone, it would be worth it. Are you interested?'

I nodded so hard I'm surprised my neck didn't snap and my head fall to the floor.

'Good,' he said. 'It's agreed then. You can move in right away. Monday. I'll pay your first few months' rent, gratis. I'll send one of my clerks over to help you with your boxes.' To seal the deal, he tossed his cherished cigars into the bin.

'Oy! Youse lot!' Phyllis bellowed from the kitchen. Portia, back to her normal, obliging self, sprang to her feet. Chantelle, who had left school to take a cookery course on the other side of London, was already in the kitchen, working as sous chef. The two teenagers began carting steaming vats of aromatic gourmet delights to the table. Portia was beaming ear from ear at the sight of all the people she most cared about exclaiming joyfully over the feast. Soon, we were all bobbing about in a comforting broth of warm emotions. We cosied up under a thick blanket of relaxed chatter. If you'd glimpsed us through the window, it would have looked for a brief moment as though we were playing happy families.

But, of course, as one of the Countess's beloved Russian writers would no doubt note (though it would take nine hundred turgid pages to say it), the family that eats together . . . gets indigestion.

Danny suddenly tapped his knife on the side of his wine glass, tearing a hole in the conversation. He rose to his feet. 'The thing is, when you're out there, all alone, lost in some jungle, behind enemy lines, you get the chance to do a lot of thinking. And what I finally realized is that love is all that really matters. And a soulmate. Which is why this old gypsy dog has decided that it really is time I settled down and got hitched. I've waited so damn long, there are cobwebs between these fingers.' He waggled his calloused digits for all to see. 'So, what I want to say is – and this time I'm sober enough to do it properly – will you marry me, Roxy? At our age, there's not so much pressure on the till death do us part, part, right?' He then fell to his knees on the floor beside my mother, pulled a diamond ring from his ironed-jeans pocket and presented it to her with a flourish.

Roxy looked at him, dumbfounded. The silence was palpable.

'So, what do you say?' Danny persisted. 'Shall we try to raise a little mortgage together?' All eyes were on my mother, who sat stiff and stony-faced. The silence in the conversation was now big enough to drive a truck through. 'Stop saying nothing in such an aggressive voice,' he teased her, as the tension mounted.

'From what I've gleaned,' Roxy finally said, 'marriage is like being dead, except you still feel the urge to go shoe shopping.'

'Well, if she won't marry you, I will . . . As long as you can keep me in the tax band to which I've become accustomed.' We all swivelled, to see Countess Flirtalotsky, who was standing in the hall doorway, Louis Vuitton suitcase in hand, having let herself in with her key.

'I keep telling Roxy that she loves me, but the damn fool won't listen,' Danny told her, before turning his full attention back to my mother. 'I adore you, woman, always have, always will.' Danny lifted Roxy's hand and placed it on his cheek. He pushed his face against her palm and kissed it with great and very grave tenderness. 'What is it you don't like about me? Whatever it is, I'll change. Is it the snoring?' he joshed.

'It's not the snoring I mind, it's the talking noise you make during the day.' Roxy snatched her hand back from his grasp.

'I can't abide people who can't tell the difference between talking and saying something. I mean, this proposal is preposterous. I still don't know anything about you. Like who you really are, exactly. Or where you grew up. I mean, I don't even know how old you really are . . .'

'I'm about 6,400 in dog years,' Danny said, patting Roxy's rescue canines, which were licking his face and fingers. 'I don't know about camel years or lemur years' – he grinned sheepishly – 'but it's old enough to know what I want, anyway.'

'How can I marry a man whose name I don't even bloody well know?'

'Um . . . that's classified information.' Danny leapt to his feet defensively. 'You don't really want to know that.'

My mother folded her arms and gave a stern stare.

'. . . Fergus,' he mumbled reluctantly.

'Christ, no wonder you changed it!' The Countess snorted with laughter. She poured herself a glass of wine and squeezed in around the table.

'Fergus! Fergus!' Roxy was hooting. 'You silly bugger.'

Jack noted Fergus's hangdog expression and rallied on his behalf. 'There's nothing wrong with changing your name. After all, the British Royal family provoked the First World War merely to enable them to change their name from Saxe-Coburg-Gotha to Windsor.'

'Don't defend him, Jack,' Roxy snapped. 'It's just so typical that you men would stick together.'

'Jesus, woman! I've apologized a gazillion times for my past. But, despite all the shit that's gone down, we still love each other, Roxy,' Danny declared. 'You know we do. Look how well we work together. We proved that yesterday. Which is why we're getting married. One of us had to make the decision, and I've decided that it's me.'

Roxy's face slammed shut. Her eyes narrowed into slits. 'Funny, because I've decided that I don't like men deciding things for me. The truth is, Danny, we don't need men. That's why we set up Pandora's.'

'But that's all changing now,' Jack said. 'Matilda's just asked if she can join my Chambers. So perhaps Danny could become your collaborator. Tilly's told me all about your latest escapade. And you and Danny clearly do work so well together.'

'You really have agreed to join Jack's Chambers?' Roxy asked me, crestfallen.

'Yep. And I've accepted her offer . . .' Jack answered for me. 'Although there's one proviso that I'm still to negotiate. You must go on another date with me, Tilly. I've taken Rohypnol, so you can have your way with me,' he joked.

Roxy speared him with a reproachful glare. 'Have you no bloody sensitivity at all? How can you joke about that, Jack, after what Matilda's been through?'

'How can I *not*? Truth is, Tilly, you're a lovely, kooky, quirky, clever bookworm of a girl, far too gentle for this big, bad world. At least when you're in my Chambers, I can take care of you and protect you and keep you out of harm's way. And Roxy, despite all your bluster and bravado, you need protecting, too. As Danny proved yesterday, by all accounts.'

A cold silence fell like a snowdrift on to the room.

My mother pushed up slowly to her high-heeled feet, pepper grinder in hand. 'I'm not sure if this thing's on . . .' She tapped the grinder, then spoke into it as though it were a microphone. 'On this day, the second anniversary of Pandora's, I'd just like to say that I was never sure if this venture of ours, the world's first two-person, mother–daughter, solicitor–barrister, boutique feminist law firm, created to fight for women's rights, would survive . . . I was not sure at times if our family would survive ... But survive we have. And with a lot of adventure, fun and frivolity en route. Plus, some victories for women. And I couldn't have had a better partner in crime – well, a better partner in *fighting* crime – than my darling daughter, Matilda.' A look of fondness spilled and rippled over her face. 'But it's never going to be easy. And I totally understand and respect any decision you make about changing your life and finding a more conventional law practice, Tilly. Because I'm way too old to change.'

It must have been the wine speaking or chronic chocolate withdrawal, because I then heard myself say 'And I wouldn't change one thing about you, Mum ... Except maybe those pink go-go boots.' I smiled.

Portia pushed her way between us and wrapped her arms around our necks. 'Well, I'd like to leave both you bonkers women ... only I just can't think of anyone I'd want to leave you for. It was sooooooo boring at Amelia's! I'm just so glad things are back to normal. Well, as abnormal as that is.'

My mother and I exchanged a melty look. The cute-o-meter had just gone off the scale – but neither of us cared at all.

Phyllis now emerged from the kitchen, staggering under the weight of a huge chocolate cake in the shape of a glittering casket, candles blazing. It had been iced pink by Chantelle and simply read – 'Pandora's'.

'Jeepers. That cake would feed one hundred Frenchwomen,' the Countess declared, as Roxy gouged out a huge hunk with a knife and devoured it whole.

'Oh, I so much prefer a woman with appetites,' Danny flirted, gazing at Roxy hungrily.

'By the way, I stole Petronella's Facebook details from Steve's computer and have posted them on a fetish dating site for geriatric kinky singles,' the Countess informed us.

'Excellent!' Roxy laughed, eating another huge hunk of cake. 'Now *that's* what I call "just desserts".'

As I sank my teeth into a giant slice of soft chocolate sponge, nothing was needed to enhance my mood of utter contentment. I felt along my veins a tingling happiness, almost frightening in its physicality.

'. . . I've been thinking about that man who's suing his wife because he didn't know she'd had cosmetic surgery and so wasn't expecting an ugly baby . . . I think we should fight it on the grounds of facial prejudice – a discrimination suffered only by women,' I said to Roxy.

'Ah yes, show me a woman who is happy with her looks and I'll show you the electroconvulsive-therapy scorch-marks,' Roxy replied.

'What? Don't be ridiculous,' Jack scoffed. 'The woman clearly deceived her husband. It's a clear-cut case of fraud.'

'Roxy's right. It's just so typical of you, always to take the man's side, Jack,' I said crossly

Jack smirked. 'Phew. I was worried we hadn't had a disagreement all night. I thought you were perhaps seeing someone else? . . . After all, fighting is foreplay for us . . . I suppose a little tiff before bed would be out of the question?'

I slit my eyes in Jack's direction, suddenly losing the urge to remove the word 'bastard' from his resumé.

'I could get some undercover info on the hubby of the cosmetically enhanced bride . . .' Danny volunteered. 'See if he's having any affairs . . .'

It was Roxy's turn to slit her eyes and level a suspicious glance at Danny. 'I thought you'd given up undercover work! See? . . . You haven't changed at all.'

'Crikey,' Phyllis rasped to Chantelle, 'I think we'd better get back to the estate, pet, where things are quieter and more civilized.'

Chantelle giggled. It was the first time I'd heard her laugh since the trial.

'Anyway, Matilda,' Jack remonstrated, 'you've just agreed to join my Chambers and I'm sorry, but we don't do pro bono work. I mean who really needs a halo? It's just one more thing to clean, right?'

My mother glowered judgementally at Jack, then raised her brows in my direction.

'I made that rash comment about joining your Chambers in my youth, Jack. People say wild things when they're young.'

'But you made that comment only an hour or so ago, Tilly,' he said.

'Kids!' I smiled at my mother and shrugged. 'They grow up fast.'

When my mother beamed back at me, Jack let out an irritated moan. 'Jesus. Where did I put those bloody cigars? I have never needed a smoke so badly.'

When the doorbell rang, the adults were too busy arguing to move from the table, so Portia answered it. She returned five minutes later and tapped her fork on the side of the glass, as Danny had done, looking grave. When we still didn't simmer down, she picked up the pepper grinder and spoke loudly into it.

'Attention! Um, sorry to interrupt the squabbling, but I have an enquiry for Pandora's.'

We all turned as one to face my darling daughter.

'There's a woman at the door whose marriage might have suffered a slight setback.'

'Why?' I asked.

'Well, she's holding her husband's penis ... but, unfortunately – um – he's not there . . .'

'Oh!' we pretty much said in unison. Followed by 'Eugghhhhh!'

'Well, show her into Pandora's,' Roxy boomed, squeezing my hand. 'Where we think inside, on top of, under, over and outside the bloody box.'

To be continued . . .

Acknowledgements

Thank you to all my legal eagles, who cast their beady barrister eyes over my prose, especially Helena Kennedy, QC, Geoffrey Robertson, QC, and Kirsty Brimelow.

Much love and thanks also go to my three darling sisters, Cara, Liz and Jenny, who endure my first drafts with patience, good humour and only minimal alcoholic bribery.

Thanks also to my perspicacious publisher, Larry Finlay, and editorial goddess Linda Evans, and all the team at Transworld, plus Brett Osmond, Karen Reide and Co. at Random House.

Thanks also to my agents Ed Victor and Maggie Phillips, as ever.

Detective Carol Davison's advice on police procedure and Mark Stephen's top beekeeping tips were also invaluable.

A special thanks to my mum, Val, for the mental aerobics of our daily crossword. To Patrick Cook and Doc for comedic inspiration. And to all my girlfriends, who keep me entertained and buoyant. But the biggest thanks of all go, as always, to my children, Georgie and Jules, who have promised to visit me in prison if Helena can't get me off (see dedication).

Kathy Lette is a celebrated and outspoken comic writer who has an inimitable take on serious current issues. She is one of the pioneering voices of contemporary feminism, paving the way for Caitlin Moran and Lena Dunham.

She first achieved *succès de scandale* as a teenager with the novel *Puberty Blues*, which was made into a major film and a TV mini-series. After several years as a newspaper columnist and TV sitcom writer in America and Australia, she has written eleven international bestsellers in her characteristic witty voice, including *Mad Cows, How to Kill Your Husband (and Other Handy Household Hints)* (staged by the Victorian Opera in Australia) and *The Boy Who Fell to Earth*. She is known for her regular appearances on BBC and Sky news programmes. She is an ambassador for Women and Children First, Plan International, the White Ribbon Alliance and the National Autistic Society.

Kathy Lette lives in London with her husband and two children, and can often be found at The Savoy drinking a cocktail named after her. Kathy is an autodidact (a word she taught herself), but in 2010 received an honorary doctorate from Southampton Solent University.

Visit her website at www.kathylette.com to read her irreverent blog, and find her on Twitter @KathyLette and Facebook/KathyLetteAuthor